Nominated for the PEN/Faulkner Award for fiction and
the Mountains and Plains Award for fiction

Winner of the Western Heritage Award for Best Novel of 1997
and the Oklahoma Book Award

Praise for *The Mercy Seat*

"Rilla Askew's first novel is earth and fire in equal measure, with the first element holding those secrets of the plains and the second the scourges visited on the land by man. It is an extraordinary story that owes its literary debt to Faulkner and its heart to scripture . . . [the novel] is ambitious in the best sense: driven by a narrative intensity that is humbling in its passion, consumed with the old-fashioned mysteries too large and too dark for most contemporary writers to go near . . . Rilla Askew is in love with this story—you can feel it in the mountains she describes, in the cold cornbread and traveling preachers and the shocking, flat-out violence—and her love is deeply contagious. I was captivated by the daring depth and fire-and-ice momentum of this novel. In creating young Mattie Lodi as God's innocent, in finding within her that dark nexus with vengeance that belongs to us all, Askew has gone after the mystery of mercy itself."　　　—Gail Caldwell, *The Boston Globe*

"Biblical echoes sound throughout . . . Askew has a fine sense of place, which *The Mercy Seat* draws upon in arresting ways . . . few can deny its relentless, almost hypnotic force."　　　—James Polk, *The New York Times Book Review*

"A powerful novel in a mesmerizing prose out of the Old Testament by way of Faulkner. Askew's depiction of Oklahoma in the late 1880s is a triumph of scholarship and imagination. And she writes with an unerring sense of myth—the way we describe our past so that we know what is right and wrong . . . Rilla Askew is a prodigious talent, and her novel is an important accomplishment."
　　　—Sandra Scofield, *New York Newsday*

"Rilla Askew's prose is so knottily wrought that it inevitably reminds you of the greatest masters of the novel. And the story of *The Mercy Seat* feels as elemental and strong as something from Greek mythology, or the Old Testament."
　　　—Madison Smartt Bell, author of *All Souls' Rising*

"Every once in a while a novel comes along which grips you with its intensity, its texture and poetic language. Such novels sweep one into the pain and suffering of the characters, and as you read you feel you're actually living the story. *The Mercy Seat* is such a novel. It's a testament to the human spirit, and it will endure."
　　　—Rudolfo Anaya, author of *Bless Me Ultima*

"Rilla Askew is this summer's Frank McCourt—a fully developed writer who comes out of nowhere, offering a godsend of a book . . . a Western saga that owes more to Faulkner than to McMurtry."　　　—*Mirabella*

PENGUIN BOOKS

THE MERCY SEAT

Rilla Askew is the author of *Strange Business*, which received the Oklahoma Book Award. Her short fiction has been selected for *Prize Stories: The O. Henry Award*. She divides her time between the Sans Bois Mountains of southeastern Oklahoma and upstate New York.

The Mercy Seat

A NOVEL

Rilla Askew

PENGUIN BOOKS

PENGUIN BOOKS
Published by the Penguin Group
Penguin Putnam Inc., 375 Hudson Street,
New York, New York 10014, U.S.A.
Penguin Books Ltd, 27 Wrights Lane,
London W8 5TZ, England
Penguin Books Australia Ltd,
Ringwood, Victoria, Australia
Penguin Books Canada Ltd, 10 Alcorn Avenue,
Toronto, Ontario, Canada M4V 3B2
Penguin Books (N.Z.) Ltd, 182–190 Wairau Road,
Auckland 10, New Zealand

Penguin Books Ltd, Registered Offices:
Harmondsworth, Middlesex, England

First published in the United States of America by Viking Penguin,
a member of Penguin Putnam Inc. 1997
Published in Penguin Books 1998

10 9 8 7 6 5 4 3 2 1

THE LIBRARY OF CONGRESS HAS CATALOGUED THE HARDCOVER AS FOLLOWS:
Askew, Rilla.
The mercy seat : a novel/Rilla Askew.
p.   cm.
ISBN 0-670-87467-1 (hc.)
ISBN 0 14 02.6515 5 (pbk.)
I. Title.
PS3551.S545M47   1997
813´.54—dc21   96–52416

Printed in the United States of America
Set in Bulmer MT
Designed by Pei Loi Koay

For my family

Thou hast set our iniquities before thee, our secret sins

in the light of thy countenance. For all our days are

passed away in thy wrath: we spend our years as

a tale that is told.

PSALMS 90:8-9

Contents

The Mercy Seat

Map

There are voices in the earth here, telling truth in old stories. Go down in the hidden places by the waters, listen: you will hear them, buried in the sand and clay. Walk west in the tall grass prairie; you'll hear whispering in the bluestem. Stand here, on the ragged rim of a mountain in the southeastern corner; you can hear the sound rising on the south wind, sifting in the dust through the crowns of the cedars: stories told in old voices, in the pulse of bloodmemory; sung in the hot earth above the ceaseless thrum of locusts and nightbirds whillowing, beneath the faint rattle of gourd shells. One story they tell is about longing, for this is a place of homesickness. The land has become home now, and so the very core of this land is sorrow. You can hear it longing for the old dream of itself. Like this continent. This country. *Oklahoma*. The very sound of it is home.

When the Choctaw people knew white soldiers were coming to force them from their homes in Mississippi, up the Great River and over the face of the earth to this unknown land in the west, the people walked for the last time in their forests and touched their hands to the trees, the rocks and healing plants, to say goodbye. They were herded on flat boats along the waterways, walked suffering over the earth, and brought longing, sickness for home, here. Others—white women, some of them—turned their faces backward, and then front, and ever after kept their eyes forward; they snapped at their children, grew tough as jackoak, and brought longing for home here. Men and women in the bellies of slaveships keened longing across the Deep and brought homesickness here.

Its name first in English was Indian Territory, and then, for a short time, it was called two territories, Indian and Oklahoma—meaning both the same thing, a redundancy—and then, again, it was one. The land took and held its Indian name, its Choctaw name, *okla homa,* meaning "red people," as the whole of the continent, changing, would hold her place names, her mountains and rivers, in the tongues that first named them. The shape of it, drawn in mythical lines by men who collaborate in illusion, is that of a saucepan, or hatchet. It lies not in the heart but in the belly, the very gut of the nation, and it contains, like an egg, the whole of the story: red people first, and black slaves among them, and soon the tide of white spreading westward from the eastern hills and mountains across the face of the plains, forsaking all behind them, to come. It is the whole of our story intensified and foreshortened, unfolding at the speed of mere months and years; the whole of our story and yet different, for Negro freedmen were strong here and prosperous; the First People, whose tongues named mountains and rivers, were wrenched from their homelands and marched here, and then when they had made of this land a home, the others came.

The story tells how they came overland or by water, by iron rail or wagon or horseback or walking, in a burst of dust and hoofbeats pounding south in the land runs, or sneaking over the borders from the east, filtering, hidden in the oak and blackgum hills like bollweevils hiding in cuffs; many came to evade the law, some to purge the bile of defeat and Reconstruction. Blacks came for freedom here, to build their own towns, their own country. Whites came for land or a new home or to sell whiskey. They came, all of them, bearing their equal measures of pride and violence and hard work and suffering; they came wrapped in decency, steeped in sour greed and hope and despair; in fear and wisdom, in tolerance and hatred, in mindlessness and sorrow and abiding faith in the hand of the Lord. Forsaking all. Forsaking nothing. Bringing it all, every bit of it, with them.

In deep winter, early February 1887, two white men left Kentucky and headed west toward Indian Territory, coming not as the Choctaw people before them—because they had to—but because they believed that they had to. When the Lodis left Kentucky, they fled quickly and quietly in the night, fleeing fear, the mind's dream, crawling guilt, and the law. They could not flee what bound them.

The two men were brothers, Lafayette Luke and John Major Lodi, and their souls were twisted together as if they'd come forth that way from their mother's womb. They had not, for there was fifteen months between them, but the elder could not remember when the younger had not been behind or beside him, following in his footsteps, doing his bidding, copying his every gesture, solid and malleable as a lump of riverclay. In their boyhood it had been Lafayette who went first behind the harrow, John following with the seed corn or starts of tobacco; it had been Lafayette who led in their games of fox-and-geese or dare goal; Fayette who darted ahead always, quick and grinning, before his slower, more lethargic brother. It was not until John's skill with a forge and hammer revealed itself at the age of fourteen—and later, after the War, as his particular, unfathomable gift at gunsmithing emerged so that men traveled from great distances to ask that gift of him, and pay him well for it besides—that the balance between the brothers shifted and changed. Slowly a discomfort built between them, and Fayette, struggling to settle again the proper equilibrium, bullied and cajoled and jabbed at the heart of his brother, and John, unable to resist, went along. But the trouble grew larger, and yet more silent, hidden between them. They did not speak of it. Their father and siblings did not see it—though their wives did, each secretly blaming the other for the trouble—but the trouble itself remained unnamed, unacknowledged; no one knew what it was.

On the night they fled Kentucky, the men carried their families with them and this brotherness that would not let them love one another nor unbind themselves. They carried it like a germ of fever in the pale shells of their wagons, across the great Mississippi, and west.

BOOK ONE

Carapace

Behold, I have created the smith that bloweth the
coals in the fire, and that bringeth forth an
instrument for his work; and I have created
the waster to destroy.

ISAIAH 54:16

This is what I remember.

My mama was crying. It was cold in the house, and so dark. I was quiet under the covers, with my eyes open. The sound came down soft in the darkness, like the sound Sudie's pups made under the porch after she tore her foot off in the fox trap and Papa had to shoot her. Before Uncle Fay pulled them out one by one, black blind fluffs and the one white one and the tricolor, and tied them inside a flour sack and threw them in the creek. That sound. I tried to tell myself it was the new baby crying, up in the loft bed between Mama and Papa, wrapped tight in white strips of cotton, soft in the featherbed, warm, crying hungry. But I knew it was not the new baby crying. It was Mama.

My eyes hurt, from the cold, from staring into the dark seeing nothing. Thomas jerked in his sleep and whimpered, scrabbled under the covers, pushed out from beneath them with his fat little arms. I lifted my hand from where it was warm under the feathertick and felt for his forehead. I was afraid for him then, more than always, more than every half second, trembling—for fever, for mystery, for what could take him—from the very hour he was born. So I felt him. His forehead was dry and naked, smooth with cold. I rolled him against me, lifted his head and slipped my arm under, held him in the crook of my arm with his face turned toward me, soft, breathing milk. On the other side of him Little Jim Dee kicked once in his sleep and got still. At my back I felt Jonaphrene's slow breathing. I held the feathertick over my brother's head to warm him, off his face so he wouldn't smother. My nose and cheekbones were burning. The hard knot cramped my chest. My mother was crying. My fingers were turning ice to the bone.

Later, Papa's voice called me.

This was all the same night.

"Matt!" Papa said. And then softer: "Mattie!"

A weight was on me, like the cold press of pond water, and I tried to fight my way up. I struggled to the top, pushing, like black swimming, and opened my eyes. Still it was dark. I looked to the window. No light filtered through the oilpaper, not even the least hint of dawn's whitish haze.

"Matt!"

Thomas twitched awake. He shuddered and reached out for me under the covers. I put my hand to him and felt his fist wrap tight around my finger.

"Martha! Git up now!" Silence, and then "Martha Ruth!" and I knew I was in trouble, because I had in those days, and still have, four names. "Git up and light the fire, would you! Mama's not feeling good."

I whispered to Thomas and slipped my arm from underneath him. My hand was asleep, tingling, buzzing on the inside like caught insects. Over my head the wood creaked in the loft bed. I pulled my finger loose from Thomas and wriggled out from under the feathertick, stood shivery and barelegged in my underslip on the cold floor. Thomas sighed and turned over. Jonaphrene rolled in sleeping to take my place.

I moved quickly over Mama's rag carpet and hunted in the dark until I found the iron poker. It stung cold in my hand like it would strip the skin back, and I traded hands, shifting it from one hand to the other while I poked the red embers. My hands and knees burned where I knelt on the cold hearthstones to blow. I picked sticks and twigs from the woodbox. The fire licked up yellow. I put two splits of kindling down crossways and stepped back to wait, dancing on the hearthstones, my arms wrapped around me. I thought then to run back to the bed and crawl under the covers, but the loft creaked again, and I waited by the fireplace, my breath small and smoky in the flickering light.

"Git dressed, Matt," Papa said. He was standing at the foot of the ladder, stuffing his overshirt inside his pants. His face was ropy, saggy with shadows, and very, very still. I wanted to ask him how come we were getting up to start day in the middle of night—for it was night then, true night, not early dark morning like Mildred or some others would tell you—and I wanted to ask Papa, but his face would not let me. And anyhow, I knew. It was part of the same thing. What made Mama lie in bed crying. What made Papa stand on the porch with Uncle Fayette and Grandpa and Uncle Big Jim Dee, talking in low, tight voices late into the night. What brought the hard knot a while ago to come live in my chest. I went to the foot of the bed and reached under the covers to pull my dress and petticoat from beneath the cold footwarmer. I put my clothes on, watching Papa.

He crossed the house and bent to put one log only on the fire. Then he straightened and pulled his hat and coat from the peg. I thought he would tell me to start the fire in the cookstove. And then I remembered. I looked to the kitchen, where the empty stovepipe hung wedged from the ceiling, openmouthed, wrong-looking, emptying uselessly into empty air. Papa lifted the latch on the front door and went out.

I waited then. A long time. I remember. The house was quiet. Papa's fire burned blue at the bottom. After that long while, me waiting, Mama turned in the bed over my head.

"Mattie?" she called me. "Mattie? You awake? Mama needs you. Come up here a minute, hon."

I climbed the ladder, my feet cold on the smooth logs. I could hardly see Mama in the heap of featherbed and covers. I couldn't see the new baby at all.

"Shhhhh," Mama said. "Don't wake her. Listen. I need you to do something for me. Can you do something?"

I nodded.

She turned in the bed again, and a small sound, like a moan, slipped from her. She held out her hand. I could see the pale line of it, her narrow arm, standing out straight in the dark. I crossed the loft, shaking. The wood of the rafters brushed the light hairs on the top of my head. Mama's hand was warm, rough as cedar where I touched it, and then Mama wrapped her other hand around both our hands and pulled me toward her. "Listen," she said. "I want you to get dressed."

"I'm dressed, Mama."

"Get dressed, Matt. Put your shoes on. Dress warm. I want you to do something for me. Go out back by the smokehouse. There's a blackgum. You know that old black tupelo tree? Look under it. Facing south. Scrape off the dirt there, you'll find something. It's not buried deep. It's just something, a tin box. I need that. Can you bring it to me?"

I nodded.

"Can you?"

"Yes, Mama," I said.

Mama let go my hand then. "Hurry," she said, and lay back, and the hurt sound came from her again. The new baby woke up crying. "Shhhh, shhhhh," Mama said, turning, and the bedclothes rustled and whispered. The baby whimpered, grew quiet. I backed toward the ladder. The rafters tugged my hair the wrong way.

"Dress warm, Matt," Mama said, as if she was sleepy. "Put my shawl on. Hurry, honey. And Mattie . . ." Real still then. "Don't let Papa see." The bedclothes rustled once more and settled. Then there was just the soft suckling sound of the baby.

The slivered moon was high and small and very white in the night sky when I stepped out the door. Frost covered the ground, twinkling dark in the starlight. A harness jangled in the barn. The sound leapt at me frozen across the frozen yard, and I jumped. I wrapped Mama's shawl tight about me and edged around the side of the house, watching the thin line of light around the barn door. The knot in my chest burned hot-cold now, like the sting of the iron poker. I hurried. Behind the smokehouse I found the blackgum and knelt on the glinting earth. Frost held the dead leaves and dirt together in clumps where I scraped. My palms hurt. But, just like Mama told me, it was not buried deep. My palm brushed across cold metal, and I dug with my fingertips and found the edges of the tin box and lifted it. It was square and silver-colored and too burning cold to hold in my hands. I wanted to open it. I wanted to know what it was that Mama kept hidden. But the box was locked tight with frost, and it was secret. Something only for grown-ups to know, like their privacies, or babies dying, and it was cold and forbidden, and it belonged to my mama. I wrapped it inside the shawl and held it close to my chest, close to the burning hot-cold place, and the knot seemed to ease or to be sucked away from me, drawn by the cold metal. I hurried back to the house.

There were seven of us in the wagon. Little Jim Dee and Jonaphrene leaned against me on either side under the quilts. Thomas was in my lap. Mama and Papa were up front, and the new little one, and the air was still dark. Do you see? We had loaded the wagon, Papa'd hitched up the mules and we'd started, and the air was still dark. We'd left the chifforobe and the pie safe. We'd left the oak frames of the two beds. Papa's big forge stood in the empty barn behind us, his bellows squeezed shut on the floor, but all the rest of it we had, and Bertha tied at the back, and her calf following, bawling. Papa's hunting dogs trotting beside. I was excited then, I'd forgotten everything, snug on the featherbed with the blankets and children. Forgotten then. But later I remembered.

The weather was changed, had gone strange, just since we'd started. In that short a time. I thought back later, and it seemed to me that the very breath of the world knew where we were going: it was not crisp, cold, and clear now, but wet, somehow warmer. I listened to the chickens cluck mildly in their crate tied to the back of the wagon, and once the old redheaded rooster crowed. I thought, *It's going to be dawn soon.* But the sky was thick black, and there was no moon now, no stars. The coal-oil lantern hung on a hook and made a yellow light pool around Papa. It dipped and swayed with the sway of the wagon.

And then there was another wagon behind us. I didn't know when it came, I was looking at the sky maybe, or talking to Thomas. But just at once I became aware of a creak and a jangle and the soft snuffle of horses in the roadway behind us. I couldn't see anything, but the sound followed, like a ghost wagon, clopping, creaking softly, hidden in the dark.

"Papa!" I whispered. "There's a wagon!"

"Yes, Matt," Papa said. That was all.

Grandma Billie stood in the yard. Her eyes looked out at nothing. Mama stood in front of her, holding the baby. Papa stayed in the wagon and wouldn't let me or the children get down. "We don't have time!" he said. He sat facing front, his hat pulled over his forehead. He wouldn't look round when I said, "Just one little half minute? Papa? Can I, Papa?"

"Hush, Mattie," was all he answered. His voice was harsh, but low and quiet, and it didn't sound like Papa. He did not look at Grandma Billie in her yard at all.

Grandma and Mama stood silent. The day was seeping gray then, opening thick and misty, with no streaks of pink in the dull sky behind us. The other wagon rolled in. I could see now. It was Uncle Fayette, Aunt Jessie, the six cousins. And all their belongings strapped and draped and dangling from the wagon. A new tarp puffed over the bed, rose up like a cloudbank against the gray sky.

A rooster crowed back somewhere behind Grandma's house, and then the old rooster in the crate started crowing and wouldn't let up. The sound of it shrieked and shrilled in my ears. Thomas laughed, and then his face fell together and he started crying.

"John!" Uncle Fay's voice came from the other wagon.

Then I heard Mama and Grandma talking. I couldn't hear the words for the riot of the roosters and Thomas bawling in my lap, just the high sound of Mama talking and Grandma's thin voice behind, and then I heard my mama say, "Mama!" and the two of them pushed fumbling together with the baby caught between them, and the baby started crying, the weak bumpy cry of a newborn, and the hard knot came back sudden inside my chest.

"Demaris!" Papa said.

Mama came toward us. She held the baby in the loose crook of her left arm. Her right hand was a fist pushed hard against the center of her chest. She climbed up beside Papa.

Papa clicked at the mules and turned their heads hard to the left and headed them out to the roadbed. Uncle Fay's wagon turned in behind us. I looked back to see Grandma Billie in her thin dress. Her eyes were empty circles looking after us.

The light was pale and sickly as we went south through Kentucky, through glittering gray fields with the frost stinging and once or twice snowfall. I didn't know when we left Kentucky. There was no mark on the earth that told us Now You Are Gone, only the hills that began to hump higher and rounder and closer together, and the dirt darkening deeper brown. I thought those hills were mountains, but Papa said no. His voice was like his own voice again, and that was another way I knew we were gone from Kentucky, though his face was yet sagging and still. He called me before first light every morning, and I cooked and we ate and loaded up all we'd unloaded the night before and went on. Mama swayed dull-eyed in the wagon beside Papa, and always her hand was in a tight fist between her breasts. She never spoke except to shush the new baby or tell me to come get Thomas. Papa hardly talked either, and because they were silent, the children were silent, and whole days we'd spend with no sound but the creak of the wagon and the chickens, Bertha's calf bawling, a squirrel scolding in a tree maybe if we passed under it. In the settled areas, dogs would start barking miles ahead of us, hearing the creak and groan of the wagon, and Dan and Ringo would bay an answer, and they'd keep that up, Papa's dogs and the unseen dogs of strangers, for a long time after we'd passed. We went fast through the towns. They were small brick and shakeboard towns, the streets in them muddy, the muffed women stopping in their big skirts on the wooden walks, staring, and the men inside the wide-open doors of the livery stables lifting their heads. We went through fast because the road did, but we didn't stop in them, not even to buy feed for the livestock. Uncle Fay would stop at a farmhouse sometimes when we saw one, or he'd send Caleb ahead on one of the team horses after we'd made camp of an evening, and when Papa called me before first light next morning, Bertha and old Sarn and Delia would have their big tongues to the earth, pulling into their mouths the clumps of hay spread on the sparkling ground.

In the same way that there was no sign when we left Kentucky, there was no single moment I can remember when we began to turn west, just the slow slide of sun to where it slanted left over the wagon in the daytime and hung a red ball in red sky before us at night. But it was after the sun moved and the land began to flatten and change that we started to come to the waters. Uncle Fayette and Aunt Jessie and the six cousins would have to wait for us by a river so we could all cross together, and then we would splash over the ford, the children wading in the icy water where it was shallow and the water swirling over the wheel rims and frothing and Mama's face going white. Sometimes if it was a small creek they would just go on over alone. They went faster in their spring wagon with Uncle Fay's horses and no cow to trail and Aunt Jessie never needing to stop and rest like our mama, so they kept getting farther and farther ahead of us, and we'd sometimes travel long after dark, with the lantern swaying yellow on the hook beside Papa, until we caught up with them camped by a creekbed and their supper already eaten and washed up after and the cousins asleep by the fire.

And then it would be the dark before first light again, and Papa would call me. I was young then, I was ten then, my life took on that rhythm. I cooked in the mornings and at night and washed up and set the children hunting firewood and tended Thomas, and when he crept to Mama and patted his hand on her breast and pulled at her, I took him away and gave him the sugartit and rocked him in my lap in the bed of the wagon. After a time I forgot to think about the home-place in Logan County or the two little graves out back of the barn where John Junior and the dead baby between Jim Dee and Jonaphrene were buried, or Grandma Billie in her thin dress, or Grandpa Lodi's white eyebrows jumping and Uncle Big Jim Dee's eleven children who were also my cousins but whose faces I couldn't seem to keep separate or remember, and I forgot to think anything about my old life at all.

Mama didn't look back, but I did. Days we traveled I sat in the back of the wagon watching where we'd just been fall away backwards, retreating always behind us, but I didn't regret it or care about it because the rhythm of my life and my family's life was the slow rhythmic step of Papa's mules. We were seven in the wagon and our animals went with us, our belongings were covered and safe beneath the tarp Papa had rigged over us—all but the chifforobe and the pie safe and oak bed frames, and Papa had left those behind on purpose, so they could not matter—and our life journeyed one life together, and so I had no reason to question or care.

Sometimes we stayed two or three days in one place because our mama was too sick to endure the bumps and jolts in the frozen ruts. In the beginning we all were sick a little, our legs wobbly at night when we climbed down, but Mama was bad sick, like poison, on account of the continual sway sway sway of the wagon, every minute, never still, never stopping, going always forward and forward, and sometimes she'd have to lean her head off the side of the wagon and throw up. And then we turned west, and Mama got sicker. We camped by a fast-running branch twisting between two low sloping hills. We stayed there a week nearly, and Uncle Fay got so restless then. He would ride out on one of the team horses in the mornings, returning at night to sit jumpy by the fire and poke it with a stick.

One night I heard him and Papa in the dark at the back of our wagon.

"Go on then!" Papa said, and his voice was hard the way it was in the dawn yard at Grandma Billie's when he would not let me get down. This was some time after the humped hills were behind us but before we crossed the big water. I might've been sleeping, because I can't remember anything before those words of Papa's. "Go on then!" Papa's voice caught me, not just the sound in it but the fact of it, the fact of the two of them in the dark at the back of the wagon when they considered we were all every one asleep. I listened with my eyes open, as I always listened to grown-up talk whenever I could get by with it, but it was that hard sound that made my chest clench with the old, tight knot. I had forgotten all about that knot, but just then in the wagon in the dark I remembered, and I knew something bad was going to come.

"No, now, John," Uncle Fay said, "I didn't mean that." He was squatting on the ground, I could tell by his voice rising, how it came from the low earth at the back of the wheel.

"Go," Papa said.

"I ain't going."

"Then shut up about it." Papa's voice grated like he meant to whisper but the hard sound pushed through him too bad and would not let him. I could hear him breathing. And then it was Uncle Fay whispering.

"I don't mean to say nothing, Son, I don't. You're my brother, we been through all this together, I ain't about to quit you. But we ain't even half out of Tennessee—"

And that was the first I knew the name of the place where we were traveling, and I said it to myself in silence in the dark in the wagon. *Ten-uh-see.* I tried to make the sound fit the low rolling hills and flattening earth, and I could not, it slipped by so fast, and when I listened again Uncle Fay was whispering.

"—get some traveling space between us, they could cross the state line anytime, come horseback, they can catch up in no time, you want that?"

It came on me then, the fear and the knot squeezing tighter to nearly shut off my breathing, because I'd forgotten somehow all through our coming, but in that moment I remembered *They* again. *They* from my uncles' and father's and grandfather's low voices on the front porch late into the night. *They* that made my mama cry soft in the loft bed and all of us to take up our home and creep south through the gray hills and west across the creeks and rivers, and all the time west, toward the red winter sun, and I did not know who *They* were, but I hated them. There was no form or shape to them, but I saw them on horseback galloping after us and we all moving slow in our crawling wagons, and my heart was with Uncle Fayette then and not Papa, because I was scared.

"They ain't," Papa said. "Jim Dee'll turn 'em off."

"What if he don't?"

"He will."

"I don't know. Could be they—"

"He *will*."

And Papa was so certain, how he said it, I believed him. I could see Uncle Big Jim Dee on the porch at Grandpa Lodi's with his shotgun, waving it back and forth in the night sky, firing, loading, and firing, and the mouth shooting red, and *They* on their horses thundering toward him and being deflected off to the side right and left. I relaxed then, my chest eased a little, and I put my hand out to feel Thomas and he felt warm enough.

"All right. All right then. Reckon he will."

Quiet a little, and I heard an owl hooting far off above the rushing sound of the water and, close by, a soft shuffle and creak of leather from where Uncle Fayette crouched at the foot of the wagon. I heard his tobacco pouch sift open. I guess Papa never moved at all. The place where he stood was quiet, you would not guess a human was there if you didn't already know. His breath and clothes and muscles, his very eyelashes, I believe, were still.

"Might be they won't hear 'im or b'lieve 'im." Uncle Fay's voice was mangled down and crammed with something. Papa said nothing. "Might be they'll get aholt of Tanner or somebody."

"Tanner's plumb to Texas."

"We don't know that for certain."

"Left before Christmas, shut up about all that now."

A stick popped in the fire between the two wagons. The branch running in the distance was a gurgling soft *husssssh.* Quiet a little while. Then: "Said he did, anyhow." Uncle Fay's voice lifting, casual, like he was just passing the time of night, but it wouldn't have fooled a baby. "Said he was leaving for Texas. Don't reckon we got a guarantee."

"It's a damn patent, Fayette!" It was like my papa spat it, like the words hissed and *ttttt*'d out of his mouth into the fire. "Ain't a goddamn bank robbery, they ain't going to chase Tanner to Texas. They ain't going to foller us down here. This is all your doings to start with. You want to go on, y'all go on. Leave me to it. If they come after us, then they come after us. She can't go no faster and I don't aim to. Y'all just go ahead. Git!" Papa's voice spitting the whisper, and I could hear him breathing then, how hard it was to choke the sound back, and Uncle Fayette coming back over with his own whisper: "Hsssht, now you'll wake 'em, it's all right, John, all right, you're right, leave it, you're right."

And then it got quiet again. For a long time. I listened a long time, and I tried to stay awake because I had to find out, to listen, to hear every one of my papa's words, because I had to know if *They* were coming or if Uncle Big Jim Dee had really turned them off to the side or if Uncle Fayette would really take his family and go on and leave us. But my eyes kept closing down, the drifting in my brain dark, the pictures sifting. I don't know how long it was before he came back again, Uncle Fayette, drawing the words out like he was dreaming at the fire, his mouth full of tobacco.

"All I mean to say, Son, looks to me like . . ."

His voice trailed off, and I heard a little *p-tttt* and the faint repeat of the same sound when the tobacco juice landed off somewhere in the darkness.

"I'd just think you could do a little something with her. Had me a wife I couldn't do no more with than a blame egg sucker, reckon I'd—"

And then he went cold quiet. I don't know what happened. Papa never moved. He never said nothing. Uncle Fayette just hushed up like he'd had his mouth shut for him. Or more like his mouth was hanging open but the words weren't ever going to come.

After a while like that, with Uncle Fay and Papa stone silent and the fire now and again popping and the water far off rushing and nothing more, my mama turned and rolled over beneath the feathertick at the front of the wagon. I heard her swallow deep in her throat, like the spit had been gathering in her mouth for a long time. I don't know how long she'd been awake.

The change came in Papa on the very morrow. I heard it in him, in his voice, how he called me the next morning before first light.

"Martha Ruth! Git up from there, quick now, we got to git on!"

He poked his head in the back of the wagon and said it so loud that Thomas waked up and shuddered and Little Jim Dee whimpered in his sleep and Jonaphrene jerked awake. Papa did not try to shake me awake easy without waking the others. He didn't keep it between us, how he did always—and I cannot tell you how he did so, it was just a feeling between us when we worked silent together before the rest were even stirring—that it was we two together, me and him, who got the family fed and coffeed and the animals fed and watered and all of us loaded up and ready, like it was our good and sweet job between us that nobody else could or would do. He just spoke loud and harsh and called me Martha Ruth. I knew the hard sound in his throat, which before had been sound only, was now something solid, permanent. Permanent till what caused it came out. The way a boil will hint itself tingling and aching under the skin awhile before it bursts open angry and sets up a permanence on the skin and in the skin that won't leave till the putrid core gets squeezed out.

Mama was different too, but her difference was harder to lay my mind hold of, because between Mama and me there was not a strong feeling. Not then there wasn't, not since the instant I started to hand her the tin box in the loft bed and Papa called "Matt!" from the bottom of the ladder when neither of us had heard him come in, and Mama and me both jumped and looked at each other, and I jerked my arm back. But I knew there was change in her, and I watched her. All I could see really was how she held her chin tight beneath the tie-straps of her bonnet. How she held the baby tight till it would whimper and wriggle and finally start mewling, so that Mama would hand her back to me to hush up.

There was one change in me, one only so far as I know of. After that night I never sat in the back of the wagon and looked behind us anymore. Not because *They* might be following on horseback—or not following, I didn't know which—not because I didn't care to watch Tennessee flattening and the earth changing behind us, but because I had to sit up close to the front of the wagon, even though it was dim and choked and cramped in the center and I could not see where we were going or where we had come from beneath the sky-dimming tarp. But I had to sit up there, right behind them, with Thomas babbling in my lap and no air hardly, no light, because I had to watch the hunched backs and clenched jaws of my mama and papa.

In a few days—I cannot tell you how many, for they all ran together the same from where I sat in the gray belly of the wagon, but it was not so many days and we did not stop again except to cook and sleep in the late evenings and Papa's voice was fixed and hard, and the knot in my chest was also back again, fixed, though not so hard as it had been but more like gutted-up twisting—within a few several days from the time of the first change, we came in late afternoon to the great water. I could smell it the whole day like old fish and pond mud. I didn't know what it was until we came over a hint of rise and I, peeking between Mama's and Papa's stiff shoulders, saw it sprawled snaking brown and wide before us.

Uncle Fay said the word, how many times he said it—*MississippiMississippiMississippi*—shaking his head at the muddy river and the day getting late and the sun sliding as we stood all of us on the bank, waiting. I saw the name in my mind, the humps and curves and dots spelled out strung out long, and the sound of the word was like the longways of the water from where it came toward us on our right, north, far up, because we could see there because the earth was so dirt-brown and flat, and it came by us and went on forever down around a curve south. But the sound in the name did not carry the width of the river, I thought, not the depth, how it was, huge wide muddy flowing brown slow and fast, like the very split in the earth, like you could never get back over it once you had got across. I thought to myself, *This is the place of no turning back forever.* I was mistaken over that. I didn't know I was mistaken, because I could not then see or dream what would happen, and I dreaded that water and could not move at all even with the men and Papa working and his voice hard and the sun sliding and the day falling colder and still. My mama dreaded it. Her face was more white than a cloudbank. The baby Lyda cried and cried.

The raftsmen had made us get out of the wagons. From our wagon they took out Mama's trunk and the iron cookstove and a few wooden crates and placed them around different places on the raft, and that wooden strapped-together raft looked too flimsy for the whole family and our animals, and the four men with their beards and slouch hats and burnt faces frightened me. I did not trust them, how they could get all of us to the far side and not lose any of us, not with the memory so close of the swirling, rushing waters behind us, and them smaller, them nowhere like this water, and in the smaller waters the whirling push and chance and struggle, the dogs swimming, and the time Bertha's calf got loose and was swept downriver bawling and Uncle Fay threw the reins to Caleb and jumped off and waded to catch her by the loose rope and pulled her kicking to the far bank. This place here was so much wider, longer, more powerful than any we'd crossed over, the smell of it strong beyond all imagining, and the day was dropping down, the sky turning purple and lowering, the air growing still. There was no wind. Cold seemed to press down on us from the heavens and rise from the earth to press us squeezed together in the middle with cold.

I hoisted Thomas on my hip. He was getting too big for it, his legs dangled nearly past my knees and he was too heavy, I could hardly hold him, but I did. I'd put Jonaphrene and Little Jim Dee to stand together near the dock where they could see, and I'd wrapped a scrap quilt around them to keep them warm together, but Little Jim Dee could not ever be still. He darted in and out among the raftsmen till Papa hollered at him to Git Over Here Right Now, and Papa's voice so hard that Little Jim Dee obeyed him and came all the way back over onto the bank and even stood still for maybe two minutes before he took off again, but he never did go back onto the raft. Jonaphrene whined over the cold, but I paid her no attention, not even to tell her to shut up, because I could not take my eyes off the water. It was purpling down in the dropping cold, a sick swirling bruise color, and I wanted to say, Papa, Papa, let's don't go, let us wait until tomorrow, and I wanted to say, Oh, please, Papa, let's go now, let's cross now and get it over before night comes and all is worse.

When it was ready finally, our goods and animals strapped to the logs, and the wagonwheels stopped with stones big enough of themselves, it looked to me like, to sink that raft of sticks, and Uncle Fayette's raft ready the same, and the two men began to pole Uncle Fayette's raft out into the current, and the two on ours motioned with their long poles, both men wrapped now in blanketcoats and high beaverskin collars so their faces hardly showed—but I knew that the one was with us, the one with black, black hair and beard and no teeth and his eyes just like slits—and when all was ready and Papa held Mama's elbow through the thick shawl and blanket and guided her out onto that pier like cordwood and over the wooden ramp to the raft, I wanted to shriek. I wanted to scream for all of us to go back, to wait for tomorrow, to do some thing or any thing other than go into the river. I did not shriek. I carried Thomas over the slatted ramp onto the raft.

The men worked in silence, their poles in the water now sliding, now lifted and rested in the iron locks, and the raftsmen not talking even in idleness, doing nothing except to watch through slitted eyes and spit. Bertha wouldn't quit bawling. The water swept us down and fast, so much faster than it looked from the bank. Out in it, where the men poled us, the river took us up like drift and swept us down, and I looked to the opposite bank where I could see tree bones outlined in the purpling twilight, but we were not going there, not going across but down the river and Uncle Fay and the others rushing on ahead, always ahead of us even in the rhythm of the water not our water, and I did not know why. I had a hidden smolder against them, even then, in the fear and thrill of not going across the water as I'd expected but down, because it should have been Papa. I believed always it should have been Papa and not Uncle Fayette in front.

I could not get my balance. Thomas was on the wet raft floor, clinging to my skirt bottom and wailing to be picked up. I couldn't hold him and hold to the iron front of the cookstove. Mama was sitting upon her trunk near the back where the raftsmen stood swaying, and

Jonaphrene was beside her with her face pinched but not crying, but the new baby surely was. I couldn't go back there and sit among their spread knees and Lyda crying. There was nowhere to sit but the raft floor, which I would not, and anyhow I could not, because I had to stand ready, there, near the front of the raft where I could see. I had to be ready in case the whole thing tipped and rolled skyward and was sucked down to the river's muddy gut. Papa walked back and forth in the narrow space in front of the wagon, and he looked from the corner of his eye sometimes back at the raftsmen, and sometimes to the opposite shore where the tree bones were darkening, and sometimes downriver to where Uncle Fayette and the others were getting on ahead. I tried to ease toward Papa to see what his face said, but the raft seemed to roll more if my feet moved, and Thomas wailed louder, and so I had to stand and hold tight to the cookstove, and I could tell nothing except frown and concentration in the way Papa held his head.

Bertha stood on the strapped logs, bawling, her nose tied to the near side of the wagon, her bony legs spraddled, and each time the raft dipped, she did a little jerking kind of dance. Her calf bawled as badly as she did but was better in balance, and old Sarn and Delia, too, stood on the raft better, their knees braced and hooved flat, and not braying either, Papa's mules, but messing bad on the raftwood, their eyes wild and rolling, and you knew you had better not be anywhere close around them if you didn't want to get kicked or bit. Because it was wrong for those animals. I could see it. They thought they were falling through heaven. And I too, that is how I felt in the rolling unsurety of the raft in the water, like dreaming of falling, like the sure clamp of earth beneath us had been ripped away and replaced with floating chaos and dread. In the other crossings, even in the swift push and rush of water, our wheels and our mules' feet had still touched the earth.

So that's how we went down the river, with Thomas and the new baby and Bertha and her calf bawling, and Papa pacing, and the air growing colder and the men silent and spitting and the evening darkening down. But there were three who loved that raft ride, and those three were Little Jim Dee and Papa's hunting dogs, Ringo and Dan. Dan wouldn't move from up front where he stood tall with his nose lifted and his tongue lolling and the tan underside of his ears showing light in the backsweep of river wind. Ringo trotted everywhere on his dumpy legs, with his nails clicking the raftwood, sniffing the raftsmen and their poles and gear and the wind and the raft's mossy cracks, getting right up near the raft edge one time to dip down and smell the water, and then backing up, trotting around again on his business to sniff our belongings, as if he thought there was danger that the raft and the river could change our family's smell. Little Jim Dee went right behind him, trotting everywhere on his short legs, and I knew Papa must be concentrating something awful because he never even told Little Jim Dee to quit.

It kept getting colder and darker. I could not smell the mud-and-fish smell, I think because it had swelled up to suck in the whole world and so now could not be separated out as river smell. The far bank did not get closer or farther but seemed to stay always the same distance, and the only change in it was how the dark sky behind the skeletons of trees began to glow red and the trees themselves jumped outlined into black. The river went bloody for a few minutes and then fell back brown, then dark again, purple, and the sandy-bearded riverman came front and lit the lantern and went back, and then the only change on the raft was how Thomas wore down to a whimper and then so did the baby Lyda, and Bertha's bawling slowed some and the calf hushed up and went to suck.

There was a time then, just a few heartbeats maybe even was all it was, but I remember it: that little blink of time when the rhythm was right. We rolled and floated in the dusk. I lost sight of Uncle Fay's raft for a while, until there was a glint far down the river in the gloaming and I saw the lantern light on the pole on the other raft swell and grow white. My hand was not so tight to the cookstove. It was cold but not shivering, not icy, and I reached down and patted Thomas the gentle soft drumming like he liked on his back. I was thinking about him, about how he would be wet on his bottom because the damp from the raftwood would be seeping up through his diaper square and blanket and gown, and I began to worry because I did not know how long we would be on the raft. I couldn't change him or lift him, not with how we were rolling, and the bit of peacefulness vanished and I began to be afraid for my brother. I looked back toward Mama. She had one arm around Jonaphrene and the shawl wrapped around both of them and the baby Lyda swaddled in her lap. It was then, when I raised my head and looked back at Mama, that I first marked the presence of the blue wind.

It didn't bother me at first—I did not understand it—but it did get my notice, how it pushed down on us from upriver, gusting off and

on at the beginning, getting stronger and more insistent until it made
me turn north to face it to keep the little hairs that had slipped out of
my braids and bonnet from beating me in the mouth. And the more
the wind rose, the more I forgot about Thomas's wet bottom. The
more the wind rose, the more the animals got excited, with Bertha
dancing and bawling again, and the chickens waking up to mutter and
rustle, and the mules, too, shuffling their hooves on the raft floor and
twitching their tails and ears. Dan did not leave his place up front
nearby Papa but he turned around in a circle a few times and sat down
on his haunches, whining and facing upwind. But it was that old rabbit
dog Ringo who got craziest from the wind change. He trotted around
the raft faster and faster, whining and jumping, with Little Jim Dee at
his tail like a trailing pup, until Ringo stopped at the raft rear and
started to bay into the wind.

The man with the black beard and slit eyes flicked his foot out and
kicked Ringo. That quick. Ringo yelped like his ribs had been broken,
and slunk tail-tucked toward Papa, yelping, and Little Jim Dee shrieked
and yelled something which I could not make out on account of the
wind and the animals and Thomas too now carrying on, but Little Jim
Dee, right there underfoot, hollering, pulled back and kicked that riverman in the knee, and kicked him again. The man took his hand off
the riverpole and did not even bend down but swatted backhanded
through the darkling air like Little Jim Dee was an insect, and sent
him tumbling, his shrieks cut off, Little Jim Dee rolling silently backwards, not making a sound.

"John!" Mama's voice split the wind, pierced the cries of Thomas
and Ringo and Jonaphrene and the new baby, all four of them howling,
and flew up to me and Papa at the front of the raft.

I looked at Mama. She was standing by her trunk, her shawl a dark
heap on the wet raft floor beside her. Mama's fist was not in a ball at
her chest but clenched at her side, and the baby Lyda was tight in her
left arm. Even in the deepening dark I could see Mama's face was
ferocious, and my heart jumped up furious like Mama's, and I was
glad. I looked up at Papa. He did not move and I couldn't see his
expression for his hat brim pulled down and the lamplight above him
shadowing his mouth, and I looked to the back again, where the raftsmen did not move either, and none of us moved but for the children
crying. Little Jim Dee lay just still on his back. His chest went up and
down, up and down, but he didn't try to get up, and he never let

out a sound that I could hear. It scared me that Little Jim Dee did not cry.

I wanted to go pick him up, but of course I could not, and I waited for Mama or Papa, one, to go to him, but they did not. I thought then Papa would rush to the back and jump on that ugly raftsman and beat him for backhanding my brother, or holler or shout or do something, but he didn't do anything. He just stood looking at Mama standing by her trunk looking at him. That was all.

At last Papa hollered, loud and furious above the wind and all the rest of it, and the sound made me jump, on account of how close he was and how I'd been holding my breath. But it was not at that rafts-man Papa hollered but at Little Jim Dee lying splat on his back. "James Davidson! Git up here and set down!" He yelled it like Little Jim Dee was still running around on his banty legs getting in trouble, and Little Jim Dee just lying there hit by a stranger, silent, his little chest jouncing like he could not get his breath. I could not fathom it. I wanted to go kick that ugly man my own self, I wanted to pick up Little Jim Dee, I wanted to do something, *something*, and I wanted Papa to do some-thing, but not what he did. "Git up now, Jim Dee," Papa said, his voice in no way softer, and then he turned around and looked down the river where we were sweeping fast into the dark.

It might have meant nothing. Everything stirred and rushed after that, and it might've melted so easy into just one of the so many times Little Jim Dee got in trouble, if not for Mama's face when she went to him. She bent just from the waist a little, holding the baby in her crooked arm, said, "Here, son," and reached down her free hand. She looked up at Papa then, and I saw it in Mama's face, how she held her eyes and mouth upon him: our Papa was wrong.

Little Jim Dee did not know it. He got to his feet, and I could see how his chin was shaking, how he was trying to keep from crying, trying to hold his chest still, not looking at Papa, not looking at the raftsman, but stepping away from Mama, holding himself still and shamed and big. Then it all disappeared and was forgotten, that quick, in the rush of wind and the riversweep toward the far bank and the men hollering and working their long poles and cursing and Papa easing to the back of the wagon to calm the mules, and the men from Uncle Fay's raft on the sandbar hallooing us in the dark. Little Jim Dee went right at Papa's heels, and you could tell he didn't have an idea in the world that Papa never should have let an outsider touch him much less cuff him, that it was not himself but Papa who had done the bad thing, because Papa never should've taken a stranger's part. My brother just rushed when the others rushed and tried to act just like them, and Ringo, too, went around the raft baying his deep voice, and maybe nobody knew it except me and Mama. But I knew it, and Mama proved me, though she didn't look at me but only hard-eyed in the dark straight at Papa. But I knew that we knew it, the two of us together, and there was a change between us in that moment.

My mind could not wrap around and hold it, or did not want to, or I could not let Papa being wrong wrap around me, and so the knowledge washed away in the grit and grate of landing, and I was glad, I was willing. I squatted down and put my arms around Thomas. It was only later that I remembered. By then the fact of it had slipped into the new way of our lives together, no greater or lesser than the fact, maybe, that Papa never asked the blessing before we ate supper anymore.

Papa did not pause when we scraped up on the sand and stilled. He hitched the mules and unstopped the wheels and drove the wagon off before he even lit the lanterns, before we hardly understood that the rolling had stopped, and then he began to load in the dark inside the wagon. The raftsmen helped him with the cookstove, but they went back upon their raft right after, laughing in their nasty language, and watched while Papa put in and took out and put in again, cursing, our wooden crates and Mama's trunk.

Uncle Fay came and whispered something low, and Papa answered short and sharp. Later I could hear Uncle Fayette down by the yellow light on the other raft arguing with the other raftsmen, and yowyowyow they went until Papa hollered down there, "Pay the man, Fayette!"

It was late, late, I don't know how late, when we moved creaking off that sandbar, and the bearded raftsmen wrapped around once in filthy quilts and lying snoring on the empty raftwood floor like dogs behind us, and the cramped space inside the wagon even more cramped and mistaken and backwards because now Mama and Lyda slept at the rear of the wagon and me and the children up front behind Papa, and the wind sneaked in upon us even with the tarp flap laid down, and I was bothered because I could not see Mama because the crates were piled up between us and the cookstove was cockeyed and Papa had loaded our possessions all wrong.

I don't know when we stopped, but when I woke the first time it was deep night and we were not moving. I raised up and eased the flap aside and looked out. Papa was nodding in the yellow circle of coal oil light. The mules were asleep in the traces. There was no moon or stars for light, and that wind was still blowing, though soft.

My heart jerked tight, and I said, "Papa?"

His head snapped up and he slapped the reins on Delia's back. Never said a word nor looked me back, and we began to move again. I could not hear the other wagon, but I laid that off to the soft drone of wind, and I snuggled back down. I was glad for us driving on in the night. It was warm under the covers with the children, the wind was the sound of forever and sky and distance and dark, and Papa and old Sarn and Delia could carry us, the wagon rocking, the wind humming, on through the night.

When I woke at first light, the wind had died completely. As soon as my eyes opened I knew Uncle Fayette and Aunt Jessie and the six cousins were not close, not just because I couldn't hear them but because I felt it, and I did not know how they could have got far ahead in such cold and wind, but I didn't care. I was glad the wind had died. The cold now was wet cold, and stronger, seeping in through the wagonsheet. I believed we would stop then and camp, for the sake of the animals if not for Papa, but we just went on. In late morning the ice came. I understood then the meaning of the blue wind, but by then it was too late to stop and camp in a place of protection, too late to turn back.

It started first as cold rain. Wet crept up from the south, light at first, just misting so I barely could hear it, and then it became rain and began to spit at the side of the tarp. I remember that, how it came at the wagon's left side where my feet were crammed and curled tight beneath me. I could hear it spitting and then spatting and finally drumming steady on the tarp. Lyda was hiccuping at the back of the wagon. I couldn't see Mama. The children were still asleep, all of them, even Thomas when I slipped my arm from underneath him and pushed back the flap to see out. No wind then, just the slant of rain from the south, the wind's absence as strong as its presence, but I did not think. I looked around, as far as I could see, and the land was as flat as a door. I cannot describe to you how that was to me. I had never imagined the earth could be so lifeless, no more rise or fall to it than a coffin lid, and no trees that I could see anywhere around. The sight of it made me breathless and dizzy and a little bit frightened because I did not know what could have flattened the earth so. The air was a strange color, too bright for the overcast, almost greenish, even in that gray spitting rain. The water muddied the frozen ruts and drenched around the side of the tarp and poured against Papa, but his hat was pulled low and he acted like he was not even wet. I could hear Dan panting along by the right front wheel of the wagon. I couldn't hear Ringo, but I knew him, how he tried to run underneath. Bertha and her calf both were bawling. Delia kicked her head back and down again, trying to shake loose the bit, the mules' hooves sucked down in the muck and the wheels clogged and spinning, and Papa slapped the reins, hard, harder, silent, never once hyahing them. Papa did not treat his animals so. Never had I seen it. He'd been running them all night in that wind, and now here he was, going on and on and on in cold rain and mud. I could not fathom it, any more than I could fathom how or why he yelled at Little Jim Dee, but I would not ask. My papa was changed so.

The wind, dead once, I thought, suddenly, even as I watched, got resurrected, and it blew up stronger than an old sinner just born again. Sound came first, the rustling shift and change, and I did not know how the sound sent itself when there were no trees to tell of its coming, but I heard it like water rising in the north, and then came the blue wind swooping down from the north and across us like an army of angels, and it met that southern rain, or else brought its own, I don't know how it happened, but what happened was this: the cold rain slanting from the left suddenly shifted and slanted the other way, straight out, and became in that moment freezing rain, and we kept going on. There was thunder rolling above us and lightning flickering in the greenish sky and jagged hail falling in pieces big as horseshoe nails and small as the tiny tips of Lyda's fingers, and the hail thumped the tarp and cracked on the wagonseat and bounced and jumped off, and Papa did not stop. The hail transformed itself round and smooth as musket balls, grew small, became freezing rain again, became sleet, became tiny frozen pellets in gravelly masses covering the earth, and us going on, going on, and air and earth and sky turning sleet again, turning freezing rain, becoming at last all together, all iceform at once pelting down together, jagged and frozen like shattered hell falling, and it went on forever, for hours or days or forever it seemed like, the whole world turning ice and white, the sky white, the earth white, and flat, and there was nowhere to turn for protection. I knew then that this—*this*—was the place of no turning back forever. This was God's glory and punishment, and I thought Brother Hoyle lied when he preached it, because this old world is not burning. The end of the world is not fire, it is rain into sleet into hail into heavenly assault of white ice like the veil between heaven and earth rent, the whole world torn asunder. I thought we would die there, all of us together. Papa did not stop.

He drove those mules balking, he lashed them with the whip, their hooves caked and slipping, and you could see the ice chunking on the traces, the reins, the mules' necks and ears and withers all gray-white and spattered, the ice getting thicker and thicker, the wagonwheels slipping and catching and spinning, and Bertha carrying on something awful, I could not hear the calf at all now, and I had to at last, I had to, reaching my arm out. "Papa!" I cried. "Papa!"

He turned only a little, a little half turn, and his face was the face of an ice man, his mustache and sideburns white with ice, his brows white, his lashes, and he looked at me and did not see me, and he turned back again, slapped the whip.

The wagon stopped, and I don't know if it was the same day or the next one, for there was no such thing as time then, only the endless now of the crossing, but I do know it was after Little Jim Dee peed the bed because that smell was all around and part of it, and I know it was daytime, for the whole of the white blinded me when Papa called me to bring him the hatchet and I pushed back the flap to see out.

At first my eyes squinted shut nearly, and this not because of the sun, for there was no sun, no light but ice light, no horizon or source or direction but just endless white blinding me. When my eyes opened all the way I could see the wagonseat nubbed with the grit of ice pellets falling, and this seemed to me a good thing, not so slick as the frozen rain. But when I crawled out onto it I could find no firm place to put my hands but the depression where Papa had been sitting, and even that place was quickly icing in, though the veil was thinner and the pellets fell with spaces of air between them and not so very fast. I could not stand up. On my knees in the well I tried to lift the wagonseat to reach in where Papa kept his tools and get the hatchet. The lid was frozen shut. My hands already that fast were completely numb. Papa was hollering, his voice rising, not hard, not angry, just coming up to me louder from where he was at the back of the wagon, and I wanted, oh, I wanted to do it quick, what he asked me, but the ice was pelting fire needles on my face and fingers, and my eyes were stinging not with sunlight but with the force of ice, and I could not lift the lid. Then Papa was beside me, his hat brim folded down gray and solid, an inch thick with ice. He said nothing, but from where he stood on the ground reached up and with the heel of his gloved palm smashed the box lid upward, hit it again, and the ice seal broke and the lid jumped. Still kneeling, I pushed the lid up and got out the hatchet, and Papa said, "No, Mattie, reckon I'm going to need the axe."

I lifted the axe with both hands and handed it down to him. Papa turned and, keeping his free hand to the side of the wagon, disappeared in the white. Dan turned behind Papa, his splayed feet slipping, his black back and tan nose grizzled with sleet, and then, stepping deer-careful upon the pelleted earth, he disappeared too.

I could hear muted whacks coming from the back of the wagon, and I wanted to know what Papa was doing. I went to climb down. My shoes slicked right out from under me when they touched the wheelrim, and my hands could not help me, for there was nowhere but ice to touch, and down I went, skidding, the ice slicing my cheek where I fell. I got up and fell again, got up, and fell, and finally bellied to the near wheel and grabbed hold of a wheelspoke. My skin stung like it would freeze to the wood, but I held to it long enough to get my feet underneath me. I could hear Thomas inside the wagon, calling me, mumm mumm mumm, how he did then, but I went on, keeping a hand to the side of the wagon as I'd seen Papa do, except Papa had gloves and I did not, and it was only because the whacks came steady and harder that I kept my numb fingers out in the pelting ice to hold to the crusted sideboard, and went back.

We must have been dragging it a long way because just seeing it you would not even know that it had been a calf. You would know it had been an animal because the rope was still around its neck and the four legs still stuck out, but it was so mangled and the hide broken and the blood congealed red and black in the filthy ice casing that even Bertha did not pay it any more attention than if it had been a frozen sack. She stood with her head bowed nearly to the iced ground where Papa had laid hay, her near eye unfocused, not closed or open, and she was not chewing or flicking, not moving a muscle. Papa was hacking the rope near the calf's neck with the axe. I could see where he'd tried to cut it with the Bowie knife, and the knife lay on the ground getting covered in sleet. Ringo was chewing at the back end of the carcass, and he would flinch and duck each time Papa swung the axe. Papa hacked one more time and the rope broke like a stick, and, turning, Papa saw me. I felt then like Ringo to duck back, but he said only, "Git the knife, would you," and wound the frozen rope up in great stiff loops around his cocked elbow and shoulder, sliding slow on the ice toward the back of the wagon. He reached to put the rope on the hook, and it was then I saw the cover pulled off the chicken crate and the hens dead in gray masses of feathers frozen on their sides. I don't know if the rooster was dead yet, for he was still upright, back under where the hide hung over a bit, but he was perfectly still, and the ice was all on him and the crate floor. Papa could not get the frozen rope to stay on the hook. I watched him fool with it for a time until finally he pulled it back down and let it drop hard over his head and shoulder, draped like a white thick snake around him, and with the axe in one hand he started back around the side of the wagon to the front. Dan trotted, slipping and sliding, behind him.

Just a quick moment then I looked around, at Ringo gnawing the cut-loose mangled red thing in the shell of black ice, and Bertha with her head bowed and unmoving near the yellow hay turning white on the white earth before her, and the chickens dead on their sides, and Dan's black tail disappearing in the white behind Papa. I raised my eyes and looked out at the great white flatness, turning my head slowly, but there was nothing to see. There was no world out there, only our world, and our world was only us inside the smell and dark of the wagon behind Papa and Delia and old Sarn going on through the white and the veil around and behind and before us only to go through, keep going through, and keep on. That was all.

I looked down at the Bowie knife disappearing under the sleet. We would need it. Flat-footed, careful, I edged over to where it lay and dug in the ice crust with my fingers, and it was like something I remembered and did not remember, and the handle stung my hand but I wrapped it in the shawl and edged back toward the wagon to reach and hold to the side of it with my free hand.

The first that I saw them, they appeared dark blue and low over the lip of the horizon. They came when the sun came, and in the same place nearly, for the sun returned first in the west, not rising but sinking below the silver blanket of cloud. This would have been near the end of the second full day past the river, I remember, because the earth where the mules trod was not white. There were trees then, and the limbs were low and bare and sheathed in crystal, dripping, and the land rolled, and the sun sank below the sky, brightening it and turning the earth blue-white and glaring, and finally draining away purple. A little south of where the sun drained away is where I first saw them. I thought they were thunderheads maybe, rolling above the earth in the southwest, but when they did not change or draw nearer, I did not dread them, and anyhow we stopped then in a little copse and made camp.

Papa shook when he got down from the wagon. He stood on the ground and his legs trembled and his hand holding to the wheel quivered like he was shaking with fever. I thought at first he was sick. I said, "Papa?" He turned away and walked two steps over to a little rise and sat down upon it. Then he lay back flat on his back. His hat fell off and gaped openmouthed and stiff on the dark earth. I could see his legs jerking beneath his britches. He said to me, his voice calm, like it was in no way unusual to lie upon the frozen earth twitching on your back, he said, "Start supper, Matt."

We stayed there one night, our first camp since we left the river, our first time to eat proper and empty the pots and rub diapers and air out the smell. It was there in that bare tree copse we left the chickens dead in their crates, thawed enough by daylight to stink and so we ate only the rooster, and it was there we left Bertha, not dead yet but dying, and I don't know why Papa didn't shoot her unless maybe he did not want to waste the powder and lead. It was there, too, as I was helping Papa load the wagon at dawn and looked up to see the indigo shapes still in the distance, that I understood they were not cloudbanks or some purple drift skyward but a part of the earth itself, humped low on the southwestern horizon, pushing up from the ground. I knew, the way you will sometimes know a thing, one swift thought that speaks the word, that these shapes were mountains. I did not have to ask.

It seems strange to me now to think how foreign they looked then, the shape of them, humpbacked, blue in some lights and purple in others, and tapered low at the ends like great shell-less snails lining themselves east and west clamped to the earth. That humped shape now is burned in my heart like the lines of my own memory, but then to me they looked strange. They stayed the same distance for days, weeks even it seemed like, never coming nearer, never going back further, but riding always at the edge of forever as we went west. Sometimes they would disappear for a few hours behind trees or a turning fold of land, but then, when I wasn't looking, they would rise up watchful on the horizon again. We had long left the delta, and the land had returned itself normal, and the weather, too, was back common and normal, for spring was blowing up real by that time, and the mud sucked at the wheels something terrible, and there were days we made almost no time because Papa had to pry us from the mud with the tree limb he kept strapped to the sideboard, while I slapped the reins on the mules' straining backs.

I don't know what would have happened if Uncle Fayette and Aunt Jessie and the six cousins had not caught up to us, any more than I know what would have happened if anything ever had been different than what it was, but them coming in the night and Uncle Fay's horses snorting and Sarn answering is one event I wished forever had not happened. I regretted it later until I was eaten up with it and I could not stop. I went back over and over in my mind and told it that they did not find us, that they passed in the night and went on to Eye Tee without ever knowing we were camped by that road in the dark. I made Uncle Fay die in the ice storm, and sometimes Aunt Jessie. Sometimes I saw all eight of them frozen tipped on their sides like our chickens, or I made them turn back. I know now the truth that nothing will make you so sick as sorry, but I couldn't stop regretting any more than I could do anything to change what happened. I believed if only I'd known, if only I'd looked hard enough, understood the meaning of the blue wind, petted Sarn so he would not answer, if only *something,* I could have made everything different. Because if Uncle Fay had not caught up to us, we would have kept on straight west and never turned south into those mountains. Because it was always those mountains, I believe that, and how they affected my mama. How they rose up around us and closed when we entered, jagged and hard-edged toward heaven, tree-glutted, rock-bound, blocking the light.

Uncle Fay and Aunt Jessie had not lost any of their animals. They had lost nothing because they didn't come through the ice storm but stayed by the river until it was finished, all finished, and then they came across the flat land melted and running warm with spring behind Uncle Fay's swift horses. I understood they were force of family that could not be got away from, and it was expected in my heart that they would swoop up from behind without loss. I was only surprised that all that while without me knowing it, Papa had been the one in front. I tried not to think the next thought, which was what it had cost us.

But they came and wrapped around us, and right away it was as if we'd never been separated, except for the way Aunt Jessie shared eggs with us, so wide and smiling it made you want to be sick. They had no milk either, never had had because they never brought their cow with them, but Aunt Jessie made smiling sure to share their measly brown eggs. And right away, too, Uncle Fay started in upon Papa.

He had a plan to go south and come in to Eye Tee through the mountains. He talked it low at night, jabbing at the fire, darting his eyes around outside the light, more restless than ever. He said it was too dangerous to go in at Fort Smith, said the Law was crawling all over the place there. He said the whole country knew Hanging Judge Parker would as soon hang a thief as look at him, no telling what might happen. And for many nights when we camped, he went on like that. Papa acted like he did not hear him, except the one time he said, looking hard at Uncle Fay in the camplight, "They ain't going to hang a man for breaking a damn patent. Are they?"

Uncle Fay's eyes went sideways. "I don't know, Son. I couldn't say. Couldn't say for sure, now. You aim to find out?"

And Papa said, soft, just under his breath then, "Don't make a lick of sense to go west by heading south."

Fayette whispered, "That's a hellhole, Son, that jail there, you ever heard about it? A man might just as druther be dead."

Papa didn't answer. He did not say another word, either then or later, but Uncle Fay kept on and kept on, every night, about turning south to get to Eye Tee. Even I knew Eye Tee was west, because we had been traveling toward sunset for weeks then. I didn't even know he was talking about Indian Territory, for he never called it anything but Eye Tee, the way my mind saw it, and I believed Eye Tee was its name. Uncle Fay spoke the sound like the name stood for Heaven, and I guess I believed it must be so.

Every day we went on, but we went slower, which I marked but thought it on account of Mama, for every day she looked paler and weaker and her hand now almost never left that shut tight place at her chest, and we were gradually turning, which I did not mark somehow, watching Mama, until the dawn we were facing directly toward the mountains, close then, rising up snail-like before us, and the rising sun back over our left. Then I knew Uncle Fayette had won.

The road wound around and up, and behind us I could see the valley falling away pale green below, and it frightened me, the earth falling away and disappearing, and so I quit watching behind us and looked only at the back of the wagon—for we were walking then, all of us, even Mama, to ease the weight—or I would walk up front beside Papa and keep my eyes to the rocky earth rolling beneath the mules' feet. The sides of the hills were hardscrabble. Uncle Fay said the road had been looked out by the loggers down in Booneville, said it was a good road, said loggers always sighted the best way to go. He lashed his horses and hyahed them because they did not want to climb. Papa said nothing, not the first day or second, nor later, growing each day more silent, but he did not whip his mules. Everywhere were great stumps of trees like fire corpses, until they began to dwindle and mix in with living trees tall as God, I thought then, and then the stumps disappeared and the mountains closed thick with woods and insects.

Dark dropped quicker because of the hillsides. Morning came later. Evenings after we'd camped I would sit for hours in shadow and watch the twilight stretch blue and starless, lingering late, high above. I knew the days were getting longer, were supposed to be getting longer, because it was well into spring then, almost summer, but I couldn't feel the sun coming back to us in those mountains at all. The climb grew steeper, and each time we crested, all we could see before us were more mountains rolling dark blue into skyhaze to the south. We never came up over a hogback like Uncle Fayette said we would, to ease down again to a smooth valley and turn west. Each day we went slower. Each day my mama was paler. Each night Uncle Fayette's mouth got worse.

It started out him talking about Mama. He never said a word directly to her or to anyone, but spoke soft straight ahead while he jabbed the fire. Said he'd heard of some kind of weak-minded women scared of their own shadow, some kind of lily women—and this is how he called it, meaning only our Mama—scared of Injins in Eye Tee, scared of a little ole biddy copperhead snake. He would talk like that, poking the fire, not saying it directly to anyone but muttering in his beard for the whole world to hear, especially Papa. I'd see him cut his eyes at Papa all the time. Sometimes he'd get up and go off awhile in the dark behind the wagons, and when he came back to the fire again, his blue eyes would glitter and his voice would be loud. Yessir, these lily women, he'd say, poking the ashes, They ain't no kind of pioneer women. Ain't the same stock the Lodis come from. Scared of some pitiful old Injins getting fat in Eye Tee. Scared of a garter snake, he reckoned. Scared of a June bug squallylegged on its back. He'd heard that, Uncle Fay would mutter, and then he'd shake his head and turn his face away from the fire to spit.

When he talked about the Injins in Eye Tee, Aunt Jessie would call little Pearline to her and stroke her scrawny head and lift her own head, looking brave, I guess she thought it, like she wasn't afraid of anything on God's earth or under it, including red heathen savages. I would get so mad then, just furious, because I knew Mama *was* afraid of Indians, because *I* was, and I would call Thomas to me and rub *his* head and lift my own face brave and courageous to the dark outside the circle of light from the fire, and it was all a lie. I was a fake in my heart, both then and later, because I finally understood that Eye Tee meant Indians, and at night in the wagon I pulled my feet up and tucked my knees tight under my chin so that Thomas beside me got nothing but hard bone to rest against, because I was afraid the Injins would sneak around the wagon and chop off my feet while I slept. Injins and Eye Tee and the darkness in those mountains were all the same to me then.

The road thinned, became a hard rutted track growing thinner and thinner, until it was two faint rails fading to nothing beside a little trickling creek in the high cleft of those mountains. We stopped and camped in the early part of the afternoon, though the light was still good, but the road was fading. The two tracks went down and disappeared like a ghost road into dark pine woods below the clearing, you could not see where they went, and it was there in that clearing that Papa and Uncle Fayette had their knockdown-dragout fight.

I know how they tell it now, Mildred and Pearline and them. I know they say Uncle Fay went on to prepare a place for Papa like Jesus going on to Heaven. I know they say the two of them made it up together, and it was all to protect Mama, but I was there, mind you. This is me here. Matt Lodi. I remember all of it. Every bit of it. Just this way.

We were camped on someone else's land, though we didn't yet know it, and at first it was three days, and then four days, and soon it was a week, and then longer. Mama did not come out of the wagon except to eat a little bite in the evening, and then she'd go back with the baby and lie down. Uncle Fay didn't even talk under his breath now but straight out, loud enough for Mama to hear from where she lay in the wagon. Loud enough for all of us. He'd put it like a question, like he was asking the ashes, and then he'd spit, the tobacco juice sizzling in the red underpart, Uncle Fay's answer. What were we going to do for food when the supplies run out, did anybody reckon? Put in a crop on the rock side of a mountain with no sun? What were we going to live on till that lily woman got well, rocks and water? Spit then, and sizzle. Wasn't but so-many miles fu'ther, just over the hog-back and down again west, but no-sir, we got to sit and starve for a woman, he reckoned. Spit.

Every night he said it, sitting on a tree stump, poke, poke, poking at the fire. I'll never forget that, the image burned harder and brighter in my mind's eye than those mountains: Uncle Fayette in his big hat with his pine stick jabbing every word from his brown mouth into the fire's spark and ashes. His boys then, Caleb and Fowler, they'd act just like him, poking and spitting, though they knew better than to speak it, but Uncle Fay just kept on and on in a singsong about food and Mama, food and Mama, like it was food and Mama that landed us up there in those mountains with the road fading before us and nowhere to go but back down like we'd come, and my papa saying nothing, saying nothing, like he never heard him, till I thought I would scream or puke from rage, and I could not understand why Papa would not *do* something. But all he did was ignore Uncle Fay like he was deaf to him, or else Papa would just go off to hunt. Every dawn and dusk he went out, and when he'd get back and had finished cleaning whatever he'd shot—mostly squirrel, sometimes rabbit, one time a slick, stringy old coon—he'd put it down by the fire for me to cook and go over to the wagon to check the supplies bin. He'd look in the box at so-much cornmeal left, so-much beans, so-much molasses, and none of it enough, and he wouldn't say a word about it but just turn away then to do some little piece of work. In the high part of day, Papa tended the animals or went off by himself and stayed gone for hours. At night he sat off away from the fire by the lantern and mended harness, sharpened tools, such niggling jobs as that.

When we'd been camped for ten or twelve nights maybe, a man showed up one morning. He wasn't an old man, I think now, but he looked old to me then, his skin washed out and wanly freckled and his hair where it curled out beneath his hat so pale it looked silver. He had great tufts of bright yellow hair growing out of his chest that stood up startled and met his reddish beard, and that was the only color upon him—that and his blue eyes—for even his clothes were washed out and pale. His voice was burred and lilting, and he scared me a little, but Papa was not scared. He went out behind the wagon with the man to the place where the woods were thinnest and squatted on the ground with him and talked for a long time. The next morning I woke up when I heard the sound of wood chopping. Papa never said a word to any of us but went to cutting trees, and in the afternoon he took Little Jim Dee to help him.

That night Uncle Fayette picked up a stone, gnawed it like a corn ear, tossed it off into the darkness. "Corn don't grow on rock," he said.

Papa said nothing.

"Some folks are fools," Uncle Fay said. He picked up his green pine stick to poke the fire with. "Some folks are fools for a woman, some are just jackasses in general, I reckon." Poking, talking loud. "Can't see it matters much, seeing as we're all going to starve like dogs anyhow. Seeing as there might be enough cornmeal and grits left to get us to Eye Tee." Jabbing like the fire itself was Eye Tee. "Ain't enough to wait for some lily woman to get some gumption about her. Ain't enough to wait for planting." Gold sparks whirling, spinning skyward to disappear in the dark. "Provided it'd do any good to wait for planting to start with, seeing as what mule-killing land I seen around here ain't going to yield a crop worth pulling nohow, which any fool ought to be able to see." Jab the flames. Spit. "Any fool but a blind ignorant jackass fool like God seen fit to give me for a baby brother."

And Papa quiet such a long time, through all of it, letting Uncle Fayette go on and say it, how we'd *all* (jab), every last *one* (jab) of us *Lo-dyes* (jab jab), flat starve to *death* (jab) there in *Ar-kan-saw* (jab jab jab). We'd *flat* (jab) *well* (jab) never make it to *Eye Tee* (jab jab), where the pickins was so easy. Spit. And on and on, jabbing, bits of fire swirling, that same night, that worst night, when Mama did not go to lie down in the back of the wagon but sat with us in the circle of firelight with the baby Lyda upon her lap and Uncle Fayette raving on about Eye Tee, where there was no law but Injin law which was no law, and Eye Tee, where Papa could make his guns, wouldn't nobody threaten to flay the hide off him and then shoot his skint corpse over a blame gun patent in Eye Tee, where it was good land, milk and honey land, you could take it slick, like plucking apples from the roadside, like picking persimmons, just over the next ridge and so-many miles west, to Eye Tee, where Uncle Fayette had it all mapped out for us to live.

And Papa quiet for just a little while longer. Then he said, his voice level, soft nearly, looking at him, "Yes, Brother, you have a way of mapping things out for all of us pretty damn good."

Then they were both quiet and it was just the fire snapping and the peepers peeping on the black creekbank, for it was already that late in the season, and then the two of them at once rose up together from opposite sides of the fire and clashed together like goats butting. They fought all over the cleared space between the two wagons, with the children crying and the cousins shouting and Aunt Jessie screaming and the dogs barking and Mama saying soft, No, John, No, John, No, John, like he could even hear her over that yelling and yapping and him and Uncle Fayette grunting, and me, I'm probably the only one who heard Mama because I was standing beside her from the moment Papa and Uncle Fayette rose up in silence, butting.

While it was going on it seemed to go on forever, and then when it was over I couldn't believe it was over so quick. Before I could realize it, Papa was on his back in the dirt, winded, with his shirt bloody, holding a hand up, palm open, in the air.

To this day I believe he let Uncle Fay lick him. I know he did. He had to, because Fayette was never big in his back and shoulders like Papa, he never had the same strength in his arms. He couldn't swing a sledgehammer like Papa or carry a deer on his neck from the deer woods nor in any way hold a candle to Papa, because my papa in those days was strong.

The next morning at first light when I got up to start breakfast, Uncle Fayette and Aunt Jessie and the six cousins were gone. They'd left in the middle of the night, the same way we'd all left Kentucky. I didn't think anything about that then, but later I did.

The first thing Papa made—he began it the next day, I remember, because his lip was swelled up like a hog bladder, his eye shut nearly, and he would grunt every time he bent over—but first thing there in those mountains, Papa smoothed down a tree stump and set a back to it and rolled it to the place at the side of the wagon where the sun touched first and stayed longest. All day Mama would sit there, her eyes following Papa back and forth while he cleared and broke ground. There was more color in her face then, her fist was loose then, though she still seldom said anything but just held Lyda and nursed her and was quiet on the tree stump and watched.

It was only a truck patch, no more than a quarter acre, but it took him a long time because that ground was so rocky, the tree stumps were many, and he broke the plow point and had to borrow Misely's anvil to make a new one, and we had only the singletree and so he could only plow one of his mules at a time. Papa put in squash and beans and sweet potatoes—he said it was too late for corn, which it wasn't, or at least not any too much later than for the rest of what we planted, and that's something else I didn't think about then—and I helped when I could. I'd go bent behind him with our seeds and potato starts, Thomas crawling in the furrows behind me, trying to pull himself up on my skirt, and Mama watching Papa with that fierce look on her. Intent. Hopeful. Like she expected any minute for him to do something other than what he was doing.

The tallow-faced man, Misely, came around every day or so and talked to Papa. It was his land we were camped on, but he let us plant there, only too glad, I guess, for the work of clearing Papa was doing, and to my knowledge he never asked so much as a half bushel of nothing for pay. He had a wife and a passel of children who were white-blond and palely freckled just like him, and shy and silent, the children more than anything. I don't recollect hearing hardly one of those children say a word. The old man's bright chest hair and his faded red beard danced and sparred with each other when he talked, and it reminded me of Grandpa Lodi's white eyebrows, how they would jump up and fidget on his forehead when he got going good talking, and in this way I liked and feared the old man Misely, and he seemed to belong to us somehow, though his tongue was so strange.

When he came in the evenings to talk to Papa, his passel of children—boys mostly, but there were three or four girls too—would trail a little ragtag tail behind him. Sometimes there'd be ten of them, sometimes eleven or thirteen, I quit even counting, and the old man would leave them to stand around outside the split-rail fence Papa was putting up. He'd step over the rails and go off with Papa, the two of them together, to squat in the dirt behind the wagon and talk. His children would stand outside the fence and look. I'd linger on the near side of the wagon, acting to be busy sorting beans or something, and I'd listen to Papa and Mr. Misely. I never found out any secrets that way, because their talk was just crops and hunting and farm stock, how a man in the mountains needed a good brace of oxen—but it was Mr. Misely's voice I listened for anyway. Just the sound of it, thick and burred and accented from somewhere which even now I can't place. So I'd act busy and listen and keep an eye on the Misely children, because I did not in any way trust them. There was something big-eyed and hungry in them, the way they stood there, their fingers holding to the rails, looking at all of us, silent, like we were the strange ones. I was sneaky, how I watched them, and I told Jonaphrene to ignore them, but she would stand in the yard with her hands cocked on her hips and stare right back at them, because Jonaphrene knew who was strange.

So the days just went on. The weather got hotter. Our provisions got leaner. Our new shoots came up slow. I knew it was on account of the poor ground and so little sunlight, though our clearing was broad and getting broader all the time with Papa cutting. I would take Thomas sometimes and go walking back along the road the way we'd come, or if he wasn't with me, so I didn't have his weight to carry, I'd climb the craggy sun-tipped ridge on the far side of the water, trying to see, trying to see, but all I could see was trees and mountains marching off in any direction. Once or twice I followed the two fading tracks along the creek to the place far below our clearing where they turned away from the water and disappeared into deep woods. I never went in there, because those were the woods that swallowed Uncle Fayette and Aunt Jessie and the six cousins, and it was the place the man Misely and his blond children walked in from, and those dark piney woods were a boundary to me. The mountains were strange, I could not fathom them, how they could be so scraggly and mean and hot in the daytime, the rocks keen with scorpions and lizards, the trees whining with locusts, little stubs of prickly pear and stunted cedar on the high ridges, and yet the water sang clear and cool on the rocks trickling by our clearing, the slopes around us hidden tall and dark and wet with sweetgum and pine. At night it got cold. I would tell myself sometimes, looking up at the black wedge of sky or along the ridge eastward, *This is not the same world as back home in Kentucky. That is not the same moonlight. Those are not the same stars.*

Jonaphrene whined at night with the bellyache, and me, my stomach cramped too, though I wouldn't tell it. I'd give my portion to Thomas a lot of times to make him hush up, I had to, because we'd left Bertha dying on the ice sheet and even though Thomas was the knee-baby and needed milk, Mama said she could not nurse him, and he would cry and cry. Some mornings we'd find a sack of snap peas or early okra by the rail fence, sometimes a full milk bucket, once a big round cake of butter, and I knew one of the Misely children had been sent by the father and had come and left it in the dark. Papa hardly ever hunted, though there was good game in those mountains and we were all hungry, but I did not ask why. Never in our lives did we ask questions of our parents, you just did not do so, ever, nobody did. But I wondered sometimes. Like why, if we meant to go on as soon as we'd brought in our little crop, why was it Papa worked so hard, all day, every day, to make that camp look like the old place back home in Logan County?

He'd built a lean-to out of rough-cut and blankets under a big oak tree beside the wagon and hauled the featherbed out of the wagon and crammed it inside. Then he went on and split rails for the fence, like the old one, to keep the mules out of the yard. He dug violets from the deep woods and planted them in a little half-moon in front of the wagon, dug an outhouse like our old one, strung a pulley rope for the washing at the exact same angle as our old clothesline had run, south and east from the house. Papa cut and sawed and toted and carried and hauled rocks and rocks and more rocks out of that clearing, and sometimes he'd call me to help him because Little Jim Dee was just too little and wild and distracted, he couldn't stay put on any task Papa set for him but would chase off after a lizard or something until Papa would get mad and holler at him and tell him to go on then, get out from under foot. Then Papa would call me to come on and hold the pry bar for him or something, and I'd put Thomas down and go help him, feeling Mama's eyes, watching.

I could not tell you the precise moment when it happened. It was just a slow waking—me waking to the change within Mama, her waking to what Papa was doing—but it changed, sure enough, how she watched him; it was not less fierce, but there was no expecting in it now, no waiting for something, and she no longer sat on her hollowed-out tree stump when she watched him, and it was not Papa only she watched.

It was that that first made me wake to the change in her—how Mama watched me. How she watched all of us children, like we were strangers, like every word out of our mouths, every gesture—the way Jonaphrene cocked her forehead and made faces, the way Thomas sucked his two fingers or Little Jim Dee tried to back up and lean against her—like all of these were ways belonging to children from some other country. I did not know what it was she marveled at in me, but she stared at me not only when I was with Papa but any moment I came in front of her eyes, and it was the same with me as with all of us—as if she had not ever seen a one of us move or speak in this way before.

And in a short time, not long after I first saw her so watching us, Mama got up from her tree stump one morning and put the baby on the pallet in the shade, and from that minute on, she followed Papa. Whatever he was doing, Mama went right behind him, her eyes fierce on him, and I thought she was helping, or trying to, but I believed she was just unabled from being sick and still and out of practice for so long. She was furious, though, you could tell that. I thought it was us she was mad at, me and the children, and I tried to do right, but I did not know what would make her not mad. I thought, too, that my mama had forgot how to work. The day Papa strung the rope for the washline, Mama did a load of washing with cold creekwater right there beside him while he was hanging the pulley. She never put the tub on the fire but just rubbed cold lye soap on the cold clothes—and her arms so thin it did not even seem she could hold a rub board, but she would not let me help her but looked me back hard—and then *slap! flap!* she flung the wet clothes, not even wrung out, just sopping in fury over Papa's newly strung washline till it sagged deep from the weight. Then she stared at us—me and Thomas and the children— dazed and furious, while she pressed her hand to her chest and caught up to her breathing, and then she turned and went after Papa to whatever he was doing next.

Every day she did like that. The evening Papa planted violets by the fence row, Mama poured the dirty dishwater on them till they drownded. When he weeded the truck patch, she went behind him with the broken pieced-together hoe and chopped the squash vines so close we lost nearly all of them. When he split shingles with the froe for the lean-to because the pine bough roof was leaking water, Mama climbed up on the bows of the overjet above the wagon—and they were not iron but just bent sapling wood, how Papa had fixed them, and I didn't know how they would hold a child's weight, but I believe my mama did not weigh much more than a child anyhow—she climbed up and balanced there, Papa frowning so with worry, but he did not stop her, and Lyda shrieking in the lean-to, hungry, and my mama perched like a bird atop the tarp-covered bones of the wagon, laying those rough shingles before Papa could hardly finish splitting them and hand them up to her, and oh, I was afraid for her then, so thin and breathing hard, balanced on the high, dirty puff of the wagon, reaching, pounding nails with the claw hammer like she would pound that fragile lean-to into the earth.

I heard them one night. We still slept in the wagon, me and Thomas and the children, but Mama and Papa slept with Lyda in the lean-to. The dogs were restless, not baying steady but howling every now and then, long and lonesome, and then they'd settle down awhile, snapping and ornery, only to raise up and howl again because of something they smelled outside in the dark. I believed it was Indians they were smelling. The children were hard asleep, Thomas snoring his tiny soft snores beside me, and I was afraid to move, afraid to breathe nearly, and I didn't know why. I had my legs pulled up and folded in front of me like always, because I was ever more afraid of losing my legs from the knees down than of losing my hair. So I was awake, hugging my knees and breathing lightly, and afterwhile the dogs settled down completely, and it was quiet. I heard my name. Papa spoke it.

"Take Matt then!" he said. "Take Matt and the baby!" He was whispering loud, though you could tell he was trying not to, his voice scraping harsh through the papery wood and blankets of the lean-to.

"How, John?" Mama's voice was so thin. Thin like the bones in her arms. "How can I? You know I can't."

"*I* can't, Demaris. *I* can't. I can't go back, you know that, but you won't ever hear it. All right then, take the wagon, take Matt and Lyda, go back. We won't wait for any damn crop. I'll take the others on."

"In what?"

It was quiet just a heartbeat, and then I heard Papa say, "I'll hire out from Misely." Quiet a little longer, and then Papa's voice coming softer, without the harsh scrape in it. "I don't know what else to do. What do you want me to do?"

"Take me home."

A rough sound, a disgust sound from Papa.

"Take me home, John."

"Are you deaf, woman? Are you stupid?"

"Take me home to my family, John. I want to go home." Mama's voice came low and steady and relentless, like she really couldn't hear him, or like she had only those words crowding her mind, no room left in it for hearing. "We've come far enough, we do not need to go farther. Take me home."

"I ain't! I done all I could, woman."

"What? What have you done but tear me from my family to bury me in these mountains? I cannot breathe, John, I can't stand up straight."

"—stopped here for you to get to feeling better—"

"—cannot breathe, you are choking—"

"—put us in a crop—"

"—me, this dark is choking me—"

"Take 'em and go back! *Go* on back if you think you're just going to die for your mama. I mean it. Mattie can drive them mules. Y'all go on back."

I thought I heard that old sound then, the sound like Sudie's pups crying beneath the porch steps, but I could not be sure, and my heart was squeezing so tight with that thought then, me going home to Kentucky with Mama, and Papa kept on, but softer a little. Only a little.

"I got to go on. I got to. If you got to go back awhile yet, you could. I believe Mattie could drive 'em."

"Not a while, not *while*, John."

"I'll just go on and get settled. When I get us a house built, I can send word. It won't take more than a few months maybe. Y'all can come by train. Won't no law be looking for you on a train, you can come easy on the train, ride it right into the Territory, I heard that, somebody said it at Booneville, they're laying tracks plumb across the Territory. Or else . . . y'all could . . . you could just come on with me now."

It was quiet a real long time, and when she spoke again, I heard it, the ferociousness in Mama's voice, like the look upon her in the days since she'd got up from her tree stump, like how she would work and destroy everything in fury, the sound thin still, seeping out of her like a leak in an earth dam. "They're little savages already, John! I do not intend to raise my children amongst a bunch of heathen."

"Ain't only heathen in Eye Tee."

"I guess you count your brother."

"Hush up about Fay." Papa's voice scratching deep in his throat, him holding it, holding it. "Don't start on Fay."

"Start," Mama said. "Start?" And I heard her move in the bed-clothes and a little harsh breath sound from her, though I did not know if it was a half-laugh or half-cry, and then her voice came back with the same wiredrawn fury. "They're *hungry,* John! Your children are hungry and you don't see it, they're turning wild, and you don't see that either. Look at Jonaphrene! Look at her hair snarled a rat's nest full of cockleburs! Your son spins around like a tongue-talker, you can't make him sit still one minute or do a lick of work, Mattie's turning into some kind of pinched-up little hull of I-don't-know-what. Look at her! Look at your daughter. She hasn't got an ounce of meat on her, she runs around here on spit and spite, lugging that baby and worrying the rest of them to death trying to boss them, the baby can't walk nor talk right, he's going on two years old, John, his legs bowed out like elb—"

"Whose fault is that?"

"Whose fault what? Tommy's bones too soft to carry him because you let our cow die?"

"That your firstborn has to be mother to your children."

"Whose—?" Mama's voice so high and frail it could be a wisp rising through the shingles. "Whose fault but *yours*—to carry us—carry us off from our *home*—to live like the very heathen of the earth—"

"You're my wife. I didn't put you in no tow sack."

"Yours and your foul-mouthed brother with his *big* ideas, his *big* talk—"

And then I did hear it. The muffled sound again. Like Sudie's pups. I lay stiff and quiet, not breathing for sure now, waiting. Trying to hear. Blood beat in my chest, my ear on the pillow. Jonaphrene coughed, and I reached over and pinched her. She said No!, still asleep, and kicked me. I put my hand on her back, firm, and in a bit she got quiet. But still I couldn't hear them. I stayed awake long after my parents' voices went silent, long after I heard Papa snoring. Stayed awake listening, for what could never be heard or said anyhow, holding my legs safe from the Indians, quiet, hardly breathing.

From that night there grew to be an edge in Papa, a jagged rough thing like the ridges all around us, and it was worse in him, and different, from his hard voice on the porch steps with Grandpa Lodi and Uncle Big Jim Dee, worse even than his face coming through the ice. He was short with me and the children—especially Little Jim Dee, it got to where he stayed on Little Jim Dee all the time—and then he'd jump all over any of us for being too loud around Mama. He worked fiercer and harder than ever I saw him, long before daylight, long, long after dark. He would grunt and move and sweat and not talk, but you could hear it in him, like breathing, like the sweat dripping from him: *More work could work off the trouble. More work could wear away that look upon Mama.*

But more work could not do it. Our mama got worse.

It wasn't that she got weak again, exactly, but more like she fell back and began to disappear inside her own mind. She sat all day in the sun, like before, alone with the baby on her tree stump. She quit pretending to work, quit watching Papa, quit the rest of us. Her eyes turned more and more inward, to herself—and down, in her lap, to Lyda, the last baby. Her fist went back tight to her chest.

And Papa just kept working. He couldn't see that each touch he tried only made Mama fall back farther. It was such a ferocious thing in him. He wouldn't get finished with one idea for that camp before he'd start in on another, and all of it to make it look like the homeplace, and none of it, none of it could do what he wanted. I could see it, but I couldn't stop it. I couldn't stop her disappearing and I couldn't stop Papa, and so I just watched and tended Thomas and tried to make the children mind and be quiet and stay out of the way.

Sometimes I helped him when Mama's back was turned. I didn't know then why I hid my helping from Mama, but I did and only worked with him when she was resting in the lean-to and Thomas was down on the pallet in the shade for his nap. Alone with Papa I worked hard. I pretended to believe the same as he did, that somehow we could make it right or please her or make time go backwards, though I knew in my heart we never could. Because the earth in that place was high and jagged and completely unyielding. Because it held back the sun. There was no house there, no graves there, we'd left the pie safe and the chifforobe. It wasn't Kentucky. But I went on and helped him, Lord help me, in secret, even though it was melting my mama. I was young then. I was ten then. I didn't understand.

Well, you know then my mama saw me.

I remember it. How she stood in the arc of the lean-to, holding the ragged pink blanket to the side. I don't know what woke her up. She stood there, one half of her, half her face, in shadow. Looking at me and Papa. No. Not Papa. Only me. There. Where I crouched with my hands on the great wedge Papa used for a chisel, keeping it steady for Papa while he carved out a new seat stump. Stood a long time, still and quiet, just looking. Then she turned slow and went back and disappeared in the dark inside the lean-to.

So that was when the last change began.

It wasn't something sudden you could see in one minute—no more than there'd been an earth mark in winter that said Now You Are Gone From Kentucky; no more than there'd been one moment when she'd known, and so I'd known, that Papa was trying to shape the old homeplace out of those mountains—it was just change slow and gradual, growing in her the same as the green crops were creeping up slow out of the earth. For a time I don't think anybody knew it but me and Mama.

It started that she kept me with her. Where for months she had sent me off with the children to keep them quiet and away for her, now she'd call me if I was away from her doing something, no matter if it was chores or cooking that had to get done. She'd ask me to get her a cool drink of water. She'd let me brush her hair. She still couldn't abide the children, even Thomas, but she held Lyda and nursed her and called me to come to her a dozen times a day.

Then, not too long—it wasn't so very long though it seemed to me then so—my mama began to talk to me. It was just a little at first, just telling me this one thing, how her mother was born in London, England, where the King of all English-speaking peoples lived. But then more and more Mama kept me with her—she would send Jonaphrene to fetch me if I dropped out of her sight—and Mama touched me, put her hand on my hair, on my shoulder, and she talked to me, the words falling each day freer and faster, till at last it all came like a hymn or a history, like a waterfall she couldn't stop or hold on to, couldn't say fast enough; she said them, she whispered them, soft and low and furious, many of them the same words, again and again.

And so Papa saw this change within Mama, and the change between her and me. He'd come upon me sitting in the hot sun with Mama, and he'd be still a long time. Then he'd say, Matt, here, put on these britches, I seen a late patch of blackberries back in that deep holler. He'd say, Matt, come with me to fetch water. Matt, I need you to come help me chop wood. Then he changed even that, and it was, Here, Matt, skin this rabbit. Matt, jump up here and load the rifle, we're going for squirrel.

Thomas, he was walking pretty good then, and he'd totter after me, whining Momo, Momo, and acting like I was his mama that didn't have time for him, when in truth it was my mama who was his mama and didn't have the will to be with him, and Jonaphrene and Little Jim Dee were turning wild as red Comanches with nobody to look after them, and that's how it was then, and I didn't even know it or see it or think a thing about it.

I look back now, I see how that time set everything in me. Set me and determined me the way next year's peaches get set in the silent buds over winter. Oh, it'd been coming a long time, I know that, but it was those days that settled everything—only then I didn't know. I was just thrilled my mama talked to me, she'd never talked to me in all my life. I was glad Papa called me Matt and cut his brown trousers off at the legs for me to wear to go blackberry picking and taught me to hunt. I was glad even, though I swatted his little hands and walked off from him, that my brother Thomas thought I was his mother in this world.

It was the last part of July—July the twenty-second—but it wasn't so very hot yet on that morning because the sun had just climbed over the eastern rim. The dirt and leaves where I sat on the ground beside Mama were still damp. That's how it was in those mountains. No matter how hot and dry in the daytime, at night the dew fell and the whole world got damp. Mama was stroking my hair with her left hand because her right hand now did not ever, not even when she nursed Lyda, my mother's hand never left that squeezed-shut tight place between her breasts. Thomas and Lyda were sleeping. I didn't know or even think about where Little Jim Dee and Jonaphrene were.

"The Billies," Mama said, "came west into Kentucky from Virginia. There were seven brothers: James and Thomas and Oliver, William, Alexander, Obediah, called Bede, and your grandfather Cornelius, who died at Vicksburg in the War. That was Eighteen Sixty-three, which seems a long time ago to your young mind, but it is not long at all. I was fourteen when my father died, and he was thirty-nine. Now . . ." Mama's skirt shifted, and her voice faltered, then she pulled her hand away from my hair. "Now," she said, and her voice waxed strong again, "the Billies came to Kentucky in the year Eighteen Hundred and Forty, and that is where Cornelius Billie met your grandmother Mary Whitsun, who was born in London, England, where the King of all English-speaking peoples lives . . . Where . . . my mama was born . . ." Fading again. Faltering. Passing her hand down her face. Rising. "Born in London, England, in the year Eighteen Twenty-seven, and traveled with her parents and two sisters to the United States of America in . . . in Eighteen Thirty, settling first in Ohio and then in Logan County, Kentucky, where Mary Elizabeth Whitsun and Cornelius Billie were joined in holy matrimony in the year of our Lord Eighteen Hundred and Forty-eight. They had six progeny, and those were . . . those children were . . ." Mama's voice trailed off into the sunlight and died there.

"Uncle Thomas," I whispered. I could feel the heat coming. "Uncle Neeley, Aunt Lizbeth, Aunt Minnie . . ."

But Mama wasn't listening. She was staring across the yard clearing to the pine brush on the other side. "When I was your age—" she started. She stopped again. Black flies whipped the air around us. Locusts whined in the hot trees. Mama stared at the brush, where there was nothing, her breath quick and urgent, as if she chased it, chased it, and could not catch and hold it.

I watched Mama's face. Her skin was brown and freckled now, like the tan spotted eggs Papa found in a ground nest one time and brought in for me to cook. Back home, in Logan County, my mama's skin had been pale as milk. "I don't aim," Mama said, squinting, "to raise my daughters in a place full of nothing but men and red heathen savages. I don't by any means intend to do it." She touched my hair again. I knew it was coming then, and I held my breath.

I had held it, this secret hope and fear, ever since I heard Papa say it that night from my bed in the wagon. Sometimes I dreamed it. I saw me sitting in the seat of the wagon, holding the mules tight in the traces, driving, driving forever back over that land that had unrolled behind us, back down out of the mountains and across the great flat place and the river, east toward the rising sun for a long ways and then, when it was time, and I would know when it was time, turning north again, traveling days, cooking nights, me taking Mama back home. I could feel something coming, and I believed we were leading up to it, there on that morning with the heat rising and the black flies and locusts and the quiet and the children gone. I thought, *Today is the day she will tell me.*

But Mama pulled her hand away and passed it over her eyes. "He thinks—" she said, her voice strong now, and urgent, but it was not to me she was talking, I only the same to her as a black fly or locust, I not then even there for a witness. "He thinks he can appease me with fences and tree stumps and wild violets planted in a clearing. He thinks . . ." She stopped again, staring, and the necessity drained slowly out of her face. She was quiet a long time, and then she said, and this to me, this direct to me but rising weak, like a halfhearted question, "I was married . . . in a dress . . . of white linen . . . ?"

She leaned back and closed her eyes, her one hand in the place where it lived in a fist against her chest, her other hand brown and limp in her lap. I heard the baby Lyda crying in the lean-to. I knew she had been crying a long time. Mama opened her eyes, wet and milky blue, and she looked down at me. "Honey?" she said. "You know it? I'm never going to see my mama again. I'm never going to see Kentucky. I'm never going to see my home."

There was a noise then. A great thrashing and yelling, like when Papa and Uncle Fayette had their knockdown-dragout, only it did not rise from the clearing around us but fumbled and smashed toward us from the deep brushy woods. Louder, and coming louder, until at last Papa crashed into the clearing, with the dogs and the man Misely holding Papa's gun and a dozen blond Misely children and our children whirling alongside him, the dogs barking and jumping and

Jonaphrene and Little Jim Dee hollering and jumping, and Thomas waking up on his pallet under the pine tree to join his wailing voice with Lyda bawling in the lean-to, and Mama's grief drowning in it, disappearing in it like a dead leaf sucked in a whirlpool, because Papa held in his two hands, above the leaping mouths and fingers, the cut and bloodied head of a bear. My papa was grinning. Blood dripped in small plops onto the rock dirt of the clearing.

"Look here, wife," Papa said. "You nearly lost a husband on this day, did you know it?"

And Mama, she did look, I know she did look. But she looked in that moment like Grandma Billie. Her eyes empty circles.

I had no warning. When the memory first started, I only saw Grandma's face toward us. Her dress thin like summer. Her eyes empty, rolled up, looking after, on the morning it would not turn morning. But there in the clearing, in the midst of the yipping and yapping and hollering and snapping, the mystery came on me for the first time, and the remembering went dark. I could not see then, only listen, because Grandma Billie couldn't see us leaving Kentucky forever, but she could hear us: all seven of our family in the wagon, and the new baby crying, Papa's tongue clicking, his voice—*hyah!*—the mad rooster crowing, wheels creaking, the mules going *thud* in the dirt roadbed where their feet fell and Uncle Fayette's horses even on the hard dirt going *clopclop*, and Mama, my mama, making that sound like Sudie's pups, only soft, softer than footfalls, so soft none but Grandma Billie could hear it.

Inside me it was thick dark, like when we started, no light in the nightsky, no moonlight, no stars. There was nothing but sound to surround me, and the sound more permanent and real than any vision, because Grandma Billie's ears were my ears, her darkness my dark, because I lived Grandma Billie, I lived Mama, and so I knew in that moment I would never see my Grandma Billie again.

I was shaking. The blood dripped, and I could smell it, and my poor papa—I can see now, I could not then, I hated him because I was in Mama—my poor papa, he couldn't help it. He just went on.

"Liked to killed me, that's what," he told Mama, like she'd ever even asked him. "Got between her and them cubs, well, *that* is something you don't want to do—" Grinning around at the man Misely. "Two of 'em, fat as little butterballs. I'd been seeing sign back in them roughs a week or so, but now, that is the *last* thing I had on my mind. Ol' Dan here jumped her out—" Kicking out at him, grinning. "I never seen anything like it. She's up a little hackberry, just a-slinging that head around, looking, trying to spot me—I was slipping around to get a good hold to shoot from, all at once, now, here she come down out of that tree slick as grease after me. I didn't have any idea them cubs were back there. I tell you what, I was wishing for something outside of that muzzle loader—" Nodding at the man Misely, turning the grin upon Mama. "I's thinking one of Fay's howdahs would've been just about right." Lifting the great mangled head higher, showing it. "Never even took the time to field dress her, just took her head off and come on back. Look here, got her right in under the chin, and her charging. Just placed my shot, hit her one time and she rolled . . ."

And on and on, telling it, kicking the dogs away, the blood dripping slow and plopping, though you could not hear it, only smell it, going plop, and after a while, plop, in round drops in the dirt. Mama just looking at his face, but she didn't see him. Mama couldn't see him. Oh, Papa. Poor Papa. Finally he saw it. He saw she wasn't seeing, but he never did understand. He just got quiet, and because he did they all did, except the babies and the meat-hungry hound dogs. Papa kicked Ringo, and Ringo yelped once, and then even the hound dogs shut up.

"Demaris. It's a lot of meat. We can salt it." Kicked Ringo again, snapping, "Back, now, you so-and-so," and Ringo just slinking there, not doing nothing. "Salt it and dry it, woman." Talking gruff, talking man's ways, and his talk just a lie he couldn't know or believe, because Papa's eyes were baffled. Because his head was tucked under. Because what he was doing was begging my mama, and her blind to him, her not able in any way to see my father. "That carcass'll see us along the whole rest of the way," he told her, and held the mangled head up like the emblem of bear meat, like the very manifestation of glory, so that it all changed in me, my heart breaking for Papa. I would have fought the whole world then, that she-bear, fought anything, to stop how it hurt to see my Papa be a fool.

Thomas was by me then, trying to make me make a lap, pushing my legs together, trying to climb on me, and crying. Not loud now but forcing it, faking it, his little lying whimper, and I opened my arms for him and made a lap for him. I couldn't even feel him on me. I just took him to make him hush up. I could hear Papa, only barely, because he was talking soft to Mama. But I could see Papa. I could feel him. I couldn't feel Mama.

Do you see? I could never hold them all at once together. Some people can do that. Some mothers can do that. It was never given to me to do that but only to love them singly and savagely and only one in one moment, and that is what I never could make any different. And so sometimes I hated them.

"We could go on," Papa said. "Tomorrow, if we wanted. We don't have to wait for crops now, we wouldn't have to stop and hunt any. We could build before winter, 'Maris. We could."

Mama shaking her head. Shaking her head, and I knew then she had come back from the darkness, she could see him, but nothing was changed by a bear's head, because it was never about meat anyhow, not for her, only for some of us some nights when the cramps came and Papa heard Jonaphrene whining.

"I aim to go home, John," Mama said. She was looking right at him.

Oh, I held my breath then. What could I do then? It would kill me to leave Papa. It would kill me to lose Mama; I would have to take her back home to Kentucky. I would have to. That's what I thought then, but of course it was never, either, about that. They looked at each other, and it was quiet between them. Between Mama and Papa, and so quiet in the whole world. No sound left but Lyda crying in the lean-to. Oh, I wanted to strangle her to make her shut up.

It was Papa first who broke it. "Matt, git some rope and come with me." He didn't move, just stood with the bear head lowered a little, the dogs slinking on their bellies in circles to come nearer. The man Misely made a small move with his shoulder, and then he got still. Me looking at Papa, leaning close against Mama, Thomas wriggling and restless in my lap. Me thinking it was about me. "There's some under the seat box," Papa said. And I thought if I did not move, the balance would stay balanced. But Mama put her hand on me. She claimed me, I thought. I expected to die then. Thought I would shatter and die then. But of course I did not. I watched it go back and forth between them, weighing heavy first on one side and then on the other, passing over the hot small space of sunlight, back and forth between them, with the Miselys and children and hound dogs and silent cut bear head for witness, until they settled it finally, their business between them. Watching each other. Mama stood up.

"Reckon you better cut up that carcass wherever you killed it,

John," she said. "I don't want any bloody bear guts strung here into my clean yard."

She took a step toward the lean-to, where Lyda was hiccupy crying. Her left hand swung up to clutch the right one in the center of her chest, and she turned and looked at me, surprised a little, and fell down dead in the yard.

I used to tell Jonaphrene, Your mama dropped dead before she ever stepped foot in Eye Tee because she'd made her mind up she was not willing to live here. I used to say, Don't forget this: Your mama died of a broken heart.

I had to tell Jonaphrene and the others about Mama because when it all happened they were too young. I'd take them down to the rocks by the water. I'd sit on the bank, upon the big slab of rock by the water, and gather the children around me. I'd tell them, Your mama was a beautiful woman, with small hands and brown flyaway hair that fell to her waist when she brushed it. Her skin was the color of thin milk with the cream skimmed off, and her name was Demaris.

Alone, on the rock, I said Mama's name in silence over and over to myself.

I told them, Your mama was married in a dress of white linen and there were seventy-three guests at her wedding, and on the night we all left Kentucky, when she had to leave behind the cherry chifforobe her brother Neeley made her for a wedding present, it was another aspect that helped crush her heart.

Your mama's mama was Mary Whitsun Billie and she was a blind woman. She went blind from a fever at ten o'clock one autumn morning in the Year of Our Lord Eighteen Hundred Sixty-seven, and she was born in London, England, where the King of All English-speaking Peoples lives.

The words Mama told me those last days were seared tight in my brain like she wanted, like she always intended, and I don't believe I forgot a single word.

We buried Mama on that Misely place in Arkansas. We marked her grave with a slab of sandstone standing up on its end. I told myself I would never forget where it was situated under that tall pine tree on the ridge above the water. I still see it.

I don't know how I would have managed at all if it hadn't been for the man Misely, because Papa just completely fell apart. It was Misely who pulled Papa off Mama after she fell down dead in the yard. He scattered the dogs where they were trying to get at that bear's head Papa still had ahold of like a baby crushed bloody between him and Mama, and it was Misely who picked Mama up and laid her out on Thomas's pallet in the shade. He set Jonaphrene and Little Jim Dee to fanning Mama, minding the flies off, and he sent one of his many whiteheaded children who were all standing around silent and gawking, sent the boy running to the house to fetch his own wife. He made me go in the lean-to and get Lyda and sat me down on Mama's tree stump with Lyda and Thomas both howling in my lap. He wrenched the bear's head out of Papa's hands and threw it over the fence for the dogs to have a feast on, he held Papa down by the shoulders and finally shook him once hard enough to ricochet his head and led him over to the shade where the children were fanning Mama and kicked each of Papa's legs out from under him and made him sit down.

That same day—I think it was the same day, it went so fast then, I can hardly imagine, but there wasn't any choice, it was just so hot— that afternoon him and two of his sons went up on the ridge far enough above the water and dug the trench where we were to lay her and tacked together a coffin made of pine planks he'd sent one of the boys home to tear out of the ceiling from the Miselys' own bedroom, which I did not know then but only much later when the woman told me, and I believed her, because I could not imagine how they could have cut and planed wood for Mama's coffin so fast. The woman came and sat beside me and taught me how to dip a clean washrag in cow's milk and give it to Lyda to suck on because she would not take a cup but turned her face away, screaming, the milk dribbling, and we all knew she was not getting enough nourishment because she hardly ever shut up.

This is hard now. My memory is hard here.

You would think that day would be seared tight above all others and it was—it is—in the first part. That morning. But once Mama died, everything just runs together like dreams or what you remember from when you were very little, and all I can recollect are different parts and pieces: the stink of bear's head, the smell of blood in the clearing, that terrible groaning sound Papa made, children bawling. I remember the sun burning a hot circle on the top of my head. I remember flies everywhere buzzing, the chink of metal upon rock, rock and metal.

I have one picture of the man Misely bending over me, his eyes bright blue, his skin pale as soap. The cracks in his cheeks ran like wheelspokes in all directions. The yellow hair on his chest jumped up from between the buttons of his shirt collar, jumped up like corn shocks, touching his beard, his voice was burred and lilting, and I was thinking not of Grandpa Lodi but of corn people, of scarecrows, of the man Misely as a haunt made of cornsilk and shocks and hard little pale kernels, and he was telling me something I could not seem to hear. This was before he made me go in the lean-to to get Lyda. This was when I stood up once to go to my dead mama and Thomas fell off my lap.

I didn't know much of human death then, only Granny Lodi laid out on the bed at Grandpa's house in Kentucky when they took me in to see her, and her mouth and eyes were sunken and she so dried and old that her dying could not seem to matter. I never saw the twisted baby born between Jim Dee and Jonaphrene that died after two days, though I'd heard my cousin Melvina tell it in whispers in the dark beneath the covers and had taken the picture I saw when she told it as my own memory—but that, too, could not seem to matter, because that baby's head had been only the size of a possum's. Yes, I knew John Junior, I knew how he coughed and coughed and coughed until at last he shuddered and lifted up a little, rolled his eyes up a little, and then was small and dead and perfect. I knew John Junior, but at Mama's death I forgot him. What I believed of death then was something of smell and red violence. I'd helped at hog killing since I could remember, had shot and skinned squirrels, had wrung the necks and plucked the guts from the insides of chickens, had watched Papa shoot Sudie between her brown eyes. I'd seen and smelled the bear's head. I had a recognition for death, but to me it was not real unless the body was broken. I saw my mama dead on the pallet, and I knew she was dead, I understood it, but still I wanted to go to her because I thought I could touch her back to life. But the Miselys would not let me. And though they were good to us and though I don't know what would have happened without them, I hated them—truly hated them—for that.

I remember sunset, and I think it was the next day but it might have been the day after, and one of the whiteheaded boys came and hopped over the gate, panting, and said to his mama, "She won't come."

I was sitting on the wagonseat where I'd climbed up because I could not abide to sit in the yard. Thomas was playing with my braids, pulling at them like reining horses. I wanted him to pull harder. I wanted him to pull till they would come off stinging in his fists. I was staring at that strange yellow twilight, looking up, my neck aching, at the strip of yellow sky streaked pink and mauve and crimson, long threads of clouds too pretty to look at, delicate, like somebody had painted them, and I was hating those clouds the way I hated the Miselys. Mama was under a mound under the pine tree up on the ridge. Papa was sitting beside her, quiet now, just sitting. I could see his outline darker against the dark hill rising above. The children were quiet in the yard.

The Misely boy shook his head, whispering to his mama. She looked up at me, and then back down at Lyda mewling in her lap. She was trying to get Lyda to drink from the cup again, but Lyda just kept crying and nuzzling the woman's chest, the cup milk running out sideways. Misely's wife surely didn't have any milk—her youngest was nearly as big as Jonaphrene—and I guess she never did have any such thing as a bottle and nipple because people didn't much have them back then and anyhow those Miselys were too poor. Lyda's crying was getting weaker and weaker, but I didn't care because Lyda was Mama's baby and I thought she might as well die too.

Misely's wife got up and came to me. She said, looking up at me, her face freckled like Mama's, "Martha—" and I hated that she called me by that name. "Martha," she said, "we sent for someone to nurse the little one. We sent for somebody, we did, but she's not able to come."

The woman's face was shut tight in the middle, and I knew she was worried, but I just looked at her and said finally to Thomas, "Quit that!" The woman stood in the yard, by the wagon. I looked at her, staring hard, full of hatred.

Little Jim Dee sidled up then. He stood close to the Misely woman, and then slowly, shyly, backed into her. That was his way with Mama, how he used to do with Mama, back his skinny behind into her skirts and lean against her where she was sitting. I was furious. I didn't know what to make of it. I hollered, "Jim Dee, get over here!" But Little Jim Dee didn't move. He just looked at me, big-eyed, filthy, his bony arms and legs still for once, his rusty fingers in his mouth. The woman touched the top of his head with her free hand. A look came over her. I don't know if I could name that look even now, but it was something like helplessness, something like sorrow, but it didn't belong to her. It wasn't like the grief was her own. She sighed and disentangled her skirt from Little Jim Dee. She went back to her son and bent down and talked in his ear.

The next day—this I know, it was the next day, because I remember Lyda screaming all through that night, her mewing cries grown fierce and hysterical, like she was being stuck on the inside with common pins—the next morning a colored woman came to the gate. She stood there, thin and silent, and waited for somebody to come open it for her. She had an infant slung sideways in a blue bandanna across her chest. I knew what she was there for. I'd never been around colored people because we lived far from town and we didn't have sharecroppers, but I knew of them in the same way you know about Indians and panthers and other things you don't hardly ever see. I knew she was a nigger woman, and she'd come to nurse my baby sister. I went to the gate and pulled it open. She never looked at me. She came in the yard and went straight to the lean-to where Lyda was yowling, and bent her neck and went inside.

In a short time the crying stopped. In a little while after that the woman Misely showed up and walked through the gate like it belonged to her and went to the lean-to and flipped back the doorway and disappeared in there in the dark.

We did not salt that bear carcass like Papa said. I don't know what became of it, if the Miselys went and got it or if it rotted in the sun, because no one ever mentioned it again. The dogs kept dragging the mauled head back into the yard to chew on it, and Misely or one of his boys would throw it back over the fence, and the dogs would find it and drag it back in, until finally somebody took it off into the woods and buried it, I guess. We lived on cornmeal and squash and sweet

potatoes once the beans were gone, because Papa did not hunt at all
now, and me, I didn't have time. The Misely woman came daily. I
don't know how she got her own work done, unless her many whiteheaded children did it, because it seemed like she was always in our
yard. She was strict on me, stricter than Mama ever thought about,
and she made me wash the children, made me sew up the holes in
their clothes. The colored woman came once in the morning, once in
the evening. Lyda thrived on her and opened her gums laughing when
she saw her, and I hid every time I could somewhere and watched.

Most usually the colored woman had her own baby with her, though
sometimes she didn't, but either way it didn't matter. She'd take Lyda
in her arms. She held her like she was nothing, like she was—I don't
know. Like she was a part of her clothing or something. Not like she
was anything bad, not like she was good, but like Lyda was just something the colored woman wore. Often she'd have her own baby and
my sister together, one nursing from each breast.

I had a secret fear, and there was nobody to tell it to. I watched
Lyda's mouth, pink and eager and hungry. I watched it open for the
long brown breast coming to it, the dark nipple, almost black. I
watched the woman's baby, his rounded cheeks, his lips soft and sweet
like my sister's, but brown and not pink. I remembered how I had sat
and watched Mama nurse Thomas, and John Junior before him, remembered Mama turning Thomas to the cup when Lyda was born,
and I saw her nursing Lyda. I remembered how even when her face
and hands turned brown from the sun, Mama's breasts remained white,
blue-veined, her nipples large and pink and bumpy, how the color of
Mama's nipple matched the color of Lyda's mouth when she opened
and clamped over it. I thought my sister might turn brown from drinking from that woman.

At night I unwrapped Lyda, checked her soft folded places, looking
for a change. But of course no change happened except how she got
more and more attached to that colored woman and would smile with
her two teeth and jerk her arms in the air when she saw her and cry
whimpering when the woman handed her back to me and walked out
the gate.

Papa was working fierce. If he worked fierce when we first got there
to show Mama something, after she died he worked ten times more.
He did not do smithwork, not even to shoe the mules hardly, but

anything he could figure out how to carve from wood he would try. I thought he was still working to prove Mama something. It was like her presence hung over him, trying to make him show what he had done in the first place was right. The woman Misely said he was working his grief off, but I didn't think it.

He built furniture like he expected us to keep it, and for a time I thought maybe we'd stay in those mountains and never pack up again and head on. He built an oak bed frame that was too big for the wagon, that there was no place to put it and it stood out empty in the yard. He built little tables, some chairs, a new pie safe. He tended our puny crops, helped the man Misely harvest his own, and fished sometimes, though he never now hunted, and still came home at night and sat by the fire whittling pieces with his hands.

Little Jim Dee was getting terrible to handle. He was wild and rough, and there was a tension, a knotted hard thing, in his bony body that never would ease up, not even when he was sleeping. He'd hit me and Jonaphrene, and if I tried to make him do something, wash up like the Misely woman wanted, he'd pitch a fit and fall down yelling. I couldn't pick him up, he'd lay there dead weight, legs and arms kicking, hollering in the yard. I gave up on him. I wouldn't try to do anything with him, and if that Misely woman tried to make me, I'd say, *You* do it, and walk off.

Jonaphrene took up with the Misely woman's girls, but she was mean with them and would order them around, say, Stand there, Do this, when they played, and they would do it because she'd slap them if they acted like they had a mind of their own. I tried to keep a rein on my sister. I thought if we lost her the way we lost Jim Dee we might as well quit trying to be a family. But it wasn't easy with Jonaphrene, because she was like quicksilver, she'd run everywhere, be under your feet like a new pup one minute and completely disappear the next. She'd stay off and gone for hours. Sometimes she'd be sweet and helpful and smile to make your heart melt, and she looked so much like Mama. Other times she'd be a pure little snot. They all took it for granted that because there was no woman in the household, I was the woman, and it was up to me to do all woman things. I resented that sometimes, I hated it, really, because I would've rather been working with Papa, but I guess I didn't know any other way. And so I tried to rein in Jonaphrene, but it was hard.

Still yet—and this seems like the strange part, the way I remember it—still, I was more free than any time since we stopped there, and sometimes I'd just sit in the clearing and do nothing, just say Mama's memories to myself. Even with both Lyda and Thomas to change and look after now and every bit of the cooking to do, plus cleaning and washing and mending and trying to stay out of the way of that Misely woman, I still had time to just sit sometimes. Because Papa let me alone. He never asked me to go off with him or help him build things, never asked me for anything or hardly talked or looked at me either, and it might've been partly true what Misely's wife said, that he needed all that work to do to keep up his frenzy, but to me, what I knew was, with Mama gone, Papa had lost his need to make me his own.

One morning I woke up—it happened just that sudden—and the world had turned cold. Frost iced the top of the wagon where we slept, crimped the leaves brown, sparkled the sandstone. As soon as my eyes opened and I saw my breath in the dim light of the wagon, I remembered.

I began to search for Mama's tin box in secret. When Papa was off wherever he went to, I picked and pawed and pilfered through all Mama's things. Papa had never unpacked Mama's trunk or done anything with her clothes, and though the Misely woman hinted several times shouldn't he Rid Himself of Those Painful Reminders, Papa ignored her, and Mama's bonnet still hung by the tie straps from a nail next to the lean-to door. There came in those first cold days a driven secret thing inside me. Every time I was alone, I went in the lean-to and lifted the lid on Mama's trunk and pulled out her dresses, her undergarments, her embroidered pillowslips and linens. I patted them, crushed them between my fingers, as if that square box could be hidden in a small secret fold somewhere. I felt the sides of the trunk with the flat of my hand. I hunted with one ear cocked for the sound of Papa's dogs panting ahead of him into the clearing. If the Misely woman came in the yard, I hurried out in the daylight and got busy with Thomas, and when she was gone I'd duck back in the lean-to and search the same places again and again. I never doubted that box was somewhere in Mama's possessions. I thought there was just some tiny seam or corner I'd left untouched last time that would, this time, reveal Mama's secret to me.

The weather turned back warm after that first frost, but warm weather did not stop me, and I did not forget again. Sometimes I would have to hunt in near darkness because a dense gray fog seeped in the wagon before first light, filtered into the lean-to through the overhang of blanket, hung close to the earth, wrapped close about us, stayed surrounding us and in us for hours because the sun on those mornings could not seem to get strength enough to climb over the southeastern rim. I hated that dank fog as I hated everything about those mountains, because they helped kill my mama. I felt it, that gray mist, like an invisible hand that would press me into the dirt at the edge of the yard where I waited for the colored woman to get finished with Lyda.

It was one of those hollow times when I did not have to work or watch children because Thomas was still sleeping and Jonaphrene was in the wagon with him, sitting up on the feathertick, drawing pictures with charred fire sticks on beech bark—she wouldn't come outside in the spitting mist that was falling, she was entirely too pinched up and prissy for that—and Papa was of course gone, and Little Jim Dee was out no telling where. So I was waiting, impatient, because I wanted to look in Mama's things before the woman Misely showed up to start her bossing, and I was irritated, too, with a slow smolder that I did not then recognize, because what it felt like was that the colored woman was the dark weight pressing against me which I could not press back, and it felt like she knew it and she had no right to know it or stop me, because what I wanted, if I couldn't search for Mama's tin box, then I wanted to watch her nurse Lyda, and I could not think of one good excuse to go in the lean-to and stay there. She did not now nurse Lyda outside on Mama's tree stump as she'd done in warm weather but came in the gate and went straight to the lean-to, the same way she'd done the first morning, stayed inside in the dark with my baby sister until it was finished, and then she'd lay Lyda back down in her wooden cradle, no matter even if Lyda was hollering, and come out and never say a word and disappear between the trees down the hill. I hadn't watched her nurse Lyda in a long time.

I had my foot on the bottom rail of the fence near the lean-to, and I hung on it, my arms hooked over the splintery top rail, and danced my foot on the cedar, shrugging my shoulders and rolling my head till I could feel the ends of my braids touch way down on my back. I dropped my head all the way forward, held to the top rail with my elbows and reared back, but no matter how I craned my neck and twisted and wallowed, I could not shrug that invisible weight off me. I got still. I was listening, as I always listened, for some intruding presence: Papa coming, the woman Misely, Thomas waking up. The woods were quiet because the air was too thick and too damp, but somehow it sounded like I heard the woman singing—or not singing, I guess, humming, because the sound had no words, and I could just barely hear it, like it came from the gray mist all around me and not through the blankets and rough-cut wooden planks. Oh, I wanted to go inside and see her. I wanted to see her singing to Lyda because she didn't have her own baby with her on that day, she didn't bring her own baby anymore, hardly ever, and so it had to be Lyda she sang to, and I thought this was how she made Lyda open her mouth and arms for her, and it got me all stirred up.

I stood there, my insides churning, my foot scraping again on the fence rail, hard—yes, hard! I could've ground that soft wood into splinters—the smell of cedar rising, my toes cramped in last winter's shoes. At once it came to me—and this without words but just the clear knowledge—that I could go in the lean-to if I wanted. I could just go in there and sit down. It seems strange to me now that I had believed a colored woman could keep me from my own family's property, but I was young then, I didn't know things then, her skin scared me and the way she never talked.

No. It wasn't that. Or it was not that only.

The lean-to was Mama's and Papa's private place, their sleeping and grown-up talking place. Their place for babies and Mama's soft crying, like the loft bed back home. It was the same as their privacies, as my own body's privacies, and it had to be kept secret, no matter from colored woman or children or neighbor or what. It was secret from me even, and I had to hide my going in there from myself. I could not show it to a stranger, not to Jonaphrene or Papa, not to no one at all.

I thought, *That woman's got no right to be singing alone with Lyda in Mama's and Papa's lean-to!* And I understood she would not stop me from coming in, nor tell anybody about it, and so it would just be between her and me. I felt a power then. I went quickly over the rough ground to the blanket hanging in front of the doorway and lifted it up.

She sat on piled quilts on the far side away from the doorway, over by Lyda's cradle. There was no sound in the lean-to but the little sounds Lyda made sucking, and I crouched still for just a heartbeat because I'd meant to say, You quit lullabying my sister! but there was nothing to say quit it about, and then I gathered myself, saying, *She's got no right to be alone with Lyda in Mama's and Papa's lean-to, I don't care if she's singing or not,* and so I ducked beneath the pink blanket and went in.

When the blanket fell, the room was dark like a cavern, and it was warm in there with the warmth of her body, but the quilt on the featherbed where my hands fell was damp. It was all damp, the whole ragged rectangular space, dank with the clouds living low on the mountain. I could smell mildew and wet earth. I could smell Lyda's baby smell a little but mostly Papa, his hatband sweat and suspenders, and under it the sharp scent of stranger which was the colored woman's smell. Mama's smell had shrunk since her death until it lived only in the folds of her linens and dresses. I knew that already. It was one thing I searched for when I went through her trunk.

I waited with my hands and knees on the featherbed till the darkness would lighten and reveal shapes to me, and soon I could see well enough to pick out Mama's trunk, and I crawled over to where it sat upon the bare ground by the west wall and climbed on it and sat. I looked at the woman, and her outline got clearer and clearer, a vertical dark shape faded at the top, the light shape of the baby crossways in the middle, until finally I could see the woman's eyes big in the darkness. I got scared then. She was looking right at me, and she didn't speak and she didn't blink hardly but just stared at me like I was a demon, an intruder, a night thief, I thought. It was quiet and too close, the two of us together in that lean-to, and I couldn't think what to say or what I'd come in for, couldn't think any clear thing at all. My old childish ways came on me, ways from when I was very little, and I trembled before that colored woman. I could not move, could not speak or think, and I could not go back out, and so I just sat trembling upon Mama's hard black wood trunk. It was a long time before she started to talk.

"She big enough now."

The words came soft, almost whispered, in the closed space between us, but still they made me jump.

"Y'all could turn her out if you wanted."

I was too trembling scared to understand what she was talking about.

"She big enough. Hear me?"

I nodded my head. Lyda's sucking noises got louder—long, smacking sounds, empty. The woman lifted my sister then, I could see it, and broke her suck with a finger and pulled her away from the breast.

Lyda whimpered, ready to start bawling, but the woman turned her around in her lap, all at the same time tucking her one breast in the front of her shirtwaist and pulling out the other, and she let Lyda have the other and Lyda settled down again, sucking. But it was strange to me, I got a strange start, because I could see she had Lyda swaddled, wrapped tight in the light blanket. My sister was too big for swaddling.

"She plenty big," the woman said again, and at first I thought she was answering me, but then I saw she was saying it to herself.

"Why don't you quit coming?" I said, and my heart stopped and started and fluttered, because I said it the same way I'd talk to Jonaphrene, the same voice I'd tell her to set her flighty self down and hush up. That colored woman was a grown-up, a grown-up, you did not talk to grown-ups in such a way, even niggers, I was taught that, or I believed I was taught that then.

The woman let out a dry little snort like *hunh* through her nose. She was not now looking at me; the white circles of her eyes held on the empty space in the center of the lean-to.

"Tell that to the doctor," she said. "Tell *him* how come I don't quit coming."

She lifted Lyda again and shifted her on her lap. Lyda made not a sound this time, was stiff and still as a cornshuck-wrapped baby doll, and it frightened me. I thought she was dead. The woman kept on. "Doctor have his own idea how come I don't quit," she muttered, and then she said other words I could not hear, and then I did hear: "He a flat fool and lying to his own self but I will not disapprise him of that." She went on in her low voice like it was not even to me she was talking but some other person she'd been talking to for hours, like me there, I was hidden from her sight only to overhear.

"Got me a half-dozen reasons," she said. "Name Dulsey and Amsar and Ivy and Nole Jean and Harold and Evangeline." Paused. Still yet did not look at me. I could hear Lyda making little pleasure sounds, nursing. *"Hunh,"* the woman said again, louder. Her head raised up, tilted back some, so that I could see her nostrils get big in the gray light. "They ain't all mine, if you want to know it." I thought then maybe it was to me after all she was talking. I thought then so, but I know better now. "Doctor have his own idea about that too." She laughed, not a real laugh but another snorting sound, a different sound, but no less a blowing out like horse breath into the dank grayness her contempt and disgust.

"What doctor?" I said.

She let out the *hunh* sound again and said nothing.

"What doctor!"

I might have screamed it, I believe I screamed it, in the dark in the lean-to. I did not think nigger grown-up, Misely woman coming, did not think anything of fear, because I just heard the word *doctor,* and if there was a doctor in those mountains my mama did not have to die. If there was a doctor we could have brought him before the last change and it could all have been different. The remembering came back on me then, the hot circle of sun and whip of flies buzzing and the smell of bear and blood and dog and Papa groaning, how he did across her, sprawled groaning across Mama like the sound tore out his throat from the wet depths of his belly, like it came from the bear's belly, like it tore out his gut, and I did think, alive in the lean-to in that moment, I thought, *Did not have to be, did not have to,* and it was all I could think. I said it again. "What doctor?" Choking, barely whispered, because I could not breathe, wrapped in her smell, and Papa's.

"Doctor," she said. She turned her eyes on me. Oh, she looked at me then. She saw me. She said, "What you talking about, doctor?"

"What are *you* talking about? What kind of doctor's around here?"

"Hunh. I ain't talking about no kind of doctor. I don't know no doctor."

Long pause and quiet but for the rain on the roof of the lean-to, the day mist now shaped like water, spatting on the wood roof of the lean-to, making sound.

" 'Cept one."

I held my breath then. Mama's trunk was hard under my legs and bottom, hard so I felt the bones like two hard knots under each side of my hips.

"I knowed one doctor one time," she said. Still she looked at me. "Name Williams. Doctored all around down by Booneville. Use to." Her eyes were pale circles like moon rings. "Don't doctor no more though," she said. "He dead." Then she looked back to the empty gray air.

I flew mad. I don't know why, because I was glad there was no doctor, because I did not want to carry *Did not have to be* in my soul all my life. But the anger flew up inside me anyhow, all caught up with her dark weight pressing out at me, pushing back at me, to keep me from watching her nurse Lyda, keep me from hunting in pure secret in my own mama's trunk.

"Unwrap my sister!" I ground it out like I would spit at her. Oh, yes, and I glared at her, but she did not have her eyes on me then and I believe did not see. "She's too big, you're going to stunt her."

"She too big, unh-huh, what you think I been saying?"

"Unwrap her!" I said.

"That baby pinch a plug out of my flesh if I unwrap her." She said it simply, unswervingly, like the truth that sun rises at morning.

"You hush!"

And she was hushed already, she stayed hushed a long time, staring at me in the dark, big-eyed, and I did not care or notice.

"Hush up this minute, I said!" like she was going on talking. "Quit singing too, nigger." I was rolling, my heart thumping. "You got no right here, to be singing here, in my mama's place. I heard it and I aim you to quit it. And unwrap my sister. Right now!"

The woman did what I said. Oh, that shifted something in me. She did just like I told her, and her a grown-up, and me just past ten. I watched her, her head wrapped in a light rag, tucked forward as she bent her neck to me, like she would kneel even to have it chopped off. Her long fingers plucked at the pink scrap of blanket. It was completely unwilling, she did not want to do it, I could see that, but she unwrapped my sister. Lyda clung on the skinny breast like a naked possum in its mama's pocket, and she whimpered, protesting, but her mouth never once let go. When the woman had the blanket pulled back, Lyda waved her arms free and gurgled. I saw her reach up a tiny white hand and lay it palm open on the side of the woman's face. She sucked, she made a little sweet sound, she patted the woman's face a few times, patted and got still, settled quiet, nursing, her hand soft and open on that black woman's skin.

I was trembling. I cannot tell you how it all swept me at once, my thoughts flapping like crows looking for something else I could order her to do because I wanted to say, Do this, nigger! and watch her do it, and at the same time hating her for how she'd witched Lyda to make her touch her like Mama, and I was frightened because I could not see why she did it, the woman clearly did not want my sister but held her like a feedsack, a lump of lye soap, a nothing, and that very idea scared me more than the witchery, and all at once I felt my brother Thomas beside me, how he used to feel, small in the featherbed beside me back home in Kentucky, how he'd put out his little palm toward me, sleeping, just to touch me, and I felt a pang for the way I used to be tender with Thomas and that pang started to swell so I had to push back at it, shove it down deep. I stood up.

"Lay her down!" I said. "You lay down my sister and get out of here!"

I couldn't stop my voice from shaking. I wanted to push her and her dark skin and stranger's smell out of my mama's lean-to, but I was too frightened to touch her, to even cross the little smoky space of distance between us. Her neck was still bent to me, and I watched her the way you'd watch a wild animal, like she might any moment jump and attack. Her skin and dark dress blended too much with the shake cedar behind her. I could not make out distinct lines, she seemed to just float in the darkness above Mama's quilts, but her head and neck I could see because of the light headwrap and collar. She was shaking, the same way I was shaking, and I suddenly thought if she spoke, her voice would tremble as mine trembled, but the woman did not speak. She slipped her finger in my sister's mouth, quick, trying to break her suck and peel her off the breast, but Lyda clung on. The woman pulled, her long finger wedged between the baby's lips and the nipple, till her titty stretched out from her chest like pulled taffy, and still Lyda would not let go. The woman made a little grunting sound, not the nose-blowing snort but something that came from her chest and sounded like stepped-on pain, and she jerked my sister off her tit like you'd pull a tick off your skin quick so as to not leave the head buried. Lyda balled up her fists and kicked and jerked her arms and started to wail. The woman paid her no more mind than a flea scratch, she just laid the baby down in the cradle, Lyda shrieking fit to burst, and stood up till her headwrap nearly touched the roof of the lean-to. Bending forward so she looked like a hunched-up old lady, though I knew that woman always walked standing straight up, she moved to the door opening.

"Wait!" I hollered at her, and I don't know why or where it came from, because I did want her out of there, wanted her gone from our lives forever, to quit singing below hearing, quit pushing back at me and smothering me with her dark invisible weight. But the word jumped out of my mouth, I think now maybe because I wanted to order her to do something else and watch her obey. I liked how that felt. Which she did, right as soon as I said it, she stopped close to the pink blanket over the doorway with her head bowed, her neck bent, and waited. Swooping and flapping, my mind hunted.

"Pick her up!" I said.

The woman hesitated, just a little bit, not even a breath's worth, but I was afraid she was going to quit doing what I told her and turn her witchery on me, and I shrank back against Mama's trunk, ready to scream worse than Lyda if she came toward me. But no, the woman turned smooth as lickins and stepped the step and a half across the empty space to Lyda's cradle and picked her up. She waited, holding my wailing sister. She didn't look at me, didn't put Lyda to her chest to try to hush her, but just grasped the baby around the middle under her jerking, flailing arms and held her straight out in front of her. Lyda kicked and cried, but she knew who had her and her cries tamped down some.

"Put her down," I said. This time the woman didn't hesitate a little bit. She set Lyda back down in the cradle, and Lyda shrieked like I hadn't heard her shriek since the next night after Mama died. "All right, now," I said. I could not get my voice to quit shaking. "You can pick her up." The woman picked her up. "All right. Set down over yonder," and I pointed to the quilt pile. The woman sat down with Lyda, still holding her like a piglet while Lyda hollered and kicked and squirmed. "Finish up," I said, and I don't even know, really, how that woman heard me over Lyda bawling, but I guess she did because she opened up her shirtwaist and gave Lyda the titty, and Lyda immediately settled down and hushed up.

Many times I've thought of what happened next. I used to think I waited too long, kept my mouth shut too long and so did not keep up my power, or that I watched her too close and so allowed her to snag me. I didn't know how it happened, but before I could do anything to help it, my strength started waning. When I spoke, my voice came out paltry. "From here on out," I whispered, "don't come back."

She made no sign like she heard me.

"You hear me?"

Still no nod of the light headwrap, no bent neck, no answer. I wanted to tell her to do something else, I could feel that power draining and I did not know why. It was all drifting back, seeping back to what it had been when I first crawled into the lean-to, quiet but for Lyda sucking, and too dark and close and full of that woman and earth rot and the smell of Papa and the baby, and I thought it was because of how she nursed Lyda, I made that connection, and I knew she must stop. "Quit," I whispered. She did not look up. The bones in my hips burned against Mama's trunk. I thought I would smother. "I mean it," I said, louder, and I put my hand over my nose and mouth and said through my clamped fingers, "Quit doing what it is you been doing to my sister, quit nursing her, quit witching her, after this morning, I mean it, you hear me, don't you never come back."

Her head lifted, and she looked at me. "Miz Misely say that?"

"*I* say it."

"Miz Misely say it?"

"No, Miz Misely don't say it! She's not our mother, she don't have no say-so. Me, *I'm* telling you. Don't come back." My words were strong, my voice thin as water and I couldn't help it. I pushed the words out squeaking into the choking air. "*I'm* going to take care of my sister." I meant it. I believed it. The woman snorted.

"Feed her with two little titties like acorns, unh-huh, fatten her on dog's milk an' cornpone an' field peas till she swell up and bust." The woman laughed. She looked at me and held me to the trunk with her white circles of eyes like moon rings, and she started to whisper: "Tell him, child, y'all don' need me, you tell him, he ain' about to let me, she too big, you tell him," and she went on telling me to tell him, and I didn't know what it was. Mama's trunk burned against me and the burning licked up hard in my bones, the room swelled, going dark, and darker, until I saw something and it was color, and the color was red and then blueblack and then whiteness, and then it was a white man in a dress coat on a street corner and I did not know why he was a white man and not just a man with a watch and a yellow mustache and red suspenders beneath his coat, and the white man pulled the watch fob from his pocket and looked at it and clicked it shut and slid it into the slit of pocket at the side of his suspender clasp, and the pants he wore were striped. Shifted, and I saw a little boy, and then a girl child, and their skins were dark like deep winter earth, and they chased each other in sweaty light, and a different girl then, her skin red as copper, her hair red, but she was a nigger, and she jumped from a yellow clay bank into brown water flowing thick and slow as blackstrap, she grabbed for a knotted rope thick as a fist, a long dangling hair rope trailing in the water from a tree limb, and the girl missed the rope so that the oozing water carried her on down, on down in the slow seeping brown, her red nappy head shining like a scuffed penny in easing molasses, and she changed and became smell, became smell only, I could not see anything, all dark, and this smell was the smell of mother, not Mama but *MOTHER,* like sweet sweat and skin and milk, and I began to weep and tremble until the light came again, became form and shape and color, and I heard a child crying and the child was me and not me crying but the grief filled my chest, filled my throat until I thought I would choke down smothered and burning, until I thought I would die from it, I tried to twist free. The earth held me, the way your foot feels sucked tight in mud, sucked down tighter and tighter, and the smell became dank rot of earth lain too long under water, became clay, became fathomless soft silt on a silken river bottom and I twisted, I cried out, but I could not pull free.

I was not dreaming. My bones burned against Mama's trunk, and I could feel it. I could taste copper or iron or some harsh taste in my mouth beneath that morning's burnt-corn coffee. I could feel the dank weight of my braids on my back. It was still me, Matt, there—but it was that colored woman's memory. I believed she was witching me, holding me spellcast, as she held my sister in her arms spellcast, because there in the choking smell of her and Papa and Lyda, who was Mama's last baby, who was Mama's last remnant of soul on earth, the woman took me inside her. I saw it. I heard it. I smelled it, these things I have told you, and I could not make it stop. I cried out, but my tongue did not make any sound. When I came to the light again, Lyda was asleep in her cradle, and the colored woman was gone.

I stood up from Mama's trunk. I didn't know how long it had been—a little while or maybe hours. I felt my legs would buckle and fold under me, the muscles trembling, like Papa on the frozen earth after the ice storm, his legs and arms twitching as he lay on his back. I looked at Lyda sleeping with her thumb in her mouth, and then I went slowly, shuffling in the moist dirt, to the door of the lean-to and looked out. Jonaphrene was at the campfire, putting sticks on, and the smoke was billowing up thick and white because the wood was too damp. I could hear Thomas crying in the wagon. I didn't see Little Jim Dee, didn't see Papa, but I knew it had been a long time, because Jonaphrene was trying to build up the fire to cook. I looked at my thin, tangle-headed sister putting wet sticks on the campfire, and the fear choked up hard in me, so that I had to holler, "Sister! Quit that! Go get Thomas and hush him! He's going to wake the baby up!"

And Lyda did wake then and set in to bawling—not from Thomas, I know, but from me hollering in the door of the lean-to—but it was all right. I turned and went to her, and picked her up to hold her and hush her. I knew it was going to be all right then, because when I watched Jonaphrene stand up from the fire and push a snarl of hair out of her eyes and blink in the smoke at me an instant before she turned and went to the wagon, I made my mind up.

I didn't care that it was coming on winter. Such a condition meant nothing to me. My mind was made up already. We had to go on. In myself there was one purpose only to all action and judgment—I had to get my family out of those mountains and on down to Eye Tee, because all was changed in the ways I saw Eye Tee, because what had been dread and void and terror in front of me became, in that time in the mountains, a place to flee to, because what was there in those mountains was too mysterious, too terrible to fight.

I began to work upon Papa.

In the beginning I thought it could be done with lies and questions, and I did so, in the early dark evening when he sat with his plate by the fire for moments, only still for those few eating moments, before he hunked into the lean-to and did not come out again until first light.

I said, Papa, that Misely woman pinched Jonaphrene today (and it was not the woman Misely but me who pinched Jonaphrene to make her hush and sit still and peel the damn potatoes). I said, Papa, Little Jim Dee hit Thomas this morning, hauled off for no reason and walloped him right off the stump (and that was true, because Jim Dee was getting rough as a cob and too mean to handle and we all knew it and stayed out of his way when we could). I said, Papa, how far is it to Eye Tee? Not far, is it? Two days on horseback? A week's ride in the wagon? It ain't far, is it? Them Miselys said it ain't so very far. I said, Papa, Uncle Fayette's waiting for us, you reckon? You reckon Uncle

Fay's got us a house built already? Papa, that colored woman says she's going to quit coming to feed Lyda (oh, not true, that one, and I would not ever tell my papa the truth about Lyda and the colored woman, but to tell that lie, the urgency to hurry up and get past it would come on me so bad I'd have to put my hand on my chest to hold down the pounding). Said, Papa, the baby's acting poorly, what are we going to feed the baby with the cow dead when that colored woman won't come?

Could've told it to the tree stump, any lie or question, and it would've done the same amount of good. He couldn't hear me because he'd already quit us. You just couldn't see it. So I went around another way. I worked and prepared everything in secret from Papa, or tried to, but I was young and stupid and it was late in the year. One thing I remember, I dragged the quilts and blankets from the wagon one morning and washed them in the creek and hung them in the narrow strip of sunlight to dry. That was stupid—I told myself afterwards it was stupid, though I never let on a bit to anyone else—because it was already deep autumn, the sun was feeble as an old woman, it stayed too short a time overhead, and the air was so cold most mornings you could see your breath in it. That night we slept tight and shivering, all of us snugged up close together, and Jonaphrene whined till I pinched her and whispered in my teeth the Injins were going to get her if she didn't shut up. Our covers were still hanging outside on the line. That night the fog came and danked them down worse, but I didn't let that miscalculation stop me. I just went on.

I packed whatever I could find to pack and put it away in the wagon. I kept Jonaphrene with me working and threatened Little Jim Dee we would leave him if he didn't stay close by. I'd told the children we were going on to Eye Tee any day now, any minute, and so they had that excitement in them and it carried all through the camp. Even Thomas was stirred up, though of course he was too little to understand Eye Tee, but he followed me around talking that language he talked all the time then, and he'd try to do whatever I was doing and I'd have to slap his hands to keep him from trying to help. I hoarded food from the woman Misely and lied to her and said the field peas were all gone, we'd used up the cornmeal, was there any potatoes left? and on and on such.

Oh, that was my sure secret preparation, how I worked on the woman Misely. I was always after her for more food, and I quit combing my hair and Jonaphrene's and I never washed any of the children or even my own self, so she had to stay on me all the time. All along I told her about Uncle Fay and Aunt Jessie, and I told her lies about Aunt Jessie like she was a gracious and Christian woman, which was not in any way a true fact. Because I knew the woman Misely was weary near unto death of us, and I took Jonaphrene and Little Jim Dee in on my secret so that when she was around they were a hundred times worse. I knew she wanted to be shed of us, wanted that with her whole worn-out being, but would not just stop on her own from coming, though I did not understand why. So I told her Aunt Jessie was waiting for us—I drew my mouth down pitiful when I told it— poor Aunt Jessie standing at her door looking out from her new house in Eye Tee, wondering whatever happened to her dear little five nieces and nephews she loved so very much. Oh, I could see that working on the woman Misely, and I believed she would work on her husband and he would work on Papa and so we could all head out for Eye Tee. That was what I thought. The urgency was in me as bad as it ever was in Papa, and yes, Papa worked like a madman, but his work was useless, all Papa's work went to no end. And as fierce as he worked on his too-big bed frames and chifforobes, that's how fierce I worked—he could not hold me a light to go by—and me just a little girl, and sneaking besides. I did it all in secret, Papa nor no grown-up understood what I was doing. I have to admit I still carry pride in my heart over that.

Mama's tin box had completely disappeared from my thoughts then. It just blinked out in those short gray days, and soon even the remem-bery of the memory of it did not enter my head. But it was always like that, Mama's secret box, from the beginning till the end of it, a glinting fleet thing like a will-o'-the-wisp, like marshfire, that could appear and disappear of its own doing and would only just come when the weather was right. At that time, in those shrinking cold days of work and my pulse drumming, the weather in my spirit was in no way hospitable to Mama's secret, because I had one thought in my mind only: that col-ored woman was witching my sister and I knew it and I could not see a thing in this world I could do about it except get us all every one down from those evil mountains and gone to Eye Tee, and I did not care that my mama had made up her mind to die rather than live there, because inside me the change had already come.

If I watched before for the colored woman coming up the track and along the water's edge in her light headwrap and brown dress and blue knitted shawl held tightly closed with one fist showing at the throat line, now I watched for her every waking moment, even when it was not time, even at supper, when she was gone for the day and would not be back to feed the baby until morning. While I worked, furious, rushing hard to get the preparations done, I watched for her, my senses on the track rising from the pine woods and not on what I was doing, and when Thomas would come up and touch me, I'd jump nearly out of my skin and have to slap him. Even in my bed in the wagon, staring straight up into the darkness with the children breathing slow beside me, I watched for her, sick to my soul with loathing and dread. She had more power to make fear in me even than Indians, because I thought if she could witch my sister so and witch me in those moments, she could come as a ghost spirit in the night. Maybe she would come singing or humming round our wagon in the darkness and turn me and the children into— I didn't know what. I could not name or put shape to what I was afraid she might do to us or make us become, but it was terrible, terrible, and it was dark, like her, and full of darkness more terrible than the vision I'd had in the lean-to.

I owned one kind of fear then, one kind primarily. I did not yet know the evils of the human heart, did not know you could cry and rail against God and have no more power than an insect over drouth or fever or blood kin turning against you. I did not know that your beloved could be snatched from you in the drawing of a breath, in the frigid new-moon darkness of a January night. Yes, I knew about Mama, but my mother's death was too big, it was the guiding force of my existence, then and always, and I could no more see it than I could see gravity. I didn't yet have the sense in me that death was the condition of all life, and so I did not fear it. And I did not much fear bears or panthers or cottonmouths, because I'd seen Papa kill too many, knew they were just blood and entrails that could be torn apart with a lead ball or a cartridge shell. What I feared above all in that time was this: the Devil, ghosts, haunts, robbers, Injins, the I-Will, niggers, soul-catchers, Satan's Army, and witches.

I stood trembling, waiting in the real times when I knew she would come, my throat so tight I could not swallow because I had lain awake dreading and fearing her hollow humming all through the night, and each morning, each evening, I suffered a start when her rising and falling shoulders first appeared through the scraggling limbs at the path's turn, because I could not reconcile the thin colored woman picking her way up the track toward me with the dark power I'd witnessed in the lean-to on that morning. Still, I never doubted. I would shove the little startled sense aside and keep my eyes upon her. If she made the lightest sidestep to avoid a tree root, I'd suck in my breath like she'd raised her arms to fly. When she came into the yard and made her way toward the lean-to, I'd watch her the way you'd watch a chicken snake crawling toward the coop and you without a hoe handy to kill it. At the same time I had all these other pulls pulling at me, the list I'd made up and carried in my head to get the work done, and that list getting longer instead of shorter so that I might at once be thinking about where I last saw Papa's pickaxe and shovel, we'd need them for sure in Eye Tee, and quick as anything I'd tell myself I better send Jonaphrene hunting Jim Dee, I hadn't heard him yelling in over an hour, and that would get me off thinking about what in the world was I going to do with Jonaphrene when it came time to comb her hair out, because it was a pure snarl from not being brushed and braided, and Jonaphrene's hair so thick like Mama's you could hardly get a brush through it anyhow and I might just have to cut it off and start over once we got to Eye Tee, then I'd begin to imagine how I might have to tie her down to make her let me do that, though of course, how it turned out, I never had to worry about that, and then here'd be Thomas trying to put the Dutch oven back on the fire, lifting that huge heavy black thing by the handle with both hands and stumbling toward the fire with it and me yelling from across the clearing, running, and him dropping it, scared, bawling, and our cornmeal mush, which would be all the breakfast and dinner both we'd have to our name, going splat yellow like vomit all over the brown oak leaves and pine cones on the floor of the clearing, and here that colored woman would just pick Lyda up like a laundry bundle from off the pallet and duck into the lean-to with my sister to cast her witchery upon her, and this all would happen so fast I just couldn't hold it. I could not hold a rein on all I needed to hold a rein to.

But I never once quit trying. I had the idea I could throw my mind and quick hands like a spun web around all these parts, and draw the children and the work and the planning and maybe even the terrible darkness under my control. I just kept on, kept on, until at last the getting ready was done, or at least done to the degree that I cared about, because I knew we would not take Papa's too-big furniture and I didn't care really about what was left in the lean-to that I could not yet pack and store in the wagon because then Papa would know what I was planning, or rather I did not care about any of it except Mama's trunk, and I had my secret plan about that. Then there was nothing for me to do but wait, and you know waiting is the hardest task in the world for a child, though I had not the least notion in the world of myself as a child, but I was that, and the waiting was finally the worst part of that whole dread time, worse even than the nights in the wagon, staring up into the dark and listening for her. Because I had a new fear and it was of a different kind: I did not believe the preparation could stand still. I feared that if we did not leave soon, the little web I had spun would begin to fray itself in waiting and start to unravel.

I would think and think what I could do to force Papa, and if not force him then what could I do to go around him, and I would come back time and time again to the fact that even if I knew or could find out where was Eye Tee, even if me and the children could get there by just heading down along the fading track into the pine woods (and oh, they were terrible in my mind, those pine woods, and how they swallowed Uncle Fayette and Aunt Jessie, how they allowed to creep forth every morning, every evening, that black woman) and on down out of the mountains and west, even if I was willing to go off and leave Papa in order to save the children from witchery, the fact was, we could not walk to Eye Tee. There was one other truth I cared little to admit, and that truth was this: I might with the help of a feedbag full of shorts and a solid tree stump get old Sarn harnessed to the wagon, but that contentious pestle-tail mule Delia was never while she breathed going to allow me within ten feet of her. No human hand had ever touched her but Papa's, and she meant to see to it that none ever did. I could not manage without Papa. And Papa would not come. I decided that this, too, was the work of that woman. It came to me that the colored woman had, sometime when I was not looking, witched Papa, witched Delia—witched all of us, to keep us there in those mountains. I pondered upon this, pondered it, until I knew what I had to do.

On the last morning we lived in those mountains, I went out early to catch that nigger woman down the hill where the little rocky track disappeared into the pine trees. I cannot now tell you what I thought I would do with her once I'd caught her. I knew only—and this not in words or understanding but just living drenched in the sense of it —that I feared her and dreaded her and felt her presence waking and sleeping and believed her to be the source of all my family's trouble, and that I longed toward her the way you long to what you can never know or touch. May be that I thought I would finally know something of her. May be I intended to leave her caught there till she chewed her foot off like a trapped animal, or maybe I thought I would kill her. Sometimes I think I just meant to frighten her off. I don't know what I thought; I know only that my going to the track on that morning had no more to do with me deciding to go than my coming on the journey with Mama and Papa had to do with me wanting to come. I had some notion in hand, doubtless, some plan or idea or talk I was going to talk, but what I made up in my young mind and told myself does not matter, because I was compelled to go hide behind a tree to catch that nigger as sure as I was compelled to boss Jonaphrene and slap Thomas and love my family beyond all reason or telling, not because they were the most important thing but because they were the only thing, the complete full rounded world to me, and I never had choice over it any more than I had choice over my dun eyes or big teeth or straight hair.

I set out early, before the night fog lifted, before anybody was up. In the cold bluegray dark I crawled out from the wagon. It was not yet quite light enough to see, or only light enough to make out lighter shapes in the night mist, but I told myself never mind over that, because the evening before, I'd put the traps handy by the near wheel at the back of the wagon and wrapped them in the last shred of pink blanket so they would not clink. I touched my hand along the rim of the wagonwheel to the ground and felt for them in the dark, and they were just as I'd left them. They clinked only a little, muffled in the blanket, when I pulled them up to myself and hugged them. I went slow and urgent, feeling with my pinched feet along the swept yard toward the track, thinking nothing except to make no noise, to not wake up Dan and Ringo on the other side of the wagon by the lean-to, and to get away from the yard before Papa came out. I had threatened Jonaphrene in the dark in the wagon to stay close to camp and keep an eye on the children and she'd better not say pea turkey to Papa or I'd snatch her baldheaded when I got back, and she'd mumbled and kicked at me and rolled over toward Thomas, and I never even knew if she heard me, but it was all coming to the end then and I didn't really care.

The dawn birds were not yet even calling. My feet found the track sure enough, but as I left the yard and started along it, the fog closed in thicker so that no matter how wide I opened my eyes I could not see a hair's breadth in front. For all my fear of Papa waking up and coming out of the lean-to and catching me—and I did not know what he would do then but I feared it—I had to ease along the track like a terrapin, holding the traps tight to my chest and trying to shush my own breathing. I heard rustling now and then off to the side in the underbrush, and I would think *bear*, I'd think *coyote, wolf, panther, rabid coon*, and still I went on, my eyes open and sightless as Grandma Billie's, feeling the earth with my feet.

When I believed myself close to the place low on the mountain where the track ran into the pine woods, I stopped and waited a long time, waited what seemed like forever, and I began to think I had to have come far enough, and then I thought, *No, maybe not, maybe not yet.* I had to be sure, and so I waited. The little rustles and skitters kept up here and there in the distance, in the murky darkness, and I was afraid. I feared the colored woman, that she would come floating in the fogbound air like a banshee, feared Ringo, that he would wake up and start howling and so wake up Papa. I feared a snake crawling over my feet, or an owl swooping down upon me, or a she-bear who would scent me and come for me as that one had come for Papa on the day Mama died. Above all I feared that the woman would come as she always came, picking her way along the track in her light head-wrap and dark shawl, and I would not be ready.

More than once I thought of turning and running in the thick mist back up the track to our yard. I don't know what kept me there. I wish I did know. Maybe I just thought I had that job to do, I believe that's how I looked at it, and a job in front of you left no choice but to get it done. What I had to do was to hold still and wait for the light to break enough so that even in that fog on the mountain I could see where I was. In time—I don't know how long: same as distance and sound and space in that murkiness, time was distorted—but in time the fog began to lighten, and by this I do not mean that it got thinner but that it began to turn white. Sun was rising, and my heart lifted with the whitening, but it was not what I could see but what I heard that made me know I had not gone down the mountain far enough. I heard a dog scratching, his foot hitting the dirt *thuthuthuthut*, his ears flapping when he shook his head. I heard the *wssssk* of Papa's suspenders as he slid them up over his shirt. I had not gone far at all, only fifteen or twenty yards down the track maybe, and my heart, beating so fast already, beat even faster. Hurrying, so that the dogs might not smell me and start in to baying, but with all stealth and quietude so those old hound dogs might not hear me, I rushed down the mountain on the faint two-lane track.

I hid myself the good way I knew how from hunting with Papa, blended myself up close to an old pignut hickory and held still like a piece of the mountain, waiting patient and stony as you'd wait for a deer. I had that feeling, you know, that excitement, that breath-holding, keen-eared anticipation, and the blood pounding and the smell of mist and dead leaves and earth and fresh pine, but my hands felt too empty. I wished then I had Papa's muzzle loader. I believe to this day if I'd had Papa's gun with me I would have shot that woman when she first came out from between the trees and it all would've been different, but for some reason I never thought of Papa's gun when I set out to catch her but only the bear trap. The other trap, the smaller one Papa used for muskrats and beavers, I took only because I saw it on the ground next to the bear trap when I was sneaking it away from Papa's tools, but it was a good thing I took it, because no matter what strength and force I put to the bear trap, I could not pry the jaws open, though I tried till I sweated in the cool white fog and grew faint from the blood swelling behind my eyes. So I set the beaver trap, which took as much strength as I had anyhow, hurrying, the jaws big around as my thigh, and I covered it up with oak leaves on the pathway and moved back through the gauze and hid. The small clump of leaves was hardly visible, but I felt it, hot and cold, burning in the white mist like it belonged to me, and I watched that place on the track.

When it came to be full light, the fog thinned some and fell back gray. I could hear Little Jim Dee above the trickling sound of the water, yelling that rebel yell he'd made up or heard along the way in Tennessee someplace, and once I thought I heard Papa's voice calling me, but I shut my ears to it and it didn't last long, and then it was just the crows and jaybirds and water in the early morning, not so very cold on that morning but just damp and gray like always, and I could not see down the creekbed very far. The shag bark of that old hickory was rough at my breastbone, even through Mama's thick wool shawl. My toes ached from where they were curled under against themselves, but I would not move to try to ease it but only chastened myself for going barefoot all summer and letting my feet get too big. *Hold still, Hold still, Hold still,* I told myself over and over in my mind like a song. I bit down on the inside of my jaw to stop the ache in my toes from getting so bad as to make me shuffle in the dry fallen hickory. I knew how to wait quiet for quarry. That was one kind of waiting I could do. I'd learned that patience from Papa. You could never be a good hunter if you didn't know that.

The shush of dried yellow pine needles, the hush of brushed homespun on pine boughs came to me long before I saw her. Through some trick of the mountain the sound shuffled up from deep in the forest, whispering at the edges of creek sound because it was of such different nature, and I listened with my head cocked, my breath quickening. I told myself it might be a ground sparrow feeding in the fallen needles and pinecones, because her step was so light, but the soft rustling came steadily on toward the place where the trees opened to the water, until I knew it was her.

Oh, I itched for Papa's gun then, my hands nearly hurt with it. I was excited because it was so much like hunting—crouched, hiding, waiting the way you must do: watching downwind in stillness for the single creature you've watched for since first light, and the creature comes and your complete soul and breath focus upon it, and all there is in the world at that moment is you drawing aim on it to kill it, or not kill it if your aim is not right, and so there is always that turning moment, and all I felt at first, watching her dark shoulders and light headwrap emerge from the darker space between the trees, was that excitement and the ache in my hands. She walked straight up tall. She did not have her baby. She stepped on the track like a doe placing its careful foot so, and just so, and she did not look down at where her foot stepped but kept her neck and eyes and shoulders tilted up a little so she could see straight ahead up the track. I was above her on the mountain maybe fifty yards, and still she looked tall, and something in that woke me and scared me and also made me mad. I could not hear the whisper of her skirts now for the gurgling of the water, but I could see her shoulders rise and fall with her hard breathing on the climb in the gray mist, and it was that, the rise and fall of living breath beneath dark blueblack knitting, that made her real beyond real, beyond quarry, and I wanted to run.

It came on me that I was alone with the nigger witch woman in the mist on the mountain, that she could turn in any way her power upon me and I had not even my sister or my family's things or my mama's trunk to protect me, that I could not even scream in time to help myself because she was now but a few dozen yards below me, and I could not run because she would see me and rise up to swoop down upon me, and I could do nothing but hold myself stiller than still, not even to breathe. I watched her. On toward me she came, and still more toward the salvation pile of oak leaves. Nearer her foot stepped, now the other, nearer, nearer still. I cursed myself for stupid, more stupid than to wash quilts in the short damp days of autumn, to allow so much to chance. Her foot could so lightly and easily step over the little pile of oak leaves.

The iron trigger sounded *ping*, I heard it in the stillness, I did so, less than a fraction of an iota of a half breath of a second before the trap snapped loud once—*snaak!*—like the jaws of a snapper and the woman let out a terrible yell. Only that once she yelled out, one long low deep gut-scratching holler, and she dropped straight down like a rock, and then she was still. The crows and jaybirds were silent. The creek even it seemed in that moment hushed up, and all I could hear was a throbbing like the beat of blood in my ears. Without thinking, I don't know why, I still don't, I rushed from my hiding place beneath the hickory to where she sat on the rocky dirt track. I can't tell you what I meant to do, wrestle her down or help her or make sure she stayed hushed so Papa would not come—I don't know even if I had thoughts to do anything—but I covered those few steps over rocks and around brush in no time, and when I got there I stood above her on the track and just stared.

Her skirts were pulled up, her one bare brown leg sprawled out straight, the other bent toward her chest at the knee, and she held her right foot in her two hands. Blood poured from between her fingers and ran down off her wrists, and it was red, yes, but showed not so red against the dark of her skin. Where it looked red was where it fell on the dirt track. She looked up at me. Her face showed nothing. She didn't look scared, mad, hurt, surprised, nothing, she just looked up at me and matched me stare for stare. I could smell her blood then above the earth smell of damp leaves. I could smell rust. My mouth swelled up dry as cotton and I couldn't swallow. Everything rushed in me, time and my own blood and fear and sorrow, how I felt when I watched Papa smash open a mud turtle's shell one time with his hammer, beating it, soft thud and crack, till it died, because it ate the bait from his trot line—only the woman was not dead but just bleeding, and I knelt down beside her like this.

I said, "My papa says for you to quit."

She stared at me a moment and then her eyes and attention dropped away as if my coming and kneeling and talking was no more interesting than the lighting of a moth that attracted her notice for a wing beat and then disappeared. She pulled a hand away from her foot and lifted her skirt edge and I could see all the way up her thigh, hard and dark and smooth as a buckeye, and she pressed the dust-colored homespun against the sole of her foot. I saw then that the trap had not caught her but bit her, had made a deep bloody gash in the back of the heel, and the bottom of her foot was lighter than the dark brown of the top part, and there were dark fissures and cracks all along the ridged tannish edge of her heel. I did not think about her being barefoot in November any more than you think about a deer or squirrel or rabbit going barefoot, but I did think then for some reason how tough her feet must be, like saddle leather, to walk all the time on those little sharp stones on the track. Her skirt soaked up red like a woman's blood rags, and when she pulled it back and dabbed a new piece I could see the bite from the trap was a deep triangle the same shape as the jaw's tooth, and the wedge gouged out of her skin was pale pink, and then it filled up red, and the red spilled out over and began to drip on the ground.

I slid my eyes away, up toward the rim of the hogback, where the sun had climbed over but had not the strength to do more than burn a bright coin in the day mist, and then I looked down at the matted tumble of leaves on the track. I did not care to witness further the little chunk of gouged flesh. I carried on talking, squatting on the track beside her, paying no more mind to her bleeding than you do to the wounds in a squirrel you are fixing to skin.

I said, "My papa said for me to tell you to quit. He don't aim for you to come up to our place not even one more time." I picked up a stick and dug in the damp leaves. "My papa wants to know what way you been witching my sister." I didn't look at her but stirred the leaves like cornmeal mush bubbling. "My papa wants to know what you aim to do with her. You ain't aiming to turn her into a nigger, are you? 'Cause if you are, my papa says we'll just have to kill you. Here, this little trap here this morning"—I looked around for the trap, but I didn't see it—"that's just a warning. We didn't even aim to do no more than that," and I pointed with my stick to her foot, but I still didn't look at her. I went back to stirring leaves and turned up a slug big around as my thumb and three times longer. I poked its rubbery back awhile, and the slug shrank up fatter and shorter and got real still. I jabbed its back, but the skin rolled. I kept jabbing until the stick went through finally, and I picked up the speared slug and flung it off the end of the stick toward the water. "Go on back down the mountain, hear?" I said. "Don't come back tomorrow. And don't you try witching her from down yonder, because . . ." and I could not think of a good threat, so I coughed the words down into faded nothing and smeared my stick around some more in the leaves. I started again. "My papa said for me to tell you he's going to take the muzzle loader after you next time. You hear?"

She made no more response than a tree stump.

"My papa *said,*" I said, and looked at her quickly, then back down at the leaves, and went back to poking them with my slime-smeared dirty stick. I shifted my weight on my haunches, scooted around some, still crouched and half sitting, and looked out over the creek. She was making me mad. "You hear?" Still she didn't answer me, and I was getting madder and madder, so I had to then, no matter the danger, I had to look at her.

Her eyes were straight on me. They were not white circles like moon rings but dark brown like blackstrap gone solid, nearly black. Her lips were the same dusk color as her baby's, the same smooth, the same big, they had the same little hitched-in dip at the top of them, but they were clamped tight over her teeth, you could see it, and beneath her skin, all along her jaw and under her eyes, the muscles shook. She held the skirt to her foot and looked at me, silent, and I could see tiny, tiny bumps along the broad, smooth side of her nose, her nostrils were flared wide open like a horse running, and all was different and changed in the gray daylight that bronzed the oak leaves and turned the dead pine needles bright orange in the track where they lay. The skin on the woman's face was not dark only but the color of deep rich cherrywood like the chifforobe Uncle Neeley made Mama, only it did not look hard like cherrywood but warm and smooth and soft, and I wanted to touch it. The feeling was strong in me, I knew she was witching me, same as she witched Lyda, but I could not make it stop. My hand just moved without my will or say-so, dropped the stick I was holding, and reached up toward her face.

The woman flinched and fell back like I'd hit her.

I heard a little *chink* sound and her shawl fell back open and her own hand came up in front of her face—this all in one movement, one moment—and I saw the pulse beating in her throat. She'd let go of her foot and it was bleeding all over the brown leaves in the pathway, and I saw then the trap lying snapped shut on the leaves where her skirts were, with a little red piece of her flesh in its mouth.

I don't know what happened.

She was too big then, too big on the pathway, she flinched away from me, huge, a grown-up, falling back away from me. She scared me worse than anything and I wanted to throttle her, I wanted to put my hands on her neck and choke her, and I wanted to run. I wanted to make her, *make her*, I was going to make her tell me, though I did not know what it was but I knew it was something, and I suddenly realized I was standing, that it was me taller than her now, but she did not flinch again nor look up but held herself still as God's breath, her foot bleeding, and she looked at the water gurgling and rushing down the hill.

I said, "How you been witching my sister? Tell me how you witch her! How?"

She said, "You talking 'bout something you got no knowledge nor notion," and it was like a sigh when she said it, a sough of wind, an exhalation. No eyeblink, no rise or fall in her voice sound, she did not look at me, I was not even sure for a moment if I heard it, and she went on like she was talking to the air or rush of water. "I don't 'spire to come up here," she said. "It ain't me or my mind. You tell him. Somebody have to tell him—he ain't going to allow me to just quit."

"Who? Who ain't going to allow you?"

But I already knew who it was, and I knew why too, because I saw him, what he did, his yellow mustache flecked wet and moving like a hump of yellow caterpillar and her skin beneath like the black breathing mound beneath the lips of my sister, and I could see it but I didn't have words for it because it was too dark and too secret, what I could not know and should not, but I asked anyhow, and it may be I whispered, I believe I did whisper, there in the washing creek sound, because you cannot speak such secrets in daylight, but I asked it to the smoked and speaking air because the words had already been thought, I said, "How come he won't let you?"

She looked straight at me. Her face muscles shook again, or had never quit maybe, I wasn't watching, but when she looked at me I could see the skin spasm and tremble the way mule flesh ripples to twitch off biting flies.

"*Hunh*," she said. "What you think? Fool don't want my milk to dry up."

She looked back out at the water and went on in the same monotony as if she'd never stopped. "Somebody have to tell him," she said, and this time she shrugged her shoulders. "Tha's all, I told you, I done did all *I* could, suit me plenty fine never have to come climb this damn mountain one single more morning, child like to bite me to pieces anyhow, she plenty big," and she went on sort of muttering so, her voice mostly even but every now and then lilting a bit in the air, and then she'd give that little shrug, and it was just how it was on the morning in the lean-to, like she was not aware in her full self that I was there. She'd tricked me with her blood and gouged flesh, I thought, because she could not feel anything and talk lightly so, and I thought it was because she was a witch woman that she did not cry or rail or scream with her flesh bit and bleeding, and her acting like she didn't much know it or care, and then I thought of the white man with the yellow mustache and my stomach pitched up sick, and the urge was coming on me again to choke her and *make* her, and also the fear. The woman's eyes lit like she'd just thought of something, but she went on looking at the water and her voice went on in the same even sound. "Your daddy got booklearning. He know how to write."

"Papa don't know," I said, my fists and mouth clenching. It was rising bad in me. "*I* know."

She nodded. "That be all right then. You write it," she said. "Have your daddy to sign." She nodded and nodded, like she was agreeing with her own self. "Tell him to give it to Miz Misely out his own hand. Make sure she say that, she have to see to it the doctor know that, it come right out of y'all's hand," and the woman carried on nodding to herself, looking out over the water. It was that word again, *doctor,* and it jumped stinging at me across the sparkling air, because the doctor was the white man and he was not dead, and I knew it and had known it and only just then remembered. "No sense to come down and talk direct to him," she was saying. "I seen him, he'd talk the skin off a lizard, he might talk y'all back."

"Who is he?" and this I know I whispered, because I heard my own *s* sound like her *s* sound sighing in the air, and the woman did not answer, and I said it louder, and it was a threat then, my fists balled so tight the nail stubs stabbed my palm. "Who is he? What kind of doctor?"

Never looked at me, her eyes only to the water, but I could feel it, I knew it, she knew I was there. It was to me she told it, not the water, not the damp air. She said, "Hunh. No kind of doctor. He ain't no kind of doctor, he lie on that how he lie on everything, but they all call him that." She went on talking, and all she told me I remembered from the witchery inside the lean-to, I saw the pictures unfolding, and I could not stop them coming. She said, "He tell my mama he a doctor when she leaved me on the back porch after Ivy got drownded, after they chased and drownded my sister for sport pleasure down home." And I saw the girl, her skin red as copper, jump from a yellow clay bank into brown water, saw her reach for the knotted rope thick as a fist, saw the water carry her down, shining, like a scuffed penny. "My mama could not survive it, she just want to die, she give me to him to keep me, carry me up on the back porch, we bofe of us crying, and then she quit when he come out the back door with the missus behind him—" And I saw the white man pull the watch fob from his pocket and look at it and click it shut, slide it into the slit of pocket at the side of his suspender clasp. "He say he a doctor, he going to pay me, and oh yes, he do. Pay me with coat hangers and tin scrap, I been saving 'em and selling 'em going on 'leven years, ain't never going to pay back what they feed me, what they say my children eat."

She was quiet then, looking at the water, looking, her foot bleeding, whispering, and what she told me next I remembered, backwards, unrolling, though I didn't know I remembered until the telling, she said, "Step out the back door first morning like God, and her behind him, and I knowed it right then—"

The mystery came hard on me, too hard, so that I smelled the terrible smell, like old fish and rank tobacco, I saw the white man step onto the porch with his yellow mustache, his pale eyes, and I knew it was *going to be him that hurt me, the missus no worse than any, I seen her before, she nervous and watchful, mouth drawed down tight like green 'simmons sometime, but it going to be him with his mustache like a yella caterpillar and ice eyes, how he crackin his knuckles, watching with ice eyes, and hungry, so the missus watch too, but her watching just same old like any old white kind of watching, it going to be him and them long big-knuckle fingers of his the way they feel around in that pipe bowl, pokin and proddin, his eyes like his fingers—*

"Stop," I said. "Stop it," because I did not know what it was, I didn't want to remember, but she wouldn't quit it, until I cried out in a loud voice, "Stop!"

The woman turned her head slow in the smoked air. She looked up at me. I don't believe she was dying, to this day I do not, but she stared at me in the way the dying stare at the living, looked at me and through me, both at the same time, like I was a ghost child, a spirit, a wisp of nothing in the air. She shut her mouth and looked back out over the water, completely silent, her foot bleeding like a pig's throat all over the track. In a little bit she looked down and it was like she just then noticed it, like the foot didn't belong to her but was just some strange something she spied on the track. She reached a hand down along her leg and wrapped her fingers around the ankle, pulled the foot toward her, turned it heel-up and looked at it and went back to dabbing blood.

That was what I could not abide. Don't you see? She'd quit me. I felt how she quit me, and me here the one who'd hidden by a hickory to catch her, who'd laid out the trap and *had* caught her and wounded her, I don't care if her whole foot wasn't wedged in, and me here remembering, *remembering*, and she looked at me and through me and away from me in such way that I was no more than a day moth nor nothing and oh, oh, the anger swelled up bad. I had no fear then, I just yelled at her, I said, "It weren't Papa, it was me, nigger, *me! Matt!* I did that!" and I waved my hands at her foot, and I wanted to grab it and shake it but I would not touch her because I knew what a danger it was to touch that dark skin. "You quit it with witching me!" I screamed so my throat stripped. "You quit! Don't you be telling me to write nothing, nigger, I won't write nothing. I got one thing to say only: You go give suck to your own baby. You leave mine alone. Don't you come back, hear? You can't anyhow, because we're leaving to-morrow, we're going to Eye Tee and you can't stop us nor nobody and I aim to tell you to quit it with your witchery, you hear me? You quit it with my sister, she's coming with us to Eye Tee," I said. "Give her back!"

She looked up at me and I knew I was changed then, I could see it in her, and I could feel it in my belly, this change in me, though I held nothing, my hands were empty, but I had something to hurt her with and I did not know what it was. Her eyes flicked up the mountain along the track, to the water on one side, the scrub brush on the other, just wherever she could look without turning her head. I thought she was looking for a place to jump up and run to, and I prepared myself to grab her if she tried to do so, but she did not tense up and gather herself nor let go of the awkward way she held her foot. She was hunked down in herself, holding still and tough like she meant to disappear, same as that slug thought it could hide from me by hunking itself short and fat. Her eyes were not on me but darting all around. Pretty quick she began to talk, and her voice too was shrunk down, a low shushing whisper, and I cannot explain to you what was in it except it was begging and not begging, and it meant to pull me in next to her and at the same time it wanted to melt.

"Cain't," she whispered. "You got to tell him, some white person have to tell him, he ain't going to believe me, I cain't suck my baby no more, doctor ain't going to let me quit with y'all's baby, he got to have that milk, he a pig for it, he ain't going to let me quit, beat me to death with them coat hangers first, I don't care, but he beat my children worse with his fists. Missy, somebody have to tell him. He kilt my baby, he going to kill—" And then she stopped. She looked up at me in the way that she saw me, changed as I was, and her voice feathered up high and light. "I ain't saying nothing against him, missy, he never meant to, just how he shook him, that's all, snap back his neck, my baby died perfect, all at once, his little soul snap out sudden, quick like you snap your fingers, that's how babies do, they souls too entirely fragile, they don't hang on to life for nothing, some of 'em, mine don't . . ." and her voice trailed off. Then a sound came, it started low and growling in her throat, like a hurt dog, and just in an instant the growl went deeper, and deeper, sank down to a low, wrenching moan somewhere deep in her gut, and then it was worse even, a deep, terrible groaning, like her breath was stopped, like the very flesh was being torn loose from inside her belly.

I knew that sound. While I watched and listened I could not recall what it was, could not place it in the belly of my father in the hot circle of sunlight, but the sound wrenched me, tore open from me like it came out my own belly, and I thought, *That sound don't belong to* HER, *it ain't* HERS! I raised up and hit her with both fists all around her headwrap and hunked shoulders. I flailed at her like you'd beat a rug, and I don't know what she did then, I don't, except I know she didn't fight me, and I believe she turned her back and shoulders to me, because I felt my fists pound soft on the wool shawl and it made that hollow back-beating sound, and I hit her head where her ears were to make them sting, and the bone was hard as stone beneath the knuckled bone of my fingers, and I hit her on the neck and wherever I could find. She hunked and rolled tighter, her soft belly hidden, and I just flew at her with all my rage and hit, and I hit, and I hit, and I was not afraid of her. And then all at once I quit, and my heart was beating so hard, my breath pounded and hurt, and then I was afraid

again, but not of her. I was afraid Papa would come, Papa! And so I
turned and ran away from her up the mountain toward our place, and
I only looked back quick that one time, so fast, and saw her rolled
tight in herself, not looking at me but her head turned to the side a
little to wait for the next hit, not making that gut sound, her foot
bleeding still.

The track had grown steeper since I'd eased down it in dawn mist,
and the fog that had thinned had somehow grown back deep. Wet
leaves slipped and slid backwards, branches clawed for me, roots
reached out to trip me, stones rolled and skidded sideways beneath
the hard edge of my shoes. I could not run fast enough from what lay
behind me, and yet, and still—and I don't know how this happened,
because I ran and ran as in a dream and could not get away—yet too
soon I heard the children playing in the yard. I stopped. Another turn
more and I would be where they could see me. A hundred yards more
and I would be back in my home and my life again, and that meant
my family, and I could not bear it. I could not look at Papa or hear
Lyda or feel Thomas scrambling to climb up in my lap. I couldn't. I
stood still a moment, just waiting a moment, bent over at the waist
with my hands on my knees to catch my breath and remember the lies
I'd already made up and forgotten which I must tell to Papa and
Jonaphrene about where I'd been gone. I was not looking at anything
or thinking of anything except trying to call back the words to tell
Papa, and I was holding still so around the curve of the track when I
heard.
    It was clearer this time, more distinguishable and certain than on
the first morning outside the lean-to, though it was not much like
singing now, nor even like humming, but it was the same sound, high
and thin and beautiful just outside hearing, and it was familiar, I knew
it, I recognized it, and it made me sick with longing and sorrow. Hard,
hard sick, and I stood crouched so with my hands upon my knees
and the world rising behind my eyes, going dark, buzzing, until I
heaved, sick to my stomach, and there was nothing to throw up, and
I heaved again, but what it was could not be vomited out from inside
me. I lay down, there, on the track that had been a road leading us
into the mountains, sprawled forth bellydown in the damp dirt and
small rocks and leaves.

It was Jonaphrene found me. Maybe I slept, I don't know. I know it was much later, deep morning or after, because the sun was warm upon my back, slanting deep. I know when she came my chest still had the shudders that would not stop or slow, that I could not control or push down, and I wanted to push them down, I wanted to make them quit. I did not want Jonaphrene to see. But she did see.

"Mattie?" she said. I could hear it in her voice, how scared she was. My face was down still, hidden in the hoop of my arms, and I would not look. "Mattie? You hurt?" And she kept crouched there beside me, I could feel her, close, her smell and breathing, her voice small, saying, "Mattie? Mattie?" again and again. Then she touched me, her hand on my back, patting me the way I would pat Thomas to make him go to sleep at night, my little sister patting me like I was the little child, and my chest was shuddering, I couldn't quit, and it made me mad so that I rolled over and sat up and said, "Leave me alone!"

But it was too late. My sister was with me already. She was in me. She'd found me and witnessed me, and she would not let go of me, nor could she, because she did not have any choice, none of us did, ever, and so I said to her, furious because I could not make the shudders stop and so the words came out cut and weak and ragged, "Don't—te-tell—him!"

She shook her head, her eyes huge, their miraculous color more gray than green then, and she whispered back, solemn, "I won't." She never asked a word but just watched me, squatting upon the ground with her skirt in the dirt and her knees high beneath her chin, her arms wrapped around them, her hair haloed out like an angel's but snarled and dark brown, until I chewed the inside of my jaw hard enough to make the shudders go slow and slower, getting farther between until they were eased almost gone. I felt tired. I felt I could lay back down in the track again and go to sleep forever. Jonaphrene said, "Know what? Papa's loading the wagon." She nodded her head. "He is."

It took some little while for me to hear her. No, I heard her, but I could not make the words make sense to me, but she went on, chattering, like it was any day or every day, except how big her eyes were, how she never took them off my face.

"He sent me to fetch you. He's plenty mad, you better watch out. We ain't any of us had breakfast and it's already 'most time for dinner, the woman never come to feed Lyda neither and she's bawling—hear her? sounds like she's fixing to bust—and Papa cain't leave her inside, he's loading everything in. He went to catch up Delia but she won't let him, she run off in the brushes and he had to just quit and go to stacking the wagon—I think that's partly how come him to be so mad. I told him what you told me to tell him, you went hunting muscadines, but he don't care. He might lick you anyhow. I never seen him so mad."

Her eyes were big and scared for me, and I turned away, not to see it, because I had enough already to carry for the rest of them. I did not want to be connected up with my sister. I would have pinched her or something, but I just felt too tired. I said, "Did Papa put in Mama's trunk?"

She nodded. I went down the list, all I'd made up in my mind to carry with us to Eye Tee, and I felt so bonesick and weary then till I was relieved—but only right then, because later I got mad about it— but right then I was glad Papa was taking up to do all my tasks and chores and last bits of packing like he'd meant to do it all along. I never for one second questioned why he all of a sudden was ready to head on to Eye Tee, right then, on that very same November morning. I believed I'd broken the colored woman's spell. It was the most natural thing in the world to me, when I stood up finally and brushed myself off and climbed with Jonaphrene the last hundred yards of track to the clearing, to see Thomas's hands filthy in the cold campfire and his mouth black with soot and Little Jim Dee running through the yard yelling and shooting a stick at Ringo and Ringo chasing him and baying and Lyda shrieking on the pallet and old Sarn nodding in the harness and Papa loading his pickaxe and shovel under the seatbox like it was his own idea.

The clearing stood empty and full behind us. I saw it when we turned—the rail fence crosshatched useless around bright air and Papa's grief furniture, the lean-to pulled loose and left tipped broken upon its side. Mama's bonnet lay crumpled half beneath it, but I didn't tell. I did not want to say anything to get Papa's notice. He didn't lick me—he never licked any of us, only Jim Dee—but he was gruff and disgusted and in a hurry, and it was the same hurry as the night we left Kentucky. We went fast, as fast as we dared to and not run up on the mules' haunches, going down, me up front beside Papa, holding Lyda, and Thomas bawling inside the wagon, and the wagon creaking and swaying like it would shake apart going down the worn track in the filtering sunlight toward the pine woods.

This was all the same day.

I did not see the beaver trap nor the pile of oak leaves nor the bear trap nor the colored woman nor her blood, though I did look, but there was nothing. I had not really expected there would be.

The pine woods were dark, they rose up around us and bowed closed overhead. Tall. The smell of turpentine stinging. The afternoon sunlight shut off like a light turned out. I was not afraid. My heart was lifted, I was light in my body, the gray weight raised off me even in the darkness of the pine woods because we were *going,* and the going was the good thing. I crooked my head back, jouncing, trying to hold it steady to look at the brightness of light, the piercing sky, high up through the treetops. The deep part of the woods was only a ways anyhow, as I'd known in my secret heart it would be, if only I'd been able to believe it, because we passed through them and out in a short time, going so fast, the mules clopping like horses, and they were poor, the skin sagging on bones, like us all, even Ringo, but the wagon was light. We were fleeing Satan's Army and so I carried myself steady, I was glad, holding Lyda, and I did not look back at the children, though their faces swayed and bounced behind me, peeking out. We came then—and this quickly, this no more than a mile past the deep edge of the pine woods—to the Misely place.

I knew it from afar off, though I'd never seen it, because even from a way up the track I could see the blond Misely dozen-or-more children running, sitting, standing, leaning all about the porch and the dogtrot and the yard. We came fast. Papa stopped the team and got down to go speak to the man Misely. The woman Misely came out one of the doors then, her hands in her apron. She came and stood on the ground close by the wagon, frowning up, her eyes on the baby. Lyda was not crying but sitting up in my lap, watching, and she liked the going in the wagon, you could tell. She was getting so big then, she was already nearly as big as Thomas, and her hair was coming in.

The woman said, "Your father sent word on, I guess. It's better, isn't it?"

Frowning, that troubled look upon her, and she went on, her eyes sweeping from Lyda to me to the children's dirty faces poking out from the wagon flaps, and around again to Lyda, talking to herself.

". . . before winter sets in? Your aunt's waiting for you, I guess you'uns need to get on?"

Wiping her hand in her apron and frowning in the sunlight and the sun edging down now so the air had that blue November tinge.

I felt strange. I'd never in my life had a grown-up talk to me in questions. I wanted to go. But I would not, could not, call Papa. It did not matter anyhow, because just in a minute he came on and before he'd finished climbing up hardly, the woman sent one of the boys into the smokehouse and he came running out with a little slab of salt pork, and she took it from him and handed it up. It was slippery when I took it, but I didn't think to do anything but just take it and hold it. Lyda bent down and put her mouth on it to suck it, her spit running down my wrist and the greasy salt smell stabbing my throat and empty belly.

Just like Uncle Fay said—and the truth of this galled me, oh, it galled me, for him to be right—it was not so very far. We drove down and down a ways, bumping and shaking, Papa pulling back on the brake to not over-run the mules and at the same time hyahing them on fast. And then not long—it was not the same day, for we left in the deep afternoon and camped on a slope at pure dark, but the next one, late the next morning—we came to a place low on the mountain where the faint two-lane track met up with a deeply rutted, hard-packed wagon road running east and west. We turned onto it, and it snaked low between mountains, going west.

We are given signs, and we do not know them.

I was looking at everything, everything, but what I should have. In the beginning I held my head tipped back, looking up. You will not credit it, that I could have forgot sky, but I did so. We lived in those mountains most seven months, and that is all the time it took for my soul to forget sky. And we came down and the world opened out, the mountains peeled back away from us like ripe edges of plum quartered and falling away from the pit, and above us the sky opened, the pale, washed November sky, and all of me lifted toward it. I wanted to shout almost. I wanted to sing. And in that I knew what it was in my mama.

This part is hard to explain.

I was not *in* her, as I had once been in her. I could not be. My mama was dead. But coming down from the mountains I understood what it was in her—and this for the first time, and this in my mind and being, not from inside her as I was on the day she died—I knew the hurt she held in her cavity twisted tight in the dark. The long valley we went through, the sweep and roll and breadth of it, was some like Kentucky, the sky was like Kentucky, and always the moon. I'd forgot even the moon in such little time, because it is not moon that molds night in the mountains—shadows do, and sound, the life of trees and the animals—and so I'd forgot to even know it.

But no. The moon was mine. I don't want to misremember.

It was not the waxing half-moon that made me think of Mama but the escape of gray rolling-away land and farms and fields in the daylight, all mixed in with trees, yes, more trees than back home in Kentucky, but they were unclothed at the approach of winter, and still you could see. The land was settled. It was tamed, mostly. There were farms with smoke rising and crops plowed under to wait through winter, the earth split open and brown. To the north and the south purple mountains humped on the horizon, but near us the grasses in the field were orange and the stumps of bushes dark brown, the daylight gray, the air and distant slopes and sky blue, and the earth, all of it, was blue and gray and brown except for the orange grasses and, dotted on the hills, the deep green of pine, and these were the colors back home in late autumn. The same. My heart pounded so fierce every minute, us going fast and the pain of Mama in me, her sickness for home, and sometimes it would rise up in me a little as if it were my own because this place did look like back home in Kentucky, but it would fade again, because it was not for me to long backwards but only Mama. My job was to honor it for her, that was all.

Four months. She'd been dead four months then. It seemed like forever.

And I knew, or I believed I knew, that if she'd only lived a little while longer, if we'd just gone on a little longer and not camped in the jagged dark of those mountains, if Papa had listened to Uncle Fay about how it was just over the next hogback and down, or if he had not listened to him about turning south away from Fort Smith to sneak into Eye Tee, or if we'd never left Kentucky, or if only, if only, if only there'd been a doctor, if only Mama had understood we would come down again to opening-out land that was some like Kentucky, if only any one other thing had been different, my mama might could have lived. And I knew, or I believed I knew, that if she'd lived long enough to see sky and fields again and smoke rising, she would have stayed with us. I believed I ought to have been able to tell her, and so the sore of her dying woke up again and I couldn't stop it or heal it, and us going so fast, and I just held on to Lyda, up front, beside Papa, and looked out around us to open land like I was looking for Mama, like I was being Mama, to look through her eyes, and this is what I was doing and how come I never saw the moon waxing ragged-edged in daylight's washed skies, or heard the whippoorwills crying at night in almost-winter when they should have been gone, or noticed the red mark like a mask upon Thomas's face.

We crossed over into Eye Tee in the depths and blue brightness of a full-moon night. This is how Papa did, wordless, and the mules hitched at midnight, going on. This is how he did all the time, driven by demons, and Papa's demons were his own, which I know now, but then I thought they were the ones behind all of us, the ones belonging to the colored woman, who was now like a haunt to me but faint and past, without power no more.

I did not know why my papa was driven. He was silent. I was so far outside him. I thought maybe it was all in his mind. I believed I had vanquished the power of Satan's Army, and so I thought Papa was only imagining and he would be comforted later, when he at last understood. I could hear him on the ground by the fire when we camped in the night. He would talk to himself, talk to himself, all night in dreams, and then, snorting a ragged breath almost like snoring, but mean, threatful, like a furious bull, he'd let go a sound. A terrible explosion in the night. Once, I heard him get up from that sound and walk off from camp—and this deep, deep in the night—and when I woke up at first light his blanket was in a loose pile on the sparkling earth. I thought he might not come back to us, but he did, appearing at dawn from nowhere, it seemed like, his face thin and weary, sagging like our poor animals' loose skins. We were driving hard west by full light. He didn't whip Sarn and Delia, but his reins shook constantly on their backs, and his dogs ran with us, and it was as if the animals were driven too, not by Papa but by Papa's own demons. And so the night we crossed into the Territory he arose from the fire and hitched the team and they didn't even shake their long ears to complain. He did not reach in to wake me, but I wasn't sleeping anyhow, the blue night too bright and the blood coursing in me like three cups of coffee, though no real coffee had passed my lips in months.

I didn't know. There were no soldiers. There were no Indians standing guard at the border. There was nothing but a silver road in moonlight, snaking west.

BOOK TWO

Testudo

And the cherubims shall stretch forth their wings on high, covering the mercy seat with their wings, and their faces shall look one to another; toward the mercy seat shall the faces of the cherubims be.

EXODUS 25:20

Take your eye up into the heavens and place it like God's there. Look down. You will see the Appalachians slanting north to south down the eastern edge of the continent; and the Rockies, the great Sierras, crumbling south to north in the west; and all across the North American landmass the force of mountains lining themselves pole to pole in opposition to the sun. Now look to the lower midbelly of the nation, where the Ouachitas slice small, east to west, like an anomalous slit of extruding navel, binding the lands called Arkansas and Oklahoma: jagged earth rising, joining in harmony the proper path of the sun. It was here, along the southeastern blade of Oklahoma's blunt hatchet, that the Choctaw people built anew their Nation. Here, bandits hid out in the sandstone caves—Belle Starr, the James Boys, the Youngers: white outlaws in Indian Territory to escape white man's law. Deep in these mountains the shriek of a panther, like Lucifer cast down from Heaven, still cuts the night air. Along the murky sloughs of the waterways you may stumble over earthen mounds shaped by the hands of the First People who lived here, and know in your bones their bones are here.

The dirt is not the famous rich red of the Cimarron country, nor the blended sienna and verdigris and salmon of the haunted Deep Fork river bottoms in the central heart of Oklahoma, but a faded yellow brown, dun-colored, dusty in summer, clayey in spring, rock-ridden in all seasons. The names of the waters are lyrical—Fourche Maline,

Poteau, Brazil—and they tumble clear and singing from the rock hills into the long valleys, where they gather the yellowbrown dust to themselves, merge with it, drink it, until they lie low within their banks in late August, sluggish, lazy, the slow murky color of the water moccasins that lurk, secretive and mean, underneath. Summers here are long; winters short; spring is roaring and changeable, for this mountainous southeastern corner is not exempt from the unstable temperatures and capricious winds that sweep, constant and permutable, over the whole of Oklahoma. In winter, the hills are blue with pine and cedar, brown with clinging oak leaves, the unclothed bark of hickory. In spring, redbuds daub the hillsides purple; dogwoods flutter white within the tangle of stark branches like distant snowbanks, until the earth wakens, quick, frenetic with a wild scramble of growing, the fields and ditches clotted with sumac and pokeweed and blackberry briars, every living inch of these hills writhing with insects and green ivy, before the dry winds arrive in midsummer, and the high, dank heat; and the land shrinks, exhausted, sere, choking. It is a long time before autumn comes to these mountains. Before cold sends the scorpions and rattlesnakes into their rocky dens and the hickories dormant, before the seed ticks stop crawling and the skins of the prickly pear cacti on the ridges shrivel in upon themselves.

In a certain cleft near the northern limits of these mountains, in the long east-west valleys between the Sans Bois and the Winding Stair, and well north of Kiamichi's jeweled range, there grew up, in the time of this story, a little sawmilling community of white people called Big Waddy Crossing. The time was near the end of the last century. The earth remains the same—a little prairie surrounded by humped hills, the ragged ridge behind, and, directly south of the townsite, the great oval lump of ground called Waddy Mountain—but the man marks are gone now, swept away by tornado and change. It was to this place that Lafayette Lodi brought his family in the spring of 1887. He came, driving his horses hard in the swelter of a May heat wave, almost directly to this narrow cleft in the mountains, chosen for no better reason than that he'd paused at a farmhouse near Heavener to beg well-water for his team in the searing heat, and the farmer had been a white man with a Choctaw wife who said he had a brother who lived at a sawmilling town called Big Waddy Crossing, a few miles north of the stage stop at Cedar, and he meant to go visit him sometime soon. Within weeks after coming to Big Waddy, Lafayette had obtained a permit to rent and do business within the Choctaw Nation, had built a log house and a shack barn, and had set his sons to work clearing land and breaking it. Then he proceeded to set himself up as a buyer and seller of goods in a goods-starved territory, and waited.

The brother came in the time of the earth's turning after autumn: the skies gray with smoke, the fields umber, branches unsheathed. He came in the same manner that the Territory changed: urgent, quick, driven. The man drove his mules mercilessly, and his face was grim, floating in the smoked dusk of late November; his mules were gaunt, his two dogs like wraiths running beside the wagon. Next to him, sitting straight on the spring seat, her neck craned, her head bare, the girl turned her face side to side, watching; the grim, pliant face with ocher eyes, molded in the image of her father. She looked just like him, though her face was still soft with the soft bones of childhood, her features muted, a little too big. It was not so much in the bones, anyway, that she resembled him—though there was that too: her nose squarish, overlarge; the dome of her forehead high-rounded and smooth—but in the set of her mouth as she frowned at the winter fields on either side as they passed. It was in her eyebrows, fiercely feathered, like the father's, though upon the child the look was black and startling, the dark hairs above light eyes meeting in the heart of her face. The likeness was most acute in the way the top of the girl's head met the air first, bouncing along on the seat of the wagon: the crown of fine straight hair pulled tight into two dun-colored braids, elongating and thinning her narrow eyes the same color as the dust-bitten earth. On her lap the baby cried. Behind her, three tiny faces peeked from the open maw of the canvas. The wagon rolled in the bruised twilight, the gray dawns; and the blue hills humped on either side, sentinels lining the path, or guarding it, as the wagon wound along the twisting, muddy tracks of the Territory, west and a little north, west and a little north, heading always toward the inaudible pulse pounding, drawing blood to blood.

They would pause at a houseplace, a farm or lone Choctaw cabin, and the man would climb down and speak a few moments to the occupants, gesturing, cupping his hand at his chin to shape his brother's beard. The girl would watch intently, suspicious, for she knew the people were Indians and she distrusted them for their gardens and square houses, their homespun trousers and cotton dresses, more so than if they'd worn war bonnets and beads. They did not match what she expected of them, and her slanted eyes would narrow more deeply as she watched a dark man with a mustache and felt hat step out onto his log porch, or pause in his cornfield, scythe in hand, the dried cornstalks quivering and rattling behind him, to shake his head or nod it, point with his eyes or stare silently, for often they did not speak English. The girl would stare at the man's wife in an everyday gingham dress beside him, the man's children gazing back at her with deep eyes, and she would hold the crying baby on her lap tighter. She would speak harshly over her shoulder to the silent children behind her, tell them to hush up. Her eyes would never leave the faces of the people until her father had turned and come back to the wagon, climbed up onto the seat beside her, and then she would turn her eyes front, never glancing back or sideways, as they hurried on.

Within a few days they came to Big Waddy Crossing. A small town, a community of no consequence, but for the fact that the brother, having set and prepared everything, awaited them there.

*T*he town was new and raw with lumber. I could smell the yellow smell of cut wood. That was the the first thing, before even the mud and dark scent where the mules and oxen had laid down their leavings. Before even we came around the curve thick with trees to witness all other signs—blue woodsmoke and jangling harnesses and the voices of men—before even that, I could smell the planking. I could hear the pocked sound of bootheels upon it. I could taste it in my mouth, and I held it there, wounded. Roughsawed and green. When the road turned, I saw two flat storefronts on one side, split-plank porches before them, a stable. The livery doors were open. Farther down, I saw two more buildings hunched raw on one side of the road. I didn't know what they were. I did not see the sawmill then but I smelled it, sifting on the cold air, clogging my nose like a duststorm, and it was that which told me. Had told me before ever I saw the new buildings. Thomas lay in the wagonbed with Jonaphrene, too still and too quiet. Papa went fast around the deep boggy curve with the mules slogging and pulling, he did not slow when the road turned, but I did not care. Before ever I saw it, I knew we were there.

Fayette waited for us like Moses on the bare porch planks, in the shade of the overhang, smoking. He looked in no way surprised to see us. He said, his eyes squinting as if he was looking into brightness, calm, not surprised, beneath his big hat in the dark shade under the overhang, his eyes slits, Fayette said, "Y'all better come in and wash up. Jess's about to put supper on the table."

We seeped into the place in darkness. This is how it seemed. Papa had to carry Thomas up the hill into the house. It was not much of a house, just shaved logs cut and stacked square to shape the one big room and the upstairs crude as a hayloft where the six cousins slept, Caleb and Fowler on the cot at one end, the girls in the bed at the other. Papa carried Thomas, his eyes shut, his little arm dangling, into the log house thick with the smell of meat and biscuits, and laid him on top of the counterpane on the bed in the corner. We seeped in in darkness, carried the fever in with us, and I did not know what it was, hidden in the shell of our wagon, secreted in my baby brother's soft bones.

Jessie watched her brother-in-law carry the youngest boy into the room, and her fearful heart knew. She watched him lay his dying boy on her own bed, heard him direct his other children to sit down yonder by the fireplace, heard his weary grunt and the creak of cane as he sat in the chair on the far side of the room, and she said nothing. Her husband called out, "Wife, you got our coffee boiling yet?" She did not move but kept her eyes on the blond toddler on the bed. The child was not sleeping but unconscious, his face pale, his forehead high and rounded, his tongue protruding between petaled, cracked lips. A red flush lay across the bridge of his nose, spreading mask-like to his pale cheeks; he lay motionless upon the counterpane, his legs bowed and thin, the tiny body stiff and formal as if laid out on a cooling board in a parlor, and the woman knew, she knew, and was powerless to cry out: Where is their mother? Where is she? Do not bring these children of death into my home!

The voices of the men filled the log room, her husband's urgent, excited, the words following rapidly upon themselves, tumbling with his cascade of Territory news; the other's slower, the words fewer, heavy with weariness, and Jessie felt the return of the bond between them that filled her with a cold, unspoken hatred for the one who held her husband's attention. Beneath the rumble of male voices she heard her daughters in a hushed argument at the stove, the two middle ones vying to stir the fried potatoes so that they might each claim to have cooked supper and so be exempt from doing dishes, and her heart was cold with fear. She laid a thin hand protectively across her quickened belly, thanked Providence that her sons were gone with the wagon to meet the supply train at Wister. Thank God for that, thank God. And still, for a moment, silent, powerless, she could not move to protect her daughters, but only turned her eyes from the boy on the bed to John Lodi sitting oblivious, exhausted, in filthy clothes and mud-caked boots, with his hat on, in a canebottom chair against the log wall.

His eldest child Martha Ruth came to him and said, "Papa?" Her tone was impatient, her small face eerily adult as she stood with the ten-month-old baby perched on her hip and shook her father's sleeve as if to wake him, though he was not sleeping, any more than the boy on the bed was sleeping, but sitting heavily in a kind of entranced stupor, gazing at his brother's spirited, talking face.

"Papa?" the girl said, and Jessie shrank in herself at the sight of the offspring wearing the stamp of the father in her expression and stance, in the scowling dark brows feathered across the pale forehead; she shrank at the casual way the child held the baby, nearly as if she herself had borne it, and again Jessie thought of the mother, weak, sickly, without gumption, as Fayette had always said of her, and she knew then that Demaris was dead. Dead! she thought. And no word spoken to mourn her or tell of her passing, and here come her half-starved children swirling into my home in the shank of winter to spread their fever among my own. The woman looked at the father and the little girl in his image tugging at him, and the enmity she bore John Lodi leapt to the child who looked just like him, and was like him.

"Papa!" the girl said, her voice nearly scolding. "You want to unload, or you want me to? It's going on dark now."

It was this, the thought of them bringing into her house the family's contaminated belongings, that unstopped the woman's voice at last, though still she had none to defy her husband or his brother. She heard John say, "We'll unload in the morning," and thought to herself, Over my dead body! Abruptly she turned to those over whom she had direction, stepped quickly to the iron stove, where her daughter Mildred was turning the popping meat, and whispered fiercely, "Take your sisters and get on upstairs." The daughter opened her mouth, a protest rising, and Jessie hissed, "This instant!"

And the daughter obeyed, seeing the ferocity of expression on her mother's face. She likewise hissed at her sisters, and the three half-grown girls untied and laid aside their bleached flour-sack aprons, collected their little sister Pearline from where she stood staring at the new-come cousins by the fireplace, and took her, whispering, in a rush of swirled skirts, up the steep pine stairs to the attic room where they slept.

Fayette, roused a moment from his peroration by the hushed activity, said, "Here, now, what's going on?" Jessie turned defiant eyes on him, her chin raised. Her husband sat astride a ladderback chair pulled away from the table, his arms folded across the top rung, and he had to turn and crane his neck to look up at her. She saw the flush on his ruddy cheeks, the sparkle of blue eyes in the lamplight, and knew he had not given his brother's dead wife more than a moment's thought, had not given even that much to the boy on the counterpane. Still she said nothing but went quickly to the stove and knocked the lid off the bean kettle with the big two-pronged fork, and it rang iron to iron on the hot stovetop; she slapped field peas on a plate for her husband, and began to spoon up the half-raw fried potatoes. With the bunched hem of her apron she carried the coffeepot to the table and poured boiling black liquid into tin cups. She plunked the laden plates on the pine slats and set a skillet of cornbread between them, and now her silence was not paralysis but the intentional silence of rage and punishment, intended for the ears of the one to be punished, and audible in the room, ringing in the thump and clatter of tin and cast iron— but only to the girl standing at her father's elbow. Fayette had turned back again, returned to his cascade of talk, and John sat with half-closed eyes, his chair tipped against the wall. The woman and the child looked at one another, and then the woman, frightened by the recognition she saw in the girl's strange dun-colored eyes, rushed to break her own silence.

"You men get up to the table and eat," she said, and thunked the platter of fried meat on the table. She went to the front door and stepped out onto the log porch to retrieve the buttermilk and cake of butter from the cold box. The sky was streaked with slashes of orange and the deep mauves of winter. Her husband's hounds stood up from the log porch and slapped their long ears awake. Down on the road, beneath the wagon, John's dogs also stood and stretched, and began to trot hopefully toward her, their ribs distinct and countable as fence slats through the coarse, mud-spattered hair. Jessie looked at the remains of the wagon, where the gaunt mules were still harnessed in the traces, their heads bowed. The wheels and sideboards were mud-caked, the whole of it filthy, bedraggled; the wagonsheet was ripped in several places, so that the family's pitiful belongings were revealed to the mauve sky. It seemed to her an obscene thing, a corpse picked at by crows, and Jessie turned quickly, the fear rising, and went back in the house.

The men sat as they had sat before, Fayette in the back-turned ladderback, talking, the other tipped against the wall, eyes closed, silent, and the anger and fear multiplied in the woman so that she nearly spat as she said, "Y'all come on and eat now!" She hoisted the crock of buttermilk to pour it.

"Wash up, Matt," John said, and grunted a little as he stood his chair down on four legs, unfolded himself slowly, seeming to fill the vaulted room, though he was not a tall man, the force and size of him contained entirely in the bulk of his shoulders as he moved across the room toward the door.

"Where do you think you're going?" Jessie blurted. Buttermilk sopped over the snuff glass onto the pine.

"I've got to unhitch the team." He did not seem to be answering her but speaking to the girl crossing the room alongside him, the top of her head at his elbow. "See to it the children wash up good, and y'all go on and eat. I'll be in directly." He paused a moment in the doorway, the girl never yet peeled from his side, the baby big-eyed on her hip, gazing around the room. "Say it's back up yonder that way?" John asked, and nodded his head in the direction of Fayette's barn on the little rise behind the house, and his brother proceeded to give him elaborate directions for the simple distance to the barn.

Jessie thumped the buttermilk crock on the table, dread and anger passing over her in waves laced with loathing for the man who would see to his mules before he would look after the fevered boy on the counterpane. And what could she do? She could not put the sick child out in the cold wagon; she could not make her husband deny his brother—not that she would not, but that she could not, for she had not that strength of will within her, nor that power with him, and so she did what women without power do. "Your food's getting cold," she snapped at her husband, the words spliced and drawn as if spat through a sieve; she turned back to the cookstove, hoisted the kettle of water to heat for the dishes, said harshly over her shoulder, "You young'uns sit right where you are. I'll bring you a plate in a minute," and proceeded to the remains of her own work and that of her daughters. She heard the log door open, felt the cold enter.

"No, now, Mattie, I'll take care of it."

When she turned, she saw John in the doorway with the sky washed lavender and indigo behind him, and the girl, unbonneted, uncloaked, trying to walk beneath his outstretched arm wedged against the doorpost. The baby sat glassy-eyed and silent on the bare puncheon floor by the door.

"You stay here with the children. Wake Tommy up, he needs to eat something."

The woman knew then for the first time that her brother-in-law did not know that his son was dying.

"Matt! I said no, now."

For an instant there was the terrible tension of the child in rebellion, and then it was gone as the baby fell over sideways and cracked her head on the wood floor; the sound popped in the vaulted room, there was complete silence, and then a high thin wail rose. Jessie, impelled by a force separate from her fear, and stronger, stepped across the room and picked up the baby, and the wails crescendoed in hysterical shrieks. The child stank of urine and mildew and sour baby-smell, and the jerking, flailing flesh beneath the soiled gown was burning hot. The woman cradled the baby in her arms, unwilling, unable not to, and paced the floor, patting the foul bottom gently, saying, "There's some sweetmilk left out yonder in the cold box. You better fetch it in before you go off tending to your mules." She didn't look at her brother-in-law as she said it, but at the children themselves, her eyes sliding around the dark high-ceilinged room as she paced with the infant, to the back wall, where the unconscious boy lay on the bed, perhaps dead or dying this moment; to the west wall, where the little girl and fidgety boy crouched on wooden crates near the fireplace, the little girl's eyes glittering bright already with fever; and near her, just before her in the doorway, the eldest girl with her stubborn face standing at her father's elbow: motherless, Jessie did not have to be told. Laid upon her by God's will, perhaps to spread their sickness to her own, and nothing in the world for her to do but accept.

"Martharuth," she said, "cut that nonsense and get in here and take this baby. I've got to see to that boy."

She went to the foot of the pine stairs, still cradling the shrieking infant, and yelled, "Millie! Get your sisters ready!" then called back over her shoulder, "Shut that door! You're letting cold air in!" She turned again to the narrow flank of stairs. "Put your coats on! Wrap Pearly up good!" There was a chorus of blurred voices from overhead, drowned in the sound of the crying baby, and Jessie hollered, "I don't care if you got your nightgowns on already, I'm telling you to get dressed!" She turned to find the girl Mattie directly behind her, and paused not a breath but shoved the baby in the girl's arms and said, "Take her and sit down on that chair yonder. I'll tend to her in a minute. Hitch up the wagon," she said to her husband, though she never looked at him; one would hardly know she did not offer this direction as well to the child. "You got to take the girls over to Mewborns'," and her husband, confused, entirely oblivious to all that the sudden rush and noise meant, sat in his same position in the ladder-back, tamping tobacco into the bowl of a cob pipe.

Jessie went for the first time to the bed and stood over the boy. He was still breathing; she could see the shallow rise and fall beneath his filthy woolen shirt. His pale lids stretched like egg membrane over the eyeballs, and when she touched him he was fiery hot, but he was not sweating; his veined skin was dry as corn husk. The scarlet mask on his face had spread to his throat. She felt someone behind her, and she did not have to turn to know it was the father, standing back a little, reluctant, looking at the child with open eyes now. She heard wood scrape wood, her husband's chair shoved back on the puncheon, and then Fayette, too, was standing there. "Oh my Lord," she heard him say, and she turned on him in fury: "Get the girls out of here!"

John gazed at his son in the same kind of stupor with which he had watched his brother's face before; he said dreamily, "My team is still hitched, Fay. I reckon they won't drop dead to go another mile or two, if you want to take the wagon."

Jessie whirled on him now, the one, as she felt it, who had brought God's curse upon her household. "No! My daughters are not touching a thing in that wagon!" She lifted her head, craned her neck toward the stairs, nearly shrieking. "You girls get a move on! Quick! Fayette, go catch up the horse, now! Martha, run out—no, you do it," she said, meaning John, though she did not again look at him, never taking her eyes from the toddler boy on the counterpane. "Go fetch some cool well-water, we got to get this boy's fever down." The baby still wailed on the girl's lap in the corner.

Fayette said, "Jess, don't you know the boys are gone in the wagon?"

Jessie turned slowly, her arm draped across her belly; she looked at her husband as if she could hardly place him. "Well," she said at last, "borrow Witlow's buckboard. Or saddle that mule you're so high and mighty proud of and ride them over one at a time. They're not touching that wagon. They're not staying in this house." Without turning, she again screamed toward the attic: "Millie! Get your sisters dressed!"

*T*he upstairs was low and slanted, with a small window at one end for light. Jessie had intended us to sleep in the wagon until Papa got a house built—she said as much later, spit it once in anger—but instead she laid a bed for us beneath her own roof, put us together on a big pallet of blankets in a corner upstairs. She kept the six cousins away from us. She did not give us their beds. There was a lamp, but my aunt wouldn't light it. She would not waste the coal oil. I don't care how they tell it. She expected us every one to die.

I would swim up sometimes in the darkness, and the darkness was red. I felt myself sweating, freezing, my bones hurting, my throat swollen, stuffed like there was a sock in it, my arms and legs trembling, and I couldn't stop. I could feel them around me, one on one side, one on the other, their little bodies burning, Thomas and Lyda. I'd hear Jim Dee ask for a drink of water, hear Jonaphrene whining, and always it was in the strange rust-colored darkness. The world before my eyes was black standing water at the bottom of a rusty bucket.

Above me I saw the face coming down. Coming down slowly. Round and flat as a skillet; round, and flat, and brown. Soft brown. Like doeskin. Like chewed leather. Her eyes tiny and glistening, and the red darkness welling, and then black, and then nothing.

I woke again, and Thomas was very still beside me. Too still. Too still beside me, like Mama dead on the ground. I heard Jonaphrene cough. Lyda was crying. Behind me. Somewhere far behind me. Toward the log wall. And Thomas did not move. The round face was there. It said something, and I did not understand. Black swimming, I could not, I could not swim up. I fell back. Later I swam again, and it was not a dream again, and I could smell him.

I put my hand to his chest. He was breathing. Tiny breaths like butterfly flutter, and his heart like a bird's beating in his shallow hot chest. No size at all, he had no size to him, bones only like sticks without flesh and nothing to him but fire and beat and flutter, and I tried to rise up, the swelling red pushed me back, laid a hand a cloak a smothering blackness upon me, and it was a dream then and in the dream my brother crawled about the pallet, crawled blind and weak and struggling like the bones of a bird without feathers, his chest inside out and the bones sharp and showing, and he whimpered, crawling, he crawled upon me and lay across my chest, no stronger than breath, than delicate eyelid flutter, crying weak like a newborn, and I could not come up, I couldn't help him, I prayed, I believed God, I believed God would save him because I could not, I could not, and he lay on the bones of my chest like breath like a bird and raised back his head lifted his face a little toward the angels like John Junior, lifted up his eyes blue and the breath left him the spirit left him and I tried to scream, my chest shrieked with scream my mouth open my face exploding with scream, and no sound could leave me because my brother's tiny dead body lay upon me, and when I woke again Thomas was crying, fullthroated crying, and Papa was standing over me, and Lyda was dead.

The face came again, dipped low over me and lifted Lyda's body to carry her away.

That was all. That was the shape of our coming. In time I could sit up and the room was not rust black but shape-filled and breathing, the slow even breaths of my brothers and sister, and in a little more time Jim Dee began to kick and scramble and pull away the covers, and in a little while more Papa picked us up one by one and carried us downstairs. That is how we came into the life and world of Eye Tee, in darkness. Buried upstairs together in that room without light. Through a black womb fevered into daylight. New. Getting born in darkness all over again.

The father carried the girl on his back down the steep stairs, her thin legs dangling, her bare heels thumping the shaved wood. He set her on a milkstool by the hearth and went back for the others. She watched him carry her brother Jim Dee, and then her sister, and set them down on the pallet, each of them looking strange, unfamiliar, their heads peaked and bare. Her brother's scalp showed in two or three places. Bits of her sister's hair stuck out from behind her ears, brown and ragged, chopped short as a man's. Mattie touched her hand to her own head, felt it, light and numb and stubby, like a nail clipped too short. She had not known when they cut it, had merely drifted up once in the darkness and felt her head slick, without weight, hard and tight and feverish on the floor. It was only when she'd awakened entirely that she knew what had been done to them. She did not care. Her fingertips caressed the short, coarse hairs along her scalp line as she watched the movement in the room.

She saw her father's legs coming down the ladder, and she knew it was Thomas he carried. She wanted to stand up and go to him, but there was a stillness on her that kept her. Her mind told her to go get her brother, but she was too light in her body, her arms and legs hollow. She could see the toddler's small hands locked around their father's neck, and his skull like an egg shining in the lamplight, but she made no move to get up. The father brought the boy and put him on the pallet where the other two children were curled together, lying quiet, blinking their eyes. Mattie could feel the blank space on the pallet that should have been her baby sister, an empty scalded place where no one would look. She knew the truth as she waited with the others by the hearth for their supper, watching the empty space like boiled pigskin in the center of the quilt, but she would not let herself think about it. She turned sideways on the three-legged milkstool, away from her living brothers and sister, away from the barren place on the pallet, and looked at the high dark arc of the room.

It was a rough log room the same size and shape as the one above, where they had lain sick with the fever. The walls were not white-washed or plastered. She could smell pine sap, see it oozing from the peeled pine flesh in the warmth behind the cookstove. The ceiling seemed far away to her; it vaulted high and distant in the dark, but the room close by was crowded and full of smells. Sap glittered on the log walls in the firelight; the humps and backs and faces of people were lit ragged, winking and dancing in shadow, and the room was jammed with supply boxes, furniture, the plenitude of her aunt and uncle's worldly goods. The whole of the house consisted only of the one room and the upper room above, dark and crowded, the walls chinked with mud. *It's only just us,* she told herself. *Just our family, that's all.* The room seemed crushed with too many people, and she didn't know why.

Her eyes scanned the room, settling at last on her aunt's profile where she stood punching out biscuits at the flour board laid over the washstand on the far side of the room. Jessie's mouth and the side of her face were lined and drawn; she punched the flour dough as if she would kill it. The female cousins were at the cookstove in a jostle, the backs of their skirts to the room, their shoulders in navy calico, the bodices all cut and sewed the same. Mattie could see them shoving each other's aprons with their elbows in secret, even the youngest one, Pearline, whose job it was to mind the flies off the table while the men ate. But there were no flies, it was winter, and the youngest one tried to belly in with the others, whining for them to quit. Papa sat at the rough-pine table with Fayette and his boys, their sleeves rolled back on their arms from washing.

The girl looked at her father's back, his thick shoulders hunched beneath suspenders. The shirt he was wearing was not his own but one stitched together of brown homespun that which she'd never seen before. Her uncle was on the far side with his elbows cocked on the pine slats, his hands tipping a saucer of coffee, his mouth hidden in the clot of hair curled round it and the saucer lip buried in his mustache and beard. His sons slouched at the sides of the table, the younger one, Fowler, on a flour keg and Caleb, the eldest, across from him in the canebottom chair. Fowler's dark face was turned on his brother, the scowl like a storm boiling, and Caleb, in a half turn, was looking at his father, trying to shape his lips like him while he sipped his own saucer of coffee. She knew it was real coffee they drank, not burnt-corn coffee like she and her father had been drinking for months in the mountains. She could smell the dark, rich odor, and her stomach cramped around it. What she did not know, couldn't see then nor understand what it indicated, was that her uncle and cousin drank their coffee from saucers that had belonged to her own mother's set of white china dishes with the rose print on the edge.

She looked away from the crowded swirl of the room to her brother and sister and Thomas snuggled together on the pallet on the puncheon floor. For the first time she saw that it was Pearline's old summer gown her sister was wearing, a light gown of thin muslin, though the floor beneath the pallet was cold as stone. She saw that her brother Jim Dee had on a nightshirt a dozen sizes too big for him, and Thomas wore only a diaper square and a piece of blanket pinned together. Jonaphrene looked up then, her dark eyes enormous as she scrambled and twisted around to sit up. Jim Dee began to fidget and twitch, picking at loose threads in the quilt top, and Thomas lay on his side, curled around himself. *Too still,* Mattie thought, *too still again.* She saw her brothers and sister changed: thin, liver-colored and hairless as newborn possums—and still she did not see all that the red darkness had done.

"Martharuth!" her aunt called. "Jump up here now and help Sarey set the table." And Jessie went on punching the powder biscuits, laying them rapidly in the pan.

The hollowness was yet in the girl's bones, but the place behind her eyes was not filled with the black swimming; the fever was gone now, she was not even cold, and so she didn't know it would happen. When she stood up, the rock hearth and the fireplace beside it fell away. There was no pain, only that lightness upon her and a little stuffed feeling deep in her ears. But the room fell away, and she didn't know what to think. She sat back down.

Her aunt called again, her voice sharp. "Martharuth!"

"Mattie," her father said, "git up and help now. You're all right."

Again the girl stood. Again it happened. The floor fell away. She held herself very still; she didn't know what it was.

Jessie said, "Supper's near about ready, child. Hurry up!"

Mattie tried to walk toward her cousin, but the log walls swooped and fell away from her. She hit the pine table where the men sat, walked sideways into it, and shook the coffee saucers splashing, the coal oil trembling in the lamp.

Her father grabbed for her, said, "Whoa, now!"

Jessie hollered, "Look out, child! What in the name of Pete is the matter with you?"

Papa had her by the back of the nightgown, and she put her hand on the table, not because she knew to do so, but because she had walked directly into it, crashed into the pine ledge without bracing or flinching because she'd had no idea it would happen, and it was the weight of the table that stopped her. She touched the top of it, the flat plane of pine with the flat of her hand, held to it with her palm spread, Papa clutching up the neck of the nightgown—her cousin Lottie's nightgown she had on—and in a minute the room settled. Her father's eyes were on her, stern and nearly black in the darkness. Mattie looked up, and then quickly away, but she felt his eyes on her, and so she tried to take her hand off the table.

Fayette said, "Ah, leave her rest, John, them kids have been mighty sick," and he slurped a sip of coffee. The wood between his elbows was wet with slopped coffee. The lip of the saucer was sunk in the mat of his beard. The girl looked at the saucer, unseeing, without recognition, but feeling it as something familiar from long ago that erupted her soul. She heard a sharp tongue-to-teeth sound beside the stove, though she didn't know if it was her aunt or one of the cousins. She did not turn to look; her father's hand was still tight on the nightgown. The room was not rolling then because she was standing still, her hand on the tabletop, her head forward a little and tilted to the side, but she knew something was terribly wrong. Her father's hand eased on her. He said, so softly she barely could hear him, "Go set down, Matt."

She turned her head, saw her brother and sister and Thomas on the pallet beside the hearthstones. She saw the milkstool and the fire burning bright, and she tried to walk toward it.

The fire sank. The log room like a cave turned and tilted away from her, and she stepped where there was no floor.

Her chin hit the wood, and her teeth jarred and stung to her eyeballs. She heard yelling, her father's voice in a shout, "Mattie!" She
couldn't answer. She could not stand up. Her uncle said, "Y'all better
let them young'uns rest," and the girl hated him as she crawled to the
fireplace and put her open palm on the flat stones. She pulled herself
onto the hearth and lay across it, warm and smooth: the warm, smooth
breast of hard stone. The room ceased to turn; the world settled. She
heard the wooden legs of the milkstool clatter and roll on the puncheon, felt her sister's hand, or someone's hand, warm on her back.
Someone was hollering, or talking, but the sound came from far away.
The hand was calm on her back, and it calmed her.

Inside, Mattie felt a slow warmth spreading, easing through her
veins, along the trembling flesh of her back, into the well of her stomach. She turned her head and saw Jonaphrene crouched on the pallet
with her knees tucked to her chin beneath the thin summer gown, her
luminous eyes burning dark as a nightjar's, the brown hair sticking up
like scruff from the top of her head. Both of Jonaphrene's arms were
wrapped around her gowned legs, hugging them. Mattie slid her eyes
round the room, and she saw them watching her, all of them: her sister
and brothers watching her, and Papa half turned at the table with his
eyes on her, Fayette's eyes upon her, and his sons' eyes, Caleb and
Fowler, watching not out of interest but because the others were looking at her. In front of the cookstove, the girl cousins had turned and
stood perfectly still in a blue-dark calico row, the eldest one's hand in
the air with the meat fork pointed up. Jessie stood perfectly still, half
turned from the flour board, one hand on her hip and the tin biscuit
cutter in the other, cocked in the same manner, caught up in midair.

Mattie knew then whose hand was upon her.

She felt it as surely as she had felt it warm on her shoulder to claim
her that hot afternoon in the clearing. She was not afraid.

The room was still, the only movement the flicker of firelight and
shadows dancing, the coal oil burning steadily in the lamp on the table,
the rock hearth swelling, receding, warm and smooth beneath her. She
could see her own blood joined up with her, watching, not afraid yet:
Thomas drowsy, wanting to sleep again; Jim Dee restless in his muscles; Jonaphrene shivering, her eyes big, trying to know if it was all
right. She could see the six cousins, half-blood and curious, and her
aunt, who had no blood in her, fearful and furious, and it was Jessie
at first Mattie knew best because her aunt's energy was strongest and
thrown at them, because she did not want them; she had no say-so

but to take them, but she didn't choose them, and Mattie saw that. She looked at her aunt, caught in the half turn: a gaunt woman with bad teeth and a rising belly in a sack apron and patched dress, glaring in the lamplight with her hand up, the tin loop of biscuit cutter like a weapon in her fingers cocked in the air. Mattie saw the two swellings inside her: fear for her own children—especially her sons; the girl could see the fierce mother-love of sons for the two who sat impatient and hungry at the pine-slat table, and of those two it was Fowler she feared most for, her fear like a claw thrown round him—and the other swelling an aimless, useless, empty anger which had no place to land but upon the unwanted children against the log wall by the hearth. The girl did not see the unborn child her aunt carried.

Stranger, Mattie thought. *Not blood kin.* She shut her eyes from the woman, turned her head.

Her legs were long on the hearthstones, long and bony, extending off the hearth to the cold dark past the fire. She felt herself awkward, her feet big, her legs too long for her body, and she thought she had grown in the red darkness, grown long while she slept in the fever. The others were talking. She heard Lottie say, "Mama, what's she doing?" and Sarah in a loud whisper, "Mama! They're still sick!" Jessie said, "You girls hush up and tend to your business." Fayette said, "Somebody pour her a cup of coffee, when's them biscuits ready? A man's liable to starve to death before somebody puts supper on the table around here."

Mattie opened her eyes again, turned toward the sound. She could see the men's legs, their boot tops beneath the table. She didn't look up for a bit, and when she did, it was to the boys Caleb and Fowler her eyes drifted. She understood then, gazing at the two brothers, what it was that made the younger one turn his scudding scowl on the elder: the dark envy that forced him to watch his brother every instant, to crave his every joy and gesture; she saw how Fowler hungered after even the cold coffee Caleb slurped from a saucer, believing in his secret heart that it was better than any coffee given into his own hand by their father, and she saw him in that moment thirsting after it, with Jessie's fear and fierce love dug in his heart like a claw.

They are half-blood, she thought. *The blood of their father and our father is the same from Grandpa Lodi, the same from Grandma* (a wisp of sticks dying with black sunken mouth on the bed back home in Kentucky), *but their mother is not blood to us. None of hers is ours. They are half-blood, that's all.*

The female cousins jostled and talked on the far side of the room. Their backs were turned again, they'd returned to the task of cooking, Mildred's arm elongated where she stretched it out to turn the fat-spitting meat in the frying pan, and the others shoving their elbows to try to stir the beans or the turnips, but Mattie could see them just as well; she knew them, the three eldest all brown-headed and freckled and nearly the same size, and the least one, little pale Pearline. *Half-blood,* she thought. It was nearly a snort in her silence, an unsounded laugh, because it freed her, knowing that they were not like her, their mama was not her Mama, and she was bound to them no more than half. The six cousins, male and female, receded to their place of no importance, no more worth her notice than her uncle's coon hounds in the yard. Papa and Fayette were talking at the table, but still Mattie did not look at them. She would not look at her father. Suddenly a new thought came to her, chilling her, wiping away her contempt, turning her legs and shoulders shivering like the fire of the fever. She began to tremble on the hearthstone.

Her father said, "Matt, get up from yonder if you're cold. Wrap up in the quilt."

She could feel him turned toward her. She didn't move or answer. Her eyes were on the four trousered pairs of legs under the table, crowded in the dark with the many chair legs and the lone dark hoop of flour keg. She thought the words again, and she pushed them away, but still they came back to her:

Papa is only half blood, the words said.

He is full blood to himself. Full blood to Fayette and Uncle Big Jim Dee, to Aunt Lottie and Aunt Myrtis, Aunt Helen Alzada, Aunt Ruth and Aunt Lovey and Melvina Jane. But he is only half blood to us.

Mattie looked to the pallet. Thomas was sleeping, his tongue bulging pink between his lips. Jim Dee and Jonaphrene were sitting close together, the boy fidgeting, picking at the cotton batting leaking from a torn seam in the pallet quilt, his legs twitching.

We are the only ones equal from Mama and Papa both together. Only us. No! (She would not think about Lyda. She shut the picture of the baby lifted away by brown hands, the tiny legs dangling, legs sticks of bones nearly, and dead. She shut it.) *My two brothers, my sister, they are the only others the same as me,* she thought. *It is us. We four together. Only us who have Mama's blood now.*

She watched Jim Dee lean over and pick at Jonaphrene's nightgown, Pearline's summer gown they'd put on her. He plucked at the muslin hem, tugging lightly, and Jonaphrene ignored him, and then he pulled her sleeve, and Jonaphrene said, "Quit!" The boy climbed into a crouch, ready to spring, to jump, to do something, and Mattie knew he would get up in a minute. He would have to. His skin itched deep to the bone. He would get up and go to the rest of them, the half-blood and no-blood, and Papa would growl at him, yes, but only a little, and Fayette would say, "Have a seat, son," and Fowler would turn his fierce scowl upon him, and Jim Dee would get his place at the table on an old flour keg or firkin, but Mattie knew he would not be able to sit there. He would get up again and roam the room and poke into things until Jessie would holler, "For the love of Pete, child, can't you for one minute be still!" And he would sit a while longer, and then he would be gone. He was her brother. She struggled a long time. But she knew she could not keep a rein on him, never would she be able to hold him, and so she let him go finally—though he had not jumped yet, though it would be years yet, she didn't know how long—but she could feel it: that it was only time and a little of what Jim Dee didn't know yet that kept him with them, his taut muscles trembling beneath his pale limbs.

She had to keep Jonaphrene. Jonaphrene and Thomas. Mattie knew it, looking at the sleeping toddler with his tongue bulging and her sister wrapped inside the sheath of summer gown like a cocoon she'd tried to spin round herself because there was no one to put a shawl on her shoulders or a quilt. Even with her hair gone, Jonaphrene was the exact image of Mama—but for her eyes, which were the gray-green of Papa's, lined in a thick fringe of straight, dark lashes. *Jonaphrene is Mama's. (Not Lyda!) Jonaphrene is Mama's own child in Mama's image, as I am, for how Mama claimed me.* Mattie felt her mother again, not as a hand upon her but as a presence, the way she'd felt her when Mama rocked her and nursed her as an infant, her mother's scent.

She knew at once what she must do. She must hitch Sarn and Delia to the wagon, take Mama's trunk and her linens and quilt tops, she must wrap the children warm.

No, but first she must find Mama's tin box—for it was somewhere, Mattie knew it, inside Mama's trunk, or hidden somewhere in the wagon: a secret square, an invisible door—and she must find it and carry it with them. She mustn't tell Papa.

It was the old dream and it had never been completed, and so she had to go on and do it, with her sister and brother, Jonaphrene and

Thomas, her most kin, Mama's most kin, just as she'd dreamed it all those months in the mountains. It could not be burned away by the red darkness. She must load their possessions, as she'd loaded and unloaded, loaded and unloaded and loaded them again so many times. She knew how to do it. In secret she must do it, and then she must drive the mules east over the twisting wagon tracks, past the log cabins and shacks, past the Indians in white people's clothing standing in their empty gardens, and east out of Eye Tee, back up into the mountains, and get Mama. She had to take her mama back home.

Mattie jerked suddenly and looked up at her father. She thought he had heard her. She thought he knew what she was thinking, and she flinched backwards in guilt, looking up at him, but Papa's eyes were not on her. He had turned back to the table, his hunched shoulders in brown homespun toward her and the children. Mattie knew where her father's eyes looked.

Fayette was talking, as he always talked, never ceasing, about his *plans,* his big doings, he was always going to do this and this and this, and Mattie did not listen, his voice only the hum of a dirt dauber in her ears, unless the words meant something about her father—or her mother, as it had been in the mountains. She saw the image then: her uncle in his big hat poking the fire. Talking. Talking. She remembered, looking up at Papa looking at his brother, and it was only Papa's back she could see, but she knew the look on him, like Fowler's, and yet not Fowler's because it was not envy but just the same manner of being captured, caught by the full and equal portion of blood from their own father and mother, caught by his brother, caught and held by his brother, as he always had been. She did not look at her uncle. She didn't have to, for she could see him, the picture of him talking, talking, talking, poking the fire with his green pine stick, and her stomach curdled around it, the sound and smell of him, spitting. A sour taste rose up in her mouth.

When they called her again, she lay still. While her aunt put the men's food on the table, while the men ate and the female cousins stood by the cookstove, piecing sneakily from the cooking pots as they waited. While the girls ate afterwards, standing, with their tin plates beneath their chins, while Fayette smoked and his boys and Papa and Jim Dee drank coffee from her mother's china saucers, Mattie lay long-limbed and silent, watching, though she pretended to sleep, her bones light on the warm hearthstones and her mouth full of yellow bile, as the people in the room spoke and moved and washed and spat and drank coffee.

It wasn't until the cold night air swept in through the door when it opened once and shut again quickly, until she heard Thomas cry and saw Jonaphrene shivering alone in Fayette's big chair at the table, until her father's voice called her, saying, "Come on here now, Matt, git up and feed your brother," that at last she pushed herself slowly up from the warm breast of stone to her hands and knees. She crouched, her bare feet beneath her, to stand, and it took only that, only her feet crouched beneath her, and rising, and the world fell. She went skittering across the dark room to the line of blue-dark calico and sack aprons.

I did not ask about Lyda, and when the children tried I shushed them. I would not let them speak her name, any more than I would speak it, or the others. None of us did. I didn't know for a long time where they had laid her. One day Thula showed me; she took me to the place far up in Waddy Holler, a cleared place where you could see down through the valley, looking east. There were other graves there. There were no markers with names, only slabs of sandstone facing heaven, each balanced on a ridge of raised stones: orange slabs cut from rock in the shape of a coffin, lying flat on raised stones to face the sky. Facing God. To press the bodies for eternity into the earth. Lyda was not under a slab but in a tiny sunken place the size of a cradle, with nameless sand-colored markers at the head and the foot. So I knew then, but I did not tell the children. I believed I understood what I was supposed to teach them.

She is dead, I thought, let her stay dead. It is not like our mama. Mama does not have a headstone in the mountains of Arkansas, I thought, just a narrow wedge of sandstone standing up on its end. Under a pine tree. High on a ridge. Lyda has two small squares of sandstone, chipped from nothing, though they are nearly perfect rectangles. That is how they break free from the earth. Two pieces of sandstone two feet apart in a field grown up with wild roses and brambles. In an old Indian cemetery in the cleft of Waddy Holler. No one is named there. This is as it should be, I thought.

I forgot nothing else, but I forgot Lyda. In my living mind I did. She dropped like a stone in water, and they all were willing, Papa most of all, and Aunt Jessie, and I let them. I wanted to, I tried to. I knew.

It was not even to escape Satan's Army, which we could not, no matter how I worked, how I tried to arrange things, washed the quilts, caught the nigger, fled the darkness and witchery. No matter how Papa pushed the mules, how quickly we fled. It wasn't hers anyhow, that colored woman's curse upon Lyda. It was ours, the mark was on us, and I knew it. I knew there would be sacrifice. We carried it with us like the fever into Eye Tee, and that is why we seeped into this place in red darkness. We brought it with us, though the darkness, too, was already here. There would have to be sacrifice, blood sacrifice. Our blood, I thought then, though I did not yet know the half of it. In the closed upper room, with Thula's brown face coming down to bear witness, with my infant sister and my brother on the pallet beside me, I did the first iniquity. I traded Thomas's life for Lyda's.

In prayer I did.

But that is not all I owe for.

The time was not long that they were caught all together in the dark vault of the log house, but to the girl it seemed forever; it seemed longer than the crossing, the climb into the mountains, the warm months into autumn they had lived in the clearing. Later her mind would roll it out and spread it like black manure laid down before planting: the pull of her aunt's mouth and judging eyes on them every minute; her uncle's voice talking, talking from the roan mat of his beard, his big belly, and later the smell on him, which the girl did not yet understand. She would remember the boys taking in after Thomas, teasing him, mocking him, and the cousins in their new calico with their peppered faces watching her and her sister yoked together in the cousins' old hand-me-down dresses, and her father gone, and all of them crowded in on top of each other, the sour smell in the house, the days and nights reeling aimlessly in a circle forever, marked only by meals and her father rising and what little light came through the tanned-hide windows.

The others climbed down the ladder in the early morning, her aunt first and then the cousins, to start the stove and sift biscuits, and her father would be already gone. The girl would lie still and watch in the dark with the fire dying. He would not light the lamp but always he'd put another stick of wood on the hot coals of the fireplace, and in time the gnarled blackjack would ignite and burn hot. She'd watch him put his hat on—not his own hat but a different one, a shapeless tan one which bore no more character in its folds than a turkey wattle—and place his hand beneath the clean cloth spread over the dishes on the table, take out a cold biscuit or a piece of saltmeat or whatever was left from the last evening's supper, and turn and lift the latch and go out. Many times he walked out the door emptyhanded. The cold air would whirl in, and sometimes she could see stars shining. Her father left well before the others came down, well before daylight, and often he didn't return until the house was quiet and dark, the others asleep overhead and the children breathing deeply beside her. Her father would take his plate from the stovetop, and sometimes it would be so late that the fire in the cookstove would have gone out and the gravy on the tin plate would be congealed. Mattie would watch from beneath veiled eyes as her father ate his cold supper and went to wrap up in his quilts and lie down on the far side of the room.

She did not know where he went in the early mornings, why he came home late; she would not ask him, and no one offered to tell her. She spent her days crouched on the pallet or the milkstool, waiting for her father to come home. Fayette had nailed scraped hides over the windows to keep the cold out, and the back door was always closed, with a heavy oak bar laid across it, and so the vaulted room was close and dark even in daylight, and rank with the smell of cooking and coal oil and Thomas's dirty diaper squares—and the others, how they smelled, she thought, because nobody could wash properly. She couldn't take care of Thomas except to change him, and then only if he would lie still for her. Even yet she didn't know what the fever had done to him, though she could hear how he echoed what she said, what anyone said, would say it back in exactly the same tone and words and inflection. She'd hear him scream and shriek when Jessie tried to make him sit on the chamberpot; see him drop suddenly to the floor sometimes and thump and crawl across the cold puncheon as if he'd forgotten how to walk. Scanning the dark arc of the log room, her gaze would settle on her sister sitting crosslegged in a cousin's nightgown on the pallet, staring, rubbing her small hand again and again down the back of her shorn head. Mattie would quickly turn her eyes away. She'd see her brother Jim Dee tromp out the log door behind Fayette's boys every morning, come home with them in the evenings and slurp his coffee from china saucers just as they did, but Mattie would not think about him, though he was a sweaty, knotted, softly snoring lump on the pallet in the night beside her; she shut him away as perfectly as she'd shut away the memory of her dead infant sister.

Each day she watched from her milkstool to find a secret time when the boys were gone, and then she'd lean over and whisper to Jonaphrene to take her behind the curtain, until at last she began to eat and drink almost nothing because she didn't want to go behind the curtain in the presence of any of them, not even the females. She waited, for her father to come home and take them out of the log house, for her mother to come again and touch her, for change of some kind, any change, and no change happened. The days and nights spun together. If she tried to walk, the room tilted crazily. She had to hold a chairback or press her hand to the table to keep from skidding sideways wild and loose across the floor. She began to believe it would be this way forever, that she would never be able to walk straight or take care of the children or go forward and do the one thing that must be done. She prayed, *Heavenly Father in Jesus' name, please, I promise, please, just let the room hold still a little while, let the floor stay put,* for she believed fully that the disturbance was not within her but outside her: the world itself, falling. Each day when her aunt was not looking, when the cousins' backs were turned, the girl would slowly, carefully, stand up from the hearth or the milkstool and take a step, and each day the puncheon slabs would fall away. She pondered it, even as it happened, even as she stepped, falling, or tumbled cockeyed in a looped circle, she'd think, *Why would Mama come here to tell me, make me remember my job to do, and then leave me locked in this house of half-blood and no-blood? to be held in their ways and smell, only to swirl and skid in this dark room with the floor falling—*

The girl could not understand why her mother would leave her unbalanced, untethered, unable to go forward and do what must be done. She believed her mother had power to change it, that from where her mother was she could do anything, and so the girl asked, in the haze before sleep, she questioned, though she couldn't have said who she asked it of, because it wasn't God or Jesus; it wasn't her Mama. The strangeness of the world falling was beyond source or telling, and she couldn't fathom where it had come from, and so she asked—but she asked no one, unfocused, her chest open in the dancing dark.

In time, there was one change. Her aunt came to her one morning and said she must get up and make herself useful. Jessie said it was no use to send her outside to draw water or feed chickens or sweep the yard, because she wouldn't do anything but pitch a fit sideways and fall down. But even a pullet lays eggs, her aunt said, or it gets eat quick for Sunday dinner, and she drew the girl up by the elbow and guided her across the floor and set her at the table to shell corn.

The girl daydreamed about what lay on the other side of the door as she sat at the table scrubbing turnips or peeling potatoes. She had an image of the raw, slapped-together town laid out on one side of the road when they drove quickly around the long curve toward it, but the memory was from before the red darkness, and that town could have been any town they had come through on the long journey or tried to avoid. She couldn't connect that memory with what lay outside the big split-log front door, which she could see when they opened it: a long scabby slope down to a creekbank with a wagon road running beside it. Sometimes the sun would be glancing off the water, making her eyes hurt, but then the door would shut quickly to keep the cold out, and the room would sink into darkness again. So the girl sat at the table and scrubbed turnips or lay on the pallet with her baby brother or hunched uselessly by the fireplace in the dark swirl and smell, thinking this was to be her life forever, thinking she was a cripple now, no good for anything. Thinking they might make up their minds to shoot her as they would a crooked mule.

Then came a warmish day in deep winter. She didn't yet know that was how it would be in this country; she couldn't fathom that the earth could turn warm of a sudden in the hard edge of winter, and then, in a day's time or an hour's time, turn back brutally cold again. She thought it must be spring.

The back door was propped open with a chair wedged against it. The front door was wide to the south wind. The cousins were doing wash on the back porch and they had her sister helping, though Jonaphrene was smaller than even the youngest, Pearline. Jessie had set the girls working before walking off to take dinner to her sons clearing ground on the far side of the creek. Jonaphrene was standing on the porch cranking the handle on the wringer. Mattie could see her through the open door. Long threads of wrung clothes and bedsheets spilled flattened through the clenched rollers into the tub. Thomas was outside on the porch with the rest of them, crawling on the split logs. Air came through the house. Sitting by the fireplace on the milkstool, she could smell light and air for the first time. Through the front door she could see the naked branches by the creekbed, the sun sparkling on the water, or, turning her head, she could see her sister cranking the wringer in the porch shade at the back. Life outside the log house slanted in from either side and split the dark room; she wanted to go out there. She craved it nearly. She could taste the soft-soap smell, and warmth and air and sunlight like God's breath where she couldn't touch it. Mattie made up her mind she was going to go out there; she told herself in that moment that she could walk forward in the strength of her own will.

She stood up very slowly. The floor shifted, as always, the room swooping and falling. She didn't try to take a step. She knew what would happen. She could hear her cousins' voices, and the chickens below them scratching and cackling in the yard. A horse whinnied in the distance, and another one answered from the rise behind the house. The empty space swooned between her and the table, and she slammed toward it, aiming wildly at the rough-pine table covered in white cloth, until she landed against it and knocked down the near chair. She didn't cry out when the table struck her in the low rib, sharp and stunning as a wasp sting. She didn't look up—though she knew the others on the porch must have heard—but shoved the cloth back with one hand and edged around the table, her palms flat to the surface, her eyes looking where her hands crept, slowly, one over the other, until she reached the far side near the back door. There was no chair.

Without pause, without a look to the others crowding at the door, Mattie edged back around the table to the knocked-over chair and went down into a slow crouch and touched it with one hand, hoisted it by the back, her left hand flat to the table, her right raising up with phenomenal strength the back of the chair. She stood the canebottom on its four legs and, hunched over to grasp the two sides of the seat where the cane looped around, she walked it, screeching and snagging on the rough puncheon slabs split from sawed logs with an old adze and never planed, because it was not her father who had laid that floor down; her father would have planed it smooth as a dresser drawer. She thumped and shoved and pushed toward the square of light, where she could see the four speckled faces peeking around the doorjamb and her brother with his two fingers in his mouth sitting on the porch floor at their skirttails, and her sister with her thin arms in someone's old dress, without a shawl or a sweater, standing in the doorway with the light behind her and no bonnet on, her naked head bare.

Jonaphrene said, "Mattie?"

She didn't answer but kept on, *clunk-thunk, clunk-thunk,* over the puncheon. The cousins clucked at one another like the gargle of chickens in the yard below. Jonaphrene stepped through the square of light, the cousins bahwking behind her, and came into the dark house, leaned over and whispered, "Hold my shoulder." Mattie did not pause or look up but kept on clunking ferociously, an inch at a time, over the puncheon. Jonaphrene said it again, a whisper: "Hold my shoulder!" The younger girl came closer, dipped her thin shoulder a little, and it was then that Mattie understood. She let go of the canebottom, reached up and took hold of Jonaphrene's shoulder, and stood straight up; she held tight to her sister. They walked outside that way.

Mattie sat on the porch ledge with Thomas crawling and tumbling on her. The porch faced the north side so that she could not see the sunlight sparkling on the creekwater or the new roughsawed buildings of the town. But it was light and air for the first time, and she breathed it like a victory, though all she could do then was sit on the porch ledge while the others did the washing. She looked out at the mottled slope of stubbly field rising north and east to a rough gray structure on the rise at the foot of the mountain—Toms Mountain, though of course she did not yet know its name—and she breathed deeply. She knew something was changed. In a kind of secret, powerful rejoicing, she sat on the porch ledge, while the others worked faster behind her, her sister turning the wringer, cranking quickly with her thin arms, and the cousins rubbing halfheartedly and pinning the laundry hastily on the line because the clouds were already rolling in over the top of Toms Mountain, the temperature dropping fast. She didn't think then of walking, of going forward any more in a straight line, but only that she had won what she had to. That evening, for the first time since her father had carried her downstairs, she ate a full supper; she ate as much red-eye gravy as her cousins. In the morning, with the wind howling from the north, the world gone back winter, she leaned over and whispered to her sister. Jonaphrene stood up, and Mattie stood, put a hand on her sister's shoulder, and they walked outside together.

In this way the girl emerged from the darkness of the log house joined tight to her sister. Not yet could she work or do the task she believed she was meant to do or go forward in a straight line. Alone she couldn't, but joined to her sister, she could walk. And they did walk, never far, never to the town or along the road or even down to the creekbank, but tethered in a tight circle to the log house. They walked to the dug well or along the path to the privy, and later a little farther, easing singlefile down the slope almost all the way to Fayette's store. The girl went with her arm stretched before her, touching her sister's shoulder, and the little one walked somberly in front, tiny, her peaked head only reaching the top of the older one's chest. They went linked in this manner through the fields and hillsides, along the pathways: a tiny solemn fairy without hair leading a blind person.

In time, they began to climb the rise behind the house to the sandstone ridge that razored east and west, cupping the community of Big Waddy Crossing in its rough fold. The sisters wore a path to the top of the ridge, where they would stand for hours with their arms linked, gazing out at the long broken valley of orange grasses and blue cedar sweeping wide east and west between the humped hills. The ridge had no English name in that time, though later it was called Baldback, and to the east it rose abruptly and became the skirt of Toms Mountain; to the west the bony spine ran a mile and a half, descending, until it disappeared in the scrub oak and cedar deep in Waddy Holler. From the ridge's open sweep the two sisters could see Bull Mountain kneeling in the west, stumps of pine and giant oak upon it where men had logged the trees out; or they could turn back to the east and see Bull Creek emerge from the far side of Toms Mountain and crawl toward Big Waddy, winding close enough to embrace the sawmill, lick the edge of town, before it abruptly twisted away to the southeast through the bare arms of hickories. Always, directly across, on the far side of the valley, the girls felt the enormous humped presence of Waddy Mountain. Below, the raw buildings of the town sat in their strange way, on one side of the road only. The rutted wagon road, which had once been the old Butterfield Overland Stage road, curved on past the town in a great boggy sweep at the foot of Waddy Mountain, and on around south, to the rest of the world.

Sometimes the warm salt wind would come again, sift up from the Gulf around the hump of Waddy Mountain, slip between the hills in the hollows as the road snaked, grow big again in the prairie, and climb the ridge to touch them warm so they could remember summer. It was not spring yet, only the lying kiss of the south wind, but on those days the two walked back and forth along the bald top, pacing, tracing their steps back and forth again, or they would range in a great looping circle, the little one leading, walking slowly, her sister's hand clamped to her shoulder, hardly a thread of daylight between them. Thus, through the winter, linked as plates in an armadillo's shell, the two walked, or stood on the ridge for hours—as long as they could manage to stay out of the log house, away from the eyes and mouth of their aunt, away from chores and the stares of the cousins—gazing down at the log house below, built, not in two side-by-side pieces with a dogtrot between, as others in the Territory built their houses, but with one room hunched on top of the other, surrounded by log porch on all sides. They gazed down at the back of their uncle's store below the log house and off to the side a little toward town: Fayette's store of roughsawed lumber split clean and yellow, like the rest of the town—as if the Lodis were a part of them. As if they were in kinship with the people of Big Waddy Crossing, but the girl knew differently, because always from the corner of her eye she could see the hunkered one-on-top-of-the-other squares of the log house.

Time doesn't go in a line forward but around in a circle and down, looped with the seasons spiraled upon themselves into Past, which is not past but Now spiraling forever, deep, like a hair rope dropping loose on itself. The season was moving along the hoop at the top— one year from the time the Lodis left Kentucky—when the Indian woman came again. It was winter still. The trees were bare, the earth smoke-gray and waiting. She didn't come along the road through the town but came straight across the top of the ridge from the west, walking, the front of her skirt gathered in her hand to keep it from snagging on briars. The sisters were in their place on the craggy out-crop, watching. The day was cold, sunlit, bitter with wind. The girl knew the woman was coming to her, and she watched, afraid, her hand on her sister's shoulder. Jonaphrene began to wriggle and squirm and clutch at her fingers, and Mattie at last made herself loosen her grip, but she could not make her chest slow, could not ungrit her teeth.

The woman was small at first in the distance. Coming, she never did get big. She came without pause directly to where the two stood. Her dress was still gathered in her fingers, an ordinary muslin dress dyed butternut brown. She wore not a shawl but a draped Confederate army blanket the color of dried clay. Her hair was wound in a black braided loop around the crown of her head. She was not much taller than the girl was, standing, her skin brown and seamed, her face round, her eyes small. Mattie smelled sweetsmoke and something else, she did not know what the other smell was, but it was old and familiar, green-smelling, and it made her chest ache. The woman looked at her and spoke, long rapid words in her own language, unfathomable to the girl.

The wind blew the yellowbrown skirt; the broken hairs cobwebbed loose from her thick braid. She didn't squint in the sunlight but looked straight at Mattie, her eyes almost even with the girl's eyes, and then she went around the two girls and on along the ridge, and down, toward the log house.

"Reckon what she wants?" Jonaphrene whispered. Her eyes followed the woman's back.

Mattie didn't answer. She thought, *She will kill me.*

She knew the woman was an Indian. The muslin dress and Confederate blanket were like those she had seen on the pig trails coming into the Territory, and she thought not of the round face coming down in the darkness but of Indians dressed in white people's clothing, walking the rutted wagontrails in groups of families, smoking in front of their cabins, the dried November cornstalks rustling in rows in their fields. The images blurred behind her eyes: blue humps of mountains rolling fast past the wagon, trails winding, twisting back on themselves, and yet always west, west into Eye Tee, and Papa driven in his mad way toward his brother, stopping to ask, again, and again, and the dark men with their black eyes and black mustaches pointing with their faces, talking low in their throats, and Lyda bawling in her lap and sometimes laughing, her mouth open, her little teeth white in her laughing mouth. She had to shut it! She had to cut the memory fast. She stuck her tongue into the side of her jaw and bit it. Jonaphrene made a small sound, a little whining sound, and shrugged her shoulder hard. Mattie loosened her hand again, and they waited, the two of them quite still, quite quiet, standing in the wind and cold sun.

They waited a long time before Jessie stepped out the back door onto the log porch below and called to them. Frowning, she looked all directions before she finally lifted her eyes and saw them. She motioned impatiently, great circular swoops with her arm, and the sisters started down the path along the ridge toward the house, the elder's hand on the younger's shoulder, the younger a half step in front and off a little to the side. The girl knew her aunt had sent for the woman. She thought it must be, at last, to kill her off like a crooked mule.

It took a moment for her eyes to adapt to the darkness inside the log house. The first thing she saw was a cleared space in the middle of the floor and the woman and Jessie standing in the center. Jessie was holding Thomas, and the boy was wriggling, pushing out at her with stiff arms, trying to get down. There was a smell in the room, a strange smell, like certain soft fungi that grow on dying branches, and on the hook above the fireplace was a small iron pot. The room was empty, the square open, and Mattie didn't know what it meant, if the woman would wrestle her down in the open square of the room to ring her neck like a pullet in a barnyard. Then she saw her cousins lined up on the far wall by the fireplace. They'd been scrubbing the floor with wood ashes—each of them wore the mark of it: four pairs of hands, four foreheads, four aprons, smudged black with ashes—though they were not then on their knees scrubbing but standing in a sooty row against the wall, staring. The girl saw then that the empty space was only created by the eating table having been pushed back for the floor scrubbing, with the cane chairs stacked on top of it, and so the cleared place did not seem to her so strange. She breathed.

The cousins stared at the two sisters, completely silent, and it was this silence that broke into the girl's shell and made her want to laugh. Jessie's daughters were never silent, under no condition but sleeping, and in this they were not like their mother but like their father, who almost never, waking, shut up. Now the four of them not only stood silent, but the four identical smudged faces were joined in unison as their eyes swept back and forth from the short, round-faced woman to the two girls standing with their arms linked in the middle of the bare floor. Back the eight eyes would sweep to the top of the Choctaw woman's head, back again to the sisters, and around again. For an instant, Mattie saw the silliness of it, the four ash-marked faces, rolling eyes. Later she would come to believe that it was just this—these four female cousins staring and sweeping their eyes in union, their mouths open, their tongues stopped—that tricked her into opening her left hand to receive the clay cup when the woman stepped forward and held it out. The cup was not Jessie's, it was not one of her mother's, but a rude hand-molded cup the same muddy color as the woman's shawl. Mattie did not protest but took it when the woman handed it to her, thinking, *My size. She is my size nearly.* The woman went quickly past her and stood by the back door. Mattie turned to look. The woman made a move with her head, twisting her mouth a little, but Mattie didn't know what she meant. She looked at her sister, but Jonaphrene was not looking at her. Her eyes were on the Indian woman.

Jessie said, "Drink it."

Mattie looked at the woman again, and the woman moved her head again.

Jessie said, "Drink it, child! Hurry up."

The girl held the smooth lip of the cup to her mouth, and it was warm, the liquid smelled of rot or musk and a little of the sharp tang of rust, and she believed surely it was poison. It was for her death, she understood that. She heard her sister's breath suck in sharply. Her aunt said, "Oh, for the love of Pete, child!" Mattie could hear the disgust, the impatience and fear in her aunt's voice, but it wasn't that. It was the titter against the back wall, like the rustle of roosting birds ready to burst forth, startled, and fly in all directions. She knew the cousins would break out laughing, she could feel it coming, and so she drank the liquid down quickly, in defiance, though she believed it would kill her; she drank it warm and fast. She couldn't close her throat on it. Bile rose, the whole of her intestines sliding, swelling into her throat, Jessie shouting, "Look out, look out now!" and her sister twisting away from her grip, crying, Thomas shrieking. The girl turned her face from the cup, the dark stink of the room spinning. She vomited loose and hot, splattering on the cold puncheon floor.

The woman came again the next morning, and yet again. Mattie did not know what hour she would come, and so when she went outside with her sister, she held her eyes west, knowing the woman would come, if not that hour then the next one, waiting each minute and watching in dread until at last she would see her walking, small, not along the road but straight across the land toward her. She didn't know the woman's name. She didn't know the woman was part Creek and part Choctaw, nor even that such mattered. Her father had told her she must drink what the woman gave her; he said it would make her well, which the girl did not believe. She thought her father was deceived by his brother, who was deceived by Jessie, who hated the children in her fearful heart, because the girl believed she had seen the truth in her aunt on the night her father carried her downstairs.

But she drank the woman's medicine anyway, allowed the woman to sing over her and smoke her, and she could not have said why, because it was not faith; it was not obedience. She believed she would die. She thought the woman would kill her, and it was not in any manner she had dreamed or heard of concerning Indians; it was not her legs hacked off, it was not being scalped or staked alive on a redant hill. The girl understood that she would never walk forward in a straight line to do what she must do and had been charged to do, and in her soul was the bleak rot of uselessness and despair, and so when the woman came, she drank what was given her to drink, did all the woman showed her to do, not because her father had told her to but because she did not care.

After the first morning, the woman did not go in the log house anymore but built a fire in a cleared place in the yard and hung the small iron pot above it; she would take peeled roots from the leather satchel she carried and put them in the kettle, and when the drink was darkly black, she would take it off the fire and kneel on the earth, facing east, and blow through a hollow reed into the bowl. After a while she would begin to sing, high and deep and complicated in her throat, and to the girl it sounded as if the woman's tongue was a foot in the back her mouth. In time, the woman would pour the dark liquid into the clay cup, one-third full, and give it to Mattie, and when the girl had vomited she would give her another cup to drink which was not rotting but bitter, but it stayed in her stomach. The girl would drink the second cup, and the woman would carry the little iron kettle to the foot-deep hole she had dug in the yard the first day and put it in the bottom of the hole; she would lay a plank and a thin blanket across it and make Mattie lie down over the kettle, her ears and throat over the kettle, and the woman would make smoke from smoldering cedar and blow the sweet smoke over the girl's face and throat four times, and then she would let her get up. She would speak to her in that unfathomable tongue, and the girl did not understand her, but the woman would nod as if she did and turn and walk off to the west over the tree-stump-ridden land.

Four times the woman came, four mornings in succession. There was no change except that in the girl the hopelessness grew worse. And then on the fifth morning, after her father had gone out the door with his cold biscuit and no gloves on, before the others came down, in the gray before first light, she awoke, and she knew there was change.

She lay motionless for a long time, trying to find it or feel it within herself, but all she could sense was a lightness, a weight gone, until at last she rolled from the pallet. She stood up slowly, as she always stood, her hand to the stones, ready for the room to reel. The others were asleep, all the household, even her sister. Mattie walked her hands up the rock face of the fireplace and stood slowly. The floor did not fall away from her. The log walls held still.

A week later the girl left the house in the early morning just after her father. She watched him as he let himself out the front door into the cold predawn darkness, and then she slid silently from the pallet, carefully, so as not to waken the others, and crept past the cold cookstove to the back door. She hoisted the oak bar from the slot quietly, the weight of the wooden bar so dense the girl hardly could lift it, and she pushed with all her force, the leather hinges creaking, and went out the split-log door. She stood a moment in the darkness beneath the porch overhang, thinking nothing, waiting, her nostrils quivering as she read the air. Abruptly she turned her face to the northeast and stepped down off the porch.

Frost crunched in the crackling grass beneath her bare feet; her breath moved before her. The sun was not yet risen, but violet light eased east over the valley smoked gray with winter—and yet turning, the girl could feel the hoop turning—as she climbed directly, in a straight line, along the rise east of the log house toward Toms Mountain. The dark hulk of the barn grew bigger, the side of it flat and black in the not-yet-light, and the girl walked directly toward it as if she'd been bidden.

This was the first barn, the one that Fayette dredged up out of roughhewn within weeks of coming to Big Waddy Crossing and had never bothered to chink. The one Mattie had watched from the porch ledge on the day she'd first emerged from the log house. It sat where the land turns to rock and jumps up toward Toms Mountain, though perhaps no one but Fayette himself would have called it a barn; it was more a shed nearly: two log walls linked by a rough shingle roof. A person could stand a hundred yards down from it and fire a shot straight through to the shaggy foot of the mountain. Already Fayette had plans to build a grand new one of native sandstone on top of the ridge beside the path where the sisters walked. He had never intended the first barn to be anything but temporary, any more than he'd intended the log house to be home to his wife and sons forever, but the girl had no thought of that, or of anything, walking toward it in the cold dawn light, barefoot in her cousin's nightgown with no bonnet on, her head sleek as a squirrel's.

She climbed on the slant, and the side of the barn angled and turned toward her so that she could see the rough wedge of paler mountain sliding into view through the open mouth. Her breath would not come right. Her leg muscles trembled. But she went on, turned the corner to the back side or, rather, the east side of the barn, away from the house, and she saw then what she had come for. The wagon was aligned perpendicularly with the barn wall, a little off north and east toward the blackjacks, and hidden. It could not be seen unless a person climbed the rise, as the girl had done, and walked around to the back side of the shed barn to see it. The wagonsheet had been stripped from the overjet so that the bows stretched like ribs from a carcass laid open against the rose winter sky. The tongue lay flat upon the ground. The wheels were stopped with big rocks. The bed was entirely empty, but for the iron cookstove square in the center, peculiar, rusting beneath the hoops in the heart of the splintered wood.

The girl stood in the cold with the sky cracking light over the valley. She looked at it only; she didn't move to touch it or smell it. She knew it was her father who had pulled out each pot and quilt and blanket. Her father who had peeled back the wagonsheet, as it was he who first laid it over the frame, as it was he who built the overjet and stretched the bows arcing. It was her father who had dragged the wagon by the tongue up the rough slope and hidden it behind his brother's shabby barn, away from the eyes of his children. She knew it was her father's hands that had stripped it, but she did not know why.

The sun slid above the world's rim then, just east, so that the land at once bronzed and turned golden, the brittle ribs turning amber; so that even the gnarled blackjacks, toed down on the mountain, began to take on color, their shriveled brown leaves and black bark glowing orange in the sun's light. The girl stood in the light a moment, expressionless, blinking a little in the brightness, and then she turned and went back to the house.

I did not comprehend that it was all gone—not just our clothes so that we had to wear the scent and feel of others, but all of it—every piece of our lives brought with us from Kentucky. I couldn't comprehend anything except that our home, which was the wagon, which had been the wagon for a year and better—a tenth of my lifetime—had been stripped bare and left out to weather while I slept powerless in the red darkness and walked crazy and bounced wall-to-wall, while I paraded back and forth on the ridge with my hand on my sister. I made up my mind, staring at the iron cookstove hunkered alone in the bed of the wagon, that I would find the secret place of our belongings, wherever it was that Papa had hid them. I imagined our blankets and boxes, Mama's featherbed, her trunk and the food bin and the black cast-iron Dutch oven, all stacked and stored in a neighbor's barn, or in one of the roughcut buildings in town. I thought even that he might have put them in a dry cave somewhere, back deep in the Sans Bois hills. I had only to find where he'd hid them, and then catch up Sarn and that ornery gray Delia, lead the mules to where the wagon was hidden behind Fayette's shed barn. I had my plan and my purpose, which was all I sought, all I looked for. I would not look at what was in front of me.

I would come upon Jonaphrene sometimes, sitting alone beside the well or along the path to the privy, with her bonnet off, touching her hand to the back of her head. She'd rub her palm down it, down it, with that terrible expression, and I would go to her and say, "Quit *that!" and slap Lottie's old bonnet back around her and tie it. I wouldn't look at that face on her, because I did not want to see it. I didn't want to know why we still wore the cousins' hats and blouses too big for us, Lottie's bonnet like an upside-down feedsack on Jonaphrene and Sarah's swallowing me, and Jim Dee chasing after Fayette's sons in one of Fowler's old slouch hats tied down over his ears. When Jessie put Thomas out on the back porch, she wrapped his head in a diaper square and pinned it and covered it with one of Fayette's old stretched-out wool socks, but I would not look at him. I wouldn't look at Jonaphrene. She'd gaze up at me while I griped at her for sitting in the sun and wind with her head bare; she'd let me tie Lottie's bonnet on her, never blinking, the look gone now—but quick as my back was turned she'd have that bonnet off again, rubbing her hand down the back of her head. So I laid it off onto grief for her hair. I thought,* She will have to get used to it, *and so I quit tying Lottie's bonnet back on her. I told myself it was like a tooth gone, how you can't keep your tongue out of the hole until the new tooth comes, and I said to myself,* When her hair comes again, it will stop. *But of course it did not.*

The first time I saw that look on my sister—I don't know the words for it: there are no words; it was not an expression, though that is the closest I can say it, but more a welling up, a rising—but when I saw it, even the first time, I turned my face away. It was at supper, in the time of the dark swirl in the beginning. Before Thula came. Before I could walk. The room was flickering. We were sitting by the hearth, as we did then, because we didn't eat standing with the girl cousins, because I could not. Nothing was unusual, nothing any different than normal except that Jessie had us eating by firelight because she said she meant to save coal oil, at least that, she said, with five more mouths to feed and it not yet the shank of winter. Fayette was still at the table, drinking coffee, and Jim Dee and his boys with him; the girl cousins were near the cookstove with their plates beneath their mouths, and Jessie by the sideboard, churning butter. Papa was gone. I turned once, not thinking anything except how to hide from Jessie the slimy bit of squirrel I could not get down my throat, and I saw it: the side of my sister's face lit in firelight, her small fine face, like Mama's, only tiny, set in china.

She gazed straight ahead, her face pale, her eyes grave in the shade of their long, straight, black lashes, her brows an even slash across her forehead, and all that dark like coal marks on her pale face because she got the best from both of them, Mama's hair and complexion and the dark gray-green color of Papa's eyes. I watched this thing, this look, lifting up on the surface, rising, as a blush does, only white, pale white, and solemn, the look on her solemn and still beneath the jumping shadows. I don't know how to describe it, even yet I cannot, because I could tell you sorrow or sadness and that is nothing like what it was, because you would just have to see her. You would have to watch how it rose up from inside her at nothing and covered her, caught and held her, and she was little then, she was just a little girl. She would gaze straight ahead, her face distant, as if she was listening, and she would be just so still and inward and full of something private and sorrowful, or lost maybe; you could not say what it was. I couldn't. Or I didn't want to. I saw it that first night, still powerless and unknowing, and I couldn't abide it. I sopped some of my gravy onto her dish and told her, "Eat!" I wouldn't look at her after that.

I shut it out of my mind. Not once did I consider it. I went every day with my hand on her shoulder like a blind girl—and yet I could see the town raw with lumber chunked on one side of the muddy road. I could see Bull Creek twisting away south and east in front of the log house, and the ragged ridge of Toms Mountain scrabbling away north against the washed sky. I could see the world, but I could not of my own will move forward in it. I could see this mark on my sister, but of my own will I turned away. When I could walk again, I kept her with me, for a little time I kept her, but I would not look at her. And then when I did not need her, I quit her. I set my face against her, and not only her but against Thomas and Jim Dee. Against the other whose name I would not speak.

Lafayette Lodi stood upon the crest of the ridge watching a pair of mules struggle up the slope against the weight of a flatbed wagon piled deep with slabs of sandstone. "You fellas yonder shove up from back!" he hollered at the two Negro men climbing slowly beside the wagon. The men stopped, each on either side, and waited for the mules to slog the wagon past, and then the two turned silently, simultaneously, and laid their palms to the tailgate. Fayette cupped his hands around his mouth. "For God's sake, Moss, lay the stick to 'em!" he yelled. "They're 'bout to set down and have a picnic!"

The driver, a big khaki-colored man in overalls and a felt hat, snapped the tip of the whip at the larger mule's withers, and the wagon lurched precariously. The animals were not matched, one several hundred pounds heavier and a dozen years younger than the other, and the unevenness of weight and pull made a hard climb harder, and dangerous. They mounted nearly straight up the hillside, for Fayette, in his impatience, had not taken the time to cut a switchback but had only had his sons widen the worn footpath with a scythe, and the steepness of slope, the clots of winter-bare scrub, the loose rock and thick mud and rough ledges jutting here and there from the side of the ridge, all added to the troubled ascent.

Fayette paced back and forth on the ridge, watching the mules' plodding progress, and now and again glancing below at the boggy road curving south around Waddy Mountain. His bright blue eyes were narrowed, squinting beneath his hat brim, and when he paused to stare in the distance at the nearly impassable road, he seemed to be smiling—an illusion created by the tic that tugged habitually at his jaw muscles, thinning his lips and nipping them in at the corners to reveal the startling white of his teeth through the mat of his beard.

Those who did not know him well—that is, those who did not happen to work for him or be related to him in the tight circle of family—thought Lafayette Lodi an agreeable fellow. His voice was warm, his broad, sunburned face open and lively. He shook hands easily and often, and the restless urgency that was the wellspring of his being seemed, to a stranger, no more than a lusty, unharnessed energy, so that Fayette—or Fate, as the local tongue spoke it—appeared to have a terrific passion for life, unmarred by fatigue or tranquillity. White women considered him handsome. His features were a trifle blunt maybe—the nose more rounded than would ordinarily be admired in profile, his complexion a bit ruddy—but that was offset by the striking animation that livened his burnt face, by the nearly sapphire color of his eyes and the rich walnut color of his hair, which curled to his shoulders, sparking the red highlights in his beard. Men found him a good drinking partner and jokester, and Fayette had the habit of asking them about themselves in a manner that seemed not intrusive or prying but as if he understood that the men, their former lives and present opinions, had undoubted significance in the affairs of the world.

In fact, Fayette Lodi had never been calculating or scheming in the manner of some white men who would seduce a man into telling his business and then find means to use that information against him. In fact, he didn't attend to the answers men gave once he'd elicited them, so absorbed in self was he that he could not, had he cared to, hear. He was driven on to the next thought, the next question, consumed by a ruthless urgency that precluded his ability to witness any other human in the world—but one. And in his haste he pushed and cajoled and hollered at those around him as a man herds dawdling cattle before a storm. There were those who grew to hate this drive in him, but Fayette's wife, at least, understood that it was not a will to power that made her husband dominate others, but the sense of being himself lashed by the unmerciful whip of time and competition and profound necessity. Fayette drove others—his wife and sons, the men who had the misfortune to hire on to him—only as he himself was driven: relentlessly, without focus or respite, and it was solely in the dregs of sleep, where he sank at night, undreaming, as a bullfrog in pond mud in winter, that he found peace.

He paused now on the bald sweep of ridge. Glancing at the road again and not seeing what he looked for, he turned his eyes down the widened footpath, cupped his hands to his beard once more. "Hell, man," he hollered, seeming to grin, his voice light, teeth showing. "I seen quicker slugs crawling! Whup up on that off mule, fella, she's near about walking backwards!"

Moss flicked at the smaller gray and checked the nigh dark one, and the wagon swayed and rolled like a drunkard, and Fayette hollered, "Reckon y'all think I oughta build her where she sets?" The snort that came from between his white teeth then sounded much like a laugh. He went back to pacing, his hand soothing the holster of the Colt he wore tucked at his belly. In his mind he could see the great rectangle of the barn outlined on the hilltop, solid, immutable, rising above the town for the world below to see. Never mind the impracticality of the steep rise, the great distance from the log house in winter. He meant to build a new house there as well, one day, not long, on the crest of the bald ridge, and the house, too, raised from native orange sandstone laid out in puzzled complexity, and permanent. His eyes darted sideways and southward, where the road curved a tan muddy ribbon toward Cedar, and on he went, continuing his restless, purposeless walk.

There was one among the three hired men slogging up the hill with the overloaded wagon who understood Fate Lodi, or understood anyway the profound nature of his hurry. It wasn't the thick-chested mixed-blood driver, who accepted Lodi's perpetual harangue as he accepted the unreasonable behavior of other white men, without opinion or rancor, because to William Moss (although he was three-eighths white himself), all white people were crazy. Certainly it wasn't the jaundiced, wiry fellow pushing lightly at the right rear of the wagon, who received Fayette's urgings with bitterness in his heart and the small, hard swellings of hatred; but it was rather the taller and browner-skinned of the two Negroes, who, under the rain of Fayette's cajoling curses, now shoved at the tailgate with the full strength of his shoulders. He never looked up but held his shoulder to the wood and his eyes to the muddy rock-clotted slope of earth, his lips pressed tight around clamped teeth.

Even hunched as he was at the rear of the wagon, he was clearly a big man—over six feet tall standing straight up hatless and bootless—and heavy through the shoulders, broad across the chest. He was hatless now, having tossed his broad-brimmed Stetson on top of the load when he first bent his shoulder to the wagon, revealing to the watery, early-spring light the high dome of his forehead, the kinked hair shaved tight to the skull. His skin was a deep berry brown that seemed to hold within its integument a burnished light, separate from external source, so that even in thin overcast, as on this day, his face appeared to be lit from within by a luminous sheen. His face now was turned sideways as he strained at the rear of the wagon, the tip of an ear skyward, the clenched plane of his cheekbone raised to the sun. His mustache—coke black and bristling, the hair of it straighter than the hair on his head—twitched like a squirrel's tail as he gritted, un-gritted his teeth. The expression, but for that grim clamping, was one of irony as he listened to Fayette's rant: he knew the man, or he knew white men like him, and it made him want to laugh. He could hear, in the back-and-forth roving, the reckless spouting, that Fayette already had the barn built and the hay in it, the cows bought, the pigs slaughtered come first frost next autumn, before he'd got the stones he must have to build it up the hill. Beneath his breath, softly, so that even the fellow beside him did not hear, the big man said, "Better get your stones set first, white man."

Fayette hollered down the hillside, "I'll have to put on a little banquet for you folks up here next Tuesday! Aim to welcome you real good when you get here next week! Mitchelltree, put some damn backbone in it, my God."

The big man grunted softly, the weight of his shoulder against the wagon. Still he did not look up, only listened to Fayette's voice rising above the dry creak of the burdened wheels. "I seen you before, mister," he said, his voice low, coming from his throat, through his teeth. "You'll not be in no hurry one a these days."

Fayette called, "Somebody's going to be shouting Glory Hallelujah time y'all get here! Somebody bound to be praising the Lord! Suggs, you better lay down and take a rest now—I hate to see you break a sweat!" In a little while he hollered, "I seen a old terr'pin get to Texas and back quicker'n y'all are climbing this little old bitty ridge!"

The brown man, shoving, his head down, huffed to the hillside, "I been to Texas, mister. Them terrapins can have it." He spat once off to the side through his gritted teeth. His voice was low still, beneath his breath, but even so, it rolled as he cursed Texas. "Damn rattlesnakes can have Texas. Let the Comanches have her," he said. "They'd know what to do." And then *hunh*, he let go a deep grunt

as he heaved the wagon harder. The yellow-complected man beside
him glanced over, but the brown man, his eyes on the brown earth,
didn't see.

As the afternoon wore, Fayette paced faster and faster, his eyes
darting down the ridge to the wagon, closer now but still well below
the rim's edge; now out along the boggy ribbon of road, which stub-
bornly would not yield what he looked for; now up to the heavens,
where the weak sun slid westerly far too quickly in the southern sky.
He shouted, "Got you fellas a little liquid freshment waiting! Looks
like y'all can't get a better move on, I'm liable to have to drink it up
myself!" And he pulled a whiskey flask from his coat pocket, uncapped
it, and took a long pull. The cajoling was entirely gone from his voice
now; the words sounded just as he intended them: a threat. He paced,
nipping from the tin flask, his eyes more and more to the empty roadway, less upon the struggling wagon, and so he was not looking when
the wagon creaked to a complete halt with the front wheels wedged
against a rough stone outcropping a hundred yards from the top of
the ridge. When he did look, drawn by the silence, it seemed to his
incensed mind they'd been sitting there an hour, the smaller mule
nodding half asleep in the traces and the big one standing hipshod on
the ledge above. Fayette began to shout. "Don't make me hafta come
down there, Moss! What the hell's the matter with you? Lay the stick
on 'em! Mitchelltree, put some gumption in it! Suggs! You two shove
up there! I can't wait till next Christmas—you lazy so-and-sos mean to
get paid, you better get them damn animals moving!"

Moss flicked the whip, slapped the reins, said, "Giddap, now, hyah,
mule!" and the high-yellow man cursed beneath his breath and pushed
a little harder, and the brown man breathed deep, the old irony twisting, turning sour, rising, without humor, to a dull, familiar rancor. He
shoved harder on the wagon's gate, turned his face to the side, and
put the full strength of his anger in it.

"Y'all swing her around left yonder!" Fayette called. "She won't
make it over that jut there, take her around!"

Moss flicked the whip hard at the rump of the dark mule, sawed
left, and the big charcoal jerked his head and released his locked legs,
turned hard, forcing the little gray, and the gray stumbled as, with a
groan and an aching creak like the cranking of a colossal windlass, the
right front wheel began to rise over the rock ledge, and the front of
the wagon began to swing left. The two men at the rear, surprised,
feeling the shift and splinter of wood vibrate clear through their jaws,

leapt backwards, the brown man, slick as a snake strike, whisking his white Stetson off the top of the load as he jumped.

"Whoa! Jeeminy, Jeeminy, look out now," Fayette bellowed. "You're gonna tip her!"

"Gee, mule! Gee! Gee! Gee!" Moss yanked the reins right, trying to compensate for the hard left and sudden lift, and then he tried to pull up altogether. "Whoa, mule, whoa, mule, whoa!"

But it was entirely too late. The weight of stone shifting in infinitesimal increments, hardly a fraction in time or distance but multiplied by gravity, magnified by the weight of itself measured in tons of earth-core, could not be held back. The rear axle snapped near where it speared the left wheel, and the wagonwheel collapsed sideways; the right forward wheel raised up, hung spinning. The tailgate split wide at the seam. The tongue splintered and turned loose from its bonding, broke free of the hounds, and the shattered wagon began to collapse downward. Moss threw the reins at the scrambling mulerumps and jumped off the seat above the wagon, as, with a quaking, locomotive rumble like that of an earthquake and a shriek of tortured wood and the hysterical, bawling bray of terrified muleflesh, two tons of orange-colored sandstone avalanched in a cloud of sanddust to the muddy flank of the mountain.

When the last of the slabs had groaned to a halt and settled, it was quiet along the ridge but for the scrabbling of the little gray mule trying to rise. Her front legs were broken. She struggled in silence, and there was no sound for a long while but the scuttering of pebbles, the hard rustling of the tall, dry yellow weeds. Stone slabs, some nearly as large as the face of a coffin, spilled from the broken bed, scattered like a great child's tumbled blocks along the slope.

Then Fayette began to shout. "Jesus God!" He danced along the hilltop jerkily, his arms loose and floundering, his head bobbing, a half-strung marionette. "You fools, you damned dunces, Jesus holy Christ!" He saw the yellow-complected man in the distance, walking fast at a steep angle down the side of the ridge eastward. "Suggs!" Fayette screamed. "Get back here! You damn Suggs! Su-u-uggs!" But the yellow man was disappearing already around the far side of Fayette's log house. "Damn you, Suggs!" Fayette shouted.

The leg-broke little gray mule had ceased to struggle. She lay on her side, heaving, still caught in the traces, the broken oak tongue jammed beneath her broken legs. The big charcoal stood beside her, head down, in silence, and the little gray made a sound now, seeming to call to the other, her little bleats alternating with, sometimes punctuating, Fayette's curses. It was as if the mare portion of the mule's nature claimed her in dying, because the sound, coming contrapuntal with the man's, was not a jack's bray nor a mule's bawl but something stranger, breathed into the cold air on heaving shudders: a high, breathy whinny, begging. Fayette's voice was hoarse now, stripped with yelling, but in his rant he could not stop. "Moss! Damn you, Moss, you damn stupid Indi'n, never get a damn Indi'n to handle a damn mule! Mitchelltree, shoot that damn mule for God's sake!" And he went on, pacing, jerking, cursing.

The big brown man, hatted now, standing erect, enormous beside the hunched and miserable Moss, climbed the rise to a level spot above the broken wagon, spread the front of his coat, and, wordless, took a large, flat-sided, thick-barreled pistol from a left-handed holster beneath the denim. Immediately Fayette stopped his cursing rant. He froze, staring, as if at a ghost or a living memory. Mitchelltree raised the great slope-gripped gun so that Fayette could see clearly the four barrels stacked two and two, distinct and yet inseparable, joined together as one. Mitchelltree sighted briefly and pulled the trigger. The big charcoal mule jumped and brayed once, stood trembling, as the echo of a single powerful shot ricocheted across the valley. The ridge then was completely silent. Mitchelltree took a step down the slope, looked at the dead little gray. The union of barrels was pointed at the large hole oozing red above the open yellow eye, but another shot was not necessary. In a deep, resonant voice, he said, "Moss, help me get that big'n loose—he going to break a leg too 'fore it's all over."

The driver, moving slow, came the long way around above the spilled wagon. Fayette called from the hilltop, "You! Mitchelltree!" but the big man did not answer. He stood at the big mule's head, stroking the long, elegant muzzle, talking softly, looking calmly into the epicanthic eye, while Moss began to untangle the twisted traces.

"Mitchelltree!" Fayette called, the rage gone from his voice now, a sound in it uncannily close to the pleading in the little mule's final whimper. "Hey, Mitch!"

Mitchelltree did not look up but went on talking softly, speaking secret words, low and deep and mournful, in the long silken charcoal ear.

His name was Burd Mitchelltree. The few white men who knew his Christian name thought and heard "Bird" when he told it, and figured him for part Indian because of that name and the sharpness of his features, because of the hint of terra rosa in the brown of his skin. A willing eye could've told them those planed features were not Choctaw or Cherokee but Anglo; that high, sleek forehead, rarely revealed, hinting already at future baldness, had not come down to him through any Indian blood. He was, notwithstanding white men's poor vision or hearing, within himself and to himself *Burd* Mitchelltree, short for Burden, as his mama, without irony, had named him, and by so doing naming not what he was to her but what others would demand him to carry, when he was born slave to her as slave in Texas twenty-nine years before. He'd been four years old when Lincoln proclaimed emancipation; five by the time Texas got around to letting her own slaves hear such news the following June; six when his mother died in her slave cabin, ignorant of the war's end or outcome, ignorant of the fact that her son's Christian name was a sly parody of white man's ideas. The name could as well have stood (though his mama was never to know this either) for the sonorous sound of Burden's voice as it would become in his young manhood: mellifluous, minor-keyed, like the sorrowing lower tones of a bagpipe or the deep dulcet moan of a bass organ. It was this resonating drone he used now to calm the big, dark male mule.

William Moss moved slowly, meticulously, trying to untangle the snarled reins entangled in the traces, until at last, glancing up the hill once quickly, he slipped his buck knife from beneath his pantsleg and used it to cut the leather in two places. When the animal was nearly freed, Mitchelltree put a twistlock on the mule's muzzle to keep him from running mad and wild the instant the collar eased off, never ceasing to croon the dirgelike chant in the mule's ear all the while, and within a few minutes the mule was calm enough that he could release the twistlock and walk him on up the slope to where Fayette stood, still staring, not at the brown man himself, not at the lone living mule or the worthless dead one, nor at the jumble of orange rock slabs spilling crookedly from the broken wagon, but intently and longingly at the gracefully curved stock of the pistol, returned to its holster now, made visible to the thinning afternoon light from beneath the denim coattail by the lift and roll of Burd Mitchelltree's massive shoulders.

If there was but one person on earth whose actions and intentions drew Fayette's full concentration, there was, as well, one object only that could snap his head around like an iron filing whisked to a magnet, pause him in his relentless pursuit of whatever notion or item he currently raced after—and that was a firing weapon of any kind. Just now, as he stood on the ridge watching Mitchelltree climb the remaining yards with a soothing hand to the mule's quivering neck, there was a miraculous confluence of the two driving forces in Fayette Lodi's existence, as two underground rivers might converge in the hidden depths of a cavern to rage and rise to the earth's crust. A great stillness settled upon him—or rather an eerie calm appeared to descend on the surface: his cerulean eyes hardly blinked; the restless pacing and hand-flinging, the cursing, were now completely stopped—but beneath the sanguine surface, Fayette's pulse thudded in his owns ears, his chest cinched tight as a tourniquet, his nerves were honed and focused, keen as a cat's. The whole of his being was riveted to the curve of the gunhandle—for he was certain, or very nearly certain, that the thick-barreled pistol the man carried was one of three or four dozen powerful weapons called howdahs that had been skillfully, cunningly, illegally wrought by the hand of his brother. Guns, their power and mystery, affect different men differently; for some, a gun is but a tool, as necessary as the plow, for the gathering of food; others are drawn to a weapon's mechanical nature, its cleverness and precision; and still others cherish a firearm's ability to enhance not only a man's actual power but his appearance of strength as well, so that men will fear him. Though Fayette Lodi's fascination—one may say obsession—with firearms held a bit of all these, it was more singularly derived from the history he shared with his brother: it had been guns that unbalanced their bonded relationship; guns that had, as he thought, given his brother dominance over him in the eyes of the world. But it had been specifically the making of the big four-barreled howdahs, copied from a model filched by Tanner and carried into John Lodi's barn by Fayette himself, with a promise of fame and mutual profit if John would but turn his skilled hands to their making, that had caused the Lodis to flee Kentucky. It was the weapon the big man carried—if indeed it was one of John's—that had wrenched away the remnants of Fayette's control over his brother, and that same weapon, he suddenly thought, watching the crosshatched grip rise and fall with the man's movement, that could return him his power.

"Good job! Fine job! Get on up here, fella, my Lord," he shouted heartily at Mitchelltree as the man and the mule crested the rim. The threat in Fayette's voice was completely gone now; he might have been welcoming a beloved, long-absent friend. "That goddamn Indi'n—" he said, and moved quickly toward Mitchelltree and the still-skittery mule, with his right hand thrust forward as if to shake the man's hand.

Not for a moment did his eyes sway from their hungry watch on the leather holster, and in the thoroughness of his self-absorption, in his complete lack of self-consciousness and the prodigious paucity of any ability within him to witness another human, he was ignorant of the directness of his gaze. Mitchelltree, on the other hand, had been alert to Fayette's lean-eyed scrutiny almost from the instant he himself had pulled the pistol, though he had no notion of its source or meaning. What he did know, from long, violent experience, was the fact that a white man's hungry eye on a black man's weapon was nothing but a killing of some sort getting ready to unfold. He ignored Fayette's out-thrust hand and eased the mule warily, quickly past him, keeping the dark flank between himself and the white man, making the move seem necessary, unintentional, until at last he stood a little above Fayette on the slant, his weight balanced, his hands free, the mule off to the side now and easy. Below the rim, a thick scuttling sound rustled in the winter weeds.

"Done good," Fayette continued good-naturedly, as if the slick side-step hadn't been executed or, at least, as if he himself hadn't noticed. "I thank you for putting the poor critter out of her misery. Don't believe I coulda got any kind of purchase from here." His tone was intimate, jovial, seeming to say that, truth was, just between friends, truth was, the loss of a forty-dollar mule was really no more woesome than the inconvenience of having to shoot the pitiful thing. "Say, that's some pistol you got there, ain't it, let me have a look at her," and he took a step toward Mitchelltree, who, already balanced, instantly spread his coattail and put his hand to the butt of the gun.

"Whoa, fella, hey, hey," Fayette chanted softly, backing slowly, hands raised, palms out, the expression on his face flickering between fear and genuine bafflement. "*Whew,* man, I don't mean nothing!"

The scrambling sound below, which was only the heavy-footed Moss climbing toward them, stopped abruptly. The land was as silent as it had been in the seconds after the gunshot, and in the silence there grew an awareness within the men along the ridge that others were standing present. The sun was nearly down behind Bull Mountain, the shadows slanting long across the silent sawmill on the creek-bank below; topaz light spread east over the orange and brown grasses twigged here and there with coming green. Nowhere in the whole of the valley was there the lonesome call of a meadowlark; nowhere the jangle of harness or the scolding of crows. The three men felt others' eyes standing ready as witness, watching, unseen.

William Moss hulked spraddlelegged on the hillside, one leg braced higher than the other on the steep part of the slope below the rim. In the amber light, his eyes, hair, skin, coat, overalls, felt hat, all seemed to melt into the side of the mountain, blending each, dust-colored, with the colors of the winter-dulled earth. He looked along the ridge west. A small round figure stood outlined in the afternoon sunslant. The figure, draped in a clay-colored blanket, might have been a stone statue, so still was it. Unmoving. Watchful. Moss himself did not move in any direction. He dropped his gaze to the slaughtered mule and the great square sandstone bones, hacked free and dragged from where the Creator had placed them in the earth, to be clustered and spilled wrongly by these men down the side of the ridge. Moss couldn't see above the rim, but he didn't raise his eyes anyhow. The tension between the white man and black man above him receded from his mind, unimportant. His shame was complete, and there being nothing he could do to hide it from the gaze of the woman on the horizon, he sat down at last in the crackling weeds and pulled his hat over his eyes, mourning, despising the too-big portion of white blood in himself that made him so crazy. Never, he thought, had it been strong enough in his heart to allow him to grow fat with cattle and dollars like Peter Conser or Robert Jones or Green McCurtain, other mixed-bloods whose white inheritance permitted them to gather the earth under their dominion. Moss's portion seemed only thick enough to make him wrongheaded and crazy, too easily influenced, a grief to himself and his grandmother. Under Thula's eyes, William Moss understood the waste of the killed mule driven dead by a white man's relentless impatience. He knew it was desecration to dig up and scatter from their rightful place the bones of the earth. The shame burned him. Tonight he would find a bottle and burn the shame deep into his gut.

The two men squared off with one another on the crest of the ridge did not feel the watching eyes of Thula Henry. She was female, an Indian, her presence on the western rim no more relevant than the warm breath of the charcoal-colored mule. They perceived, rather, a presence suited each to his separate story. Burd Mitchelltree knew suddenly in the stillness that the white townsmen of Big Waddy Crossing were gathered at the back of the roughcut building which housed the post office and stage stop. He didn't turn his eyes, but he felt them, lined up as they were in their broad-brimmed hats in the store's crooked shadow. He knew they'd been there for some time, that they'd begun to gather even before the gunshot, had drawn together behind the storeback with the first rumble of rocks from the wagon. Without looking, without the need to look from this distance, Mitchelltree felt their white skins, their light eyes watching in anticipation and judgment, and in that awareness he perceived the surface of his own skin, acute and tender, like a smoldering surcoat laid over bone and muscle, a warm membrane stretched taut across cheekbones, sheathing ears and neck and lips, encasing the brown hand holding the grip of the gun. Although his own broad-brimmed hat covered him, and his high-heeled, arched boots braced him, and his heavyweight denim jacket cloaked him, Burd Mitchelltree felt himself naked on the bare ridge.

Fayette, for his part, locked as he was in his word-rant, his obsessed focus on the howdah, might not have been aware of the townsmen for some time, if not for the one who had walked up at the last and joined the mute, watching line. As the silence seeped past Fayette's rattling voice in his own mind, he sensed the one who stood off to the side a little at the end of the row of men, with his hobnail boots planted wide in the tan mud and his slouch hat pushed to the back of his head, looking up. Fayette turned his eyes from the armed man facing him and looked below at the town. All he could think of was to wonder how his brother had managed to come along the road from Cedar without Fayette himself seeing, for he believed he had watched with a hawk's eye the whole afternoon. Mystified, pondering, he slowly dropped his upheld palms and reached to his back pocket for his flask.

Immediately Burd Mitchelltree's hand tightened on the gunhandle, the smooth plate of the trigger, but he could see the flared grip of the Colt tucked unmolested in Fayette's waistband, and for an instant he waited. He was a black man naked on the ridge. To draw the gun was to fire it, to fire it was to kill the man and be instantly picked off by a Winchester from below, or chased and lynched if they could catch him, and for the minutest flickering instant, Mitchelltree calculated the distance to the mule, thinking to draw, shoot, and roll under the mule simultaneously, cursing the terrible weight of the gun even as he determined the density of briar thicket and scrub oak down the back side of the ridge and the likelihood of escape through it; he prepared completely for death or a killing in the seconds it took for Fayette to reach behind himself and pull the flask from beneath the back of his coat. Mitchelltree had no more than a heartbeat to halt the half-drawn gun when he saw it was whiskey and not a weapon that Fayette reached for; he froze then, his skin burning beneath the white eyes lined up below, his hand spasmed on the gunhandle, rage and contempt mingling, a muscle twitching along his jawline. He felt a change below, a flicker of movement. Caught by the jagged motion at the edge of his vision, Mitchelltree turned his watch from the Lodi before him to the one who had broken off from the line of men, torn free like a piece of riverdrift, and now made his way alone to the foot of the rise, where he began slowly, methodically, to climb the ridge.

The earth, which had paused for a moment on its axis, now rolled heavily forward. A chorus of crows could be heard cutting the air above Faulk's not-yet-plowed cornfield, mocking one another, languorously laughing. A low murmur arose from the line of men behind the post office. Girlish voices grated high and harsh in the dirt yard behind Fayette's log house, for the Lodi females, too, having heard the rumble and muleshriek and gunshot, having crowded one another in a phalanx of sack aprons and crossed elbows from slit of window to open doorway to back porch, now emerged fully from the log depths to witness the unfolding of events on the ridge. William Moss stood up on the hillside, slowly, never raising his hat brim or looking at his grandmother, and walked off away from her watching eyes, east, in the same direction and at the same steep angle taken by the yellow man. He skirted deeply the four chattering, bonneted faces, the silent, gaunt woman, the two short-haired little girls standing off to the side with their arms around each other in the yard; he stumped across the muddy road and disappeared on the far side into the creek bottom.

The man in the slouch hat continued to climb the rise, seeming in no hurry, and yet he covered the ground swiftly, his head bowed in the honeyed light. He paused at the spilled wagon, stood awhile looking down at the dead mule, disappeared briefly from Mitchelltree's sight as he negotiated the steepest part of the slope just below the rim, and then his tan slouch hat and suspendered shoulders appeared again, and he came on, mounting slowly, his eyes never leaving his brother's bloodshot blue ones. Without shifting his gaze, Fayette slipped the tin flask back beneath his jacket, wiped his thumb and forefinger down either side of his mustache, seeming to grin tightly at the man cresting the rim. It was then that Mitchelltree understood that he himself was no longer in it. From the instant the slouch-hatted man had broken from the line of watchers, he—Mitchelltree—had ceased to exist for them. He knew that whatever intention Fayette Lodi may have had when he came at him, it was gone now, disappeared in the blazing focus on the one who stood now, unblinking, shoulders heaving slowly, on the bald ridge between them.

The man was not especially tall, though he gave that impression because of the way his shoulders curled in on themselves, hulked from the weight of their own mass and the unconscious effort to conceal it. He was unbearded, his olive skin sallow with lack of sun. Beneath the soft brim of tan hat his eyes were dark, nearly slate-colored, sober. Mitchelltree could see the resemblance now: the same brushy brows above long-lashed eyes the same ovoid shape; the same bluntness of feature shared from the same mold—tinted sapphire and copper and rouge on the lively one, dull with the colors of the earth on the stubbled plane of the other—and yet the two were clearly brothers, as nearly alike as two sides of a dollar. Mitchelltree released his grip on the gunhandle infinitesimally, sucked in a slow, steadying inhalation. If he did not relax exactly, at least he uncoiled the invisibly coiled springs in his hamstrings. This was theirs, then, something between these two white men, brothers. He took an easing step back.

"Mitch!" Fayette said, the cajoling false heartiness returned to his voice now, though he never moved his eyes from the stern eyes of the newcomer. "This here's my brother John. John, this is—fella's name's Mitchelltree, he's a good hand, he—" and Fayette's voice rose in volume and pitch as the other suddenly turned his back and walked over to where the big coal-colored mule stood. "Got him a peculiar-looking pistol you might— Hey. I meant to mention to you about that mule, Son, I sure did. Didn't have time yesterday, you run off so everloving early. That stupid Indi'n— Listen here, listen, next drove comes through I'll get you a fine big new one. She wasn't worth a plug anyhow, too blame little. Too old. Say, what I wanted to tell you, this fella here, he's got himself a powerful big-barrel weapon you might want to take a look at. Find it a little interesting, I'll bet. John, listen, that mule . . ." And his voice trailed off. While his brother's back was turned, Fayette slipped the flask out, took a long swig, capped it, returned it to his front coat pocket this time, wiped his mustache with thumb and forefinger again.

"I'll swun to my time," he went on, fortified, his eyes bright, "that blame fool Indi'n, I'd like to take a piece out of his hide. You seen him run off. Listen. I didn't have no choice, John. I had to send them boys on to Fort Smith yesterday morning, wasn't nothing else to ride to the depot but that old yella mule of mine. I can't trust them fool boys with my good saddlehorse, you know that, not to tie up at Wister for four days." He paused a minute, waiting for some sign from the other, but John continued silent, back turned, examining the big mule. "I hate how it turned out, Son!" Fayette called out. "I really hate it!" His eyes followed the movement of his brother as he ran his hand down the big mule's neck, along his coal back, touched the raw places where the harness had galled. "Listen." Fayette kept on, talking loud and fast at his brother's back, and John never saying a word or looking at him. "Listen. How'm I going to get them rocks hauled without I had to borry your mule? Tell you what, Son, you can just have that yella mule when them boys get back with her. She's a hunnerd-dollar mule, she is, I don't care if I did give but thirty. I could get a hundred for her from Clyde Coffy next Tuesday. You can have her, minute them boys get back from the train station! Worth ten of that little gray piece of dogmeat!"

Still John did not look at him or speak, and Fayette kept on, unwilling in his soul, but unable to stop the words flinging themselves from his erupting mouth.

"Tell you what, Son, what I mean, you can have that black'un right yonder! Now, that is some mule, he'll go good with that old Sarn of yours, he might learn him how to act!" He pulled the flask out, no longer attempting to hide it from his brother, who, in any case, kept his back to him, checking the mule's teeth, his ears, lifting each leg singly to examine the small neat hooves, as a man looks over horseflesh, preparing to buy. "I give Frank Slaughter fifty dollars for that mule yonder," Fayette sang out, "and skinned him alive on the deal! The very damn day we come into the Territory! The very damn day, me and Jess and my boys. Plus I threw in that old sorrel we drove in here to boot!" He paused for a breath. "He's worth a hundred if he's worth a dime, Son! I'll just give him to you, call it even! You can't ask for no fairer deal than that! Tell you what, you put yourself to plowing some around here instead of calleywomping off to Cedar every damn morning, I'll throw in that new harness, so help me I will! Set down to a little plowing maybe, help feed some folks around here 'stead of traipsing off to Dayberry's, who ain't kin nor friend, he don't mean a thing in the world to me—" Fayette took another deep slug, the flask tilted way up, nearly empty. "You've got some mighty twisted notions, Brother, that's all I can say—some pretty strange ideas our old daddy would not be too happy to see." His voice turned mincing, mocking. "Got to go off to *Ce-e-edar* before daylight every morning. Got to work for *Da-a-ayberry . . .*"

And on Fayette went, his voice sliding with the quick changes inside him as the warmth spread in his veins, not showing in expression or gesture but evident only in the tone of voice that slid from cajoling to ingratiating to a timbre harsh with contempt. His voice drummed down finally, turning threatful.

"What the hell you need a mule for anyhow?" he growled. He drained the last drops from the flask and tossed it off toward the north side of the ridge—though later he would retrieve it, scrambling in the winter weeds upon his hands and knees, craving what burning drops might have been neglectfully left. "You need a mule like you need a damn hole in the head. If you don't take the cake! Moping around about a damn dead worthless mule when you hain't had a bridle on her in six months!" This accusation despite the fact that the other had come driving into the Territory behind that very gray hardly four months before. "You ain't aiming to plow, don't tell me you aiming to plow, I haven't seen you step foot one in a field since you got here." Never mind it was not the second week of March yet, the broken fields around Waddy an unplowable bog. "Got to run all off to *Cee-dar* and work for the other fella when you and me could be making money aplenty, and I don't mean setting on a little puly cottoncrop!" Here, Fayette's hands patted his front and back pockets without his brain even knowing they did so, searching for what was not there. "You don't do a thing with them mules anyhow but set 'em in the lot and feed 'em! A animal's got to earn its keep! All I'm doing, I'm letting that Delia mule earn her keep instead of setting in my feedlot eating my blame feed. I can't help how it turned out, that's no fault of mine, that damn Indi'n, I'm going to have it out of his hide before it's all over. Listen here! Ain't no law in this country says you can't make them same exact weapons and get a better dollar, get ten times the dollar we did in Kentuck! Ain't no law in this country period, so far as I can tell, but you don't somehow seem to want to hear it! You and me could make a fortune, but no, you got to run off to Cedar and work for pittance, leave my poor wife to take care of your pitiful young'uns, ain't a sickly one of them that's right in the head." Now his voice softened, turned almost gentle. "Whyn't you put your very God-given talents to work for your family, Son? What the hell you think He give 'em to you for?"

John, throughout the course of this final rant, had made a slow turn toward his brother. He still bore no particular expression on his features, the smooth, bland aspect unchanged on the sallow plane of his face—but Mitchelltree saw at once the cold black smolder that burned at the back of his slate eyes. Fayette must have seen it too, for his voice transformed again, thinning, curling into a fine wheedle, but with the same relentless, out-of-control urgency. He held his hands up, palms out, bouncing them in unison in the air at his brother.

"Naw, Son, now listen. Listen. I don't mean nothing. I've talked till I'm blue in the face, you won't hear a word from me. But listen here, folks'll buy that blamed howdah in this country. I keep trying to tell you. This nigger here"—and now he gestured at Mitchelltree—"he's got aholt of one somehow or another. I'd swear to it. If it ain't one of yours I'll eat my Colt. Ask him. Fella, what I want to know"—Fayette turned to Mitchelltree, his voice and attention sliding as if one thought and word melted naturally to the next—"where'd you get aholt of the likes of that gun?"

It was the first time his eyes had left his brother. John Lodi, as well—as if the words about the weapon had at last registered—withdrew his dark smolder from Fayette's face, and the two of them turned as one to the brown man who stood nearly a head taller than each of them in his high-heeled boots and big Stetson, his powerful legs set, coat front spread open, hand clenched on the grip of the gun. Both pairs of Lodi eyes studied him, not battling each other now, but united, and Mitchelltree grasped that, if he'd been out of it for a little while, now he was back in it, grandly, the suspicion of the two white men turned on him at once in tense scrutiny, the suspicion of the row of white men down in town honed on him the same, all of it old and familiar. A peculiar glowing sensation descended on Mitchelltree, a dread recognition like the aura an epileptic receives in the moments before a seizure; he felt that what was to unfold in the next moments was something old, inevitable, and wearisomely familiar.

"How'd you come to own it?" Fayette asked, casually, as if he might be asking about the weather down at Hartshorne last week.

Mitchelltree was silent. He knew the prudent thing, the smart thing to do was to tell the simple truth: He'd bought it off a horsetrader in Texas a year ago, had given twelve silver dollars and a Spanish saddle for it the day before he hit a white man in the head with a shovel and lit out for the Indian Territory—but that killing had nothing to do with ownership of the pistol, which he'd acquired in a legitimate cash trans-action. Nothing more.

"Say?" Fayette asked.

"I believe that'd be my own business," Mitchelltree said slowly.

"Well," Fayette said, "my brother and me was just wondering. Won-der if we couldn't take a look at her."

"No, sir." Mitchelltree's voice rolled in his minor key. "Don't be-lieve I'd care much for that."

"What I mean," Fayette said, seeming to grow flustered, "I ain't asking you to hand her over. Me and John just kinda want to take a look-see. He'll know if it's his. Just pull her up easy where we can take a little look at her." The cajoling tone had never been friendlier, more charming. His teeth flashed white in his beard.

Mitchelltree's mind raced; his eyes flicked back and forth between the two men. He had little doubt he could outdraw the half-drunk Fayette, but the brother was a less certain entity, the dark look un-decipherable but, Mitchelltree thought, dangerous—and the two were separated by twenty yards. Still, with a pull of the trigger, the gun's movable striker would fire the remaining three powerful barrels in rapid succession, without need even for the slight betraying flinch of a cocked hammer. All that was required was to clear the holster, aim broadly, and fire hard and fast, as a British dragoon might fire on a pair of close-charging lions in the Sudan, for this, although Mitchelltree could hardly know it, had been the original specific purpose of the weapon's design. But experience had made of Burd Mitchelltree a relentless cal-culator, a cautious gambler, and compulsively, as Fayette carried on persuading and cajoling, the big man registered the distance to the two men standing wide apart in front of him, noted Fayette's free hands relaxed at his sides but inches from the Colt single-action (Mitchelltree wagered single-action) tucked in his belt; he laid mental odds on where the seemingly unarmed John Lodi might have a weapon hidden about him, and multiplied all this by the distance to the doubtlessly armed batch of white men lined up within rifle distance below. Mitchelltree cogitated, cursing in his mind the horsetrader with drooping auburn mustache who had, in a similar cajoling vein a year ago in Texas, convinced him that the power and terrifying look of the weapon would compensate in any human situation for lack of distance and accuracy, for the fact it held only four shots—and concluded that the sole rea-sonable recourse for a Negro man in such a situation was to give up the gun.

". . . you wouldn't know it," Fayette continued, "but he damn sure is."

Mitchelltree wasn't listening. He waited for a pause in the flow of useless language.

". . . have a little look-see, that's all," Fayette said, and hushed, seeming to wait for an answer.

"You welcome to a good look at her," Mitchelltree said, his voice and eyes level. "From hell."

The mournful voice was not defiant, not prideful, not even sullenly resentful. It held only the tone that had caused the speaker such trouble in his life—the very sound the good white men of Texas had not been able to tolerate and had more than once nearly killed him for, culminating in the crushed skull of an anonymous redheaded ranchhand with a big mouth near Denton just over a year ago—for Burden Mitchelltree's marvelously soft voice vibrated, subtle and deep, with the ironic timbre of contempt. In the year 1888, on the continent of North America, within the boundaries of the country called the United States, the only place for a black man of Burd Mitchelltree's temperament, blessed or cursed with Burden Mitchelltree's voice, was the Indian Territory. And here he had fled, here he lived, and here white men flowed already and relentlessly over the border, bringing the old histories with them, and Mitchelltree was weary of them and the hatred he felt in them and for them. Fayette was silent now, staring hard. John Lodi still had not spoken. Mitchelltree expected at any moment for one or the other of them to draw, and he welcomed it; he waited. To pull his own gun was to fire it, to fire was to kill one or both of these white men, and in turn be killed by the brother or the men in the town. Not either/or, Mitchelltree could see that, but both at once, simultaneously: to meet the Creator in the act of destroying His most precious and paltry creation, and be doomed for eternity to hell. Thus, silently, waiting, Mitchelltree reckoned. Tension coiled in his wrist, neck, legs, the strong bones in the back of his hand. Tight. Anticipatory. Prepared.

It could have been no more than Fate Lodi's unconscious fingers returning to probe his back pocket for the absent bottle; it could've been a flicked mule ear, the sound of a cabin door being shut in the distance, could have been any such innocuous twitch or flicker that allowed Mitchelltree's tense gunhand to fly free and begin firing. There are such seeming accidents that change engagements between humans and thus the unfolding of individual stories, and so the very spin of the world; it could have been, for all the elements were here: fear and obsession and men locked each in the cave of his own history and will, and so easily it *could* have been—but it was not. The small turning, the seeming small accident that changed and directed the lives of the three men triangulated on the ridge, was only the high, thin sound of a child's voice calling from below the hill's rim.

"Papa."

The three men in unison—even the bleary-eyed Lafayette—obeying an ancient edict stamped on men's souls to protect the seed of the species, paused and turned as one to the sound of the child's voice.

"Papa."

The sound was not plaintive, not tremulous or frightened, but calm, unshrill, and yet somehow demanding in its calmness, mounting slowly toward them up the hill. John Lodi's profile was toward Mitchelltree now as he turned from the mule and stepped to the edge of the ridge. "You kids git on home now." The voice croaked a rough monotone as if the cords were knotted with disuse. "I mean it now!" He took off his hat, peering down, and Mitchelltree saw the thinning hair, the soft line of forehead revealed belly-white at the hatline above the sallow face. "Matt." The tone was the same as the child's: not hollered or requested, but a statement. "Hear me. Y'all git on back to the house."

The child's voice came again, a bit closer, a bit louder, almost husky, but no less calm, answering in the same flat tone. "Papa." And then the two small faces appeared above the rim, the two ratlike heads—girls, Mitchelltree could see, little girls with boys' heads in overlarge gingham dresses—and they walked singlefile, the younger before the elder, and the elder with her hand clamped to the smaller one's shoulder. Neither of them could be over eight or nine, Mitchelltree thought, little pale skinny white children, half scalped.

They came on, mounted the rise, and stood yoked together, looking up at their father as he stepped back from the edge; they appeared very small, very grave, in the sun's dying flare. Their father, hatted again, did not look down at them but looked off over the valley, blue now with shadows, as the sun's retreating rays fingered only the high peaks of the hills. There was something wrong about the children, Mitchelltree thought, something beyond the peculiarity of close-cropped, naked heads emerging from gaping neckholes of gingham—something even beyond the way they stood so unchildlike and still on the great expanse of cleared ground, arms linked, touching each other as if to do so kept either of them from skimming away on the air like a puff of milkweed seed. Mitchelltree watched them, repulsed and troubled, and then the older—or anyway the taller, the one who had walked behind as they came—spoke again.

"He killed Delia," she said. Clearly the words were spoken to her father, but she did not cast her eyes up at him. A sickly child, hatless and coatless and thin as a stick, she clung to her sister, but she stared directly at Burd Mitchelltree with unblinking eyes the color of yellow clay.

"You young'uns get on back to the house," Fayette said. His hands began to twitch toward his empty back pocket, but Mitchelltree, intent on the girl, was not looking at him now.

"You killed our mule," the child said, not an accusation but a statement, flat and familiar, as if she'd given her name.

"Matt," the father said.

Still not looking at him, she said, "Papa, he shot Delia."

"I know it," the father said. "Y'all go on back now. I'll be there directly."

"He shot Delia in the head," the child said. She continued to stare at Mitchelltree, unblinking, without accusation or anger but placidly, in the stillness of that unchildlike calm—and yet beneath the stillness, as in the slagheap at the back of her father's eyes, there was a fierceness beyond the power of her thin bones and few years.

Mitchelltree had no means to perceive the true nature of the child's reaction; all he could dream of as cause for such ferocity was the idea that the gray mule had been her particular pet. Immediately a warmth flared in him, part pity, part anger, sparked not by the child herself—for she was too strange, too alien, a white rat-child in any case—but by his own memory of the bloodied remains of a red pup he'd had once in boyhood, shot by a Texas rancher for no better reason than that the pup chased his calves. In this way individual past overwhelms history, collective memory, and Mitchelltree, in pity, had turned to her before he hardly knew he would speak.

"I had to, child. The mule's leg was broke."

"You shot our mule."

"Hush, Matt," the father said.

"He shot our mule."

And then, "You killed her. You killed our mule." She chanted the words in a thin monotone as the sun's lingering rays withdrew at last behind Bull Mountain and the blue shadows covered the hill. The other one, the tiny girl with tremendous dark eyes changing gray to green beneath straight lashes as she turned her head from her sister to Mitchelltree and back again, took up the chorus. "You killed our mule," said the little one. "You killed our mule," from the older child again. They piped in unison, the sound high and unceasing, like a hidden pondful of spring peepers on the side of the hill.

"You girls hush up now," Fayette called. "What's the matter with you, good Lord!"

John, still not looking at his daughters, said, "Matt, hush."

And abruptly the children did hush, but they never stopped staring. The ocher eyes of the older child did not blink or well tears; she was not weeping, not sorrowful; something different emanated from her, like a cold, miniature hatred. Mitchelltree witnessed it but still could not fathom that the child was absorbed by an obsession greater, more unyielding even than that of her uncle, more consuming in its degree of singlemindedness—for Fayette's obsessions, except for the two constants of guns and his brother, were erratic, leaping from this to that, guided only by the happenstance of whatever came before him; but this child had a singular obsession, driven by the feel of her mother's hand on her shoulder, and the death of the little gray mule had ground it to a terrible halt.

Mitchelltree heard his own voice roll on the ridge again. "Child, that mule was going to suffer a terrible death for a long time before it go on and die anyhow." He was shamed even as he heard it, at the defensive tone in it, but the words came, unbidden, hulking nearly in their embarrassment, in the way that only a child can shame a man. "That mule had to be shot."

"Get now!" Fayette came toward the girls, swatting his palms together as a farmwife shoos chickens, saying, "You young'uns got no business here." He came unsteadily along the ridge toward them, and then stopped when the girls turned and stared up at him. His hands swerved seamlessly from swatting each other to patting the deep pockets in the front of his corduroy coat. "John, mind your children. You see what I'm saying? This is just what I been saying—look here how they act. Martharuth, this ain't your business. Take your sister and get on back to the house. John?"

"Looks to me like you're the one better mind your own business." The brother's voice was low-key, quiet, his eyes honed on Fayette now, and once again Mitchelltree felt himself fall out of their existence. Fayette spat.

"That ole mule wan't worth a toestump, and you know it. I told you. What'd I tell you? Look here, it's dark. We got to get them slabs hauled up the mountain first thing in the morning. First thing in the morning. Tell you what: that black mule right yonder, he's yours. Quick as we get these blame slabs hauled. You loan me that old Sarn of yours, let me just borrow the use of your wagon about a day's time, that mule yonder is yours. Tomorrow morning. I'll get me a nigger to drive 'em, I'm not trusting no more Indi'ns. Hush them girls up."

But the girls were silent, and for a heartbeat on the ridge there was nothing but silence, and then Fayette, unable to help himself, had to keep on. "You going to take a look at that howdah or ain't you? I reckon you don't even want to know if it's one of yours. Hell, it's bound to be, I seen your handwriting all over it. That goddamn Tanner, I bet you he made off with a flat dozen. Listen here, Son, we got to pay attention to business here, take a look at something that matters a little bit. Forget that blame mule."

"Something that matters," John Lodi said, his eyes keen on his brother. His face was still unfathomable as he repeated the phrase. "That matters. Yes." Slowly he turned to Mitchelltree, said calmly, releasing the words one at a time into the burnished air, "Mister, if you don't mind a minute, I'd like to take a look at that gun now. We don't intend anything. Just want to take a look at the mark on it. I'll give it right back."

Mitchelltree nodded once, though later he would wonder why. Pondering it, he would conclude that there'd been something about the directness in the cracked voice, maybe, that told him this one spoke the truth. Or he would mention to himself the presence of the two children, strange as they were, bound together on the edge of the ridge between the two white men. In fact, he was never fully to understand why he suddenly gave that brief acquiescent nod to John Lodi before he eased his head in the direction of the shadowed men behind the post office wall and said softly, "Let them down yonder know."

John Lodi looked at him a moment, and then turned and called down the hill. "Blaylock! We're all right up here now! Y'all may as well get on back to your business!"

A voiced floated up in the twilight.

"Fate? Y'all got everything under control up yonder?"

Fayette waved his loose hands amiably over his head.

Mitchelltree held his right hand out from his body, and with his left lifted the checkered grip by two fingers and pulled it free of the home-made holster. John stepped toward him to take it. The children never stopped staring, although it was not at the enormous four-barreled pistol they stared; the gun held no fascination for them. They'd grown up around guns, the making of guns, the sound and smell of guns all their lives, and the lure of them held no sway over their souls. It was Mitchelltree the two children continued to stare at. Fayette took a step toward the weapon, eagerly, but by then John had hold of the gun. He broke it open at the breech, checked the three remaining cartridges, turned calmly, almost gently, and yet too fast for anyone to understand what he meant to do, and, without aiming, shot the charcoal mule once in the head.

The girl began, in the warmth of the earth's turning, to walk. She would sneak out of the house without her sister, each day ranging farther and farther, though Jonaphrene would call her sometimes, would see her walking quickly away from the log house and try to run after her. But the girl went on, relentless, unseeing, driven in her inheritance as she'd received it from her father: her birthright stronger than the blood union that had left her naked without the feel of her sister's thin bones beneath her hand, touching, so that for a month and more after Thula Henry's coming, she had continued to walk joined tight to Jonaphrene when she could have walked alone. All was changed in the twinkling of an eye, a gunflash, as Matt became at once unyoked from her sister and driven forward by the killing of the mules.

On the crest of the ridge, with the black man before her and Delia dead by his hand on the hillside, and Fayette's big mule dead by her own father's hand, the change had come on her. She did not know when her arm slipped from around her sister. She watched her father give the gun back to the black man and, without a look or word to his brother or his two daughters, turn and walk straight down the side of the ridge toward the town, and before she knew she had done it, she'd left her sister and followed him. She followed him along the road toward Cedar until she fell too far behind and the night dropped too dark, and then she found her way back to her uncle's store at the end of the row of town buildings and slept behind an empty cracker barrel on the plank porch.

The next morning, when she awakened at first light, she stood up and immediately stepped down off the porch, not east toward the log house, but south toward Waddy Mountain. The old hound dog Ringo saw her from his sleeping place beneath the store porch, where he slept separate from Fayette's dogs since the black-and-tan, wounded in a coon fight and suffering from blood poisoning, had been shot by the girl's father and buried in the yard. The beagle trotted down the hill behind her, followed her, waddling, as she crossed through Faulk's field.

Thus began the girl's restless, ceaseless roaming. She would leave the house early, the dog following, and walk until she could walk no longer, along the rocky slopes of the hills beside the valley, or she'd follow Bull Creek to where it joined the Fourche Maline, and then walk east until she was too weary to turn back. She would sit on the clotted bank then, with the sun warming her naked head, and look at the elm buds pricking red on the bare branches, the peachleaf willows swelling pale green. Her eyes would follow a cardinal darting through the cedars, a thousand shimmering insects skimming the water's surface, dancing in the changing air, but the girl did not see. She would turn her gaze to the hills, where the flowering trees daubed the ridges sweet cream and raspberry, but she had no eyes for the rush of life, could not see how the earth scrambled to cover itself. She was caught alone in the words of her own mind, and those words were like a chant or a prayer, though there was nothing of God in them but only the repetition of thoughts shaped in monotonous rhythm. *Papa put them in a cave somewhere. Safe from rain. Safe from moths and rust and summer dirt daubers, safe from the pilfering fingers of Fayette's boys. I'll find them in a minute, our quilts and clothes, Mama's trunk, I'll load up the wagon. It's just over that next rise. Beyond that cedar yonder. No. On the other side of that sandrock ridge.*

The girl's chanting thoughts did not include what she would do once she'd found her family's belongings, how she might carry them to the wagon, or the wagon to where they were hidden, now that Delia was dead and old Sarn nodded his aged dreams in the shed barn alone. The destruction of the mule, rather than being the event to end her determination, became, instead, the act which sealed her obsession. She would find their things. She would load up the wagon. She would drive east into the mountains and get her mama; she would carry her mother back home.

On she went, walking.

Her aunt forbade her to leave if she could catch her before she got out the door. Jessie would stand with her palm laid across her swelling belly, saying, "Get right back in here this minute, child, there's work to do!" The girl would look up at her, unblinking, and turn and go out the door. The woman's voice was no more than a lone hornet to her, or yellow jacket, buzzing: one could give a nasty sting if you did not stay out of its way, but one could not kill you. She believed she knew the truth in her aunt. She was not afraid of the woman, but she did begin to rise and leave the house earlier so that she might not have to listen to her aunt's buzzing whine. As soon as she heard her father leave, the girl would roll from the pallet. She did not have to take the time to dress, because she slept in the one calico she had to wear; she didn't have any shoes. She'd go to the table, as her father did, and place her hand beneath the cloth and take a piece of cold cornbread or biscuit, turn and lift the latch on the front door, and go out.

Jessie began to complain bitterly in the evenings to her husband that the girl would not work, that there was something wrong with her, but Fayette raised his head only once, said, in Matt's general direction, "You got to pull your share around the house now," and turned back to his coffee.

So Jessie determined that she would, no matter what, she *would* speak to John about the girl. She waited up for him one evening. She'd left his supper on the stove and blown the lamps out, but for the one on the pine table, where she sat, sewing, when her brother-in-law came in. The rest of the household was long abed, her sons and husband snoring upstairs. John did not speak but came in heavily and, seeing her, hesitated a moment and then went to the washbench. He returned to the table, pulled a chair out, and sat down. They didn't greet one another. Jessie gathered the bulk of the muslin sheet she was hemming and put it on the table, stood up and went to the stove and fetched his plate, placed it quietly on the oil cloth. She dipped up a glass of buttermilk from the ready crock and set it before him, then took up her sewing again and sat.

She said, "You're going to have to do something about that girl."

John looked at her from beneath his slouch hat, chewing, but still he did not speak.

"She hadn't done a lick of work since I don't know when," the woman whispered. "Stays off and gone from daylight to dark, won't do a thing in the world I tell her." She was silent a moment. "I can't have that, I'm sorry."

The man still didn't say anything. He took a bite of bacon, picked up his cornbread and crumbled it into the buttermilk.

Jessie's fingers moved faster and faster on the sheet. "The rest of them act just like her! She shows out, and the rest of them act just like her. We can't be feeding a bunch of young'uns that won't work, I don't care whose they are."

The man turned his dark look on her, and immediately the woman fell silent. There was no sound in the room then but a moth that had come in with the night air, batting around the table, thumping softly against the hot globe of the lamp, falling to the wood. John pushed his plate away, leaned back against the chair slats and reached in his front pants pocket for his purse. The room sounded with the hard thunk of coin wrapped in leather when he set it on the table. "I give Fay twenty dollars Friday," he said. "Have my children eat more than that?"

"Oh, it's not that. It's not just that." The woman hesitated, her hands still, then the sound burst in a harsh whisper. "The child don't act right!" The words spat into the room. "She hadn't acted right since . . ." Jessie's voice trailed off. She picked up the sheet again and went to sewing in fast, tight little stitches.

The man turned and looked at the children on the floor near the hearth. The girl immediately twisted around on the pallet and sat up.

"I don't know what to do with her," Jessie said, still sewing. She looked at Matt, seeming unsurprised to see her awake and listening, sitting up on the pallet with her gown tucked over her knees. The woman went on talking, as if the girl were invisible. "From the minute she quit having fits, or pretending to have fits—"

"Fits. She hadn't had no fits."

"Well, whatever it was, whatever that bouncing around and falling down was about—"

"She quit that."

"No, I know. That's what I mean." The needle paused, and then the woman clasped the sheet around and dropped it to her lap. "She's fine now, she could help now, but she won't stay put. She won't work. She runs off the minute you leave in the morning, don't come back till nearly dark, and I know good and well you know it. Lord only dreams what she's up to, because when she comes trailing in here for supper she don't have a thing to show but scratches and stick-tights in her skirt tails and, day before yesterday, a bleeding foot. Look there, the child's face is getting dark as a you-know-what, I can't keep a hat on her. I can't do a thing in the world with her. You're going to have to do something because I can't and I don't aim to, I've got all I can say grace over now."

"Nobody's asking," the man said. He didn't take his eyes off his daughter. In a bit, he said, "Mattie, y'all been running off every day like your aunt tells me?"

The girl looked at her aunt, at her aunt's mouth, not pinched but tucked in at the corners as though she might any minute break into a smile. She waited for her father to speak again, but he said nothing, and at last she said, "I been out."

"Out where?"

"Outside."

"Doing what?"

"Walking."

"Walking where?"

"All over."

Her father looked at her. He was turned halfway around at the table, his hat pushed to the back of his head. The girl could see his eyes clearly. "What is it you been doing while you been out walking?"

"Hunting," she said.

Jessie snorted. The girl continued to look at her father, unblinking.

"How come I don't ever see any game?" he said.

The girl didn't answer.

Jessie said, "You don't see no game because she's lying through her little yellow teeth."

"Jessie!" Fayette hollered from upstairs.

The room was still, just the soft mothwing thump and flutter. The girl knew then there'd been no snoring for a long time. Her brother Jim Dee was awake, lying very still on the far side of the pallet. Her sister was breathing quickly beside her, her face covered with the blanket. The girl felt the cousins rustling awake above.

"Get up here and get to bed." Fayette's voice from the upper room was not a shout this time but cold, uninflected. The wood overhead creaked.

The woman looked at her brother-in-law, but he didn't look back at her. She folded the muslin sheet and bent to put it in the sewing basket on the floor. She stood then. Before she turned to climb the stairs, John said softly, but still loud enough for the woman, for even the ones upstairs to hear, "If you aim to hunt, Matt, I believe you better take my muzzle loader. Y'might have better luck."

The girl heard her aunt grunt, the wind bursting from her gut as if she'd been kicked.

"Another thing," the man said, looking at the girl, his voice stern, his eyes bright in the firelight. "From here on out, wear a hat."

So the girl began to carry her father's rifle. From the hand-hewn nail beside the fireplace in the mornings she would take whichever slouch hat came beneath her fingers and slap it on her head; she'd sling the powderhorn by its leather thong across her thin chest, hoist the long-barreled gun to her shoulder, and walk out the door in the dawn light just before or after her father, turning her face up to him sometimes, her mouth slightly open, as if she would speak but could not. Once, she put her hand on his arm and he paused, one foot upon the stone step, and looked at her. Matt turned her face away quickly, whistled for the old beagle hound Ringo, jumped off the log porch, and walked off with the dog west. It was as if her mouth was stopped when she was alone with her father, stripped of voice and will to ask him what had happened to their belongings. It became the same within her as the memory of the baby sister, lifted away in the red darkness, taken away, disappeared, unspoken of, as if the child had never lived. To ask was to remember, to learn, to hear what she didn't want to know, and so she would not ask.

In the dark of night she stole a pair of trousers from one of the boy cousins and hid them beneath the pallet. Afterwards, in the mornings, she'd take them with her, wedged tightly like a narrow bedroll beneath her arm. When she was out of sight of the house she'd unroll the homespun trousers and put them on under her skirt—to save her legs from the briarbushes, she told herself, but in the depths of woods far from white eyes, the girl would gather the ragged expanse of calico skirt in her arms and tie a knot with it around her waist so that she could stride fast on her skinny, hickory-hard legs, unimpeded by anything more than the stone cut and scrabble of rocky earth; she used the pants pockets to hold wadding and lead. If the old hound dog scared up a rabbit and ran it around by, the girl would shoot it, but that seldom happened, because she didn't go quietly through the woods; she would not wait for Ringo to head a rangy swamp rabbit in a great loop back to where she stood, but walked in her relentless and driven manner, snapping sticks, the swiftest and broadest way to cover the earth. One time she shot a cottonmouth swimming toward her on Bull Creek. Another time she took the head off a gray squirrel flattened tight to a tree trunk, its tail twitching. She did not bother to go over and pick the squirrel up. It was not game to her then, not food or pelt, but a gray tail on a mockernut hickory, twitching.

The land turned over hot and dry. Before green had settled on the earth that first spring, the long grasses began to wither. Dust coated the blackjacks and cedars. Elm leaves shriveled and crimped brown on the edges before they'd hardly unfurled. Everywhere dusty land terrapins crawled on the dusty roadbeds, scritched slowly through the dry grass in the ditches, moving each with webbed neck stretched out and head lifted, following its own imponderable purpose. Some whites who'd lived awhile in the Territory talked about the great number of crawling terrapins, the fact it was more than a month too soon to see them crawling. It was common to see hundreds in the high heat of late June, fumbling their lone journeys along the choking roadbeds: crawling for water, some said; hunting a partner, said others—though the Muscogee people knew the land turtles were only returning home to their stomp grounds for Green Corn ceremony in the time of the full summer moon. But never had folks seen so many crawling so early, and they spoke of it, some of them, a little in fear, shaking their heads. The year was too new for that migration. The weather was too hot for early May.

Thus, in the aptness of Providence and the story's unfolding, it was cold when the girl found the cold, empty wagon, but hot on the afternoon she found the charred remains. She came upon them near the place called the Narrows, the narrow cleft south of town where the hills lap together and form the pass to Cedar. The blackened circle lay sheltered low on the east side of the mountain—this was Bull Mountain, not Waddy: the western twin shaped like a kneeling buffalo slumped toward the earth. At first the girl could just make out a dark patch on the ground through the grid of pine trunks and pin oaks; she and the dog were coming down through a part of the mountain that hadn't been logged yet. The old hound labored down the slope in front of her, panting and wheezing and trotting his fat and aged self, and Matt in her man's hat and boy's trousers, with the blue bunch of skirt tied in a knot at her belly, followed at a slow pace, her face red and sweaty, and the long barrel of the muzzle loader too loose in the crook of her arm, dipping nearly to the ground with the force of its own weight. She could see the black place on the earth, she could smell it, charred and bitterly rank from old rains, but she couldn't see the size of it or the size of the clearing. She thought it must be an old Choctaw cabin burnt to the ground. Then she came down between the trees and saw it, too small to have been a cabin, and the shape wrong: a very nearly perfect circle, laid out on a bald rock face, open to the sun.

She stood a moment. The dog went snuffling and sniffling around, but soon lost interest and trotted over to the shade beneath a pine tree and lay down with his tongue out, panting. The girl looked at the charred circle impassively, blinking slowly in the hot sunlight, hardly curious: in the great self-absorption that closed her eyes to all but that which served her secret purpose, she nearly missed the very thing she'd walked the hills and valleys endlessly seeking. She did not know it or recognize it but merely gazed at it a moment and turned away, turned to walk on down the slope toward the road curving at the base of the mountain, thinking nothing, thinking only that she might go back along the road, no matter about the dust and the terrapins and perhaps people passing, because it was just too hot. She stopped, caught by the smallest bit of sunglint off metal. It did not show perfectly, blackened as it was with soot and ashes and dulled in the tan dust, but some part of it, the edge maybe, caught the bright sunlight in one narrow streak, and Matt saw it even as she was turning, like quartz in a roadbed far off. She was caught and held by it, nearly as if the glint on the earth were singing, and she knew in the same breath and heartbeat what it was.

The dog stood up and stretched, shook his ears flapping, ready to trot off in whatever direction he sensed in her, and then he too stopped. He stood quite still, looking at the charred circle, whining. Matt lowered the rifle to the ground barrel-first, the stock sliding heavily in the crook of her arm; she placed it flat in the dry weeds before she turned to walk barefoot over the crunch and shift of ashes to where the box lay, tilted sideways, in the center of the sooted pile. Still she did not understand what she was standing on, but she knew what that black square was, shaped square still, holding the boxed shape of its integrity, not melted but only blackened like a sooty lamp chimney, and warped a little along the bottom edge. Somebody had laid it there—or thrown it—after the fire was nearly dying.

The girl knelt in the filth and the crumbling cinders rank with the smell of charcoal. Her hand trembled when she reached for it. She dug quickly in the ashes, her fingers turning black, to free it, and picked it up, cradled the box to her belly, where it blackened the knot of calico and the flat pane of shirtfront. The tin was warm from the sun's heat in the cold ashes, like living flesh. The girl understood then what she was kneeling on. She turned her head slowly, looking at all of it, the whole blackened circle: her mother's embroidered pillowslips and linens, the cedar wood from the trunk, their crockery and wool blankets and the seven quilts pieced by Grandma Billie, all the objects of her family's lives brought with them from Kentucky, burnt in a circle of fire while she had slept in the red darkness. And she knew it was the same as the circle of white ice, coming through it with Papa, the same and its opposite, for both were the point of no turning back forever, but the first had been ice and white and eternal, and the last black and fire and small. The first of God's making, and this—she knew it, she had no hint of doubt about it—from the hand of her family.

It was not Papa only, the girl thought.

She could see then the aunt's raw, red knuckles folded over, the hands lifting a straw-filled crate away from the pile of goods on the ground, setting it to the side before the coal oil rained down, shaken like rain onto the pile by her uncle's hands, and her father's. She saw the fire lick up quick and yellow, burning nearly smokeless in the cold November light.

The girl held the tin box tightly in the wedge of her left arm, and with the other hand she dug in the ashes, past the crumbling, hot, dry surface, deep into the black muck where even the hot May sun could not reach. Her fingers scraped past the shards and shreds of what would not burn, past melted shoe eyelets and her father's chisel and the iron clasps of her mother's trunk, past the formless chunks of charcoal, into the dank mass, cool and black and stinking, in the depths of the black circle. For a long time she knelt so, with the tin box warm against her left side and her right hand buried, trying to feel what these lumps were, trying to read with her fingers, as the blind would, with the sweat running in her eyes and the hot May sun burning the back of her head through the slouch hat. She stirred the damp remains, the sift and silt of what they'd made their lives from, charred and melted past all knowing, each lump with no more form to it than a clump of river-rock or stinking clay.

Not one thing to keep here, she thought. *Nothing to save.* She knew the completeness with which those hands had piled every item, soaked each piece with kerosene, how thorough and deft they had been. There was no grief in her, only the beginnings of anger, rising in small, hot waves from her stomach through her chest and face. She turned over a clumped mass that crumbled black between her fingers and fell open, smoke white, where the feathers sifted out: a lump of Mama's feather-bed, too thick and damp with down to burn properly, too dense. Matt touched the singed feathers with her finger. She smelled the burnt animal smell. At once she knew where the tin box had been hidden all those months, riding soft and discreet, like the unborn, from Kentucky into the mountains where her mother died, and then on along the pig trails, in secret, unknown, into Eye Tee, sewn tight in the ticking seams.

The heat of the box burned against her, and she set it down on the black pile. With her clean hand, her left hand, she tried to pry the lid open. There was no lock on it; there had never been a lock: not on the morning she'd uncovered it from the frozen earth beneath the blackgum, never while it rode a thousand miles, buried again, soft in the featherbed where her mother rode swaying and sick above; it was not locked by a human lock of tumbler and iron, but sealed with heat and rust. Sealed with the closure of her mother's death. And her sister's.

"Lyda." She spoke the name aloud: the dead name, unspeakable. She thought suddenly that the child's remains, too, were buried here on the pyre with the rest of it. If she dug deeper she might touch the fragile crisps of burnt flesh, the stripped bones, the tiny arcs of ribcage and scoop of plated skull no larger than a turtle shell.

The girl scrambled to her feet and wiped the muck from her blackened arm on the knot of her cousin's dress, the fear rising and, beyond that, or above it, or beneath it: the rage. She wanted to kick her mother's tin box, wanted to smash or break it. She picked it up with both hands and threw it, but the pile of ashes was soft as mush, the ashes would not resist it, and so she looked around quickly and spied the gun where she'd laid it at the edge of the circle. Stepping quickly over the coal and ash, the sound crunching beneath her bare feet so that she thought even then she could be walking on the bones of her infant sister, Matt moved toward her father's rifle. She picked up the gun, turned and sighted along the long barrel, quickly, too quickly, and pulled the trigger. The tin box jumped and tumbled a few feet. The report rang through the hollow, up the side of Bull Mountain.

The box was only a half-dozen yards away, but she had barely grazed it. She was sobbing then, not in grief but in hot waves of anger, her shoulders shaking. *Stupid!* she thought. *Stupid!* She'd missed with the rifle from less than twenty feet. She'd been too stupid to figure out where her mother had hidden her secret. *They burnt it all anyhow,* she thought. *It don't matter. There's nothing to carry.* Nothing to load in the wagon, no team to hitch up, nothing to sell to buy a new mule, and the sun was too hot, she was sweating, and she hated them, all of them. She saw then her aunt's hands unpacking the straw-bound stacks of white china from the slatted crate, Jessie's hands setting each piece gently in a tin washtub, pouring a gallon jug of turpentine, gulping, over each milky plate and saucer, the thin lip of each cup decorated with a delicate print of rosebuds, to soak in turpentine on the back porch of the log house for three weeks. In winter. While the girl and the children slept upstairs. She knew how it was then, how it had been—*She stole Mama's china!*—and the wrath swelled up more fierce.

Tipping the gunstock to the ground, the girl took a step forward and reloaded by habit, with the barrel at an angle because she could not reach it standing straight up on its end; she uncapped the horn with her teeth, poured powder into the muzzle too fast, spilling black on the scoop of her hand, down her arm, filtering, sifting black grains to the charred earth; she licked the wadding with no spit in her mouth, seated the ball with the first thrust, and went on jamming the ramrod down the barrel, again, and again, and again. Her eyes were glazed, staring at the far side of the circle, where the dog had found an old mottled terrapin crossing the cold coals and was uselessly worrying it. With the cap set, gun loaded, Matt's eyes cleared, and she could see the dog whining and sniffing pointlessly at the box terrapin. When his nose came close the creature would pull its leathery neck back and shut itself away, and when Ringo backed off, the old terrapin would emerge and move on again, slow and relentless, undaunted, following its own secret and imperative purpose. Matt hollered at the dog, "Quit that!", the rage rising, settling its focus now on the hound's animal ignorance, to sniff and paw at a useless land turtle when their very lives lay in a burnt circle around them. "Hyah!" she cried. "You, Ringo! Get over here!"

The dog paid her no mind but went on nosing at the closed shell, snuffling beneath it with his snout as if to hunt the passage through its belly. Matt reached them just as Ringo turned the terrapin over and began to paw at the yellowed plate of its underbelly. Swinging the heavy gun by the stock with all her force, she swatted the terrapin shell with a dull thunk that sent it spinning and skittering across the ashes; she kicked at the dog, but he ducked back out of her reach, and crying and sweating so that she could hardly see, she went to where the tin box had tumbled and picked it up. There was a shiny silver gash, a small silver streak clean across the top where the lead bullet had nicked it. She held it tightly, her mind running pictures: she would take it to the dry creekbank below Bluff Hole where the still, slow water lay, deep, mud-colored, and throw the box in the unmoving water. She would clean it and shine it, and carry it, held high in her hands, above her head, into the log house and chunk it down on the puncheon floor before Jessie and Fayette and the six cousins; before the astonished and sorrowing eyes of her father. She would find a black tupelo somewhere in that dry, tree-clotted country, and bury the box in the earth beneath the gummed branches: she would hide it from their eyes, all of them, blood and half-blood and colored and Indian, the white people of Big Waddy Crossing and Eye Tee, the world. She thought, *There's this, then. I'll take this when I go get Mama,* though she hated the tin box as powerfully as it is possible to hate what is only dead metal. And she knew she would do none of what she saw behind her eyes, but only sit down with it upon the ashes (though she thought she couldn't bear it, not here, on the burnt corpse of her family's belongings): she would sit on the ashes and pry the box open. Or break it open. Or shoot if she had to shoot a hundred times.

Both her hands were black now from soot and gunpowder as she turned the box over end to end. There was no clasp on it, no place visible where it should open, only a tight seam running square around. With one hand she unknotted the calico, and then she sat down on the pile of ashes and nestled the box in the scoop of skirt across her lap. The anger was seeping away now, draining, as a wound does. The dog had found the terrapin again, in the dry weeds beyond the circle; Matt could hear his little huffing whine. With the stubs of her fingers she dug into the seam and tried to work it open. She scraped the line clean with a stick, pressed against it with her thumbs, held the box like a canning jar in the crook of her arm and tried to pry apart one corner. For a long time in the sun's heat, she didn't look up. She could feel the sun sinking past its high point, hear the dog snuffling at wood's edge, but she didn't raise her frowning eyes from her work. Sweat beaded the curve above her tightly clamped lips; she worked slowly and steadily, without urgency, but the box would not open. It was only when she stopped finally, the sweat burning her eyes, and let the box fall still in her lap, when she sat with her fingers unmoving, touching lightly against the seam—only then did she feel the lid loosen. She picked the box up. Then it seemed to come too easily, one side sliding noiselessly against the other, without edge or friction, silently, and before she could realize it or stop it, the tin square came apart in two pieces in her hands.

Outside, the box was smeared black still with ash and the sweat of her fingers, but inside, the tin walls gleamed clean and pure, silver. Carefully, the girl set the lid on the blackened earth beside her; she cradled the lower half on her lap. Nesting in the bottom lay a clutch of crushed papers and ribbons, some other items, whose reason or purpose she could not fathom: a penny snuffbox, a stub of pencil, a small oval eyeglass case the color of midnight sky. The box could not have been on the fire long, because the edges of the papers were barely singed. She sat for a long time, just looking, holding the base in her hands. She waited to feel something.

Ain't even burnt hardly, she thought.

She sat still awhile longer, waiting.

It was Jessie, then, the girl thought. *She must've threw it on at the last.*

The girl tried to call up an image of the gaunt slit-mouthed woman, her aunt, slinging the gleaming box on the dying flames, but she couldn't see anything. The dark place behind her eyes gave her nothing; she saw only this unfathomable clutch of yellow papers, the cheap penny snuffbox, a pencil: her mother's secrets in the face of the real world hot and stinking and dust-crusted around her. She wiped her hands on the tail of her cousin's skirt before reaching in to take out a little rolled wedge of newspaper. She unrolled it. Inside the yellowed triangle lay a twig of ashwood chewed to a round, ragged knob on one end. Matt recognized its character, what it was—somebody's snuff stick—but she couldn't comprehend its purpose, what reason it could have for lying in the secret place of her mother's keepsakes and memory. She rolled the snuff stick back up carefully and placed it in the box lid; she reached for the cheap snuffbox and, with some effort, unscrewed the rusted cap. Inside were four used wooden matchsticks, the knobs of their heads spent and black. She screwed the cap back on and placed the snuffbox beside the wedge of rolled paper in the lid.

Slowly, meticulously, the girl examined each item. She picked up the stub of pencil and studied the knife marks where it had been sharpened, licked the square of lead extruding from the end, placed the pencil in the box lid. She turned the eyeglass case over and over before she snapped open the hard navy shell. Within, delicate as gossamer against the blueblack velvet lining, nestled a little pair of wire-rimmed spectacles half covered by a soft strip of white cotton. She brushed the cotton strip off the lenses, gently, with the end of one finger. They were so dainty, so tiny. *They'd fit Jonaphrene,* she thought. Tiny little round eyeglasses the size to fit a doll. She reached for them with her charred fingers and held them in her palm. Then, with the slow, practiced gestures of sacrament, never taking her eyes from the sunglint on the thick lenses, she took off the shapeless hat she wore and placed it carefully on the ash pile beside her, opened the eyeglasses, and wrapped the wire crescents behind her ears. The spectacles were so small they pressed a tight seam against the girl's narrow face. She turned her head from side to side, and her warped and misshapen eyes turned with her. She sat so for some time, turning her head slowly, an anomaly too old to be child, too slack-boned and tiny to be grown: a thin otherwordly creature in skirt and trousers with chopped-off hair and ocher eyes swimming large behind glasses. The girl held still and waited for her vision to clear, but the dust-coated trees down the mountain remained a drab swirl of verdigris. The blackened circle she sat upon stayed a blurred shadow. She couldn't see the world outside herself—the dog, the outline of box lid, the clutch of papers in the silver bottom—any more than she could see the moving pictures in the dark place behind her eyes.

As carefully as she'd donned them, the girl unwrapped the wires from behind her ears and removed the spectacles; she replaced them just as she'd found them, nestled against the velvet as in a miniature cradle, half blanketed with the wedge of white cotton. The case snapped shut with a popping sound that echoed along the ridge and startled silent for a heartbeat the steady hum of insects, and Matt placed the eyeglass case on the box lid next to the other items. She stared at the several articles lined up on the tin lining, thinking at any moment their meaning would come clear to her. No clarity came, no revelation, not even a moment's logic to explain the correlation of items or their reason for being within her mother's life. Matt turned her eyes down to the cache of papers in the box bottom in her lap. She thought, *This here will tell me.*

Again she wiped her hands on the skirt hem. She reached in the box and pulled out a handful of letters, released from their bond of ribbon, scattered in a loose cluster. The singed paper began to crumble beneath her fingers, and gingerly, with more delicacy than would seem possible to the hand of an eleven-year-old, she lifted the tin box and laid the letters gently in its place upon the filthy swatch of calico across her lap. As she turned to set the box to the side, her eye was caught by another something, half visible in the bottom beneath the scattered papers. Again Matt wiped her hands. She reached in and pulled out a cracked leather purse, unclasped at the top where the two tarnished brass heads did not quite meet. With two fingers she spread the mouth of the purse open. Crammed inside were several wads of crumpled paper, brownish knots aged and singed and crinkled, and when she drew them out and spread them on her knee, she knew them to be paper dollars, though they didn't look like the few U.S. paper dollars she'd ever seen. Delicately she touched them, opening the fragile crisps with a fine, fingering touch. Printed across one, crinkled and faded but decipherable: the name VIRGINIA above a half-draped woman holding wheat shafts, seated upon a horn of plenty; in the corners, the numeral 10 and a round portrait of a beardless man in a high collar. On another, a man straddled a prancing horse beneath the words DEO VINDICE. In scrolled letters the crumbling paper declared that the *Confederate States OF AMERICA* would pay the bearer on demand the sum of FIVE HUNDRED DOLLARS, dated *Richmond, Feb 17th, 1864.*

The girl unfolded each crumpled note. Some of them sifted to ash beneath her fingers, as if, having been brought to the point of combustion and unaccountably halted, called back from destruction by an icy breath, now, touched by human warmth and the sun's heat, they must at once continue their disintegration into dust. But even as they crumbled, she read the numbers: hundred-dollar notes, five hundreds, fifties, all stamped with the mark of the Confederacy, all worthless, as even the child knew; as even the raw, red-knuckled hand that had pulled the roll from the leather purse and sifted hurriedly through the bills before crumpling each in a furious wad and cramming it back in the darkness, as the intelligence behind that hand, had known. Worthless even on the day of their printing.

In the heat and sound of a thousand rasping cicadas, the girl was transported to the hot clearing in the mountains of Arkansas, to the repetition and voice of her mother, and the girl heard what she had been lessoned by rote so that the rhythms and words were an eternal present, her mother's voice chanting, rising, falling like the asking voices of locusts: *James and Thomas and Oliver, William, Alexander, Obediah, called Bede, and your grandfather Cornelius who died at Vicksburg in the War. That was Eighteen Sixty-three, which seems a long time ago to your young mind, but it is not long at all, I was fourteen when my father died, and he was thirty-nine, I was fourteen which seems a long time ago to your young mind but it is not long at all.* Matt stared at the Confederate note. Richmond, Feb 17th, 1864. *your grandfather cornelius who died at vicksburg in the war that was eighteen sixty-three which seems a long time ago.*

From the cluster of letters amidst the treasury notes she plucked a thick piece of paper folded in thirds, and opened it to discover that it was not a letter at all but a child's penmanship practice, the scrolled alphabet repeated in upper case and lower case between stiff lines ruled with charcoal. She folded the thick paper and placed it in the box lid, reached for a folded semitransparent sheet, brown and thin as the skin of an onion, through which she could see dark blue scratches. Her breath held as she unfolded the friable page. The hand was beautifully penned in slanted *o*'s and sweeping tails and elaborate curlicues, the indigo ink faded in places and smudged illegibly in the creases, but yes, it was a letter, dated in the upper corner Oct 21st, 1861.

Dear Wife,

We are camped near Leesburg where on this day since I have witnessed the awful spectacle of a thousand bluecoated lemmings leaping madly routed down the bare face of Ball's Bluff to their deaths in the swollen waters of the Potomac and have rejoiced to witness victory fierce and sweet as Manassas and to cherish the knowledge that though it will be finished soon I have not missed the fight. The regiment will receive orders within the hour I'm told and so I write in haste, though my grieving spirit tells me had I a thousand hours, a preacher's tongue, a poet's pen to ink my sorrows, I could not begin. Look you to Proverbs where the Creator's poet tells us of a virtuous woman whose husband's heart doth safely trust in her and he shall have no need of toil, it is not thy virtue wife I suffer fearing but thy willingness to loyalty & trust, and what will you tell our children when their kinsmen call them traitor? Shall you tell them to deny their father as you have denied your husband? To deny the will of Logan Co. and all its patriots who know where our allegiance lies? My grief that your brothers have turned blind eyes to the True Cause, have thrown their lot with the North when our very souls & wills & manner are southern bred, this bitterness is nothing to the sorrow of my life to have a wife who sets her face against me, and with no more somberness of mind or wit of thought than the platitudes of those who deem it Christian to take a man's property and grind his will beneath their feet. But I would not constrain you wife, nor vex your spirit when you are soul ma and pa both unto our children, it is only when I see the ladies here in the land of my birthplace who would fight before their men and at their sides to death, my grief renews. But thou wert always a contentious woman, the Holy Book tells us that a continual dripping on a rainy day and a contentious woman are alike, whoever restrains her restrains the wind and grasps oil with his right hand. I would not be a fool besides all else, and in any case will return soon and then we will dress this wound to heal it or cut it out but meantime I will not desist to write and do you so the same for separation of will is not severance. I carry my Testament and pray daily and would admonish you to do the same, and so saying and prayerfully I remain,

Your Husband

Matt folded the thin sheet along the creases and placed it beside the other items in the box lid. She unfolded another, thick-coated and stiff. In a different hand, one blocked and bluntly square, someone had written on a torn piece of wallpaper:

MY BELOVED I HAVE HIRED A FELLA TO PASS TO YOU THE NEWS I AM LIVING AND NOT KILLED. WE PAST A STREAM WHERE A PANTHER DRANK BY A DOE BOTH JUST DIPPING THERE HEADS AND BREAKING THE SURFACE AND I THOUGHT TO MYSELF THIS IS HOW IT IS GOING TO BE OR HOW IT SHOULD BE WHEN THE LION WILL LIE DOWN WITH THE LAMB. I HAVE NEVER SEEN SUCH A BATH OF KILLING.

No signature. No date. She folded it and placed it next to the others in the silver square, reached for another paper, where a childish scrawl declared Roses are Red Violets are Blue Honey is Sweet And You are To. Another contained a recipe for chess pie. When she unfolded another, a lock of very blond, curly hair tied with a pale ribbon fell to her lap from a charred printed leaf. To the girl's eyes it seemed that the burnt edges of the page were blacker, more distinctly charred, than the browned tinge at the edge of the others, and there were blurred blue marks on one side where a hand had underlined words and phrases. Matt looked to the top of the page, where the name EZEKIEL, the numbers <32 27> were inscribed. Quickly, uncomprehendingly, she scanned the passages marred with smearing blurred lines:

20 They shall fall in the midst of them that are <u>slain by the sword</u>: she is delivered to the sword: draw her and all her multitudes.
21 The strong among the mighty shall speak to him out of the midst of hell with them that help him: they are gone down, they lie uncircumcised, <u>slain by the sword.</u>
22 Asshur is there and all her company: his graves are about him: <u>all of them slain, fallen by the sword:</u>
23 Whose graves are set in the sides of the pit, and the company is round about her grave: <u>all of them slain, fallen by the sword, which caused terror in the land of the living.</u>

The girl's eyes darted back and forth and down, finding the same words underlined again and again:

<u>slain by the sword</u>
<u>all of them slain</u>
<u>fallen by the sword</u>
<u>which caused terror in the land of the living</u>

unto the last lines:

27 And they shall not lie with the mighty that are fallen of the uncircumcised, which are <u>gone down to hell with their weapons of war: and they have laid their swords under their heads, but their iniquities shall be upon their bones, though they were the terror of the mighty in the land of the living.</u>

Folding the Old Testament page along the creased squares, she slipped the lock of blond hair within and put it away. On another partially

burned Bible page separated from its binding were the listings of family
births and deaths and marriage dates, printed in a strong sweeping
hand, the words and order just as her mother had taught her. Inside
the last delicate and half-singed page the girl opened, in a hand unlike
the others, another letter began *My beloved*—

Without judgment, she read.

> —*my dearly beloved, which you are not and never shall be, this I
> see as I have seen all else here among men, but it is not that which
> I put my hand to tell you but what is revealed within the torment
> bequeathed to me through no fault or petition, the Curse charged
> to me which I have in days past petitioned Him to remove and
> He would not, now I know it is not mine to ask. We are dying,
> we all are dying the flesh melts from our bones daily as snowwater
> drips from the eaves and I care not, for Thou art with me Thy
> rod and Thy staff they comfort me Thou anointest my head with
> oil my cup runneth over, there is no goodness and mercy.*

Without wisdom, without comprehension, her earth-yellow eyes skimming back and forth, the girl read . . .

> *We have killed one another in the violence of our souls. There is
> no reason else. All that has been told us is falsehood and deceit. I
> have seen Cain's armies and Laban's armies and the sons of Jacob
> the thief, and care not, for that which now is, in the days to come
> shall be forgotten. Our very House is divided brother against
> brother not in God's vengeance nor the Just Righteousness of
> Cause, for there is no Cause but Pride and Violence, which are
> meager in the unfolding of the Face of the Lord. Thus, the Will
> of the Lord that Kentucky lie astraddle the Cause each North and
> South which is illusion, so that we have owned the limbs of the
> Sons of Ham and yet not their souls and a curse is upon us, we
> have joined with the Might of the Union for the sake of Union to
> be united with our brethren, which also is deceit and illusion, for
> "if a man say he love God and hateth his brother he is a liar."*

. . . until she began to know without language or comprehension, to
hear with her soul what she saw in the place behind her eyes: a pale
skeleton of a man seated upon the fetid earth in tattered trousers faded
to no-color, shredded high above his ankles, flapping in a high breeze

like the unsolid limbs of a scarecrow, and in his cracked fingers a stubbed pencil pressed to page, and in his shallow breath the urgency of the dying; she knew that he suffered the mystery, as she herself suffered it; that he carried unto madness the same gift and curse to breathe the soul of another; that he held, as she did, the rolling vision in the dark place behind his pale eyes.

"Moreover your little one which ye said should be a prey and your children which in that day had no knowledge between good and evil, they shall go in thither."

Abruptly the child stopped reading. The paper fell, crushed between the small, blackened fingers, unattended in her lap. She sank, spiraling, into knowledge that was beyond her understanding, truth that was beyond her wisdom, seeing that the writer was a man kin to her—kin to her mother—a blond specter with yellow eyes, and yet his was not the hand that had penned the indigo script chastising the faithless woman, though the kinship was there too, so that the words were a distortion of the same cadences and rhythms from the same pulse of blood, and she saw within the spiral Grandma Billie, blind and heavy in her shapeless dress in the dawn fog; it was her grandmother who had been the faithless woman, the contentious woman who set her face against her husband, and he died at Vicksburg, died at Vicksburg in the war. The blond specter swam forward but he did not see Grandma Billie, and the girl knew the blood kinship was not there. She struggled, trying to twist free of the spiral, and could not, any more than she could walk naked on the earth freed of the very blood and breath within her, mingled within her in the burden and protection of blood, calcified in the carapace of family.

The girl sat on the blackened earth without presence in her body, without power over the images rolling behind her eyes, listening without judgment as a child listens to a tale that is told. The blond wraith had loved her mother, these scratched words had been written for her mother and to her mother in her mother's girlhood from the long travail of a madness unto death, and the girl felt his hand shake with fever, not from a soldier's wound, though he was a soldier, but fevered with madness and hunger; she saw the ghosts of men groaning nearby on the fetid ground, sprawled in acres in a great space around him, and he was blood-kin through her mother's father, and the searing sight in him was the same behind her own eyes—the same and yet different; for in the blond wraith the vision was madness, and in the girl it was only like remembering: a deep and unfathomable memory in the blood. She remembered that the blond soldier had loved her mother, she remembered he was dying; she remembered the weeping and wailing and gnashing of teeth upon prison ground deep with the stench of dying, far away to the east, and the memory rolled back, and back, the numbers increasing, the voices crying, and the girl knew she could not know these thousand lives from before her borning, how they had spoken in the world or walked, not gestures, not scent or warm breath, but only that they were hers and she theirs, and kin.

The vision rolled deeper; she was not she but one hiding, in fear, hiding; it was a cottage with whitewashed walls and a hewn oaken table, and one hid beneath the oaken wood of the table, for the enemy roamed without, and the one hiding, coward and afraid in war, crouched beneath the oaken table, trembling, heard voices, the voices of women; and one hid, afraid, shrinking in terror, the women's voices coming to the door, entering, three peasant women in scarves and woolen dresses, moving about the cottage to prepare food, a mess of pottage, a mess of pottage for the one hiding, the coward, the soldier, until they became and had always been Holy Women, to protect and guide the one, to save the one hiding from the enemy on the fields, the green fields, the fetid fields all around, and as one watched, the faces of the Holy Women changed, darkened, became all the face of the Choctaw woman, and they held each of them out to the one hiding the clay cup.

The girl's eyes rolled back in her head, her head slumped forward, and she fell into darkness.

Mattie stood at the top of dark stairs in a house that had belonged to her long ago, so long ago, and her mother's voice called her from the root cellar.

"Mattie? Mattie. Come here a minute. Mama needs you."

"Mama?"

She stood at the top, staring down into the darkness where the wooden steps descended lower and lower and disappeared in blue-black velvet.

"Come down here, honey."

She was afraid. It was too dark, the stairs too steep. She could not remember what the cellar looked like at the bottom. "Come get me, Mama!"

"I can't come there, Mattie."

"Come get me."

"I can't. I need you. Come down here where I am."

"Who is he, Mama? That man?"

"Nobody. A cousin. Come down, honey. Mama needs you."

"I can't, I can't, I'm too afraid, come get me. You come get me."

"I can't." Her mother's voice was fading, moving deeper into the cellar.

"I been waiting for you, Mama. Every day I been waiting."

"I can't climb those stairs again, sweetheart."

"Come get me, Mama!"

"I can't."

Her mother's voice faded into silence. Mattie opened her mouth to call her and she could not; she could not follow her mother's voice into the darkness so that she might know the meaning of burnt matchsticks kept in a cheap snuffbox, a child's pair of eyeglasses, worthless treasury notes in a cracked leather purse. She could not know who the blond wraith was, blood and not-blood, half-blood—a cousin, dying on bloodless ground—because she could not know her mother's life, not lived nor told nor unfolding in the strength of imagination nor in dream or vision. Her mother's life was locked away from her, eternal, as she was locked away from all others, as we each are locked away from one another in the pores of finite mind and skin, and though she was dreaming, or trancing, her eyes closed, the ocher irises darting and twitching beneath the pale film of her eyelids, her thin shoulders slumped, her head forward, palms open at her sides and the backs of her hands on either side touching the blackened circle of goods that had been their lives, now burnt and rank with weather, and though she did not know and would never know that she did so, for the first time since her mother's dying, the child wept.

*W*e did not go from the home of our mother, living midst her salves and crockery and placement, into each of us our own home to create it newly born from our inheritance. We didn't make a home of habits and objects. I didn't, and I should have, because I was the one who remembered, because I could see the pieced quilt like Grandma Billie's with the B turned backwards which had lain on Mama's and Papa's loft bed. Inside me, in my memory, was the picture of Uncle Neeley's cherry chifforobe and the clothes arranged as Mama arranged them inside it, and rows of canned cobbler juice in glass jars marked with pencil in hot wax as Mama marked them, as her mama had marked them and lined them up on cloth-covered shelves, which I did not think to note or question because in winter there was cobbler because there was always cobbler in winter because it always just was. I could see Grandma Billie's front room with the two tatted yellow doilies on the armchair and in the kitchen the curtains of embroidered flour sacks tacked up to close off the pantry, which Mama also bleached and sewed together and embroidered the same and hung them in front of the wood shelves off to the side of our cookstove because we did not have a pantry door. I remembered all of it, the placement and shape and smell built by Mama from her own mother's habits brought and married to Papa's, I remembered it but I did not re-create it, because I did not think it was important. I could have, I believe, if I had had Mama's things to live among.

No. That is not true. That is not true either. I have made up my mind to tell it, and I will not lie if I can help it.

I was set already, my nature and my will. Papa was too much in me, which I wanted, which I chose of my own doing, or I allowed. I'd seen Mama create our lives in our home in Kentucky, watched her set her jelly jars here, her crocheted doilies there, her violets in a half-moon in the yard, and I carried none of it with me, except in words. It was my job to teach them, Mama had given me the words to teach them, and I believed it was words only I was meant to pass on.

I took them with me, down into the low secret places, to sit on the flat stone where the creek widens and deepens. I gathered the children around me. I said, Your mama was married in a dress of white linen and there were seventy-three guests at her wedding, and on the night we all left Kentucky, when she had to leave behind the cherry chifforobe her brother Neeley made her for a wedding present, it was another aspect that helped crush her heart.

When your mama was a young girl, I told them, she suffered from nose-bleeds, and she had one so bad one time she lay in the bed three days bleeding and they all expected she'd die. (Hush, now. Hush.) They cut your mama's hair (yes, as they cut ours: the same: listen) and made her to lie with her head back and stuffed herbs and poultices in her nostrils and not one thing helped. Finally an old nigger woman, a house nigger who then belonged to some neighbors, told them to fashion a lead necklace in the shape of a hog's liver and hang it from a leather thong about her neck, and your mama's papa did so, and they hung it around her and she quit bleeding and lived and never had another nosebleed again.

Your mama's name was Demaris.

(Demaris, the crows calling, Mama's name singing south in the water.)

She had small hands and brown flyaway hair that fell to her waist when she brushed it.

(Like your hair, Jonaphrene, you got your dark hair from Mama.)

Her skin was the color of milk with the cream skimmed, and her name was Demaris.

(Demaris. Demariss. Demarissss.)

A girl of fourteen. She was a girl of fourteen when her papa died at Vicksburg, which seems a long time ago to your young minds but it is not long at all. On the night of the day her papa died in battle, your mama woke in the darkness to the sound of knocking. She slept with her sisters then and the others did not waken, but your mama was the middle child and her papa's own favorite, and what she heard was three slow knocks on the hard wooden footboard of the bed. In this way she knew her papa had been killed, though the family did not learn of it till some long time after.

(Sit _down,_ Jim Dee. Listen.)

Your mama's mama was Mary Whitsun Billie and she was a blind woman. She had lived forty years when she went blind from a fever at ten o'clock one autumn morning (of a sudden, I told them: do you see it? like the closure of Heaven) in the year of Our Lord Eighteen Hundred Sixty-seven, and she was born in London, England, where the King of all English-speaking people lived.

On the bank beside Bull Creek I taught them. On the great slab of rock by the water. I told them, Your mama dropped dead before she ever stepped foot in Eye Tee because she'd made up her mind she was not willing to live here. I used to say, Don't forget this: your mama died of a broken heart.

We didn't have Mama's things, but I had my own mind's memory— not Mama's memory, mine!—every minute I had lived and seen and known that could not be burned away. Not word memory, not picture memory, but hand memory, a way of doing, because I was ten when we left Kentucky. I was big enough. I gave none to my brothers, but that did not matter. I think it did not matter. But I gave none to Jonaphrene, gave her words only and not work, not a way to set the jelly jar on the shelf so, and in this way I robbed her. She could have shaped a home if I'd taught her. That is not what I taught her. It is one of the ways I failed her, my sister, because she was the one most stained by it and I let it happen. Out of my own will, I turned my face away.

Never did I tell about our belongings burnt in a black circle. Never did I mention Mama's tin box, or what was inside it. I lifted the box from the burnt place, kicked the dog back, picked up Papa's rifle. I carried the box pressed tight against my belly beyond Waddy Holler, past the Indian houses at Yonubby, deep into the long blue ridges of the Sans Bois. For two days I walked, to a place I knew I could find again because the ridge is naked. From a great distance you can see the tumbling rocks scattered on the south side of the hill. There, in a shallow cave, I laid it. I dug the earth with my hands, buried Mama's box with my blackened fingers, to wait for the time of returning. I marked it with a small chunk of sandstone standing up on its end. Like her grave in the mountains of Arkansas. Waiting, like Mama herself, for the time I would have everything prepared and ready to go.

In late September a white man named Tanner crossed the Red River near Tulip, Texas, and traveled north through Indian Territory leading a train of thirty mules. He skirted the active coal-mining settlements around McAlester and made his way through the dry, crackling valleys over the course of several days to the crossroads town of Cedar, where he dismounted at noon, tethered his sorrel gelding to the rail next to the wide-open doors of the livery stable, and tied the lead mule beside it so that the train of thirty mules was strung north along the street in a balky, messing, multihued line nearly to the new depot in the heart of the town. He entered the darkened door of the livery, where John Lodi was bent at the back end of a plowhorse, fitting a shoe. Tanner nodded to the livery owner pitching hay from a small stack into a manger near the archway and started across the dirt floor.

"Help you?" the owner called, but Tanner waved one gloved hand behind him as if to say, No, that's all right, I can get it myself. He paused a few feet away from where John Lodi hulked with his head down, the horse's left rear leg lifted, the hoof caught between his knees. It was some time before Lodi looked up, though the measuring ordinarily would take no more than a few seconds, but at last he raised his head as he eased the hoof to the floor. He nodded once at Tanner, without expression, and with the tongs carried the cooling horseshoe to the forge, heated it a moment and laid it on the anvil to mold it with a stroke or two. He turned to the horse and lifted the leg again and placed the shoe. The smell of burning hoof scorched the stable air. There was a faint sizzling sound, soon lost in the *cling* of the hammer, and the shoe was quickly set and nailed, the nails trimmed off, clenched, and rasped smooth, and John Lodi had already begun to loosen the clenches from the worn shoe on the horse's other rear hoof before Tanner spoke.

"I seen waste in my life," he said, "but this beats anything."

Lodi picked up a pair of nippers and pulled off the old shoe, dropped it on the floor so that it made a dull *pluck* in the dirt as it hit, withdrew a straight-edged bone-handled knife from his apron pocket, and began to trim the sole.

"There's pearls before swine," Tanner said, "and gold in a tin mine, but John Lodi doing farrier work is about as useless a proposition as I've seen in a while."

The livery owner, a small, spry man with a long mustache and a face like a Cooper's hawk, stepped from the hay pile and said, "Wha'cha need, mister?"

Tanner didn't look at him; his eyes followed the deft movement of Lodi's scarred hands as they scraped the outer edge of sole, trimmed the frog deep in the cleft, and in a twinkling, replacing the knife with the nippers, began to trim the hoof wall. The owner sauntered nearer. He leaned on the pitchfork tilted on its end, prongs bedded in the dirt, seeming casually interested in the present job, as the stranger was interested, though the owner doubtless had seen his employee shoe a hundred horses, oxen, mules. J. G. Dayberry's front-thrust face matched Tanner's in focus and direction, but his bright eyes beneath the overhanging brow were keen on the newcomer. He understood three things about him: one, that the man had traveled far, and had done so recently and in the company of considerable horseflesh (the stranger's scent alone could have told this fact); two, that he was a close acquaintance of John Lodi, had known him from his pre-Territorial past, and called on a familiarity John Lodi had no wish to renew (his words and Lodi's insistent ignoring of them, and him, told that fact); three, that the man was crooked as a dog's hind leg. This Dayberry knew without knowing precisely how he knew it, but he was more sure of this last fact than of the other two put together. J. G. Dayberry had a sixth sense as acute as a redbone's sense of smell, honed on nearly two decades' worth of experience as a liveryman in a territory peopled almost entirely by law-abiding Choctaws and outlaw white men—and women, if you counted Belle Starr, which Dayberry did, for reputation if not accuracy, for most folks knew (as Dayberry's sixth sense knew) that Belle Starr was not much of an outlaw but only a hellion who traded in borrowed horses from time to time. Dayberry knew, too, of the truth concerning honor among thieves, and who kept it, and who didn't unless it was to his own best advantage, which was hardly true honor, and he knew who had not an ounce of it in his veins, and this muttonchopped stranger here who stood in his creased hat and foul clothes watching John Lodi shoe an old plowhorse was one who bore not a driblet.

So the livery owner's interest was piqued, not least because in the ten months John Lodi had worked for him he had never witnessed a Lodi acquaintance, friend, or family member coming around. It had never occurred to Dayberry that the man's past would be of the shadier variety—though certainly it should have, he thought now, that being the condition of half the white men in this country—but John Lodi was just so plainly scrupulous, to a fault. To the point of peculiarity, really. For instance, if a customer came by to make payment on his stable fee or some kind of smithing or farrier work he'd had done and Dayberry didn't happen to be in the stable, Lodi would tell him to come back at such-and-such a time, when Dayberry would return. If the fellow tried to leave payment, Lodi would ignore him, repeating to come back such-and-such a time, and would go on with whatever he was doing. He simply would not lay a finger on a dollar that didn't belong to him. If the fellow insisted because he didn't fancy to make another trip, he had his money ready now—this happened with Angus Alford and Jim Mewborn, a few of the more stubborn ones, before word got around—Lodi would seem at first to sull up and balk, but then he'd turn his slate eyes on the fellow, and the fellow would begin crawfishing, saying, yes, I believe I'll just stop back by such-and-such a time. There were other evidences of Lodi's acute probity. He wouldn't shirk a minute's work while Dayberry was paying him, would eat standing up working the bellows or some other job, and half the time did not even take a dinner break at all. Dayberry had never given much thought to this trait in his employee, except to be a little disgusted with him for his stubbornness sometimes: Dayberry knew the man was trustworthy; John Lodi didn't have to work so hard, to the point of alienating customers, to prove it.

Lodi went on rasping the hoof wall; the stranger watched him with the close eye of an apprentice learning a trade, and the owner watched the stranger just as closely.

"Got a little something for you," Tanner said at last, low, as if continuing a conversation. He was still hunkered over at the waist, watching, not moving an eyelash or a muscle.

Lodi took from his apron a U-shaped iron level and placed it against the bottom of the hoof wall to check it, picked up the file and began to rasp again. The stranger was growing agitated, Dayberry could feel it, though the man still stood as before, unmoving, the rank smell of him swelling to overwhelm the odor coming from the far side of the unmucked stable where a half-dozen horses were stalled.

"Your brother's one told me to come by and leave it. Up to me, I'd leave it right in front of that fancy new barn. I got to go up yonder anyhow."

Lodi lowered the horse's hoof to the floor, turned, took a side step, lifted the hoof front-first, rested it upright on his aproned knee, and began to rasp smooth the rough edges around the old nail holes on the outer edge. The maneuver put the horse's behind between his face and that of the stranger, and Tanner straightened then and spat on the dirt floor.

"You finish up this mighty important business you're at, come on out front. I got to get on."

He turned and sauntered out into the bright noonlight, and Lodi lowered the hoof gently, turned and backed his rear to the horse's rear, crooked the leg backward at the joint again, and cradled the hoof sole-up between his knees to fit the new shoe.

Ten minutes and more passed, and Lodi made no move to lead the shod horse out to the corral in back of the livery, as he ordinarily would, but left the old dobbin haltered and messing where it stood while he turned to the forge to work up a new set of shoes. Dayberry, keenly curious now, returned to the manger and slowly, a quarter forkful at a time, filled it, sensing Lodi's every move, though he never turned his bright, alert eyes toward him. From where he stood near the open archway, Dayberry could see the stranger leaning on the rail beside his spent sorrel, rolling a cigarette. He could see the lead mule, a big blue-nosed sumpter with haunches like a bull, and behind it the head and forelegs of the next one, though he could not see or imagine the train of thirty lined up through the town, until Field Tatum came scuttling in—Dayberry saw him in the street, scooping a wide berth around the muttonchopped stranger—and spoke excitedly in his ear.

"Blocking entrance to my store!" Tatum whispered. "A damn forty-mule train lined up single file from here to the depot! Folks are gathering, but can't any of them get to my door!"

Dayberry had no doubt that it was not to enter the spanking new doors of Tatum's Mercantile that the people were gathered but to gawk at the string of mules, though he knew there was no point in trying to convince the mercantiler of that fact. He eyed John Lodi, who never looked up from the clanging he was doing at the anvil, and suddenly the little hawk-faced man's curiosity to know what that muletrader out yonder—if indeed he was that—had to do with his employee rose up so fiercely that abruptly he shooed Field Tatum out the door and, eyes bright, tone light, he called out in a singsong, "John, would you quit that a minute and come take this manger out back? I got a bunch of animals to feed this afternoon—I can't get to all of them!"

This in itself was entirely unusual, for Dayberry had hired the man strictly as blacksmith; he'd never called on him to do one thing about the livery that did not have to do with iron. He watched Lodi's thick forearm pause an instant on the upswing, then continue down, up again, and down, rapidly, drawing out the heated bar. Dayberry stabbed the fork in the pile and crossed the floor, coming easily, gently, as one approaches a fractious horse, and when he was near Lodi's elbow, he spoke again.

"I'm asking you," he said. "I need a hand."

Lodi finished turning back the heel calk on the new shoe before he set it to the side, placed the sledge neatly on the floor, leaning against the anvil brace, and moved, without a glance at Dayberry, to the filled manger. He hoisted the heavy cradle to his shoulder, though Dayberry's flat cart stood ready nearby, and started out the door to the temporary corral around back. The owner followed, not merely from curiosity now but because of the strange sense of protectiveness that had passed over him as Lodi bent his head and shoulder to lift the manger. A foreboding was on him, on Dayberry, a sense that trouble was coming and he'd got his fingers into it and messed with it when circumstances would have been better left alone. He followed and stood in the doorway and watched Lodi in the bright sunlight move to the inside of the hitching rail, close to the stable wall, with the manger hoisted on his shoulder between himself and the string of thirty mules. The stranger ducked beneath the rail, limber as a garter snake, and planted himself in front of him. Dayberry moved quickly, but when he reached the two the trouble was already seething, for he could hear the contempt in the one and the anger in the other, and he could not get between them in the crowded space behind the rail.

"What you do with it after that's your business," the stranger was saying. "Up to me, I'd give you a good horsewhipping, 'stead of buying you a new mule."

"Out of my way, Tanner." John Lodi's voice was low-keyed, quiet, tight as a coilspring. Dayberry couldn't see his face or the other behind him, the two men were so close to the same height, and in any case the triangular bulk of the manger blocked his view, but he heard the deadliness in Lodi's voice. "I got work to do."

"Work." The stranger's voice was greasy with contempt. "You call it that, maybe." He spat lightly and flicked the flattened end of his cigarette into the road, where it smoldered briefly and was soon snuffed in the thick dust. "Aim to muck out the stalls when you're through?"

"I said it once, I'm not saying it again."

"A man could be sitting as pretty as any man in this country, he wants to set around and shoe a damned old plowhorse for a nickel, I don't know. I'd have to say he's a fool or a coward, one."

"Go on."

"Or else crazy, might be. I don't know. Strange-eyed to me."

"Go on."

"Ain't nothing to go on about." Tanner spat again, not a deep spit but a little picking one, as if to get tobacco flakes off his tongue. "Fay and me already got our deal settled, he's the one so hot to have you in on it. I don't give a damn, myself. You're both weirder than Lucius." Rapid-fire staccato as he spat several times again. "I can't fathom either one of you, him or you neither. But that's not my business anyhow. My business is to complete my little proposition here, which I just done."

Still, the stranger did not move to allow Lodi to pass. Dayberry could see the townspeople, male and female, white and Indian, gathering on the far side of the street at the edge of the wagonyard. The line of mules was clearly visible to him now, as fine a looking conglomerate of young healthy muleflesh as he'd ever witnessed, strung from south to north along the dusty main street of the little town, the new and old town: old with the Choctaw council house and the whipping tree and the Butterfield Overland Stage stop which had marked Cedar on maps of Indian Territory for years; new with the recently laid train tracks, the weeks-old redbrick depot and the mercantile, and

Dayberry's own livery, which had stood its place for nearly two decades, a long time—an eon in the quick life of the Territory—but changing itself now, growing: the new blacksmith shop already framed out on the north side of the stable where the old corral had been. The town, like the Territory, was transforming. White faces outnumbered brown in the wagonyard across the street. Dayberry's sense in that moment was that, really, he'd already messed in it, he might as well go ahead and try to fix what he'd messed with, and as the other two continued to stand stock-still, the edge in the air rising, the livery owner called out to a young man he spied in the small crowd on the other side of the street. Even as he did so, the old curiosity welled in him: What business proposition? What kind of a deal? What did these many mules have to do with it, and what did that pearls-before-swine remark seem to mean? Dayberry was hankering for answers, but he tamped down his curiosity, swallowed it like cud to be chewed over later, as he called out across the street.

"C.H.! Come over here and give us a hand!"

The young man, a lanky sandy-haired fellow of about sixteen, stood in the crowd, gawking.

"Come on now!" Dayberry called. "There's two bits in it for you! I got nineteen head of stock to feed, and John here's got to get back to work!" Then he spied another man. "Mounce! Where the devil you been? That nag of yours's been finished an hour ago! Come get him or I'm going to charge you a stabling fee!" And Dayberry withdrew from behind the rail and circled out to the street, where he pushed his keen-eyed face in between the two men, saying, "John, just set it down around back anywhere; I got to figure out some type of a system a little better than what I got. Mister"—he turned his bright eyes and regal nose to the newcomer—"if you aim to board them mules you'll have to talk to Culpepper yonder at the wagonyard; I'm afraid I am completely full up." And he clapped a hand on Lodi's shoulder, swelling with the strain of hoisting the manger, said, "Tell you what, John, set her down right here. I don't aim to have my prime blacksmith toting hay if I can help it. Carston here can tote that manger around back. Here, son." He turned to the young man who was then crossing the road in a low rising of yellow dust. "Go in yonder and get that little cart of mine I got rigged and drag it out here. A man don't need to break his back toting hay to a handful of horses. Mounce!" he called back over his shoulder. "Come get that critter of yours out of my barn!"

And J. G. Dayberry, with his jovial voice and spry movements and intelligent face of sharp eye and deep brow, altered the moment. The stifling air shifted and changed, became of a different variety, the tension focused on the livery owner himself now as he ordered folks around in his quick, good-humored voice, until at last Tanner ducked back beneath the rail and sliced the dust a quick step or two to where the lead mule was tied. From the halter he loosened the rope that connected the rest of the train to the big blue-nosed sumpter, and leaving the mule where it stood and looping the rope around one gloved fist, he untethered his gelding, mounted, walked the weary sorrel out into the street, and turned its head north. He did not speak as he drew the ragged long-eared slant-eyed multihued train in a great turning loop across the wide street, but as he rode north out of town on the old Butterfield Stage road, he shouted back over his shoulder, "It ain't been fed in a couple of days, Son! You better give it some hay from that manger you're toting!"

When John Lodi finished work in the evening he came outside through the double doors of the livery, hatted, coatless, unarmed, an empty sorghum pail dangling loose in his fingers, and turned to his left without so much as a glance at the big black mule still tied to the hitching post. In the slanting shadows he walked north, as he did every evening, along the dusty road out of town.

The sun had lowered itself beyond the mountains by the time he neared Big Waddy Crossing, and the withdrawing light, gold-glinted, greenish, seemed to trick the eye and impart glory to the dust-dulled familiar, to the powdered ribbon of road, the iridescent pines and empty oak trees, the driblet of creek, low-muddied, glowing, crawling away east. Even before he rounded the long curve he could hear the commotion—men's voices, his brother's bright and brusque, above the others. He neither quickened nor slowed his step but continued on at the same steady plod which was his rhythm, not rapid nor staccato but iambic, monotonous, like the slow beat of a tom-tom, or the pulse of blood. He heard first, and then saw, as the trees opened, the back end of the mule train once again lined through the town, this near-town, this community of white settlers with its five slapshod buildings raised on one side of the road only, their backs against the hillside, the sawmill in the failing light silent, and a dozen men gathered at the

204 / Rilla Askew

head of the mule train in the low swirl of pale dust in front of his brother's store.

No one had lit a torch, none had brought forth from an unlit interior a kerosene lantern, so that, as dusk came on, the figures ahead of him blended with it, silhouettes blurring and fading to blue, and then dark blue, purple, indigo, navy, sparked here and there with the red ends of cigarettes and white fireflies dancing. In the black line of trees along the creekbank the whippoorwills were whillowing. The men in their nearness to one another could perhaps see and distinguish faces, but from the distance he knew only his brother. He could feel the abrupt gestures, the tilt of head and broad hat brim, the voice; he perceived without having to strain through the darkness, knew him in the bones of his being, as a lover knows the beloved in a crowd at a great distance, as one knows one's own reflection in a draped parlor mirror. Sound was muffled in the dusk, drowned in the relentless whillowing, but he knew without sound, as he knew without seeing, what his brother was doing.

On he came walking, one foot set rhythmically, unerringly, in front of the other.

From the time of his arrival in the Territory he had held to this rhythm, his mind empty of words, only marking the cadence, one foot in front of the other, eyes never looking at anything except the ground where his foot stepped. He saw almost nothing but that narrow space before him, as a man with a growth on his eyeball can see only where the growth has not spread. In this way he was able to live, this means he had discovered, not from will but from necessity, from his nature, which resisted words, resisted thought in language; which, in the twisting of grief, was unwilling to allow even that which is most human— the ability to plan and look back, project and regret—as if the meted portion had all been doled to his brother, to make his brother fired with language, paralyzed with future, locked in past, and these not genuine past or future but only that imagined in the volcanic language of Fayette's own mind. His brother's voice in the dusk was nearly a constant. A flip-lipped blur as of an auctioneer, a distant swarm of insects, and John Lodi walked on, hearing without listening, seeing without sight.

He neared the weary line of mules, strangely still in the growing darkness. Holding to the right, he could feel the road surface change beneath his boots as he traversed the clay portion of curve that would turn boggy in wet weather; he could smell the mulesweat and leather, the droppings on the cracked crust. The droning voice in the darkness heightened and changed. He knew that his brother was aware now of his coming, and he intended, without word or pause, to continue past the glut of men and mules and restive horses to the log house some twenty rods distant, mount the stone step and go in at the log door. He intended, but he could not. Without a glance or an acknowledgment, his brother drew him. The droning voice ceased the selling, paused and waited, and the air shifted. The men standing about in the road parted. John Lodi walked in among them, his eyes on the square of log house nearly black in the distance, walked forward in the tricking purple of first dark, in the night sound and murmur of men and tree frogs and the snuffled stirring of horses, until he was nearly on a parallel with the crowded storefront, where, scourged and lashed on by the despairing cry from the creekbank to *whip poorwill,* he looked up at his brother. His step faltered. His eyes were turned up to Fayette on the east end of the porch above the roadbed, one arm about a cedar post, the tight-gritted grin showing white in the twilight, yet he saw his brother not present on the porch but darting behind a weathered barn playing dare goal, pulling him with him into the hayloft, the pigeon's nest falling, straw raining, the nest in his own arms, upside down, cradled, pushed from the rafter by his brother, and in the nest of straw and bird mess and feathers when it was turned over a tremendous coil of black snake, and Fayette running, running with the pitchfork to kill the rat snake. There was the sound of a baby crying.

"Son," Fayette said from the porch darkness, "what the Sam Hill are you doing walking? I ain't expected to see you afoot."

A light was lit then, swelling yellow inside the store, so that Jessie was made visible, backlit within the open doorway, and behind her the white-collared blur of dark bodices which defined her older girls. Her infant was crying, and she stood in the doorway, bouncing and patting it on her shoulder. Because the light was behind her, he could not see her face. He saw his daughter Jonaphrene on the porch above the top step, with Thomas hoisted at her chest. The boy's legs dangled to the porch floor. His daughter's hair had grown out so that it nearly reached her shoulders; her limbs and torso had grown long and thin. Fayette's boys were perched on the porch rail, their hats tilted forward, cocked each at the same angle over one eye, and he saw his own son Jim Dee among them, indistinguishable from them but for the restless energy that made him unable to hold his swaggering pose; his son's leg jittered up and down, jiggling against the swimming dark below his booted feet.

"Where's that blame mule I just bought you?" his brother called down.

He willed himself forward; he walked on, but his step was mis-weighted; he couldn't seem to find his proper rhythm. His eyes were open, but the evening had grown dark. He moved through the shifting crowd of men until he was well past them and the house was nearing in the darkness, and he left the soft roadbed, climbed the rock-stubbled incline to the sandstone slab step, crossed the house porch.

Tanner sat at the table, hat off, his taffy-colored hair mashed flat. He was eating a hunk of pie, washing it down with slugs of coffee. "Evening," he said, his mouth full.

John went to the washstand, set his lunch pail on the floor beside the butter churn, dippered water into the basin, and rolled his sleeves back to the elbows.

"Fay get them mules sold off yet?" Tanner asked.

John hung the gourd dipper on its nail, reached for the lye soap. The water in the basin turned grayblack and murky as he scrubbed soot and forge dirt from his hands, and still the flour-sack tea towel blackened when he dried his hands on it. He had not yet removed his hat. He looked to the top of the stove; there was no tin plate of food there. The cookstove was nearly cold.

"They're not the best in the world to feed a fellow," Tanner said. "You'll about have to make do. What I done anyhow." He forked up another wedge of crust.

John saw the remains of apple pie in the pie-safe through the open tin door dotted like swiss eyelet with pin holes punched in the homely shape of a half-moon and stars. Punched by Jessie. He had watched her, one Sunday afternoon in the summer, on her hands and knees in the shade of the porch punching the sheet of new tin laid out flat on the porch floor. Kneeling on the porch floor punching tiny holes with a homemade pick, her mouth gritted, dotting the tin with a half-moon and stars.

"Coffee's cold, even," Tanner said. "He's had her over yonder all evening." He took a slurp of coffee, followed by a bite of pie. "Pie's good, though."

John stepped over and closed the pie-safe door. He bent to the nearly empty woodbox and gathered a few splits of kindling, opened the firebox and poked around in the ashes till a glow started, then put the kindling in on the halfhearted coals. He went out, leaving the front door open behind him and Tanner visible at the table near the oil lamp, mashing the back of his fork on the pie crumbs and lifting them to his deeply mustached mouth.

Standing in the dark beside the woodpile he saw his brother, trailed by the skirted covey of females, coming along the road from the store. In the distance he saw the boys driving the mule train up the mountain toward Fayette's barn. John gathered an armload of stovewood and turned to climb the rise and go back into the house. When Fayette and Jessie and the daughters came in, John had the stove started and was stirring flour and eggs into batter. The woman did not acknowledge him but gave the infant to her oldest girl and immediately went to the washstand and lifted her apron from the nail and tied it on. She took the wooden spoon from her brother-in-law and stirred the batter, turned and spat on the stove once to see if it was hot.

"Sell them all?" Tanner said from his place at the table.

"Not hardly," Fayette answered.

"Not hardly," the boy Thomas said.

Fayette put his hat on a wall peg, sat down in a near chair to take his boots off. The daughters in a fluid motion moved each to a practiced task: one to grease the griddle, one to slice the bacon brought in with them from the well box; one held the baby on her shoulder as she set the table, while another went out the door with the empty bucket. Jonaphrene took the paring knife when Jessie held it out to her and sat at the table to peel potatoes. The smell of heating bacon grease slowly salted the air.

Fayette grunted, pulling a boot off with both hands, one each gripped around the heel and toe. He set the boot on the floor. "How many days we got to get word around, you reckon?"

"You reckon?" the boy Thomas said.

Silence a moment as Tanner eyed the little boy at the the end of the table, leaning across his sister's lap. "Not many," Tanner said finally. "None, maybe."

"None baby," Thomas said, looking up at Tanner. The boy's head cleared the top of the table. He was big for a three-year-old, a blond, broadfaced toddler with a blandness in his features like a newborn, his forehead high and smooth, his eyes pale blue, wide open, almost devoid of expression, as if he saw everything around him new in each moment and had no experience to weigh it or judge its meaning. Tanner shook his head. The boy spooked him.

"How many you get rid of?" he asked Fayette slowly, never taking his eyes off the little boy's pale blue ones.

"Five's all." Fayette grunted, tugging at the other boot.

"Five, Saul," the boy said immediately, almost before the words were finished and in just the same tone and inflection, but with that minute split in the placement of vowel and consonant, the slightest increase in the sibilance of *s,* so that the meaning seemed changed, and Tanner, growing ever more uncomfortable, shoved the empty plate across the table and leaned back in his chair to tug his tobacco pouch loose from the waist of his breeches. Glancing at John Lodi, motionless, still hatted, beside the front door, Tanner took papers from his shirt pocket and began to roll a cigarette. John stepped to the side when the middle daughter came in with the water bucket and carried it, her shoulders sloped with the weight, across the room to the washstand, but he did not make a move to come on into the room himself and sit down.

"I figure we can sell a dozen or so Monday," Fayette went on, "provided that idiot Moss'll do like he says."

"Do like he says," the boy said.

"Monday? That's day after tomorrow. I ain't hanging around till day after tomorrow, pardon me, I'm sure not."

"Sure not."

". . . said you'd have a bunch of buyers ready. You better get them here tomorrow, you aim to sell 'em, and you better aim to sell more than a dozen if you intend me in on this type of a deal."

"Type-a deal."

"Tomorrow's Sunday," Fayette said. "Folks don't buy on Sunday. You the one come lollygagging in here on a Saturday—"

"Saturday's the day folks come to town buying. They ain't bought on a Saturday, they ain't going to do it on a Monday!"

"On a Monday, yeah," the boy said.

"Goddamnit, get that kid out of here!" Tanner exploded. "I'm going to wring his weird little fool neck!"

"Fool neck."

The room was silent for a moment but for the hiss of flapjacks just poured on the griddle. Slowly, quietly, but with great menace in his voice, Fayette said, "Jess, take the girls and go upstairs. I'll be there directly."

"Dreckly," Thomas said, never taking his unblinking eyes off Tanner.

Jessie opened her mouth but said nothing. She set the hot griddle to the cool side of the stove, the flapjacks still smoking, bubbles popping; she looked once at her daughter Mildred and stepped across the room to the table, where she took the boy by the hand. "Leave it," she said to Jonaphrene, and without a word the girl left the milky potatoes to rust on the tabletop, the peelings curled in a pile beside them, and followed Jessie's skirt and her brother's toddling legs to the far side of the room, where the hems of the girl cousins' dresses were already disappearing up the stairs.

Tanner said, "Well." He pulled a wooden match from his shirt pocket, struck it on the tabletop. He spoke from the side of mouth, around the cigarette. "I can't talk business with some fool kid mocking my every word."

John made an aborted move, quickly strangled, seeming to half come at Tanner, half turn to go out the door, and then he stood motionless again.

"We got to get some things straight around here," Fayette said. The menace drained from his voice, slowly. "First place, that's John's boy, and he ain't mocking you. He can't help that, and I'll thank you to keep your trap shut about it, or about anybody else in my family. You ain't doing business with my family, you're doing it with me, and maybe John here if we can persuade him, which you taking in after his boy ain't going to help. Second place, there's no call to start in on such stuff before we even eat supper." The threat was entirely gone from Fayette's voice now, or covered over, ladled with the familiar cajoling tone. "These kids are hungry. *I'm* hungry. I don't like to talk business on a empty stomach." He surveyed the room from his chair in the corner, his gaze coming to rest finally on his brother beside the door. He was sober, completely, Fayette was, and he seemed ready to say or ask something, his brilliant blue eyes questioning, but John's eyes held steadily to a section of rag carpet about three feet in front of him. Fayette at last returned his scrutiny to Tanner.

"All right," he said. "We got started, let's finish her up. Say what's on your mind."

The man at the table drew hard on the cigarette pinched between his thumb and forefinger, said, "All I mean to say, you aim me to be the one risks his neck bringing a string of animals through the Territory, you better have some buyers waiting at the end of it or we got no deal."

"You'll get your buyers," Fayette said.

"That's what I know." Tanner dropped the cigarette to the floor beneath the table, ground it with his boot. "Question is, when. Might leave the both of us wishing different if a U.S. marshal happens along about day after tomorrow wanting to know where you come by such a pretty mess of mules for sale marked by that peculiar-looking brand."

"Ain't no U.S. marshal going to happen along day after tomorrow, or no time."

"How do you know that?"

"I know it, that's all. Listen here, you keep to your end of it, I'll keep to mine. I said I'd take care of the selling, I'll take care of it. Selling's my middle name, and you know it. I just need a little time. Not every Tom around here's got sixty or a hunnerd dollars to plunk down on a good mule. We got to get the word around."

"You're supposed to get the damn word around before I got my neck on the line holding 'em."

"You get a little more specific about when you'll be pleased to show up, I might do so, yessir, I just might."

"Hell, I can't get any more specific. What you want me to do, send up smoke signals? Took me a damn week just to find a opportunity to wade those animals across the river. Thirty mules is not exactly invisible."

"Well."

"Well." Tanner began spitting the little front-of-tongue sputters that were his habit when irritated. "All I know is, it's a good way for the law to get wind of what become of thirty missing army mules."

"Law ain't going to get wind of it."

"I don't aim to be here when that happens."

"I said the law ain't going to get wind of it."

"How do you know that?"

"*Ain't* no law here—hadn't you figured that out?"

Tanner laughed. "You tell that to the sixty men Parker's done hanged."

"All right now, hush up and listen. Sol Clayton's the deputy for this district. He ain't going to bother us, all right? Now, that's all I'm going to say about it. You can't be comfortable with that, why'n't you run on up to Eufaula or somewheres, come back when you got your mind a little more at ease. I'll give you your cut then."

"Oh, *hell* yes. I'm sure about ready to do that."

"All right then. Bide your time and leave me take care of my end of it. Now, what I asked, how long you reckon before them mules are missed from off that trail drive? We'll just calculate from there."

"Don't you hear nothing? I said it took me a week to cross the Red; they been missed a helluva long time before that. On top of that, you got me stringing the whole mess of them right up before God and the whole damn town this afternoon—"

"Whoa, now, I didn't tell you to take them mules into Cedar—"

"Said for me to leave that coal-colored one for your brother, how else am I going to do it—"

"Coulda left the rest of 'em hid someplace—"

"Oh, yeah, twenty-nine mules is *easy* to tie up and hide. Come back and find every damn one of 'em stole and all the risk I took gone for nothing, you and your damn charcoal-black mule."

That black mule was an old bone of contention between the two men. It had been Fayette's specific request on the July afternoon they'd first hatched up their plan together; it accounted, in fact, through no fault of its own, for the partners' first venture in stolen horses turning out to be stolen mules instead. Fayette had insisted on that big black sumpter. "Wherever you find one," he'd told Tanner, "I don't give a damn how long it takes. Big and charcoal black, them's my two requirements. Don't bother to come traipsing over the border without one," he'd said, and Tanner had bellyached and griped and finally agreed, and when at last he'd located the animal, all the rest of the twenty-nine had been there alongside it, and so he'd just taken them as well. Now, however, he felt he had some justification for resentment—and blame if things didn't turn out right—because mules in general had not been their original deal.

"If it was horses and not a mess of ornery mules I was dealing with, we'd be sitting a whole lot prettier, I can tell you that. Wouldn't be having to beg for buyers, hang around and wait a week."

"I didn't ask you for no thirty mules," Fayette said. "I asked you for one, damn it, you were on your own what you stole after that. And I blame sure didn't tell you to string the whole bunch of 'em through Cedar—"

The two went on for some time, carping at each other like an old married couple, and neither noticed John moving until the door opened and shut quickly and they looked up both at once to find he'd gone out. As one, the two men scrambled to their feet and followed to the porch, where John stood on the east end looking out over the valley at the three-quarter moon rising, low-slung, side-tilted, on the horizon. Fayette came in his stocking feet to the porch rail, said, "Son, just listen. All right? Hear me out, would you grant me that?"

John did not answer but neither did he make a move to turn and step down off the porch and leave, and so Fayette took the stillness for acquiescence.

"All right then," he said. "Now. I ain't asked you about that mule, and I'm not going to. That's your lookout. Whatever you done with it's your own business. I give it to you, you can turn around and sell it, give it away, shoot it in the head like you done the other one, I don't care." None who knew Lafayette Lodi would believe he'd give anything freehanded, unconditionally—even the youngest in the household knew he gave with the left hand only to take back with the right—but Fayette himself believed it in that moment, and the jovial tone in his voice rose as his head swelled with his own largesse. "I bought it and Tanner brought it," he said, as if it were a gift from the two of them. As if John had not heard their carping. "That ought to even us up square on the mule business. All right?"

He looked east along the moonlit road, empty, and then west, where he thought he saw figures approaching in the distance.

"Now," he said, the urgency coming on him, "we got a little something else to parley with you about. No, now, listen, listen," he said as John stirred, seeming ready to move to the slab step. "Listen. I am not asking you to do a thing in the world that's illegal. Hear me? I'm not. What I'm thinking, I'm thinking about getting into manufacturing. Right? I'm not talking about that howdah—that's a good weapon, that's a fine weapon, there's need for just such a weapon right here in this country. Now! Now!" He held a hand up, spoke faster as John grew increasingly restive, though it was not any particular movement his brother made, but a shifting in the shoulders, a tension Fayette felt twisting as in his own body. "John, listen, they's a thousand patents have run out years ago—Smith and Wesson, Colt double-action, I don't know what all. We're not talking about infringing no more patents. Hear?"

He felt the tension in his brother rise to a peak and hold still. Tanner shifted weight on the dark porch behind them. Boot leather creaked. Fayette heard cigarette papers sifting one against the other, a faint whisper back by the door.

"I don't aim to do that," Fayette said. "We had our little go-round with that, didn't turn out too pretty." He eyed the figures approaching from the west, three of them, coming in the moonlight but still too distant for Fayette to recognize. Absentmindedly, entirely heedless of what his words meant or the cost his brother had paid for their previous venture, he went on. "Lawsuits is one thing. I don't give a damn about lawsuits, it's them blame death threats I'm not too partial to. We're going to do it different this time." He turned to his brother, clearly visible beneath the porch eaves but for his hat-shaded eyes, for the moon was still low. Fayette said, "We can't make no real money with you building one measly gun at a time for a fellow. We got to get into manufacturing like Remington, Smith and Wesson and them. I been studying on it, I know just how we'll go about it. We got to get a little capital ahead, that's all, start slow."

He could feel his brother listening. Still, he knew him so little— though he felt him keenly and genuinely—that he misinterpreted all that he felt. In Fayette's mind, his brother's rapt listening was tied to interest in the possibilities as Fayette himself saw them, inextricable from the garnering of money and prestige in men's eyes. Never could he dream that the listening was in his brother's hands as he stood in the moonlight, the memory in his hands working intricacies—not the rough broad-stroked work of shaping horseshoes and pounding wheel-rims, but hands with precise strength forging the mechanisms of weapon, the many chambers of revolver balanced and sleek to spin freely, line up perfectly; powerful fingers honing smooth the brass plate of the trigger; deft wrists turning, rifling the barrel; and the beauty of the piece when the creation was finished, held and balanced in the hands for no more than a few moments before it must go off to live where it would in the world, the hands turning then to another bar of iron, a new piece of hardwood. Fayette had no means to comprehend the past now rising in the one who would not look back, coursing through the living joints and fingers so that they clenched and unclenched in the blue darkness at his brother's sides.

"Capital's the key, Son," Fayette said. "Me and Tanner's got a little proposition going to take care of that end. You don't need to think a thing about that."

John continued silent, unmoving. Tanner came forward then, leaned against a porch post, one boot crossed over the other at the ankle, arms folded, cigarette dangling, unlit, from his mouth.

"There's three things a man needs in this country, John, am I right?" Tanner said. "Four if you count women, but we ain't elected to go into that business. Not yet we haven't anyway. So not counting women, it's three things men need: guns, whiskey, and horses. Am I right?" His voice in the bluelit shade of the overhang was almost musing, philosophical, and he looked up into the blackness of the eaves, oblivious to the growing menace in Fayette's glare. "Now, some would say otherwise. Some would say a man's got to have a little excitement thrown in, and they may have their point for the likes of *them,* I suppose. That's the type would be given to wanting to rob a bank, you know, or a payroll train, something like that. There's those say that's a good way to go, they'd say it's easier to hide a saddlebag than a herd of horses, and certainly they got their point. But banks are a dangerous business, John." He spoke like a teacher. "There's so much gunplay involved, which some are partial to, I know that, but I never have been. Let me just get in, get out, do my business when folks are sleeping." He struck a match to the cedar post, cupped his hands. His mustached and muttonchopped features jumped briefly in the flare. "My opinion is," he said, speaking tightly as he puffed rapidly, several quick inhalations to ignite the tobacco, "the three of us make a good team. We were good in Kentucky, we're going to be better in this country. Quit laying all our eggs in one basket, use what different talents we got. Three things a man needs, and we got every one of them covered. Fayette's got the whiskey business covered, I just leave that to him, he knows all about that."

Fayette said, "Tanner. Shut up."

But the man had warmed too keenly to his subject. "I'll handle the horses. That just leaves you to make up your mind: are you with us or against us?" Tanner flicked the spent match into the darkness, turned to face out toward the valley, with his forearms propped on the porch rail. "Everybody's got their own talent, John. Sometimes they don't even know about it till the right opportunity shows up. Now, you take me, I been an entrepreneur in many areas, you know that, but I have to say I found my calling in horse trading. Or mule trading, I don't care. Whatever's available. It's just a knack. I guess you'd call it that. I always was a good hand with stock, but I don't believe I ever would've guessed my real talent if I'd never left Kentucky. Opportunity's like that." He chuckled. "Y'all should have seen me slip in that line and cut them mules out, and never a bawl or a whimper." He went on chuckling deeply, almost silently, in his throat as he brought the cigarette to his mouth; once again his features seemed to jump in the brief ruddy illumination as he drew on it, long and deep.

"Tanner," Fayette said. "Shut the hell up. I mean it. This don't concern you."

Tanner rolled his eyes, pursed his lips beneath the drooping hair, shrugged his shoulders as if to say, Your business, and grew quiet, looking out over the valley. The three figures had neared enough that Fayette recognized his sons and nephew now, coming along the road, but the recognition did not ease his urgency; rather the imperative increased, not because of who approached but simply out of their proximity, the fact they would soon climb the stone step and enter the blue darkness beneath the overhang and, in coming, shift the timbre, the air. Fayette felt he must get an agreement out of his brother before the change came; he felt vulnerable in his stocking feet, and he spoke rapidly, without pause for breath or thought.

"Forget that business, Son, that don't have nothing to do with you. He's just blowing off. Now listen, listen a minute. What I want, all I'm asking, is just help us at the outset, let us get started, half the profit's yours—or no, I mean a third of it," he said, as Tanner abruptly turned to stare at him. "What I mean, your equal share. We got to make models, you know, show 'em around, you're the one can do that. We got to hire on some fellows to work for us, you're the one can teach 'em what they need to know. I can't do that neither. You got complete free rein too—what I mean, whichever kind of pistol you want to make, rifle, whatever you like, it's just up to you. Once we get going, you can do what you want, quit us or keep on, it don't matter, the profit's yours. I don't believe you can ask for any fairer deal than that. I'll get the capital, I'll get the materials, whatever you need, just say the word, we're going to get it—blackpowder, silver, ivory, you name it, you just tell me what you want. I'm going to build us a building, see, just as quick as I get that new house built, big long building right up there behind the sawmill. This little community's going to be famous, you know it? And they ain't a thing illegal about it; I'm through with all that."

He was entirely oblivious to the lie. Though he had, less than a month previously, caused to be buried in the straw-strewn dirt floor of the old barn a tremendous oak vat from which golden and extremely potent corn liquor could be withdrawn by a vinegar pump hidden behind a ruined horse collar on the east wall; and though introducing ardent liquors into the Indian Territory was a crime found by federal law to be nearly as heinous as horse stealing, punishable by stiff fines and imprisonment; and though there were close to two dozen stolen U.S. government mules at that very moment stabled in his new stone barn on the crest of the ridge, Fayette believed he told the truth. His intention was legitimate concerning the manufacture of weapons; he had no mind to re-create the kind of situation that had caused them to flee Kentucky. Bootlegging and horse stealing were merely means to an end, and so they could, to Fayette's mind, be dismissed.

"What say, Son?" he said. His toes curled against the porch floor as he watched his brother's face. He sensed the wavering, felt him almost persuaded, and Fayette's heart lifted—but once again he mis-interpreted what he perceived; he believed it was his own assurances of legitimacy and the promise of profit that made John waver. If he'd understood that it was the work itself that tempted—the urge in the very muscles to return to what they knew best, the hands from ado-lescence craving the feel of file and chisel, iron and wood—Fayette might have said something that would have pushed his brother into a promise to do that which he'd sworn nearly two years past he would never put his hand to again. John's word, once given, would not easily have been withdrawn, and the old inextricable binding, Fayette's dom-inance and the proper balance, as Fayette saw it, could have been renewed far more easily than even Fayette himself could imagine—if only he'd understood what he sensed. Instead, feeling victory in his grasp and believing it his, he said, "Patents is a nuisance, but we'll act legitimate fair and square."

He did not see his brother stiffen, grow yet more coldly breathless and still.

"No more borrying somebody else's design unless we know a hun-dred percent sure it's run out. You can't make no money that way anyhow, fending off lawsuits and what-have-you, but I'll tell you something—manufacturing is the way to go. I have sure figured that out. You were making, what, seven, eight guns a month there at the last? That's nothing, that's not a drop in the bucket compared to what we can do. We're going to be rich, Son, and we don't need no how-dahs to do it." His voice grew wistful with regret. "Too bad, though, if you think about it. That is a fine weapon." He shook his head. "There's some power in that gun, now. You can blow the top off a bear's skull with one of them barrels and have three left for target practice. That one I got off that ni—" He stopped abruptly, slapped an imaginary mosquito on the back of his neck. "Lord," he said. "You reckon it's ever going to frost, kill a few of these critters?"

He paused a moment, gazing out into the moonlit yard, his mind on the big four-barreled pistol he'd bought off Mitchelltree on the ridge and now kept hidden from his brother's sight beneath the horsehair mattress in the crowded room upstairs. The fact that he could not brag and show it about to the townsmen of Big Waddy galled him. "Should've kept them." Without even a glance at Tanner, whom he'd long suspected of selling that very howdah to Mitchelltree—of taking, in fact, more than a dozen of the weapons when he lit out for Texas, and selling them, and sharing not a penny of the profit—Fayette turned to his brother. John's face was shadowed beneath the porch overhang, for the moon had now risen above the roof rim. "We should've kept one or two of them. I shouldn't never have listened to you on that business. We could have hid them—just for our own pleasure, I'm talking about. I don't mean to sell."

The fading smolder of an old resentment licked up, breathed upon by memory; the image quickened in his mind of the charcoal mule, dead on the ridge, its forehead exploded by the .54-caliber shell. "You got some mighty strange notions, Son," Fayette said, his voice balanced between ire and wonder. "Mighty strange." Then, as if to extinguish the image with heartiness and false camaraderie, and unwilling to perceive the icy stillness in his brother beside him, Fayette slapped his hands together, saying, "Well, well. Enough about all that now—we got other things to look upon." He spied the three boys climbing the incline of the rocky yard. "Caleb!" he shouted, trying to force into his voice the familiar joviality. "You get them mules took care of good like I said?"

"Yes, sir," the tallest boy answered. The three trooped up the steps, nearly identical in their swagger, and spread out to take their young men's positions about the porch, moving confidently, the eldest with an inflated sense of his own manliness, his brother Fowler in perfect imitation of that self-importance, and their young cousin in wiry, awkward imitation of each. Caleb crossed the porch, his boots making an exaggerated sound on the rough wood, and squatted on his haunches beside the door. He tipped his hat to the back of his head. His brother eyed him briefly and then moved to the porch rail, climbed up to perch there casually as on a yard fence, and Jim Dee, for an instant torn between them, at last took his own position against a cedar post, arms folded in complete and unconscious imitation of the mutton-chopped stranger leaning against the post by the porch steps.

"Water 'em good?" Fayette asked, and the eldest nodded, and the younger two nodded. "Put out some shorts like I said? I ain't going to stingy 'em on feed, never mind if they are going to belong to somebody else come Monday. I mean to see sleek livestock, I want to see me some fine muleflesh fat as fall taters when I put 'em up for sale—" He suddenly remembered the big black mule—not the dead one but the new one he'd gone to such worry and expense, as he just then recollected, to present to his brother. Despite his earlier intentions, Fayette turned impulsively in John's direction, said, "I hope you fed him up good, that black mule I bought you, before you come off—"

Abruptly he halted, confused. He could not comprehend why he suddenly felt as if he'd stepped out onto the porch naked. John's face was turned away, looking east, hidden in shadow. Fayette felt it then, an absolute coldness there, a blackness beyond telling. He floundered a moment, felt he needed to get back in the house and put his boots on, though it was late, way past time for supper, time for sleep really, and he remembered the unfed females upstairs and his own unfed belly and the bacon growing limp in its own grease on the back of the stove. He had to get back into the log house, sit at the table, see his wife at the stove cooking, his daughters in an impatient row beside the washstand, his sons with their sleeves rolled back looking up at him over their saucers of coffee. He had to put his boots back on.

"Lord have mercy!" he cried. "Don't tell me I'm about to plumb forget to feed myself!"

Only his brother heard the fear in the forced heartiness of the explosion.

"Tanner, I told you I don't like to talk business on an empty stomach. Man alive, we got to feed these boys. Got to feed ourselves. Son—"

It was to his son Caleb he spoke, not his brother, and he saw no confusion or inconsistency in it, nor did any of them, even the two he called by the same appellation; Caleb knew his father meant him. In fact, there was only one among those on the porch who noted—was burningly aware at every moment—that Fayette called both his eldest offspring and his brother Son, and that one was Fowler, the younger, who longed to be called by that name and never in his life had been.

"Get up from yonder," Fayette said, "and y'all go on in the house."

Slowly Caleb stood, and as he did so the other two slid from their positions.

"Tell your ma to get them flapjacks cooking," Fayette continued, the heartiness gone from his voice now, the sound only gruff, domineering. "Folks are famished. We're going to starve to death if she don't put some food on the table. Tell her to get a move on. We got one or two things to clear up here, and then we'll be on in." He felt his woolen socks rooted to the porch floor, feared he could not move them upon his will to do so. Feared what would happen if he tried. "Git now!" he said, though the boys were already moving. "Tell her to hurry up with that grub!" Fayette felt the last remnants of his will surviving only in his ability to give orders, and he continued mouthing at the boys until they'd gone in the house and shut the door behind them. He could hear voices inside, the baby crying, his wife hollering down from upstairs, but the sound was too far distant. There was that coldness, that blackness swirling about him, and he was confused, terrified by his own inability to move. He heard a new sound, below him in the yard, a labored panting, and looking down, he saw his brother's fat, aged beagle trotting heavily around from behind the house. Something in that sight inched his rising terror higher; his throat was dry, he could not make spit, could hardly speak, and he feared even his voice would be stopped in a moment so that he'd have nothing of self left, nothing left of will.

"Son!" he croaked. "C'mon back out here!"

In a few seconds the porch was sliced open with a square of yellow lamplight, widening, widening, and Fowler poked his head around the log door. He did not come out but stood craning his neck around the doorway, looking up at his father.

"Bring me that jug yonder behind the safe," Fayette said.

The girl was out there somewhere in the darkness. Her presence was as distinct as the sound of the dog wheezing in the yard, though John Lodi could not see her, did not know where she was hidden; he knew she would not come in until the porch was cleared. He looked at the moonlit sideyard, east along the strip of road to the low, rocky ford where the trickling remains of creek crossed it, twisting away into shadows. The trees were bare, not with the coming winter but with the drought that had stripped them before August was well ended, and their limbs cast a grotesque web over the exposed stones of the creek-bed, the sunken trickle glinting in moonlight. He heard the log door open again behind him, the pock of the boy's boots on the porch floor, the unstoppering of the jug close by, nearly at his elbow, and then his brother's throat moving, a choked, chugging gurgle. In his nostrils the smell of liquor burned, and above it the sweet, pungent drift of to-bacco, the rank odor of old dog, the dust-dry crumble of oak leaves. His senses were grown suddenly acute, so that he tasted even his own spit. He heard lungs breathing, the swallowed phlegm in his brother's throat; felt the crack and pop of cartilage in his own knuckles as his hands curled and uncurled at his sides. It was as if he'd awakened from a long sleep—not as one wakes luxuriously at morning, drawn unwilling from the familiar country to that other landscape beyond dream, but as one jerks awake in the night, snapped alert by the sound of something crashing, glass breaking on the far side of the room in the dark. His heart beat in staccato rhythm. In the yard below him he saw the marked hairs, coarse and distinct, on the dog's back. His tongue was bitter with the taste of iron, metallic and foul, from ingested ore, smoke, solder; from not having eaten for many hours. Always, in and around the other sensations, was the sound of the ceaseless whil-lowing: *whi-ip poorwill whi-ip poorwill whi-ip poorwill whi-ip poorwill whi-ip poorwill whi-ip poorwill*

He could feel her out there somewhere in the darkness: hidden behind a tree's silhouette; crouched in the black shade of the rain barrel. Without turning his head from the clear wash of moonlight, he said, "I have sworn once to make no more guns. I'll make no more." He turned, moved past his brother, with the jug upturned on his shoulder, past the boy with scowling face in porch shadow, past the man with arms folded beside him, and stepped down off the sandstone slab of step.

*T*he dry ground was lit blue in the moonlight, so bright you did not need a lantern. I came down the path slowly, stopped beside the smokehouse when I first heard their voices. I would not go forward into their air and breathing. My thought then was only to wait awhile, until they had all gone to bed. I could see them on the porch, the three man-shapes outlined in the darkness, and the slimmer forms of Fayette's boys slouching, though they didn't matter, and Jim Dee, my brother, whom I could feel. Papa was beside Fayette, and back a ways beneath the porch overhang stood the stranger, but I thought that he, too, did not matter. I recognized him from before, back home in Kentucky, when he would come slinking around our barn where Papa worked the bellows, the fire hot in the forge, and the barn bitter with the smell of iron and solder. Slinking like a skink, Mama said, because she did not like him. I could see him outlined against the lighter space in the yard beyond the porch ledge, his arms folded and his drooping mustache covering his skink mouth.

It was Fayette I knew first, from where I stood beside the smokehouse—my uncle trying to throw his web around Papa, slinging it out from his gut as a spider spews silken threads from its belly. I could feel Papa his prey, trapped, kicked softly in a spinning circle, a cocoon of soft silk wrapped tight so that the life juice could be sucked from him. Papa's hands clenched and unclenched in the shadows behind the porch rail.

I forgot to hold Ringo, and then I wouldn't whistle softly to make him come back when he waddled away from me down into the yard. But it did not matter, because Papa knew I was there. So I came on, closer, moving slow in the shadow of the smokehouse, fast across the bluelit yard to the ribbed, narrow shade beside the well. I saw the boys stir, Caleb and Fowler rising to go in the house, and my brother in his caught way behind them. I told myself I would go back up along the path to our wagon waiting in the moonlight behind the shed barn, our wagonbed empty except for the cookstove, which I slept next to sometimes when I could not make myself go in the log house. But I knew I would not go up to the wagon, though I wanted to, I longed for its splintered, hard emptiness, bare in the moonlight, but I did not go there, because it was then that the mystery came on me, as I crouched beside the dug well. I had known that it would. I'd felt it coming, the way you feel season-change coming on a new wind.

The picture was dark at first, darker than the shadowed place beneath the porch roof, much darker than the yard, but I knew what it was: the gun Papa made, the big four-barreled pistol, sandwiched in a dark place, hidden. I saw the mule's forehead explode red. I could smell it, the taste of iron and powder, and I didn't know which one of them held this in his memory. It was not my memory, though I had witnessed it, yes, but I'd seen the back of Papa's elbow, his hand stretched forward with the gun at the height of my eyes; the image in the dark place was from someplace directly across, and higher, standing close. I let the pictures and the smell wash through me—that was the only way; you could not fight it—and then I understood it came from both of them. At once and together. I had entered the two of them at the same time, Fayette and Papa, because the remembering could not be separated, because they held it in union between them, as two parents hold equal between them the memory of a dead child.

The hair-rope hoop coils around and down, as it must, each season dropping looped upon self: the curve of hoop spiraling toward winter, cresting pale, coiling downward toward spring, the long green arc of summer, and each year, irrevocable, rising toward winter again. It was late fall—metal skies, dark brown tree limbs: November—three loops from the time of their coming, almost four from the night the Lodis left Kentucky, when the woman Thula Henry came again. She came this time not across the land, walking, but in a buckboard carriage driven by Jessie's son Fowler in yellow spats and a new bowler hat. It was Jessie who'd sent for her, as it had been Jessie who'd brought her to the log house the first winter, but for a different reason—and yet in its essence nearly the same. She meant the Choctaw woman to do what she herself could not, to heal a mystery she could not understand.

For three years Jessie had watched in silence, from a distance, as John Lodi's children grew wilder and stranger. She'd thought that when she and her family moved out of the log house and left John and his children to it, her mind would be shed of them. She'd thought that her new five-room home, framed out and finished with kilned lumber and real glass freighted from McAlester, which Fayette had hired built, grandly perched on the slope above the store, would remove thoughts of the unwanted and undisciplined children. But each day she watched from her front-room window or the steps of the store and saw the condition of the log house deteriorating, the yard unswept and growing up with brambles, trash lying about in the dirt, on the porches, and every morning her brother-in-law walking off to work at Cedar while the filth spread and the children grew more untamed. She watched the girl Martha take her sister and the younger boy down by the creekbank, where they would disappear for hours among the sycamores and peach willows, to emerge at dusk in a pitiful little procession climbing the rise to the log house. The older boy, Jim Dee, was sometimes with them, more often not, and he ran wild through the town, would bowl a grown white man off the wooden walk in front of the post office or follow her own sons when they went to Wister to the depot, running along behind the wagon until they stopped and allowed him to climb up. Jessie didn't know what the children ate or how they kept themselves. They did not attend the new subscription school and she believed they didn't wash often, though the few times John brought them to church meeting at the schoolhouse they were clean, the two boys in starched overalls and the girls in clean, plain gingham dresses with their hair braided and bowed, the boys' hair parted and slicked down. But something was very wrong at that house, the town knew it, Jessie knew, and at last, when the old beagle dragged a rotting opossum carcass into the yard and it lay stinking for two days before John found it and buried it in the field across the road, Jessie determined she would take matters in hand. She'd gone to the log house in the early morning before the children could scatter, had crossed the log porch with the strange sensation of entering her own past, and knocked at the door.

It had been the younger girl Jonaphrene who answered, and Jessie stared at her, wordless. The girl was starkly beautiful, as a colt is beautiful, but with an unnaturalness about her that made the woman exceedingly uncomfortable, because it was a long-boned and aquiline beauty, an adult beauty, not that of a nine-year-old child. The little girl stared at Jessie rudely—without even a word of greeting, because the children had no manners whatsoever—and failed to ask her in. Hemming and hawing, Jessie had finally stuttered out that it was high time for the children to go to school, that their uncle would pay the dollar subscription for each of them if their father could not manage (though she had already determined that she would save out the money and pay it herself), and it was then the girl Martha had come to the door. She'd stood behind her sister and lifted the door hanging loose on its leather hinges, scraped it open wider, silently staring, as rude and unmannered as her sister, and Jessie had stammered her message again. She could see through the open doorway that there was no furniture in the room beyond what her own family had left behind when they'd moved out: the rusted iron cookstove John had hauled down from the old barn, a busted ladderback and two wooden crates turned over to sit on, a flour keg, a pile of folded quilts on the floor by the back wall. She'd been stunned for a moment; it was one thing that had never occurred to her, though she'd known they were un-couth, but she'd never dreamed John had not brought another stick of furniture into the house. There was not even a table to eat at, though she could smell beans or peas cooking, saw a black Dutch oven steam-ing on the stove. She saw, too, that the house was dirty—not unsan-itary, not filthy, but cobwebbed and dusty, the floor covered in soot and dirt and wood leavings, what a woman must strive against every minute because of carrying in stovewood and toting out ashes, because of yard dirt and leaves tracked in with every coming and going—but clearly no one had striven here. The girl Martha stood staring up at her from behind the door. She was small, hardly taller than her sister, though she must have been almost fourteen, and tough and yellow as a corn kernel. She'd remained silent as Jessie spoke again of school, and then she'd answered politely, "Yes'm, I'll speak to Papa." Then, without a word of pardon, she'd lifted the log door and pushed it closed in Jessie's face.

The following Saturday afternoon—almost as if by design or pur-pose, Jessie thought later, for the Henrys did not often come in to Big Waddy, almost never traded at her husband's store—but the very next Saturday, the Indian woman had come into the store for flour and a tin of molasses. The idea had struck Jessie from nowhere, watching the woman ease sideways along the crowded aisles with her head tilted back, looking up at the tinned goods and plow points and bolts of cloth on the shelves. Jessie had come from behind the counter almost immediately; she gave no thought to what she was asking except to hurry up and finish with the business, for Fayette or one of the boys would be back soon, and she had negotiated quickly and efficiently, promising her five yards of quality cotton from one of the finer bolts behind the counter, and the woman had agreed. Jessie did not consider that she'd hired Thula Henry once again to heal sickness—the woman, in any case, would not take payment for that, or she hadn't three years earlier anyway—but Jessie thought she was making a simpler agree-ment; she believed she had hired her to come clean the log house.

When she sent Fowler to Yonubby to fetch Mrs. Henry, she'd made him promise to not tell anyone, meaning, as both he and she knew, to not tell his father. Jessie didn't question to herself why she did not want Fayette to know—there was so much she had to keep from her husband—but she told her son to bring the woman directly to the store, to keep hushed about it, and then he might take the buckboard on to Cedar if he wanted, and, as with so many secrets between them, the boy did just as she asked. He drove up in a cloud of khaki dust and buckboard clatter, drew the reins up sharply, and waited impatiently for the Indian woman to climb down. He was off with the team and buggy before the woman had hardly cleared the spokes, and Jessie called after him, "Mind what I said now!" She stood on the porch, her arms wrapped around herself, one eye on her youngest child toddling about the porch floor, as Thula Henry, wrapped in a red blanket and holding to her chest a leather satchel, slowly climbed the store steps. Jessie bent and grasped the toddler by the back of the collar as the little one wobbled toward the porch ledge. She said, "Come in, Miz Henry, let me just get my wrap."

The woman waited inside the door, seeming to look at everything and nothing, as Jessie carried her toddler to the back and placed her kicking and yelping in her eldest daughter's arms. "Watch the front," Jessie said. "I'll be back in a little bit." It was not necessary to tell Mildred—to tell any of her daughters at any time—to not speak of things to their father. Jessie took off her apron, folded it and laid it on the counter, reached for a thick knitted gray sweater lying on a shelf, and put it on. She made her way rapidly between the crowded rows of boxes and barrels, kegs, harrows, singletrees, stacks of buckets and tins, to where the woman stood in her wool dress and blanket, peering upward, expressionless, seeming oblivious—or, in any case, without opinion—regarding all that took place in front of her, and at the same time acutely alert. Jessie started out the door without speaking and was halfway across the porch before she remembered what she was supposed to be doing. Quickly she turned and entered the store again, where the woman still stood, apparently not having moved an eyelash, just inside the door.

"Millie!" Jessie called. "Bring me the mop and that big bucket. And one of them corn brooms hanging up over there." Surely they've got soap and water in that house, she thought, and then, on second thought: "Bring me a box of them soap flakes too!" she said, and then did not wait for her daughter to put down the little one and do as she'd directed but went on into the store and gathered the items herself. She handed the mop and box of soap to the woman and started out again with the broom in one hand and the bucket stuffed with clean rags in the other, and this time the woman followed behind her.

Jessie led the way across the sloping yard toward the log house. They left the store's little wedge of swept yard and moved east directly across the land. For some reason Jessie did not want to go along the road, and the Indian woman followed without protest, the two of them picking through the burst pods of milkweed and clutching cockleburs, their skirts filling with legions of beggar's-lice, their sticks of mop and broom pointing skyward, as they made their way slowly across the orange and umber November field.

Again Jessie experienced the peculiar sensation of entering her own past when she mounted the stone step. It was not pleasant: she had worked too hard to leave that bone-hard existence; she did not like to reenter it, and even as her shoe touched the wood of the porch, she hesitated. But there was that sense of duty in her—or this is how she thought of it—a nagging sense of Christian duty which she could not escape. And something else. Something about the girl Martha and her hard eyes and her hard little chest: the girl was coming into her time, Jessie knew it, she had raised too many daughters, and the child had no one but a father to guide her, which he would not nor could not, and in any case most of the time he was not even there. It was up to Jessie to do something, and this was more important, deeper and more urgent than the children's dirt and wildness, but she knew no other way to start than to begin by cleaning up the house—as if cleaning could wipe away the soiled years and lack of raising, she thought— but really, she knew no other way. She half hoped the children would be gone, half hoped they would be there, and knew not why she wanted either, but there was no answer when she rapped her reddened knuckles on the split-log door, and the relief swept her like a wind.

She entered the room that had been her home for the first terrible year and a half after they'd arrived in the Territory—the rough log room wherein she had scrimped and saved and struggled to put enough food on the table for her children, where she'd worked day and night, trying endlessly, futilely, to keep them and the crude, sap-glittered, mud-chinked, bark-littered house clean—and went straight to work sweeping almost as soon as she came in. She started at the cold, cinder-strewn hearth, moving the corn broom roughly over the sandstone, the scarred puncheon in front of it, because she did not want to look at the room—dark, as it had always been, and hollow now, empty, the unfinished ceiling arching away. The Choctaw woman came in behind her and stood in the center of the room, watching. Jessie could feel her there, not moving, not working, just watching, and at last she stopped, exasperated, and said, "Well, what are you looking at? What are you waiting for?"

The woman said, "Me think you hire me him for to clean 'im up."

Jessie nearly exploded in disgust. "Oh, for Pete's sake. Yes. Me hire you to clean him up. Talk English. Here!" And she thrust the broom at her.

It wasn't just that the woman's English was abominable—or seemed to be anyway, although Jessie had always had, even in that first year, the sense that Thula Henry could speak the King's English as well as any white person if she wanted to—and it wasn't just that she didn't care to be paying an Indian five yards of good cotton to stand around and stare at her in disapproval. It was . . . it was the taut strings twisting her spine into knots; the shudders running rivers beneath her skin; her teeth—the twelve that remained to her—gum-gritted and aching. It was . . . she didn't know what it was, but when the Indian woman laid her satchel aside, dropped the mop to the floor with a clatter that echoed in the bare, high-ceilinged room, and took the broom from her and began sweeping in just such a way as to nearly literally sweep her out the door, Jess Lodi was grateful.

She stood on the log porch a moment, a little confused, but relieved, as if a dreadful burden had been removed, and recognizing suddenly that she had done all she could do, she stepped down off the porch and picked her way back across the land, home.

The white woman was right about Thula Henry's ability to speak English. She could speak it precisely as well as she chose to—had learned not only to speak it but to read it and write it at the Wheelock Academy down by Broken Bow—but she preferred her father's brand of English, and she used that when she had to speak the distasteful language at all. Thula Henry was Choctaw, yes, for her mother was Choctaw, and she spoke Choctaw predominantly, lived with her mother's people near the Indian Church at Yonubby—but it was her father's English she spoke when she had to; it was from her father's people that she had received certain gifts of knowledge.

Her father had been a Creek man, a Muscogee man, who'd come down into the Choctaw Nation soon after the Removals and settled there, taking a Choctaw woman, Thula's mother, to wife. He had fathered Thula, whom he called Tooske, in the winter of 1837 and lived with them nine years, taking up Choctaw ways, farming—but each summer he'd returned north to his native grounds at Kialigee town for Green Corn ceremony. And each year, going, he stayed longer, coming back to Choctaw Nation later and later each autumn, until the year Thula was nine, when he did not return at all. For two years her mother waited, and in that time she did not hold the Big Indian Cry, would not take up mourning or receive another man. Then, the summer Thula was to become eleven, her mother put her on a fine horse, gave her a pistol and a leather satchel of food—this selfsame satchel she'd laid aside on a flour keg to take up Jessie's broom—and sent her to Creek Nation to bring back her father. She had not brought him back, for he was dead, shot on the sandy banks of Skunk Creek by a Cherokee man he was drinking with, and Thula did not grieve him, for she understood it was because he was supposed to be, in his language, *hilishaya,* or medicine man, that he had to die like that. Long before that time, he had taught her. It was from him she had learned the everyday forms of healing—not spirit healing, not the songs and powerful medicine, but how to use the slippery-elm bark for cleansing, the uses of blackroot and chiggerweed, how to smoke the sick person or make a sweat. But her father had told her early on, from the time she was little, that he was a bad man who did not do as he was supposed to do. He had never worked bad medicine, did not use the gift that way, but he'd let the white man's fire demon take him when he was a young man, and it had thiefed his soul; he had no defense against it, though he would become sober a good long time before Green Corn, had to be clean to take ceremony, to purify himself, to receive the black drink and dance—but always afterwards, the thirst would come on him bad again, and he would go down in the Deep Fork River bottoms alone, or with another one also caught by that demon, and so he betrayed the gift. It was because she understood this that Thula did not grieve her father, but she stayed four months with her father's people, and it was during those four months that she had listened to the drum, the singing, the *saka-saka* of the turtle shells strapped to the shell-shakers' legs as they danced in a circle around the sacred fire; only one summer did she drink *osofki,* dance the ribbon dance at Green Corn, take medicine—but she'd held the truth of it inside her spirit all her life.

From her mother she had one kind of mind and thought and being, for her mother's people had received the Christian faith early, had embraced it from the first teachings brought by white missionaries to Mississippi and carried it with them into the new Nation. There was something in Christianity that spoke to the understanding in her mother's people, and now they were Baptists, for it was the Baptists who'd sought out hardest and tended fiercest their souls to keep them from hellfire damnation, and Thula was Baptist, and she brought her children and grandchildren to the all-day camp meetings at Yonubby, and they were each baptized and took the Lord's Supper when it was offered, and it was through her mother's faith that Thula understood the Holy Trinity, how the Creator and the Son and the Spirit were one—but it was from her father, or, more truly, from her father's people, that she understood the Sacred Four. Thula Henry knew that the number Three left the sacred hoop broken; it was not whole in the ways formed by the Creator: the Four Directions, the four seasons, the completeness echoed in the four brush arbors built for Green Corn ceremony on the sacred stomp grounds. Thula Henry's Creek soul recognized the Fourth Part, the portion left out by white men and Christians in their search for the spirit—and yet this knowledge did not divide her. There was no conflict between stomp dance and baptism in her spirit, but only, as she understood it, the marriage of two spirits within her, and it was right in her eyes. She worked as she waited for the return of the girl and her brothers and sister, sweeping the leaves and ashes from the corners into an open circle in the center of the room, but she knew, if the white woman did not, that her purpose concerning the girl with yellow eyes was not to clean the log house.

They came at evening. Thula had built fire in the fireplace and put meat on to roast. She cooked the *tanfula,* the hominy she'd carried with her in her satchel, in the Dutch oven on the the iron hook above the open fire and put shuck bread in the hot ashes to bake. There was time for fasting and time to feed the body, and the time for fasting was not now. Almost she could feel the girl hesitate on the roadbed when she looked up at the chimney and saw the gray smoke. Almost she could feel her move forward slowly, and then her step quicken, believing it was some other one who had built fire in the house. And so they came. Thula heard the small feet running across the porch. The latch lifted, the heavy door was shoved inward, and the children, bounding in quickly, came to a tumbling halt, stumbling one into the other behind Matt, who stopped still in the middle of the floor.

For a very long time the girl and the woman looked at each other. There was recognition in their gaze—acknowledgment from the time of the clay cup healing, from the day of the death of the mules on the mountain, yes, but it was not that. Caught in the circle of leaves and ashes on the floor of the room warm with the smell of meat and bread roasting, the girl remembered what she had pushed away for nearly a quarter of her lifetime: the brown face coming down in the red darkness, *round and flat as a skillet—round, and flat, and brown*—the hands lifting away the tiny body with arms and legs like sticks, dangling. It was this Indian woman who'd been with them in the fever, who had stayed with them and nursed them when Papa was gone and the others shunned them; this woman who had given them medicine, smoked them and sung over them, so that they had lived—they had all but one lived. And so it was this woman who had witnessed her secret sin.

Every nerve and fiber and instinct in the girl's being told her to run. Turn and run out the door, run out into the prairies and hills and creek bottoms, never return to the log house till the taint of the woman was gone and her smell gone, and the sight of her eyes gone, if it took forever, if Matt never came back to the log house forever. And the girl could not move. She felt herself caught in the circle as tight as a mite in an orb spider's web; she could only look at the woman whose eyes nearly met her eyes—for Mattie had grown tall in the first decade of her life, but from the time of the earth falling she had not grown, and so she and the woman were the same height nearly, hardly more than four and a half feet tall, the girl only perhaps a half-inch taller, and the two stared in recognition at one another, brown webbed eyes and ocher eyes, each in some way bearing kinship to the other. For the woman recognized the girl too. She had known it in an outside way a long time, had thought it maybe even from the time of the fever, but now she knew. The girl was charged with the gifts of the spirit. Thula had never seen this in a white child. She had never seen it in anyone but her father and her firstborn grandson, and they both were dead.

The other children, held only a shocked moment by the silent web between the two females, quickly swarmed the room, led by the urgently hungry Jim Dee, who smelled and saw and heard the hog's leg sizzling and dripping on the spit inside the fireplace and, giving a little shout, rushed over there. The boy Thomas came behind him, big and pale and handsome, his smooth countenance bland as an angel's, and he was nearly as tall as his wiry, sandy-haired brother, heavy, dense in his bones, though he was not fat but just big, solid, like his father, and, like his father, he moved always in a slow, rolling gait. And then it was Jonaphrene, torn by her desire to join with her sister—in their profound link that whispered in each other's souls without language, she knew Mattie was caught and could not move—but at last the compelling urge of the body won out in the younger girl, and she went to the spit, where the boys were tearing at the meat with a knife and their bare fingers, burning their own flesh, and said, "Wait. Wait! Let me get a fork and plate."

Jonaphrene started across the room toward the pine shelf where the improbable stacks of delicate white china stood amid clusters of tin utensils, candle stubs, the father's shaving mug and razor strop. Thula broke her gaze away from Mattie, came around her to the kitchen area, and took the fork and the chipped plates from the younger girl's hands. With only a word or two in Choctaw she made the children settle down and stand in line before the fireplace, and she served them, great heaping plates of pork and *tanfula,* or "tom fuller," as white folks called hominy, big crisp hunks of shuck bread. The boys went each to his place, Jim Dee to tip back against the wall on the rope-mended ladderback, Thomas to his place behind the door, to eat wolflike, not speaking, and Jonaphrene took her plate to the cold cookstove and ate tiny delicate bites of the pale hominy, her back to the room. Thula filled a plate then for Matt and took it to her, where she stood, still unmoving, in the circle of ashes. With gesture and sound and expression, the woman made it known to the girl that she should eat; she made it known to the other children to take a second helping, to carry their empty plates to the bucket, and she calmed them, made friends with the two boys almost entirely without language, as very young children make friends with one another without need of words. She calmed all of them but Matt, who continued staring at her with wide eyes, knowing eyes, frightened, but Thula Henry went on working patiently in the room, in silence, continued even when the children's father came in after dark and began asking questions. She gestured and shrugged and filled a plate for him, and pretended to not understand, until at last the man talked himself into his own answers, said he would speak to his brother tomorrow, and did not ask again, not even when she pulled her red blanket from beneath the satchel and wrapped it around herself to sit on the floor beside the hearth when the children climbed the steep stairs to settle down on their pallets. On the morrow, and on the morrow following, Thula Henry cooked and cleaned and cared for the children; never did she cross the clotted field to the store to receive her length of cloth from Jessie. Her reason to remain was not connected to the white woman, nor to any human demand or payment. Each day Thula worked in silence, in patience, for she had a large purpose, and she knew God's time was long.

The word went out in the cold moon of January. The Wilderness Preacher was coming to hold services down below Latham's Store on the banks of the Braz-eel, as the little river was called. Among the Indians it was known as far away as Nashoba and Skullyville, and it was noised about a great deal among the white settlers as well, for the Preacher's fame was broad in the land then, and the hunger for spiritual food and for entertaining diversion in I.T. was great.

It was not the proper time of year for brush arbor meetings, not in the cold teeth of winter—the proper time was the long lingering evenings of midsummer, when the crops were laid by—but Brother Jonathan Fingers, who called himself and was known as the Wilderness Preacher after his most often quoted text from Ecclesiastes and his passions for baptizing and for eating wild honey, did not pause in his soul-winning for the seasons to pass. Satan, as the Preacher knew, did not take a vacation in winter. The Preacher himself had just come from the recently opened Oklahoma Territory, where sin and corruption flowed as freely as the whiskey in the many saloons and dance halls, where the wild tribes of the west practiced their heathen rites before God's very face upon the frozen wind-stung prairie, and so he had determined to go down into the mountains among the Choctaw, who were known to be more receptive to the Word of the Lord, and to live in well-heated and tended log cabins as well, and in any case the mountains were farther south. He sent word out before himself in the form of posted handbills in English and a Chickasaw runner among the Choctaw church communities, and by the time of the new moon in February, the people of the Sans Bois, black, white, and Indian, all knew the Wilderness Preacher was coming, and where he would set up his camp meeting, and when.

On the appointed Saturday which was to be the first night of the revival, whites and Indians (not those of the African race, for Brother Fingers did not consider he had been sent into the wilderness to teach the Sons of Ham; that was left to their own preachers, because true Christian missionaries had all the flock they could tend to between the red heathen and the white sinners, and in any case, the communities were not to mix: it said so in the Bible somewhere) began to gather from all directions. They started out in the early morning in their buckboards and farm wagons, on horseback, muleback, entire families walking, to gather throughout the day and on into the evening beneath the leafless arbor set up on the banks of the Brazil, coming to receive the Word of the Lord from the mouth of the Preacher on the first frosty night of the February new moon.

Of course, the white people of Waddy gathered with them. Fayette and his boys came for sport, his wife and daughters for loftier reasons—not excepting the notion among the four young women that the famous Wilderness Preacher's Day of Pentecost Brush Arbor Baptism Revival & Camp Meeting would surely be the most apt place in the Territory to show off their new winter muffs. Several families started out well before daylight to drive the nearly twenty-five miles from Cedar, though John Lodi was not among them. On the first day of the revival he walked south at dawn from Big Waddy Crossing to work at Dayberry's as he would on any ordinary Saturday morning; nor did he make any attempt to see to it that his children attended the camp meeting either. In fits and starts over the course of the past three years he'd made occasional stabs at civilizing his youngsters by cleaning them up for Sunday morning service at the schoolhouse at Big Waddy, but his efforts were without heart, because they were without faith, and so he did not persevere; he was not capable of sustained effort in that area, though his tenacity for all else was nearly beyond reason, and the youngsters did not fight him because they knew it would not last long.

However, conditions had changed in the log house since the coming of Thula Henry. She did not bother with Matt, did not seem to make any effort concerning the girl in any manner, for Thula knew the time was not yet. But every Saturday afternoon she cleaned up the other three children and walked with them in the waning afternoon light two and a half miles to her log home near the Indian Missionary Baptist Church at Yonubby so that they might be present and ready when the bell in the church yard began to ring Sunday morning. The huge brass bell, standing free in the yard at the top of a wooden stilt-like scaffold, would begin ringing in the early morning, and from all directions the people would come walking, the three white children lined up before Thula Henry, along with six of her grandchildren, making their way the quarter mile from her home to the one-room log church surrounded on all sides by screenless frame cookhouses. The children had to sit still for hours and listen to the Choctaw preacher preach the Gospel in Choctaw, but this was acceptable to Jonaphrene, for there was a powerful ascetic streak in her that responded to the mystery of the Word spoken in an undecipherable tongue, and it was acceptable to Thomas because everything that came before the boy's eyes in the world was received equally, and it was all right with Jim Dee because he could play games with the Choctaw boys around the cookhouses when church was over, and the food, when they finally got to it in the late afternoon, was good.

So it was Thula Henry who insisted that John Lodi's children attend the Wilderness Preacher's brush arbor revival, but when she got the children ready for the journey, she somehow did not deem it necessary to tell their father, who in any case had left the house at dawn before she began her ear scrubbing and hair plaiting, that they were traveling not to Yonubby this morning but nearly all the way to Bokoshe, on the banks of the Brazil, a day's ride away. She did, however, tell the girl Matt. In English she told her—not the broken English of Thula's Creek father, but the form as she had learned it from the Presbyterian missionaries at Wheelock Academy forty years before.

"We're going to church now," she told the girl. "Won't be back till day after tomorrow." Thula stood in the road in front of the house with her hand on the halter of an ancient fat white mare she had borrowed from one of her sons for the journey. The three younger children, scrubbed and red-faced, perched dangle-legged on a blanket on the mare's back. "You come go with us," Thula said.

The girl stood at the edge of the yard, looking down at the four in the roadbed. She had just come from Toms Mountain, and she was dirty-faced, in a pair of trousers and a felt hat, holding a leather thong twisted around the tail of a dead coon. She stared at her siblings, especially her sister, saying nothing, but in Matt's eyes was accusation. She answered nothing, and Thula, looking hard at her hard eyes, shrugged her shoulders and turned to walk east along the road, walking before the mounted children in the cold early morning with her hand on the halter, the braided circlet on the top of her head hardly reaching the mare's nose.

They walked nearly eighteen miles on deeply rutted roads, and in some places no roads at all, through the valleys of the Sans Bois to the appointed place below Latham's Store. Sometimes Thula rode, but she feared for the old pony's endurance, and so, riding, they did not go much faster than the woman—or the girl coming behind them—could walk. They stopped twice to eat from the leather satchel Thula carried, and so it was well dark by the time they arrived in the place of the brush arbor, and she could hear already the singing, see the lantern light from a great distance. Coming nearer, she saw the many glass bottles tied to the trunks of trees around the cleared space of the brush arbor, the bottles filled with kerosene, rags stuffed in them, burning, and she smelled the cut wood. Thula tied the mare to a tree at the rear of the conglomeration of buggies and wagons, lifted the children down one by one from the mare's back, drew a feedbag from her satchel-of-many-things and hung it around the mare's muzzle, and walked forward toward the light, holding the little boy Thomas tightly by the hand.

The brush arbor of the Wilderness Preacher was made in just the same way as the brush arbors on the stomp grounds at Kialigee town, though here the arbor was not four separate ones laid out around the square in the Four Directions, but one, and the covered space was much larger: a great open tabernacle of post oaks hewed into forked poles and placed equal distance apart, smaller poles laid across at two-foot intervals, and brushy limbs and bushes laid over all. Thula thought it was through the smiling grace of God that the night was dry, frost-bitten, the stars twinkling in the black sky above the leafless branches, for if it had been a night of sleet or cold rain, that discomfort surely would have fallen through the barely clothed sticks onto the worshipers gathered to hear the Lord's Word. But the making of the brush arbor, though it was winter, was the same, and the purpose was the same, even if the white preacher knew nothing of purifying the body, preparing the body to heal it so that it might receive the spirit, but that was all right, because *Chisvs,* the Great Physician, had known that part, and Thula knew it, and all was well, as it should be, in the woman's eyes.

Thula Henry lived in two worlds simultaneously—not just Creek and Choctaw, Christian and medicine, church and stomp grounds—but in the presence of the Unseen in every moment, more real, as her heart knew, than the Seen. She understood that all had been formed balanced by the Creator from the beginning, that it was only humans who tipped and unsettled the balance, that *Chihowa's* gift of grace allowed for even that. She walked toward the square of the brush arbor as reverently as she had stood outside the sacred circle of swept leaves and dirt at Green Corn forty-three years before; this was not duality in her but union, because she believed it had been given to her to see all things not as separate, but as one. Taking the white children with her, she walked forward without acknowledging the several white men, including the children's uncle, scattered here and there among the shadows outside the square of light, surreptitiously sipping from jugs drawn quietly from beneath blankets in the backs of their wagonbeds. Nodding only once or twice, she walked past the Indian people sitting in their wagons or on homemade stools or standing around outside the rim of the tabernacle. She didn't acknowledge the woman Jessie, seated halfway down the aisle, when she turned her drawn face and looked up, shocked, her mouth open with singing, stopped open, as if she would say something. Thula ignored the little boy dragging on her hand, pulling, his head turning this way and that as he tried to shrink away from the numbers of people, the light from the kerosene lanterns hanging on poles inside the arbor, the smells. On in between the rows of hewn, backless pews filled with white people the woman walked, her eyes forward, leading the ragtag row of children to the very front of the tabernacle, where sawdust was spread on the cold earth beneath the empty log pews directly in front of the pulpit.

She made the children to sit down beside her, and they did so without grumbling, even the wildly restless Jim Dee, and Thula opened her mouth, singing "There is power! power! wonder-working power! in the blooood—of the Laaaamb!" along with the congregation. When the many voices swung into a chorus of "In the Sweet By and By," Thula Henry sang the words in Choctaw. The children, having heard it for more than three months then, sang *"Kanima-a-ash inli ho-o-oh"* right along with her, and the Preacher, who had, after all, been sent to save heathen, nodded benevolently at them from where he sat on the raised platform behind the pulpit—though the song leader, a short red-faced white man from Dog Creek with hair in a fringed circlet around his bald pate, frowned horribly at them, not because they sang in Choctaw but because Thula and the children were sitting on the mourners' bench where the wicked were to kneel in repentance of sin at the end of the service, and where those baptized with the Holy Spirit were to roll in the sawdust when they began to talk in tongues.

The Preacher stood up. The congregation hushed to silence, a slow fade of coughs and rustles and closing songbooks among the few who had brought them. The song leader retreated to the back of the platform and then, under the quick glance of the Preacher, descended entirely from the pulpit area to seat himself on the far end of the same mourners' bench where Thula and the children sat. The Preacher stepped to the pulpit, which was no more than a post oak stripped and hewed square, topped with a flat piece of pine. It, like everything else at the camp meeting, had been quickly hand wrought by the deacons and devout members of various white congregations of numerous denominations—Baptist, Methodist, Church of Christ, Pentecostal—for several miles about. In a territory so new to white settlement, there was as yet little condescension and tension between denominations, though that time would come. The Preacher, tall, crow-thin, shaggy-headed, handsome, placed one long thin hand on the pine pulpit, raised his head, flashed his eyes, and began in a resonant, rich voice to pray.

"Our Father and our Great God, as we approach the Throne of Grace this evening, we'd just ask that You'd look down upon Your poor Servant—"

Heads quickly bowed, eyes closed, most caught unawares by the unexpected invocation, and then hardly had the congregation entered a state of prayer when the Preacher shouted, "Vanity!" and the consciousness of the crowd lurched abruptly awake.

" 'Vanity of vanities, saith the Preacher; all is vanity'!" the Preacher cried. He lifted up the great black leather Bible he carried, one long-boned finger caught near the center in the Book of Ecclesiastes, though he had no need to open it and read from it, for the words of his most favorite and illustrious text were inscribed on his soul. " 'I have seen all the works that are done under the sun,' " he boomed, " 'and behold, all is vanity and vexation of spirit'! And what meaneth the Preacher by that? Useless! That's what he means. Useless. Everything on this earth is useless, every small or large thing under the sun is useless, without the Lord. There's no getting around it. I don't care what you do. Oh, you can try to get around it: you can gather unto yourself the wealth of David. You can get the wisdom of Solomon, wisdom's not going to do you a bit of good. Listen!" and he opened the Book and laid it flat open in his great splayed hand, but he never looked down at the printed words. " 'For in much wisdom is much grief! and he that increaseth knowledge increaseth sorrow! For there is no more remembrance of the wise than of the fool forever, seeing that which now is, in the days to come shall all be forgotten! And how dieth the wise man? as the fool'! You hear what the Word of the Lord is saying? Wise man dies just like a fool! Y'all might just as well be fools. The Book says that. Y'all might just as well set down and quit working. It doesn't make a bit of difference to God, because it's all vanities to the Lord of Heaven, and He says it right here!" The Preacher raised the Book over his head. " 'I gathered me also silver and gold and the peculiar treasure of kings of the provinces! and whatsoever mine eyes desired I kept not from them! Then I looked on all the works that my hands had wrought, and behold! all was vanity and vexation of spirit! and there was no profit under the sun'! You hear that? 'No . . . profit . . . under . . . the sun . . .' "

He paused long and lingeringly between the words, his great shaggy head lifted toward the arbor roof. "Vanity," he whispered. "Vanity of vanities. All is vanity." He closed his eyes, shook his head. And then he thumped the Book closed and began to stride back and forth on the platform, his long shoulders humped beneath his black frock coat, his voice winding up to preach. And the Preacher did preach. He preached high and preached low, preached Sin and Salvation, slid from Hellfire Damnation to God's Forgiving Mercy, from Joel crying "Awake, ye drunkards, and weep! Howl, all ye drinkers of wine!" to Christ promising the disciples He would send the Comforter to abide with them till He should come again. If Brother Fingers knew a mighty lot of Scripture, it would have to be said that his biblical scholarship was a bit slippery, in that he freely blended the Old Testament with the New and could not seem to get settled between Judgment and Grace. It was not only Ecclesiastes he fancied himself after but John the Baptist as well, trying in all desperation to make straight the path of the Lord. He knew he was a Voice Crying in the Wilderness—it said so right on his handbills—and he wore, not camel hair, camels not being native to that country, but a leather girdle about his waist at least, and a buffalo robe in cold weather, and he ate wild honey when he could get it (though he eschewed locusts, which were more than plentiful in the Territory), and he went about baptizing many Indians and a considerable number of outlaws in the name of the Lord. On the other hand, the Preacher's primary method of baptism—especially in cold weather—was the baptism of the spirit, which he invoked and exhorted in his sermons, whereas a Bible scholar would have noticed that John the Baptist did his baptizing with water and in any case had lost his head long before the Day of Pentecost, when the true believers began to talk in tongues. Still, the order and references mattered little to his congregation, and the Preacher carried on, crying out to the Holy Spirit to come lay hands upon them, and every few moments punctuating his sermon with the phrase "Vanity of vanities!"

(without an iota of irony, for he had not a clue in the world he was vain), because he understood, along with Ecclesiastes, the pure, dull emptiness of life without the Lord.

Before the two-hour sermon was finished, Brother Fingers had reduced himself to sackcloth and ashes, quite literally, through a bag of props he kept at the rear of the platform, and if he'd had a coat of camel hair he surely would have put it on. By that time, too, the front of the open-air temple was crowded with believers raising their palms to God, faces thrown back in ecstasy and the reception of the Holy Spirit, many speaking the jaw-tight, back-teeth-gritted glory of God in the language of the Spirit, and even on that frostbitten February night there was a considerable amount of sweat balling up the sawdust at the front of the tabernacle, and there was much shouting and singing and praising the Lord, and the Holy Spirit was so manifestly present at the camp meeting that many wished in their deepest hearts for summer so that they might find a good long serpent to handle, as had been promised to the true believers in the Book of Mark, though of course the local reptile population was all well denned and asleep. The Preacher had not yet even begun to give the invitation. There might be many more dozens of poor sinners, he knew, still nailed by sin and hardheartedness to their log pews, resisting the call, and the Preacher, sensing the hardheartedness and corruption still out there in the audience, began to try to make a sign to the song leader to come up to the platform and lead the remnants of still-seated congregation in the powerful invitational hymn "Just As I Am," which never failed to pull a few nails from the recalcitrant rear ends of unbelievers still tacked to their seats by sin and self-will, and the Preacher did look yonder to the song leader, who was somehow not intent on the pulpit as he should have been but peering off at something to the side beyond the square of light. It was not only the song leader from Dog Creek who felt the presence outside the brush arbor in the darkness. Thula knew her. Jessie, seated far back behind the raised hands and lifted voices, knew her. And the girl Jonaphrene.

The Preacher paused, sweating, trying to carry the whole of the tabernacle into silence, but those filled with the Holy Ghost down front could not feel the Preacher's direction, drenched as they were in the filling of the Spirit apart from the vain world, so that the speaking in tongues and the shouting Glory! Praise Jesus! went on and on while the girl came from the dark outside the lanterns, came toward Thula walking slowly, directly, without coat or sweater, her hat gone, her face more soiled than it had been in the morning, and she walked directly to the mourners' bench unobserved by any but the song leader and Jessie, her own siblings, and the Choctaw woman whose story and responsibility were bound up with hers.

Jessie stood up and came down front as a sinner comes to the altar to be washed in the Blood of the Lamb, but she did not bend her head and kneel in grief and repentance. She stood, staring, as the girl walked forward and stood directly in front of Thula Henry, talking, speaking a language that was not the sound of tongues spoken by those baptized by the Holy Ghost all around them, and Jessie thought it was Choctaw maybe, or French, but it was not Choctaw, she knew the chopped sound of Choctaw, and the fear was rising in the woman Jessie and the powerful wrenching of compassion that she dreaded and would have none of and that made her want to cry out. Thula Henry knew that the tongue the girl spoke was not Choctaw, nor any language formed of the intelligence of humans, and it was not the language of the Pentecost either, but it was nevertheless a part of the Great Mystery—the language of the Fourth Part—and this, too, was the language of God. As her tongue moved, rapid, guttural, the girl suddenly grew rigid, as if every muscle and tendon in her small skinny body at once tensed and became frozen; she did not lift her palm or face to God but fell straight down solid as a ninepin, straight down to the sawdust, and her entire body began to twitch and tremble and shake on the earth.

When Fayette lifted her from the sawdust floor to carry her out of the tabernacle, the girl's head fell back on her thin neck as a dead songbird's will dangle, tendonless, from its downy, unbeating chest. He stumbled, walking out into the darkness, and Jessie came behind him, her hoarse whisper chopping the air: "Careful!" She reached around his shoulder to support the girl's lolling head. Behind them on the platform the song leader led the invitational hymn, his eyes darting now to the side at the departing family, now back over his shoulder at the Wilderness Preacher, who knelt behind the podium, his crowlike body hunched in sweating prayer. The song leader's hand moved in a monotonous, ponderous triangle through the kerosene-lit air; his mouth moved, his eyes darted, as the voices of the congregation lifted mournfully inside the tabernacle, swelled out into the darkness. "Ju-ust as I a-am, without one plea, but tha-at Thy Blood was shed for me, and that Thou bidst me come to The-ee, O Lamb of God, I come. I come."

Thula sat beside the girl in the bed of the wagon as they drove home beneath the terrible spangle of stars in the winter-black sky. The girl was perfectly still, perfectly limp beneath a spread blanket. Jessie drove, her eldest daughter beside her on the spring seat, holding her sleeping youngest; scattered about the wagonbed, the other daughters whispered in the darkness; the half-intoxicated Fayette mumbled to himself, leaning against the tailgate in the back. The two sons had hours before disappeared from the camp meeting with a bunch of older wild boys from Bokoshe; they would not come home until well into the next night. The team picked its way along the rutted road as John Lodi's three younger children, mounted one behind the other, nodding with sleepiness, trailed behind the wagon on the back of the fat mare. Now and then Jessie would cluck softly from the spring seat, flick the reins. They stopped once to put the three children into the crowded bed of the wagon after Jim Dee, having fallen asleep, nearly tumbled off the mare, and then they drove on slowly in the stillness of the new-moon darkness, drove in silence for hours, no sound but the jangle of harness, the soft thud of hooves on the winter-hard roadbed, and once, far off in the distance, the chilling screech of an owl in the dark. They did not reach the log house until first light.

John watched from the porch. His eyes were ringed dark, his chin was covered with stubble. He wore his hat and a thick shirt beneath his suspenders, but he did not have on a coat. The air had lifted, begun to blue slightly with the coming of daylight, and John stepped off the stone slab of step as soon as he saw them cross the creek, was at the foot of the yard slope when Jessie halted the team. He saw Thula hunkered near the front of the bed and so knew the answer to his question before he spoke it, but he said the words anyway, ground them between his teeth at Jessie, a powerful accusation in his voice.

"You got my young'uns with you?"

"They're here." She was too weary even for anger, and turning on the spring seat, she nodded at the clumps of sleeping blanket-covered bodies tumbled one upon the other—her own daughters, John's children, her husband snoring open-mouthed and rank in the cramped bed at the back. Only Thula was not sleeping. Only Thula sat up, her hand on the girl's shallow, barely moving chest beneath the blanket, her fingers touching the pulse place at the girl's throat. She looked at the father, said, "She gone some place. Gone to get her lessons, maybe."

John carried his daughter into the house and laid her on a pallet beside the fireplace. The Indian woman followed and sat down on the puncheon floor next to where the girl lay curled around herself in a stillness that was like unto the stillness of death. The log house was like a house where death had visited, for the children moved about the room slowly, swimmingly, as if in a dream, and they talked in hushed whispers. Even Jim Dee did not forget the solemnity of the situation, excepting only when he was outside the house, when he would dart and run and play as usual. John sat on a nail keg on the log porch, staring out past the bare tree branches at the fast-running Bull Creek, and Jonaphrene cooked and ate a little and fed the boys, but John and Thula did not eat.

On the second morning, Jessie came. She dreaded that house and the goings-on inside it, but she couldn't keep away. Her brother-in-law was sitting on the nail keg on the east end of the porch when she came into the yard, but he didn't acknowledge her, didn't move his eyes from the distant water or speak to her, and so she climbed the stone slab and hurried past him, also without speaking, and, without knocking or calling out, lifted the latch on the log door and walked in. The younger girl Jonaphrene sat with the boy Thomas on her lap on a box beside the cookstove, and the older boy was not in the room, but the Indian woman sat, wordless and motionless, beside the girl. She didn't speak or acknowledge Jessie any more than the father had, and Jessie went immediately and stood over her and the thin form on the pallet.

They had covered the girl with a threadbare quilt, faded, flat as a sheet with years of washing, the cotton batting leaking from the seams in several places, but even beneath the thin quilt Jessie could see the awful, twisted shape of the girl where she lay curled on her side, knees drawn toward her chest, the hands clawlike and curled inward just below her chin. The child's face was set with an immobility that was like a death mask, the eyes closed, the membranes stretched taut over the eyeballs, and there was no movement at all beneath the pale blue-veined lids. Jessie couldn't see any rise or fall of breath beneath the drawn-up arms. The figure on the pallet reminded her of the translucent discarded brown shells of locusts one finds clinging with drawn legs to elm bark, the brittle castoffs which crumble so easily at human touch, but when she reached down to lay a hand on the girl's forehead—a gesture that caused the Indian woman to suddenly make a harsh, unintelligible sound in her throat—Jessie felt the skin beneath her palm as cold and hard and dense as white marble.

"My God," she said to Thula, "she's dead, for Lord's sake. Dead! What are you doing?"

Thula didn't answer. She didn't even look up at her but kept her eyes on the lifeless girl. Jessie stared at the woman and the empty shell on the pallet, and then she looked around at the stark, wood-littered barrenness of the room, the pine shelves, the folded pile of quilts on the floor against the back wall. The eerily beautiful little girl and the pale little boy stared back at her from their seat on the wooden box in the corner. Jessie could smell the sweaty outdoor smell of children's unwashed bodies, the tang of stale bacon grease, the musty odor of Thula's herbs, and the sweet scent of cedar smoke, but she didn't detect yet the smell of the dead. Still, she hissed at the Indian woman, "You got to get that child's body out of here! She's starting to stink."

The woman looked at her, said calmly, "Not dead. She gone to the other world."

Baffled, more than a little frightened, Jessie looked around the room again, and not knowing what to say, what to do, she turned and walked out the door and went hunting her husband. She couldn't find him for the longest time, but at last, climbing the worn path behind the log house toward Toms Mountain, she heard the muffled sound of his voice rising above a hollow, steady thumping inside the shed barn. Jessie hurried across the barnyard, rushed in through the open archway, and was stopped by the powerful odor before she recognized where it came from: the open trapdoor leading down to the dug room, where her husband and two of his men were at that moment making a run of whiskey in the crude copper still hidden beneath the barn floor. She turned immediately and walked back out into the sunlight and stood fifty feet outside the open archway, calling her husband's name. From the day he'd started his men digging up the old dirt barn floor two years earlier, Jessie had lived within the notion that if she didn't admit to her waking mind what her husband was doing, it would never call down trouble on her household, and so she'd never yet come within acknowledgable distance of Fayette's operation in the shed barn—but the woman was frightened by the strange unfoldings in the log house far beyond her fear of the illegal trappings of her husband's bootleg business, and she kept calling his name until he emerged from the dark square. She could see anger in his face, but even that didn't stop her, and before he'd traveled the fifty feet across the dung dust of the old barnyard, she was whispering out loud in a harsh and grating whisper: "Lord God Almighty, Fay, you got to do something. You got to *do* something—they've every one gone mad. He's gone mad, your brother, he might—oh, Lord, I don't know what any of them's liable to do. That child is *dead*."

Fayette stopped in front of her, looking hard at her, the anger whisked off his face so completely it might never have been there.

"What?"

"They got that child on the pallet she's all crimped up dead as a cricket, that crazy Indian woman is sitting there, those kids are sitting there, your brother's out on the porch, they haven't even washed her or laid her out. They're acting crazy, just plain weird. They—that Indian woman said she's not dead. She is dead. I know a dead child when I see one. Go see for yourself. You got to do something, Fay—that corpse is going to start to rot."

And Fayette turned, went back inside the darkness of the barn a minute. When he came back out, Jessie could smell the faint whiff of corn liquor, but he walked on past her and down the gently sloping wagon track to the back porch of the log house. He climbed the rickety steps, tried the back door, which did not open, and then continued on around the side porch to the front of the house. Jessie stood on the little rise for more than an hour, watching the back of the log house. There was no movement but for the smoke rising, drifting, curling blue from the rock chimney, now and again the fat old beagle, asleep in the sun at the side of the woodpile, scratching an ear. She could hear the muffled voices of the men inside the barn behind her, the half-breed Moss laughing, and the other one—an Indian too, from the sound of him, from the sound of how they laughed together, that Indian kind of laughing she could not abide, like everything that was funny to them was some kind of big secret Indian joke—the other one laughing too, and hushing him. She knew they'd got into her husband's whiskey, but since she could not allow the knowledge of her husband's trafficking in illegal spirits into the front of her mind, she had to block out also the sounds of his workers procuring for themselves in his absence a free drunk.

Finally she saw Fayette in the near sideyard, coming around from the front of the house. He climbed toward her without looking up at her, and she had the sudden cold thought he might be as loco as the rest of them. She met him halfway down the path, and when he stood in front of her, he ran his eyes along the path, up to the shed barn, past that to the foot of Toms Mountain, back down to the fading wagon track.

"Well?" she said.

He wouldn't look at her; his brilliant sapphire eyes darted up the yellow slope again to the barn's mouth.

"He . . . he says she ain't dead."

"She's *dead*, Fay. Good Lord, go in and look at her."

"I did," he said.

"Well, is she or ain't she?"

"I don't know. Looks dead to me. They say not. That Indi'n woman says not. I don't know. I didn't smell nothing."

"Oh, for Pete's sake!" Jessie said, the plosive exploding into the now fading daylight.

"Well." Fayette turned his head, let his eyes wander back down toward the log house. "I don't reckon it's going to hurt to wait till she starts to stink." There was a burst of low chuckling laughter from the depths of the barn then, and his head snapped back around, his eyes to the barn door. "Let's give it a day or two," he said as he began to stride swiftly away from her up the track. Jessie could hear him cussing the men as she made her way down the path a few yards, and then she cut west straight across the land above the log house.

She stayed away for a day and a half. She went about her work in her own house, bossed her daughters, and her sons when she could find them, minded the store, but her thoughts every minute were on the dead girl and the Indian woman inside the log house. There was no one to turn to in this lawless country, she thought, no white sheriff within a hundred miles to come haul that corpse out of that house and make those people bury it, and plainly she was not going to get any help from her husband; she'd have to take matters into her own hands, of course. But how? She awoke the following morning with a plan. Within a half hour she was climbing the slab step with a wedge of mirror from her daughter Lottie's broken vanity set tucked into the pocket of her apron. She'd marched across the field between the two houses with a gritted determination to make that father see the truth for himself, but John wasn't sitting on the nail keg on the end of the porch as she'd expected; neither was he inside the house, and even this mild discrepancy between her mind's rehearsal and the unruliness of reality was enough to make her hesitate as she crossed the doorsill. Jonaphrene and Thomas were in their same places beside the cookstove, Thula Henry was hunched in the same crouch beside the body on the pallet, as if no one had moved, no life or time had proceeded in the two days since Jessie had been there. She went immediately, even with that horrid hesitation about her, and stood over the woman and girl again.

"Mrs. Henry," she said, "this is . . . this is . . . We can't have this, you got to let that child go. I don't know what . . ." Her determination slipped further in the face of the woman's fierce concentration. "You been mighty good to come take care of these young'uns, but . . . Mrs. Henry? You can go on back home now. Right this evening, if you want to." Jessie lifted her eyes, swept the room with them, lowered them to the Indian woman again. She saw for the first time that the woman's lips were moving, hardly perceptible, the lips shaping inaudible language, her face very still. "Mrs. Henry!" Jessie cried. "She's dead. You ain't going to bring her back from the dead! Look here!" From her apron pocket she drew the irregular palm-sized triangle of mirror and, bending down, held it in front of the girl's colorless lips. The mirror's foiled surface remained clear. "Look!" she cried. "No breath. See? No breath!" But even as she cupped the trembling wedge of mirror, she saw the cloud come, a tiny spot no larger than a dime, blurring the looking-glass surface, and a sickening sensation drained her, a sinking heartsickness and fear. It was worse than death, she thought, a thousand times worse than a dead child, and her mind reeled with condemnation, with judgment, with comprehension of the sins of the fathers—the sins of the fathers and the mothers, she thought—visited on the children. The fear was dark in her, a rising, clutching thing in the pit of her belly, for she knew she herself was alive with her secret iniquities, the fear biting, clawing, because of her own sons, what could become of her own sons, and her daughters, in the face of God's judgment, if such a thing could happen to this girl. She dropped the mirror on the pallet, straightened, and walked quickly out the log door.

But she returned again in the evening. She could not stay away—she didn't know what it was or why—and she prayed. All through the afternoon she kept up a silent pleading with God to relieve her of the bondage of that family, even as she cooked a pot of beans and hamhocks to carry back across the clotted field to that same maddened family locked in the taint of the log house that had been her house and was no longer, and she did not know why she must carry that burden. She struggled, she railed, she pleaded, she resisted; she hated them with a terrible hatred and thought of taking one of her husband's many guns into the log house and putting the barrel to that form's pale cold forehead, thought of shooting all of them to put them out of their mad misery as you would gladly shoot a hydrophobic dog, and then the terrible pity would rise over her and she would beg forgiveness, to be forgiven her trespasses as she forgave those who trespassed against her, which she did not, and she knew she did not. This knowledge only caused the biting fear to rise again, and all of this in silence, in the silent orison of her mind pleading with the Almighty to forgive her, to relieve her, to take this cup from her, as she unwrapped new bolts of calico and slid them onto the store shelf, directed her son Caleb to clean out the ashes from the woodstove, took money from customers and made change with her hands hidden inside the cash box, climbed the worn path from the back of the store to her own house to check the water in the beans and tell Millie to put on a pan of cornbread, descended the worn path to the store again.

It was coming on dark by the time she carried the heavy cast-iron kettle across the field, although it was only four or four-thirty, but the day was gray and short with winter. John was back in his place on the nail keg at the end of the porch, so she knew he had not been gone to work when she'd come in the morning, because he never returned from Dayberry's before eight or nine o'clock. She hoisted the heavy kettle up the step with both hands on the white dishtowel wrapped around the handle, and then waited at the door for her brother-in-law to get up off the nail keg and come open it. There was a calmness about her as she stood with her arms stretched to their full length and strength, burdened with the weight of the pot of beans, as if her silent struggle throughout that gray February afternoon had left her with a certain equanimity at least, if no understanding or peace. Her brother-in-law held the door for her, and when she entered the lamplit room she sensed the change immediately. She didn't know what it was at first, for the Indian woman still sat beside the drawn form on the pallet, and though the boy Jim Dee had come in, he was as quiet and watchful from his place on the far side of the room as the other two little ones. Jessie carried the pot to the stove, where the Dutch oven squatted with its lid propped to the side a crack, from which creviced darkness floated the whangy, aromatic wild scent of boiled game. She hoisted the bean kettle to the rear stovecap, drew from beneath her coat the crumbling, towel-wrapped square of cornbread that she had carried in the scoop of her pinned-up apron, and laid it on the cooler surface at the back of the cookstove, turned to face the room. She saw then that John stood above the pallet looking down, just as she herself had stood a few hours earlier; that the Indian woman's lips were no longer silently moving; that the girl's eyes were opened in half slits, the whites showing at the bottom. The drawn limbs were eased a little beneath the thin quilt, though they still crooked toward the center of the body, and the labored breathing was visible now in the rise and fall of her chest, audible in the lamp-hissing silence of the room.

"Well," Jessie said, that calmness still cloaked about her which she did not understand. "She's better, looks like."

"Yes," John said.

"Well." It was quiet a minute, except for the girl's breathing, the lamps hissing, a stick popping in the cookstove. "I brought something. These young'uns need to eat."

"We thank you," John said.

"It's just beans and cornbread."

"We thank you," he said again. There was no hint of sarcasm or hidden grudge in the words, but rather a kind of hazy detachment, as if he meant the thank-you but didn't quite comprehend it. "Jona-phrene."

The little girl got up from her box near the stove and went to the pine shelf by the washstand, reached up on tiptoe to gather down the china plates.

"Here," Jessie said, and she took the plates from the girl. "You two wash up," she said, meaning the two boys, and she proceeded with what she could do, what she knew to do, filling plates, cutting bread, lifting the iron cap with a fork because she couldn't find the cap lifter, and shoving more twigs in the hole to make the fire hot for coffee, as if the three forms on the other side of the room were invisible to her. It was only after she'd got the children fed, started the dishwater heating, set the younger girl to sweeping up cornbread crumbs from around the stove, that she went over to where they held their positions, posed and motionless as a painting: the man standing with hat on, the woman crosslegged on the floor in a red blanket, the stick figure curled on its side with arms and legs drawn up. It was then that Jessie saw, beneath the taut membranes of the half-opened eyelids, the girl's sightless pupils roving about the room. A powerful physical revulsion swept over the woman, a sickness that was like the nausea she'd felt a dozen years before as she'd watched Demaris give birth to that pinheaded baby, a retching of soul and belly in the face of what was not normal. She said—croaked actually: she could hear the awful sound in it, her voice like an old woman's—"Y'all better eat something." The strange calm that had descended on her as she'd climbed the porch step with the bean kettle was entirely gone now, fled, whisked dry away, replaced with that sickening recoil of the senses and a cringing sense of defeat: she was too weak, too weak: she could not abide it. She turned abruptly and went to the stove, began to scoop beans out of her kettle onto a couple of tin plates. She slapped stringy spoonfuls of boiled meat from the Dutch oven—rabbit she thought it was, though the dark flesh was boiled off the bone and it was hard to tell—onto the plates, broke the last piece of cornbread in half and put a piece on each of them, stood a moment at the stove, her shoulders heaving with deep, gulping breaths, her back to the room. She could feel the children off to her left, watching her, could feel John's eyes on her back, and the Indian woman's, and time swirled around her, the past as present, eternity, her self bound forever in that house before the stove in the corner with a child of death somewhere in the room.

"Y'all eat now," she said, without turning. Her eyes were on the rusting elbow of stovepipe where it crooked to vent out the log wall in front of her face. "Girl," she said, meaning Jonaphrene, though she did not look at her, "put the beans in the cold box when they get finished. They'll sour on you if you leave them out overnight. I'll come get my pot tomorrow evening," and she turned slowly, carefully, moved across the open space of the room without turning her eyes, and when she reached the log door she said, "There'll be somebody come fetch it tomorrow," referring to the kettle again, and she pushed on the door, went out, promising herself she would never darken that threshold again.

That was on the evening of the fourth day.

Before dawn on the morning of the fifth day, John arose fully dressed, as he had lain down at midnight, from his pallet on the far side of the room. He lit the lamp, looked over at the woman keeping her sleepless vigil near the fireplace, at the still form beside her, and could see the slow rise and fall of his daughter's chest. The fire was burning strongly, so he knew the woman had moved a few times in the night to feed it, but from her position and expression it appeared she had not moved or slept at all. He looked down at the near pallet where his other three children were sleeping. Jonaphrene had dragged her blankets downstairs the first night, and the boys would not sleep in the upper room alone, and so they all slept in the single room together. The three younger ones drew their slow, untroubled breaths with their mouths open, their faces placid, soft with the transfiguring perfection of sleep. Quietly John slid his suspenders up over his shoulders and went to the woodbox for kindling. He shoved a few sticks onto the cold ashes in the cookstove, twisted the bent nail in the stovepipe to open the flue, reached for the box of sulfur matches on the pine shelf.

"Papa?"

He started, glanced quickly over his shoulder. Jonaphrene was sitting up on the pallet beside her sleeping brothers. She hadn't unbraided her hair the night before—had perhaps not braided or unbraided it for days—and the two flattened plaits were cockeyed, loosely woven, with a thousand stray hairs pulled free and radiating wildly about her head. She shivered in her thin nightgown, squinted in the lamplight, rubbing her eyes. "What are you doing?"

"Nothing, honey. I got to go to work."

"Is Mattie better?"

"She's better. Hush now. Y'all go back to sleep."

"Is she well?"

"Not yet, honey. Soon. Go back to sleep."

The little girl said nothing more while her father got the stove started, ladled fresh water into the granite coffeepot, spooned grounds from the grinder into it, and set the pot on the stove. When he started out the door into the predawn darkness with the empty drink bucket, she called out again, "Papa?"

"*Hssht,* honey!" He stood with his hat on, his hand on the latch. "What?"

"How come you're going if Mattie ain't well?"

He was silent for a moment. "I got to," was all he said before he opened the door.

"Papa?"

He stood with the sky blooming gentian behind him, the cold air welling into the room. The crow of a rooster off east somewhere rode in on the cold air. A black look was on him, an icy, merciless expression that seemed to have nothing to do with the little girl sitting up on the pallet. "What."

"Is she going to die?"

Her father didn't answer. He turned and went out, drew the door closed behind him. When he came back with the full bucket, the black icy look was gone from him, and he set the bucket on the washstand, ladled water into the tin basin, proceeded to strop the straightrazor he drew down from the shelf. He took his hat off and laid it on the countertop beside the bucket, lathered quickly, and began to shave off the five days' growth of facial hair that had gone beyond stubble to the scratchy beginnings of beard; he scraped his chin, forelip, upper neck entirely by feel, as he always did, for there was no mirror—or none but the small triangular wedge Jessie had dropped earlier that morning, which Jonaphrene had picked up from the quilt and hidden away in the folds of her own pallet. It was while he was shaving that the Choctaw woman spoke aloud for the first time since she'd followed him into the house as he carried the girl.

"Take them little ones with you," she said.

John paused, the razor in one hand, the fingers of the other hand feeling gingerly the edge of the hairline in front of his ear. He looked at the woman. Her head was uptilted, the thick coil of braid like an ebony crown on top, and her eyes, black and small and depthless, stared evenly at him.

"I got to work," he said.

"Take the little ones with you," she said.

They looked at each other a long time. It was a strange union, almost collusion, between the two of them, and yet there was antipathy as well. He did not like the Indian woman's ways, her smell and smoke and songs she'd sung to heal his daughter when the girl could not walk straight, to heal all his offspring, but one, in the time of the red fever. And yet she had healed them; she could heal Matt, if she would, he believed that, and never moving his eyes from the woman's eyes, he said at last, "Jonaphrene, wake up your brothers. Y'all get dressed." He took his hat from the washstand, put it on, and went out the door to bring in wood for the woodbox.

A half hour later, as the man and the three bundled, sleepy children started out into the pale light of first dawn, the woman spoke again. She didn't lift her eyes from the figure on the pallet this time, didn't bother to look up and hold the man's eyes.

"Keep away four days," she said.

So then it was the girl and Thula alone in the shell of the log house. The girl and Thula alone, as it had been in spirit, as it should now be also in the body, and Thula understood that there was something she must do, but she did not know what it was. She didn't know a song for this sickness. She knew no herbs or healing but had prayed in silence, without medicine, for four days. She had fasted. She went again and again in her mind to the passage of Scripture she'd found on the first night, and then she would turn from the Word to her understanding of where the girl's soul roamed, and Thula's own soul was troubled. As Jessie strove in spirit with her God, so Thula Henry struggled, but her striving was of a different nature than the white woman's, for within the Choctaw woman a trembling had begun, marked by that duality which had never been a division within her but which now cut her thoughts, separating her from her own understanding. For Thula knew of this kind of travel in the other world. In Indian way, she understood fully where the girl's soul was. In Christian way, this could not be so. It was the inescapable force of this duality—not of more than one God, but of more than one world—that conflicted Thula's spirit and threatened to destroy her peace. She knew that Matt's soul had been captured and carried to the world of the dead, but the world where the girl now dwelt was not like what the preachers preached of heaven and hell, as God had ordained them, those two only, with no other place for the departed to dwell. The girl was not in heaven or hell, no more than she was present inside her body. She was in the other world.

If the girl had been Indian, Thula would have sent for a certain *hilishaya* of her father's people, who would risk his own soul to follow her into that world and bring her back. But it was a white girl curled on the blanket; no medicine of that power was going to work on a white girl. If she could have, Thula Henry would have arisen from her place beside the hearth, gathered all her things into the leather satchel, and gone home. But she felt herself tethered to the form on the pallet by a strand invisible and profound, shining, unseverable but by God's hand. All she knew to do, all she could do, was pray. And she did pray, watching through the day as the pale squares of sunlight crept west to east across the floor; she prayed on into the night, pausing and rising only to feed the fire, into the coming of light through the oilpaper-covered windows the next morning; she prayed on, and on, but she questioned within herself the quality of her prayers, the strength of them, even as she moved her lips silently. Again the words came to her from the Scripture as she had taken them the first night: *Chitokaka ma! sai yimmishke; nan-isht ik a sai yimmo ya is svm apelvchaske.*

Toward dawn of the third day that she'd been alone with the girl's form inside the log house, Thula took out once again from the leather satchel her Choctaw Testament and read by firelight the passage in Mark. Her eyes skimmed the first part of the story where one of the multitude came to *Chisvs* and said, Master, I've brought you my son who is possessed by a spirit, and wherever it takes him it tears him and he foams and gnashes his teeth and your disciples cannot cast it out, and the Master answered back, O you people of such little faith, how long am I going to suffer you? Bring him here. And when the child was brought to Him, the spirit saw the Master and knew Him and threw the boy down and tore him and made him wallow on the ground, as the girl Matt had wallowed on the sawdust floor of the brush arbor, and when *Chisvs* said, How long has he been like this? the father answered, Since he was a little child, and many times it's thrown him into the fire and into the water to kill him, but if you can do anything, have compassion on us and help us.

Here it was, here, that Thula's eyes paused, and she strained in the flickering light to read the words in Choctaw again and again: *Mihma Chisvs ash osh chi yimma hinla hok ma, na-yimmi hokvno nana akluha kvt ai i yumohma hinla hoke, im achi tok. Mihma vlla ya iki yash ot mih makinli no nishkin okchi mihinti hosh chitolit, Chotokaka ma! sai yimmishke; nan-isht ik a sai yimmo ya is svm apelvchaske, achi tok* ("Jesus said unto him, If thou canst believe, all things are possible to him that believeth. And straightway the father of the child cried out and said with tears, Lord, I believe; help thou mine unbelief.")

Chotokaka ma! sai yimmishke; nan-isht ik a sai yimmo ya is svm apelvchaske.

"Lord, I believe; help thou mine unbelief."

Thula's eyes moved from the Scripture to the drawn form on the pallet, where the girl's eyelids were fully open, the sightless pupils now darting minnow-like from side to side, now roving aimlessly about the log room, tracking what was not visible. Thula looked to the Scripture again. The words told her that when the Master cast out the spirit, it cried and rent the child and tore him and left him as one who was dead, and the people all said, The child is dead—just as Jessie, the man Fayette, even the children's father, once, on the first night, said of the girl—but *Chisvs* took the boy by the hand and lifted him up and he arose. *Chisvs* took him by the hand and he arose. That clean. That sudden, from the hand of the Savior; one had only to touch the hem of His garment to be healed. He had given power to His disciples to cast out spirits, but they could not cast out the spirit that had hold of that child, and when they asked why they could not, *Chisvs* answered, This kind can come forth by nothing but by prayer and fasting.

Thula read the words again. By nothing but by prayer and fasting. If thou canst believe, all things are possible. She had prayed. She had fasted. She had believed.

But she had not believed enough.

She had not believed.

Here was the source of the striving in her spirit. She understood it, though she couldn't say its name. It had grown from such a tiny place, like the mustard seed that can move mountains, only it was faith's opposite, and she could not even say when it had come. Not when the girl had fallen on the sawdust floor speaking the language of the Fourth Part. Not during the long ride in the wagon, or the first days and nights when the girl had lain as the dead, for at the beginning Thula had sat beside the pallet entirely balanced in her faith, as she always had been: patient, praying, believing that *Chihowa* would reveal to her what she must do. But the Creator had revealed nothing, and at some instant—she didn't know when—the uneasiness had found that small chink in her faith, and crept in. It was like *Impashilup,* she thought. The Soul Eater. The ancient one who would find a little nick in a person's soul, left there by bad thoughts or too much sadness, and *Impashilup* would creep in through that tiny hole and eat that person's soul. Thula did not feel her soul eaten, gone, destroyed, but unbalanced, struggling in this place of doubt. Not that she doubted the hand of one Creator over all, or *Chisvs* as Son and Savior, or the Son's power to heal, cast out devils, make one who was dead to rise up and walk; she didn't doubt that *Shilombish Holitopa,* the Holy Spirit, dwelt now upon the earth as Comforter in the hearts and minds of Christians. But Thula Henry knew this was not all of the Unseen.

Through the fasting days and nights she'd sat beside the empty shell upon the pallet, and in the silence she would hear a stick crack or a rustle or a small thud on the opposite side of the room in the darkness, and she would know it was *Bohpoli,* the Thrower, one of the ancient ones who had followed the *Chahta* people from their homelands to the new Nation, and she did not know why the Thrower, who lived only in the woods and deep forests, was in this house. Another time she heard the low, scuttering sound of the little bantylike spirit, the *lokhi,* of her father's people, as it came into the house and ran past the curled figure on the pallet, calling softly, lokha, lokha, lokha, scuttering around the room beneath the cookstove and washstand in search of ways to make its little mischief, quickly past the pallets on the far side, and then, as if discovering it had no business here, on out through the back wall, calling the whole time its soft lokha, lokha, lokha. Thula had been deeply troubled by these ones coming into a white house; that would not happen. That had never happened, so far as she had ever heard. Now, sitting in the flickering darkness on the dawning of the seventh morning, as she held her Choctaw Bible open in her lap, watched the girl's eyes roam about the room, Thula understood it did not matter about those white people; white people would never know or hear them. It was her own presence inside these walls, and the unease within her, that drew them. She had been taught they were of the Devil, or the old superstitious ways of the people, and the Choctaw preachers said the people had to turn away from such things, they had to forget about all that. Thula knew she must turn her face away, she must not believe them. And yet they were here, in this house; she knew the purpose of their presence as surely as she knew the white girl on the pallet journeyed in the other world. The ancient ones had come to bear witness of the Unseen, that Thula Henry might not forget.

"*Chotokaka ma!*" she cried out. "*Sai yimmishke; nan-isht ik a sai yimmo ya is svm apelvchaske!*"

Through the morning and noontide and afternoon she repeated the words, knowing, even as she prayed, that it was not for the girl's lost soul wandering on the other side, or that Thula's own faith and prayer and fasting might bring that soul home, but that the surety of that faith might return to her. The peace of the Comforter had departed her, and she did not know why or when; she was left unbalanced, divided in her spirit, and the cause was the Fourth Part, the existence and truth of the Fourth Part, which had been within her always, but never had it caused her to be caught in this place of disequilibrium and doubt. *Chotokaka ma! sai yimmishke; nan-isht ik a sai yimmo ya is svm apelvchaske.* Lord, I believe; help thou mine unbelief. Lord, I believe; help thou mine unbelief. The words were a dry, empty pleading, and then the words of her prayer changed, became a Creek song, one she knew of her father, but it, too, was cracked and dry, and it was not for the unconscious stick form on the pallet, but for her own unity, her oneness, her balance, that it might return to her. And then the song left her, and all sound left her, but she did not stop praying; in silence she prayed. Night came, and the woman went on praying, and even as she prayed to That which she could not help but believe in, she doubted that her prayers would be heard.

Late in the night, at about the third hour, Thula arose to put wood on the fire. It had begun to rain, she did not know when, for she had been deep in the place of wordless prayer, unaware even of the girl's slow, steady breathing beside her, unaware of the sounds and creaks and rustles within the house or the calls of winter night creatures without—the tortured screech of an owl, the yip of coyotes. But now, as she came to wakefulness in the physical world, the drumming on the roof above the upper room entered her from a great distance; she heard, nearer, the harsh patter on the porch roof, the sound small and quick, needlelike, the rain hovering at the point of freezing. In her bones, her joints, the places her muscles wrapped around her backbone, she felt the rain's ache and knot, and it took her a long time to unfold herself, for she had been sitting crosslegged a long time. The room was cold and pitch dark, the fire down to a few embers bedded in a deep mound of chalky ash; she had not shoveled the grate since the man left. The woman could see nothing, could not even see to make her way to the woodbox. She couldn't see the girl, but now she could hear her, the slow, deep breaths that were like a sleeping child's.

Slowly Thula unfolded her legs, pushed herself up from the floor, grunting, and as she did so her blanket dropped from her shoulders. She stood at last and made her way by feel to the far side of the room, where the lantern stood on a small square shelf above the man's pallet. By feel she picked it up at the base, carried it across the room slowly, feeling with her soft leather soles before her, to the shelf above the washstand where the tin of sulfur matches stood. In the dark she set the lamp down. In the dark she struck the match, and the area around the washstand leapt quickly to detail in the small yellow flare. When she'd lit the blackened wick and placed the globe over it, the room swelled to a brightness that seemed out of proportion to the strength of the one lantern, and Thula's eyes squinted at the sudden light. It hurt to bend at the woodbox, where there were only a few sticks of stovewood left amidst the cluttered twigs and bark at the bottom. She was faint with fasting, faint with the too-quick return from the place of silent, hopeless prayer, and she lost her balance as she reached for them, had to catch hold of the cold edge of the cookstove to keep from falling. When she turned with the two sticks of stovewood cradled in one arm, the handful of twigs to feed the embers in the other, she saw the girl's eyes watching her. The fragile body still lay curled on its side, but the limbs were no longer crooked inward. One hand had slipped from beneath the quilt she lay under, rested on the edge of Thula's red blanket where it had dropped on the floor. The girl's breath sounded in the room, deeply drawn and even. The woman moved forward, slowly, watching the ocher eyes as they followed her, the slow rise as they tracked her approach, and Thula knew the girl was not looking at something in the other world but at her, Thula Henry, as she came, knelt on the puncheon floor beside the pallet, placed the dry twigs on the orange coals, and blew on them until they began to smoke.

By the time the man returned with the small children at evening, Matt was sitting up on the pallet with the red blanket wrapped around her, sipping broth from a clay bowl. Jonaphrene ran toward her the instant she came in the door, but then stopped shyly a few feet from the edge of the pallet and stood with her hands behind her back. Matt looked at her sister, said nothing. She turned her eyes up at her father, looked at him a moment, glanced then at her two brothers, and went back to sipping the brown broth.

And the world returned to normal—to what was normal within the realm of that home and family: the older boy ran and played in the woods as usual, or chased after his male cousins, with the younger boy stumbling along behind until the teasing would become too unmerciful and Thomas would run back, silent and panting, not crying, to the log house. The father continued to leave the house before daylight and come home well after dark; the younger girl sat in her dreamy reverie beside the hearth or the cookstove, or followed her older sister's directions as she bossed her in how to clean a squirrel or sweep off the front porch. Matt herself seemed unchanged, but for the bone thinness and the pallor that had come to her in the winter darkness, painting her skin an ethereal bloodless yellow. But even that disappeared in a short time, and within a week and a half the deep amber color of her skin was back, and she'd returned to the restless, ceaseless roaming that marked her existence, sometimes hunting, sometimes not, occasionally taking the aged beagle with her, as if the time of her near death on the pallet had never been. Every few days she would take the younger children and disappear the whole afternoon into the brush along the creekbank, and Thula would watch them from beneath the porch overhang as they trailed singlefile across the road, and each time she watched she thought she would go back inside the house and gather her belongings in the leather satchel and go home. But each time, when the children came in at first dark, they smelled the meat roasting and the *tanfula* cooking and found Thula Henry sitting with her handwork beside the fire.

Jessie did not come again, but often Fayette would be there, following John through the door as he came in from work, or showing up a half hour later, and the children's uncle would sit on the mended ladderback tipped against the wall for only a moment before he'd get up to rove restlessly about the room, prowling and pawing at their few pitiful belongings—the shaving mug and razor propped on the top shelf, the chipped china saucers, the metal pitcher on the washstand —though he seemed not to really see the things he picked up and handled but to be touching them thoughtlessly, unconsciously, as one caresses an old scar. Always, he would be talking. Talking. The Indian woman watched him. She recognized the unnaturally bright eyes, the overloud voice, as he blustered and tried to cajole his brother; often she could detect the faint sour-sweet smell. When he was in the room the unease within her would stir up, get stronger. This was still a house of sickness, which Thula knew if none of the rest of them knew it; in her soul she knew it, and she knew it was very bad, very dangerous, to bring the destructive power of liquor into a sickhouse. She watched the children's father as well, not understanding why he would let that bad force come around his frail and vulnerable children.

But John seemed to pay his brother almost no mind, and Thula watched that too, how the more John ignored Fayette, the louder and more restless the other would become, striding aimlessly about the log room, talking, talking, and she thought, watching him as he roamed, insatiable, unable to be satisfied with whatever he picked up or looked at or ate or spoke, that this was the same in the girl, in her restless, aimless walking, the same in the father as he worked, the same in the jittery limbs of the boy Jim Dee, and Thula Henry thought maybe it was the same in all white people; maybe *Chihowa* put that hungry restlessness in all white people for a purpose, though she could not see what that purpose might be, because it seemed to make too much destruction. But the Creator's will and design had ever been unfathomable, and in her deeply troubled spirit, Thula did not try to comprehend. It would be like trying to comprehend why He sent His Son to such a little bunch of people in the desert, and then when that news went out, He let it be spread with so much killing—or why He let all these white people come swarming and devouring as locusts so that now there were three whites to every Choctaw in the Nation, taking the Nation's coal and trees and unbroken earth—or what He meant her to do with that girl.

Thula had given up trying to comprehend that portion; she was no longer patient and faithful, believing He would reveal to her His purpose, nor was she submissive, as she had been, to her part in that purpose—but still she did not seem to be able to leave. Nor did the children's father ask her. Never once had John suggested, whether by word or silence or gesture, that she was not needed in this house, that it was time for her to go home. The two continued in their unspoken collusion—the man, without argument, allowing her to take the place of mother for his children because he would not take a wife; the woman staying because, when she was alone in the log house, when she would begin to gather her herbs and her second skirt drying by the fire and her red blanket in preparation to go home, a bad feeling would come on her, a strange, indefinite foreboding, which would not depart until she settled back some way to stay. Not that she found peace in staying—her peace had entirely departed from her in the seven days and nights of the girl's sojourn—but the disturbance in her soul was easier when she did not try to fight.

She would speak to the girl sometimes, in the evenings before the father came home, when the younger ones were asleep in the upper room and it was just the two of them alone in the quiet beside the fire; she would say in a facsimile of her father's English, "You got some job to do. The Creator given you some work, you going to die you ain't done it," and repeat the same meaning in her mother's tongue. Sometimes she would read aloud from her Choctaw Bible, or smoke the room with sage and cedar, make her offerings of tobacco, but even as she did these things she felt her own soul dry and barren; she had no faith in the words coming from her mouth, no faith even in the cedar smoke, the songs that seemed no longer to belong to her. It was as if she had been sucked dry of all forms to do the Spirit's work. Once, she asked the girl, "What you seen yonder? What is it look like?" and then was shamed at her own question and immediately held her tongue. The girl looked back at her with almond eyes, answered nothing.

One morning Thula's eldest son George came and stood in the yard and called her to come out, and when she stood on the porch and looked at him with his big hat in his two hands and his black hair streaked with gray in the wintry daylight, and his face which was her own face gazing at her with that question, the longing in her to go home was so sharp she thought it would cut her breast in two. She went back in the log house and got her satchel, leaving even the chiggerweed roots she had just dug drying beside the fireplace, and walked with her son as far as the sawmill on the east side of Big Waddy—but the pull was too strong in her, that terrible sense that there was something she must do, and she was afraid. Thula stopped her son with a hand on his arm, looked up at him, and the two faces were equal in the gray light, the same round form and blackness of eye and glabrous skin, the woman almost two feet shorter and the son's head grayer, but the expressions on the identically formed features just the same, and she said in native tongue, "It's not finished. When it's finished I'll come." She turned, leaving her son standing in the dirt road, and went back.

Thus the end of winter passed. The hoop was arcing toward the earth's renewal when the man Fayette followed his brother in the door one night with a large powderhorn hanging from his neck and a grotesquely fat rifle of many barrels in his hands. Thula was sitting alone in the silence. Her Bible was open on her lap, but she was not reading the words. The younger children had been put to bed upstairs; the girl was not in the house, had not yet returned from her day's roaming, and Thula felt herself waiting, as she was ever waiting. Sometimes she thought that this was all that was asked of her, to wait, in bewilderment and turmoil, because the Creator was testing her as He tested His children in the Old Testament; other times she thought the soulsickness in that log house had crept inside her skin.

She paid little attention to the gun the man carried—though it was a tremendous weapon that held the force of great destruction within its iron pores—because it was sometimes Fayette's habit to bring a gun into the house and show it about, demonstrating its mechanisms to his brother, who hardly watched, and as Fayette snapped open the breech or spun the smoothly revolving cylinder, he would keep a constant hungry eye on his brother, who seemed to take notice of that least of all. But Thula was alert to the man himself from the moment he stumbled in the door, exhaling the sour smell before him, because she saw that the liquor was on him bad this night. It was the same as she'd seen it in her grandson Moss, as she'd seen it in her father, in old Cinnamon John who lived at Yonubby and sat in the yard of the church with his eyes blurred, looking to heaven, weeping, and trying to sing the old songs: as if the liquor itself were a spirit that got into the drinker and walked in his form, though crooked, and spoke through his mouth, though slurred, but a bad spirit itself whose only purpose was to destroy the carcass it inhabited and any human souls around that the spirit could find a way to touch. She closed her Testament and set it to the side, but she did not stand when the men came in. This was part of the silent agreement she held with the father: she cooked for and tended only the children, and the father might eat the leftovers in the food warmer above the stovetop, but he would serve himself—which he did now, first washing up at the washstand—but Thula's eyes were not on the father but on his brother as he roiled and raged about the room.

"When you going to get some damn furniture?" Fayette said, and he lurched in a looping half circle toward the crate box in the corner. "Man cain't even find a damn place to seddown!" But Fayette didn't attempt to sit on the crate but rather upended the multibarreled weapon on it so that the stock rested on the pine. "You gonna like this one, I reckon. It's a damn blackpowder muzzle loader, like that blame ole contraption you got yonder," and he waved a flapping hand at the longrifle resting on two big iron nails above the front door. "Fellow could make pert near any kinda gun on the face of the earth and still yet uses a old muzzle-loading Kentucky rifle, I reckon he just likes to mess with it, reckon maybe twelve times that many barrels to pack and load oughta satisfy him in a weap'n. Eh?"

He winked broadly, held it like a squint as he turned a glinting sapphire-and-ruby eye on the woman near the fireplace and, seeing the impassivity of expression there, allowed that same lit eye to travel around the room, roving, unfocused, as if it were the eye that were drunk and the man chasing after it, until at last it found his brother standing in front of the cookstove with a tin plate in his hand. Fayette blinked an instant, and then he said, almost with surprise, "Looka here now, Son. Look!" Swaying a little, he lifted the powderhorn that hung from the thong around his neck. The large end of the horn, where it had once met the bull's skull, was sealed with a leather skin stretched tight as a drumhead; the sharp point had been snipped from the tapered end, and that end was capped with a snug hand-carved horn cap. Fayette pulled the cap off with his teeth and spat it onto the floor, where it plinked against the wood and rolled, and he began to pour blackpowder from the horn into the many barrels, loosely, messily, the powder sifting in a fine black rain over the fist that held the muzzle end of the big gun. He kept up his rain of words as he poured, sometimes slurring, sometimes pronouncing them cleanly and carefully. "Got this off a ole boy 'tween here'n Fort Smith, old trader I don't know what some kind of prospector or something, said he was. Said he was. Volleygun. That's what he called it. English volleygun. From England. I bet you this thing's a hunnerd years old, y'reckon?" He righted the powderhorn a moment, squinted at the barrels, upended the horn again, and continued to pour. "Give 'im two dollars, 's all he said he wanted. I th'ew in a quart of whiskey for good luck. You could scare the bejeezus outa somebody with this thing, couldn'cha? Man alive. Open up twelve barrels at once on their gizzard, just blow 'em to holy hell."

He reached with clumsy fingers into the leather pouch at his waist and drew out a lead ball, dull and pewter gray in the lamplight, and with several tries managed to align it with the round rim of one of the barrels, pushed it in, reached for another from the pouch. He'd poured a tremendous load of powder in each, and Thula saw him put two balls in some of the barrels, none in others. Several times he fumbled the one he was trying to place, and the ball would drop from his fingers, thunk, and roll cleanly on the wood floor. He withdrew the rod from the pipes beneath the nether barrel and rammed it down the twelve, sloppily, missing some of them, doing others two and three times, as the tone of his words changed from boyish thrill to the bitter whine of accusation.

"Could jus' lay this in a man's face, I reckon a man might do about whatever you ast him politely to do then. What kinda hole you believe twelve barrels at onced is gonna make in a man's belly? 'M'ona show ya right here in a little bit. I come to give you a little demonstration." And he continued jamming the ramrod hard, haphazardly, hit or miss, into the barrels. "Blasts 'em all ever' one at once, this thing does. Course, somebody knew what he was doing, he could figure out how to make him a twelve-barrel shotgun could just fire however many barrels a fellow wanted, nine or seven or the whole blame bunch if a fellow wanted to blow somebody to holy hell and be done with it. Couldn't he?" Fayette turned the glistening moistness of his eyes to his brother again. "Somebody been given a talent he don't even want to use it for the betterment of himself or his children who been living in a pigsty without even no decent furniture, won't use it even when his own blood and kin asks him, asks him polite as a gingerlady, that's the kind of fella's about as stubborn and stupid as a pig himself. Y'reckon? Son?"

John spooned a pale clump of hominy into his mouth. His eyes were on his brother, his features without expression.

"Man with that kind of talent, he wouldn't even have to use his brains that hard." Fayette paused in his ramrodding, gazed steadily, evenly, across the room, his bloodshot eyes still glistening but the sway of trunk and slur of tongue, for the moment, calmed. "He could just forge a good simple type of a weapon people could use in this country, let the other fellow distribute it like he wants to, make 'em all a living. Make everybody a decent way to live. But no-sir. No-sir. Man like that, he don't care a damn what's to become of his family. Man like that, he's got to run off at the first sign of some little old patent trouble, some stupid little no 'count thing." Thus had Fayette twisted in his mind the old trouble that had caused them to leave Kentucky. The sway was back in his torso, and he spat once on the floor, returned to jamming the rod again and again, remembering, in the blaming necessity of his besotted mind, that it had been John who'd fled fearfully across the land, driven by phantasms, he himself who'd been dragged along in his brother's wake.

Thula Henry, watching, understood that the man Fayette had been naming something in his mind's language for a long time; she did not need to listen to the words in their harsh tongue to hear. This one had nurtured and built and nourished something until it swelled up big, fully grown, but it had become something different from the seed that had begun it. Watching the two men, she saw the children's father standing before the cookstove with the hominy plate in one hand, eating steadily in a slow, unvaried rhythm, lifting the spoon without pause from plate to mouth, back to plate, the sound of tin scraping tin making a ticking, monotonous rhythm in the room. On his face was a shadow of the black, cold look she had seen as he started out into the predawn darkness on the morning before the girl had awakened from the other world. Thula turned her eyes to the face of the drunk man again; she watched him draw the ramrod from the last barrel, fumble to replace it in the pipes, give up finally and, with an oath, drop it clattering on the floor, among the loose musket balls, the powderhorn cap, and spilled powder, all the while watching from slit bloodshot eyes as his brother ate in that slow, undeviating rhythm. Thula saw that the man Fayette was nursing a very old wound. She saw that he'd been feeling and re-feeling that same grievous wound for many years. It wasn't formed from outside himself, hadn't been given to him that way, but was a remembered stab-hurt entirely of his own making, and

Thula saw this in the same way she saw that the liquor was not, as she'd thought (as she wanted to think, because of her grandson, her father), a separate bad spirit come into the man's soul to make him act so, but a sly force that knew how to trick the bad thing that dwelt there already to come out.

Fayette grunted as he hoisted the volleygun. "You just need a little demonstration, Son, reckon?" He raised the heavy muzzle unsteadily, pointed the twelve barrels at his brother, held them there a moment, then swept the heavy aim in a wide, clumsy arc across the room to the west wall; he held an instant on the small square of window before he pulled the trigger and the poorly packed and excessive blackpowder in the twelve barrels exploded, and the smell and roar and splinter cracked beyond sound, reverberated in the log room, swirled and settled at last into smoke and silence. Then from the upper room there came the high thin wail that raised, spiraling, into a child's scream. Through the hole, where the splintered wood jutted down like eye-teeth into the gaping place that had been solid log, the cold night air seeped in.

For two days thunderstorms raged in the valleys of the Sans Bois as if God Himself were venting His fury. An enraged yellowgreen light followed and preceded each drenching, each rain of hail on the earth popping and dancing, each roar of wind. In the night, lightning's fingers splayed and forked, heaven to earth, back to heaven, unceasing, so near in the blackness their crack and splinter was one with the light, and the aftermath of rumbling rolled for minutes until it was interrupted by the next crack. Trees fell, smoldering. Barnroofs blew off and tumbled toward Arkansas. The daywind blew hard, warm and wet and cool, from the southwest—the balmy mixed roiling winds that for eons have blown twisters into this quick-change, irascible country— and each time the wind paused in the charged light, Thula Henry would step out onto the porch and look to the top of Bull Mountain to see where the tail would drop from the black clouds. Twisters did drop to earth from that two-day spate of storms, all over the Choctaw Nation, at Skullyville and Honobia and Tuskahoma and Swink—but none here at Big Waddy Crossing. None here.

For two days the family and the Indian woman were bound together in the shell of the log house. Not Fayette—he'd gone out soon after he'd blown the hole in the wall, immediately after John stepped across the room, took the volleygun from him, and said, too calmly, his voice controlled, icy, "Reckon you'd better go on home now." Deflated, small in the gray smoke choking the room, his mouth working, Fayette had slid out the split-log door beneath his brother's cold, calm, black stare. But John and the four children and Thula Henry were confined by the coming-one-on-top-of-the-other assault of storms. And it was like this—not one constant storm but a relentless series of different storms, each with its own wind and shape of hail and sound of drenching, with only the false promise of ending between each. The first had approached disguised as a cold spring rain within an hour after Fayette left. Matt had come in, driven by the rain, and found the little children sitting up swollen-eyed and wide awake beside Thula, the room still smelling of blackpowder, and her father carefully nailing a piece of blanket over the ragged hole in the west wall, his movements slow and precise. She did not ask, and no word of explanation was spoken. The girl slapped the water off her hat and hung it on the peg beside the door, went to the stove for her cold food.

It was late that night that the temperature began to rise, driven by the southwind, and the sky split and began to pour water. John tried to walk to work the next morning, but he returned within a half hour, soaked, saying he could not wade through the boggy place on the curve, it had become a rolling swamp, and he would try again in a while. But he did not try again that day because the rain poured and drenched, pausing only long enough to gather more fury before it rushed to pound the ocherous muddy earth again. To the east Bull Creek raged over the road, spread an eighth of a mile wide, crawled moiling up toward the yard.

On the second day the two girls emerged from the house about noon and stood just back from the slanting downpour that whipped beneath the porch overhang, and then the father came out behind them, then the two boys, and the woman last of all. The girls stood shoulder-to-shoulder looking down at the livid, moving water, the two figures almost exactly the same size, though the elder was fourteen, the younger barely nine, both of them with faces beyond their years and the bodies of children. Their arms were linked as they'd been linked when Thula first saw them on the ridge. They stood thus for more than an hour, while their brothers played about the porch and their father paced the far end, looking west for the glimmering of light that would signal the storm's lifting. Suddenly, for no discernible cause, Matt pulled away from her sister, turned, and began to pace about the porch in the same manner as her father, though with less seeming purpose, gnawed, as Thula knew, with that terrible restlessness that made her all the time need to walk and walk.

Toward evening the last storm retreated east, chased by the sun in the widening slit of western sky. It was too late for the man to walk to work at Cedar, and his restlessness matched his daughter's, their faces turned each toward the retreating clouds streaked orange and crimson and deep muddy violet, or west to the beryl sky where the sun burned, or out at the very earth itself, transformed by the storm's fury, unseen, the green infant leaves and grass blades sprung from the grayblackness. Bull Creek still roiled beyond its banks, the road below the house was a muddy bog crossed by yellowbrown rivulets, but everywhere the smell and sound of the transformation were evident: in the murmur of people's voices on the porches in town, in the smell of verdure and the cacophony of songbirds and crows and bluejays announcing the storms' departure, spring come. For the father and the daughter on the log porch the hour of release from the storm's grip was almost worse than the two days of its holding, because it was followed too soon by the coming dark.

But at dawn the next morning John walked off to work at Cedar, and soon after, Matt took the old slouch hat down from the peg beside the door and went out, descended the stone slab of step and started directly toward the moiling waters of Bull Creek, which had receded from the yard but still swelled beyond the bank. Thula stood on the porch and watched her, watched the old hound dog emerge from beneath the porch, slapping his ears, and begin in his feeble way to trot after the girl. She turned and hollered him back once, went on. The dog waited a little bit, and then he continued behind her, fat and slow and determined, trailing at a distance. But when the girl waded right into the brown waters of Bull Creek, waded to her thighs at the ford and kept on going, the beagle stopped. He stood a minute looking after her and then turned slowly and waddled back toward the house.

The girl did not come home that night. She was not there at dawn the next day when her father left to walk to Cedar. He rose, shaved, dressed, and then stood for a half hour on the porch with the light coming, agitated, angry, not yet fearful. Thula came outside, looked off east where the man was looking. After a while she said, "She be here in a little while." He nodded, neither of them looking at the other, and finally, as dawn was breaking, he stepped down off the stone slab and walked west.

At midmorning Thula saw the girl coming. From the open doorway she watched Matt cross back over Bull Creek, wade through the water, lower now, still filled with tumbling sticks and brickle, muddy, but shallower on the road. The girl's slouch hat was missing; her face was blank, her mouth thin and cracked. A terrible dread came over Thula as she watched Matt wade up from the water and into the yard. The girl walked directly to where the ancient beagle warmed himself in a patch of sun beside the woodpile, and sat down and put her arm across his rolling back. The straight dun-colored hair was pulled back from her face in a leather thong at the base of her skull; her skin was parched-corn yellow. Her eyes were entirely empty. Thula thought, looking at her, that the girl's soul was gone. Not gone traveling, as it had seemed when Matt lay on the pallet, but gone altogether, disappeared: sucked from her form as the marrow is sucked from a chicken bone by a starving man.

"*Impashilup,*" Thula said out loud.

But she knew that was not possible. The ancient ones cared nothing for any human but Choctaw. It wasn't possible that the girl had encountered the Soul Eater on one of her solitary roamings in the creek bottoms and, that little nick being there, *Impashilup* crept in to devour her spirit. That was not possible, Thula knew it. But she didn't know what other encounter of the Spirit could strip a form so cleanly; she didn't know what could have happened to this white girl. The trembling came hard upon Thula, and a strong sense of helplessness in the face of what was beyond her knowing; there were certain things the Creator had not given to the people to know—had not given to her, Thula Henry—and the trembling of doubt increased, quaked large, to include her own purpose, what she'd believed she had already known. Her eyes were on the hollow form in the yard, on the girl's thin hand resting, motionless, against the dog's flank. Thula could do nothing to retrieve hope for that emptiness; she knew no medicine for a thieved soul. The woman turned, not as if she had been released but as if she forced herself, one soft-soled foot set before the other across the porch, washed in the invisible trembling; she went back inside the log house and silently began to gather her herbs and cedar and tobacco and place them inside her leather satchel.

BOOK THREE

Plain Chant

There are, it may be, so many kinds of

voices in the world, and none of them

is without signification.

I CORINTHIANS 14:10

Grady Dayberry

They tell it a hunnerd ways, as many ways as you'd care to listen, but I don't believe there's many still living that knows the real story nor even a fraction of it. Tales get blown all out of proportion, you're liable to hear anything anymore. But if you want to know what happened, I'll tell it. I witnessed a good portion myself, we all did, the whole town—well, what I mean, I didn't see the actual incident but about as near to it as a person would want to. I was just a boy. Whooee, that's the first man I ever seen killed. But what I didn't see and what I'm fixing to tell you, I heard direct from my daddy, and you know my dad was a well-respected man in this country. You know he was never known to carry tales. It all happened right here on the street in front of his stable, what used to be my daddy's livery stable, and I guess he seen more of it than any man living, and what he didn't see he knew about in the first place because John Lodi worked for him nearly from the day him and his family come into this part of the country and in the second place because my dad was a perspicacious man.

They lived up at Waddy, these Lodis, what we used to call Big Waddy Crossing—and it didn't cross nothing, just a big boggy place on the old Overland Mail Line, but they called it that, I don't know why. Might've been one of these old Choctaw names got knocked out of whack. Might've been on account of how Bull Creek runs through there, but Lord, Bull Creek wasn't nothing to cross even way back then. But it was Big Waddy Crossing, or so they called it—well, it's not even a ghost town now. Nothing yonder but the stone foundation of the school and a little piece of the teacherage. Sawmill burnt in Aught Six, and then that cyclone come through in Forty-five, blowed everything plumb to the other side of Toms Mountain, and that was all she wrote for Big Waddy Crossing. But it started out to be some kind of a little old town, and these Lodis all lived up around there. I believe according to my daddy it was the one brother come in first, the one they called Fate. Don't know where they come from—well, you just didn't ask a fellow where he come from nor why back then, everybody had a story and the majority of them might not've been too pleasant—but they just migrated into this part of the country and settled in their families, first the one brother and his family and then the next one and his. That's how a lot of folks did. Now, my family is a bit to the unusual, because my granddaddy come in here early, way back before the Civil War even—the War of Rebellion, was how he used to call it. Come up from Texas on horseback, Grandpa did, married his first wife and opened his little trading post up yonder at what we used to call Old Cedar when there wasn't nothing but Indians and colored people hardly anywhere around here—but when these big batches of white people started coming into the Nation, a lot of times they'd trickle in one piece of the family at a trip. They tell me that's how there got to be so many Tannehills around this part of the country. Tannehills didn't breed all that many Tannehills once they'd got in here, they had a good headstart long before that. I heard it was six brothers all dribbled in here a piece at a time from somewhere, spread out over ten or eleven years, but a lot of families would do like that. First one bunch would come in from Alabama or Mississippi or wherever they come from, and then they'd send word back how good and easy life was here in the Nation—and it wasn't, not so easy as all that, but I reckon it was easier than what some of them left—and here'd come the next bunch, and so on, and I reckon that's how these Lodis did. It's a pretty common story.

But, now, John Lodi was a widow-man, and that was something a little bit unusual. There were plenty widow-women around in these parts, I expect, even then, but a man without a wife didn't usually stay without one for long, especially not if he had young'uns, and John Lodi did. You'd need somebody to take care of your children, do the woman work, unless you had a big old grown girl—which Lodi didn't have nothing but two little bitty ones, they tell me, and one of them never did act just right—but even if you did have a girl big enough she could take care of the young'uns, you'd still want a wife to answer a man's natural instinct, unless you meant to ride all the way to Fort Smith. Now, when Lodi come in here there might not've been all that many white women falling all over theirselves to get a husband, I know that, because that'd been in Eighty-six or Eighty-seven, or anyhow John Lodi went to work for my dad in Eighteen Eighty-eight at the start of the new year, but there was bound to have been a few white widow-women around. Men died easy back then. Or you might send back home for one, for your dead wife's sister or somebody, or a man could get an Indian wife if he had a mind to, and a lot of them did. Made your permit papers unnecessary, you didn't have to go through all that rigmarole—they put you through the hoops, these Choctaws did now, you had to have a certificate of good moral character signed by ten citizens, pay a hunnerd-dollar license fee, renounce the protections of the laws of the United States, I don't know what-all. But John Lodi, he come in here without a wife, white nor no color, and that little parcel of motherless children, which is unusual in itself, because a single man might come in here by his lonesome or a family man might lose his wife to birthing onced he'd got here and get him another'n right quick, but a widow-man with children would usually just piece them out to relatives before he come into the Nation, or else he'd stay home. John Lodi never so much as tipped his hat to a lady on the street, that I ever heard of—not because he wasn't a gentlemanly man but more like because a female creature was something invisible to him—much less kept company with a woman, so far as I know. So that aspect was a little odd, but there was more to it than that.

It was highly unusual for a man to live in one community and work in another in that time, but John Lodi did. That was another characteristic from the outset that was strange. Every morning for I guess it must've been close to nine years he walked the whole way from Big Waddy to Cedar and then, turn around, walked back home by coal-oil light after dark. That is a distance of seven and three-quarter miles, people, and it could be plenty rough in the winter, I can tell you, but that's not even it. In those days, see, a man worked for himself. You didn't go out and do public work, you just *were* something, sometimes several somethings—farmer, sawmiller, blacksmith—just whatever it was you knew how to do. In the time I'm telling about, that was so. Oh, you might have to go off from your family, say, and locate your sawmill-set off up in the mountains till you'd logged all the timber out, and then you'd come home. If it did happen you worked for somebody—it wasn't common but it wasn't entirely unheard of, these coal miners did it around here for years, but coal miners is a different breed altogether to what I'm speaking of, and anyhow, back in that time, they was foreigners or colored nearly to the last man—but if you was a white man and you did go to work for another man, why, you worked close to home. You didn't go traipsing seven and three-quarter miles to work like a hoehand from daylight to dark for day wages. And if through some mismanagement or misfortune you *did* have to go seven and three-quarter miles to work for a fellow, well, you about moved your family over yonder and built them a house. That's just how folks did. Plus, too, John Lodi was bound to have a saddlehorse or some kind of old mule—well, come to think of it, I know they had a mule or an old plowhorse or something because folks talked about how awful it was him putting that little girl to plowing and all he had her doing up there—but you'd never see him on one. I never seen him anything but afoot, and a man in that time just didn't do like that. And now what compounds that little mystery to my mind is what the man did for a living, because what John Lodi knew how to do—I don't care if I am telling it on my daddy—John Lodi was the best blacksmith this part of the country's ever seen.

My dad was a pretty fair hand with a tong and hammer, but he couldn't hold John Lodi a light to go by. Nobody could, not in that time, not to this day. I ain't seen anybody yet who could meet him. You'd just have to watch him work a forge to believe it. He'd take that piece of iron out perfect, I mean, just the right minute—he could tell by the color, had it down to the very iota—and, mister, he'd go to work on it, mold it like riverclay, just practically smooth it around with his hands. Didn't use his hands, of course, used regular smithing tools like any man would, it just appeared nearly like he was using his bare hands. That's how smooth a hammer and tongs'd fit 'em. That's how easy they'd beat and clang—bang! bang! bang! there's your shoe fitted perfect, he wouldn't have to measure but once. My dad had plenty of tools—he started fooling with iron early, maybe age eleven or twelve —but he just didn't have the touch for it like Lodi did. Dad was skilled, see, but he wasn't an artist. He didn't have that knack. Mostly he just liked to shoe horses—he was always a good hand with livestock, now that was one of my daddy's main skills—but he just turned all the other ironwork over to Lodi quick as he got him hired on. But my dad had garnered tools over a lifetime and he owned about any size hammer, ballpeen, crosspeen, sledge, or whatever, had any size chisel you'd want, and if he didn't have the right size for what was wanted, why, Lodi'd just take an hour or so and make it, but the man never would own a single tool he made. He just never would. Well, that was another thing that was strange.

See, now, John Lodi could've pretty near had the run of this country as far as blacksmithing's concerned. He never did have to work for my dad. I don't reckon he could've afforded to buy a forge and anvil when he first come in here, but a man as skilled as he was, I believe he could have made what he wanted if he could've got ahold of the iron. I know he could. He could make any tool you'd want, from froe blade to swage block, just anything, and he worked at day wages for my dad. Well, that's plumb daft. Now, Daddy wasn't daft, he kept him on because folks'd come clear from Bokoshe or Bug Scuffle for John Lodi to make them a plow point or bang out a wheelrim or shoe some ornery old mule. And he was fair with him, Dad was, paid him honorable wage for all that, but it wasn't nothing to what Lodi could've made on his own if he'd had half a mind to, and he knew it and we knew it, and nobody said a word.

Well, we didn't worry too much about all that business—I didn't, I wasn't but twelve when the killing happened and I'd been around John Lodi all my life—but even Daddy and Granddaddy, I don't think they thought too much about it except to mark it and chalk it up to Daddy's good fortune. There was plenty odd men with odd stories all around in these parts. Still are. But after the killing, people started in talking about how odd it was, him living at Big Waddy and working at Cedar—you know how every little thing'll take on a new light after a killing—odd him never marrying, odd how he treated that girl. That'd be his oldest girl, I mean to say. Now, that is probably the most peculiar fact. I can't swear to it personally—I never seen her but once, that morning at the hearing, and the girl looked just normal to me—but they tell me she took spells. I don't know what it was, if she layed down on the floor and went to frothing or what. I never heard anybody describe it, they just told it like this: she took spells. And she dressed like a man, the girl did, wore pants and a slouch hat and a man's shirt and everything, but I've got my own speculation about that. She wasn't no prize to look at, see, and she had to know it, and I believe that's how come her to take after Belle Starr. We all of us youngsters were pretty taken with Belle Starr in those days. She'd been dead, I don't know, five or six years maybe, shot in the back—now, that's another killing got told around plenty—but that didn't stop us admiring her, and we played Belle Starr and Cole Younger, or Cherokee Bill or Bill Doolin or the Daltons, or just any other of our famous citizenry, me no less than the rest of them—I pretended myself into a bank robbery and shootout more than a few times—so to my mind that's as reasonable an explanation as you need for it. Everybody knew Belle Starr was ugly as a saddlesore and did her outlawing in britches, dressed like a man.

But anyhow, they didn't talk so much about the idea the girl was strange—though plenty of them said that too, after the killing they tsked over that like they'd watched it all along—but what they did the most headshaking over was how her daddy treated her. He treated her just like—well, I don't know how to say it. About like a son. But that's not even right either, because he didn't go around teaching her or bossing her, he treated her more like she was a partner to him. You'd almost want to say like a wife, but that wasn't it neither, because he took her hunting, had her plowing and whatnot, about all you'd expect out of a son, but they tell me he'd be as like to ask her advice on something as tell her what to do. Treated her maybe about like a brother, I want to say, or something like. She could even do a little farrier work, some of them said, though I don't know if I believe it. That girl wasn't as big as a minute when I seen her at the hearing, and she was fullgrown by then. I can't picture her shoeing a plowhorse or something, but they tell me she could. But anyhow, Lodi kindly kept her with him, they said, when he wasn't working, especially after some of them died and the rest of them just went to rot and ruin, about like you'd expect.

They come in here with the fever, you know, that entire little mess of children—well, I don't know what kind of fever, we had every kind of fever known to man burning our children up back then—but this Lodi bunch carried it in with them, Dad said, liked to worried that community to death. Had reason for it, Dad said; said you'd hear about the fever in one family, next thing you know it'd be spread all through the community, just hopping from housetop to housetop like a wildfire, and before you knew what hit you, you'd have a dozen little graves out back of the house. But look at that now. I've studied this some, see, put my mind to it a little bit on account of my dad was so close to the situation, and I've got my theories on that too.

Now, folks say that family was strange, and they were, maybe, but you look at this a minute. All right, say you was to come into a new

part of the country and first thing happens, your children take sick—
not one thing you can do to help it, they just take sick, that's all, and
pretty much like to die, and one or two of them do die—well, now,
that wasn't so uncommon, we didn't have no doctors to speak of nor
medicine nor nothing. Children died a lot back then. Everybody did.
But, now, say the result of your children taking sick and dying on you
is the entire community shuns you, just won't have one thing to do
with you nor your young'uns—now, how's that going to make you
feel? How're you going to act?

I don't want y'all to get the mistaken impression here. In general
folks are good to help each other out in this part of the country, they'll
show up for any sort of tragedy, take food to the house, and they did
better back then even than they do now. Had to. You just couldn't
survive hardly without you helped one another, and you didn't be-
grudge it neither because you never knew when it'd be you or yours
was going to be the ones needed the help—so I don't have a precise
explanation for how come the community of Big Waddy Crossing to
shun these Lodis so bad, at least not after the fever'd passed and there
wasn't no danger, but they did so, my dad told me that. But, now,
here's the odd thing: they didn't shun but one half the family, and
that'd be John Lodi and his. They tell me Fate Lodi was well thought
of in that community, folks traded with him and all. It was just the
one fevered family folks acted like that about. I wouldn't know, I never
went up to Big Waddy in those days, but, you know, stories get started,
no rhyme nor reason to it, might be just one of these chicken and egg
deals—did Big Waddy shun them because they's strange, or did they
get strange on account of everybody shunned them? You'll have to
answer that question for yourself, but me, for my part, I like to think
it's that little dead town's notions, whatever they was, made these Lodis
turn in on theirselves.

I liked him. John Lodi. I admired him, I guess. He was good to
me, for one thing. I never did know those young'uns, and they
wouldn't've been young'uns to me if I had known them, they was every
one I believe older than myself. But we didn't go school-hopping over
to Waddy at no time back yonder—wasn't any need to: Cedar was
already bigger than Waddy even then—and I never did see a one of
them young Lodis, all but that day and the morning of the hearing,
wouldn't know them on the street this minute, if any of them's even
still living. Don't know what become of them neither; they all kindly
disappeared from this country after that. Wasn't many boys anyhow—

I believe the brother had a couple or three, but that Lodi name just died out, the way some of them do around here. Some families, like these Tannehills, they grow up a bunch of boys and spread the name all over creation, but there's other families used to belong around here, the names have all died out. You'll see them marking a tombstone at the Cedar cemetery, maybe a whole fencerow of tombstones, but you won't meet a Grange coming or going, nor a Lodi nor a Phelps.

But here's the kind of man John Lodi was.

All right, I'd've been maybe—what? Ten or so, I reckon. It was pretty well before the killing but I was big enough to know a few things and not forget. Not that I ever forgot much, let me say. My memory hadn't ever been a weak part of my brain. Well, all right, I'll tell you just exactly. I was ten years and eleven months old when this happened, now how's that? Here's how come me to recollect: I turned eleven years old on the twenty-fourth day of December, Eighteen Hundred and Ninety-four. That's right, Christmas Eve. I was my mama's last and best Christmas present, she always said that. All right now, the killing took place March the third, Eighteen Ninety-six, your history'll tell you that. You can go look it up in the *Woolerton Eagle*—my, yes, they had a newspaper in Woolerton at that time; this country was getting plumb settled by then. All right, so this is how I calculate it: the little event I'm fixing to tell you happened along about Thanksgiving, and I know I had to be at least ten because my dad said he wasn't getting me no rifle till I got big enough to justify, and if I'd ask him what that meant, he'd say, When you can load it singlehanded, and I'd say, I can do that now, Dad! (I probably started that when I wasn't over five or six), and he'd say, Not till you can see over the muzzle with it standing on its end, and if I'd ask him when that would be, he'd say, I reckon when you're ten. He told me that all my life, from ever since I got to wanting one, which is from before I can remember, so there's no doubt in my mind I was ten. I'd been ten a good little while and I hadn't got no rifle yet and I was just chafing at the bit.

All right, I'll just tell you the truth over it. I didn't care two beans about a rifle at that time. What I wanted was a pistol. I wanted me one of these Colt double-action revolvers because I reckoned myself an outlaw—that's how I played, see—and everybody knew these outlaws had to have their sixshooters when they went to rob a bank. But I never even pestered my dad about a pistol because it was just out of the question; he aimed for me to have a squirrel gun. Now, I'd be turning something in December, I was going to have a birthday in one month, and I know the killing didn't happen that next spring because I used that gun all through the summer and I know Lodi was still working for my dad then because him and me went coon hunting the next fall. So this here happened November, Ninety-four, I was ten, going on eleven, and I come into the livery one evening after I'd finished my chores.

Might've been four o'clock or so, because it was already starting to frown up and get dark. What I mean, evenings was short. It was one of these overcast November gray spells, you knew it was going to be black as midnight under a iron skillet in about an hour, and the wind was fixing to whip up a little storm. Lodi was sitting there at the cold forge, working a piece of wood. He didn't have no ironwork to do, there wasn't nobody sitting around the shop waiting for him to finish up their go-devils or whatever they'd brought in for him to fix for them—now, this was highly unusual. They was always somebody in that shop. A blacksmith shop back in those days, it was pretty near like your barbershop would be in this time, or your cafe. Men just liked to gather around there, I don't know why. Well, you always had a few folks waiting for their ox team to get shod or something, but there'd be other men just happen by and set a spell around the stove where it was warm, or squat over yonder in the straw, gossiping and whatnot. They just gathered like that.

All right, see, now I'm going to have to sidetrack on this a little bit, I reckon. Y'all don't remember my dad's livery, but it was right down here yonder across the tracks—well, they was more Cedar south of the railroad in that time than north here on Main Street. The hotel and everything was down yonder, and my dad's livery was there. Well, now, when he built that place he built it for the stage stop. He didn't care to do more than shoe a few horses, and he'd stable your mule or your horse for you if you was to need to hole up at Cedar—started that for the outlaws some, though he told it he did it for the men laying the tracks—so what he put up mostly was more stable than blacksmith shop, though, sure, he had him a little handmade forge. When Lodi hired on to him, Dad had to knock out that whole north wall, and what he done, he built a new stable over yonder and opened the whole of the old part up for Lodi to have him a shop. Look here, John Lodi was about as good a woodworker as he was a ironworker —a good smith was in those days, because if you was working wagons, you was working wood—so he needed plenty room to drive them wagons in. Needed room for the big forge Daddy had hauled in from Saint Louis.

Oh, a good blacksmith was a well-respected man back in those times, he had as high a outlook as a doctor maybe, or a judge would right now. Well, you just had to have 'em, you couldn't get by without one, everything depended on him, your farming and livelihood and getting around. So, you look here at this irony a minute. John Lodi was maybe the most respected blacksmith in this whole part of the country, and they'd come from all over to have him do their work for them, wood or iron either one, they'd set around here same as they would at Hartshorne or Poteau, any good blacksmith and livery. But they never did warm to him one bit. They respected him, don't get me wrong—and the men flocked here, they hung around my dad's livery as good as any stable around, but they would settle theirselves mostly over in the barn part and watch Lodi work from there. They didn't try to pass the time of day with him nor nothing, they'd just lay out over yonder and watch. Now, Dad, he was a friendly man, always was, and they'd jaw with him and he was always glad to set a spell and talk. But it was nearly like there was a line drawn where that old barn wall used to've been. Them men wouldn't come over it hardly but just to tell Lodi what was needed, and then they'd back off. And then they called the man strange.

So anyway, this particular afternoon I'm speaking of, there wasn't no customers around and my dad wasn't around because he'd gone to Brown's Prairie for some kind of horse-trading business—now, I knew that already, I knew my dad wasn't going to be there and wouldn't likely get home before the next morning—and maybe that's how come me to go around. I don't know why there wasn't anybody else around, unless folks just knew my dad was gone and they reckoned they'd just wait to get their work done till they knew he'd got back. Well, Lodi didn't have any work he'd ought to do nor would get paid to do, and it was getting dark outside and raw—but do you think the man went on home before the snow come, like any normal man would? Not a chance of it. He was working day wages, and my daddy's day wages said a man worked till six o'clock, that's how Lodi'd worked it out with my dad. So even without him with a piece of work to do for nobody, he still set there in the shop. And he was working wood by the forge, and that forge was flat cold as ice. Wasn't nothing to heat that big old barn but the woodstove over yonder, you'd think he'd've gone over to sit by it, but his place was by the forge there at his bench, and that's where he set.

Well, I come in, see, and I don't know what-all I had on my young mind, I can't for the life of me remember that. Probably I just meant to watch him work a bit without my dad around to find me something useful to put myself to, I don't know. I did like to watch John Lodi work that iron; it was just like a miracle to me. I had the thought in those days that if I didn't turn out to be an outlaw I might learn me some blacksmithing, but of course I never really did. Oh, I can make you a good fitting for a mule shoe—I always did prefer shoeing a mule to a horse, even if they are ornery sonuvaguns. Their feet's just so little and neat, hardly any trimming to 'em, just give them a lick or two and that's it. You don't have no trouble with them if you know how to act—but I never did have any real skill for it. About like my dad. But you know, when you're little you'll think anything, so I thought I'd turn out to be an outlaw, but blacksmithing was my second choice.

So here I was. I blew in with that wind rising, bang! that old rough-cut door slammed behind me, liked to whupped me in the butt. He looked at me, never missed a lick with the plane he was using on that piece of wood.

"Son," he says, and nodded. Hands never stopped.

"Evening, Mr. Lodi," I says.

He was bareheaded, and you didn't hardly ever see him like that. Well, it wasn't warm in there, not hardly, not with the forge blowed out, so I don't know why he was sitting there without a hat. He was pretty near a bald man, or he didn't have too much hair on top; you'd think he'd a been cold. I can see him just as well. Looked odd, you know, because he wasn't an old man but his forehead was near as smooth as glass, it slicked right back yonder, like what little hair he'd got was crawfishing back from his brows. His eyebrows was about as brushy as new wood. He near looked like two different men with his hat on and hat off. With it on, his eyes would go all shaded, and he'd look, in fact, if you can believe it, more like an old man than he did with that forehead shining, on account of how the shadows under his eyes would do. It was strange. Take the hat off, his eyes would lighten, he'd drop about twenty years. Isn't that something? He'd appear younger-looking with his hat off and that bald pate just a-shining than he looked with it on. Made him look . . . I don't know . . . easy. Soft,

I almost want to say, though you knew good and well he wasn't a soft man—but that light forehead of his, it'd look nearly as soft as a little child's. That's how it was.

So I don't know, I felt easy with him, how he had his hat off, and—now, I don't know why, because it wasn't any too warm in there—I took mine off too, and took a step over toward him. Ordinarily I wouldn't. Ordinarily I'd do about like the rest of them, just hide and watch. Who can explain it? I just lay it off to him sitting there without a hat. But he didn't bite me or nothing, so I took another step. You know he was working by kerosene. They wasn't no electric lights in that blacksmith shop—no electric lights nowhere any closer than McAlester I reckon at that time. You just had your lanterns and your natural light from the big door, if you were in a position to stand it open, which not in that weather you were not, so the light was pure yellow yonder, sitting on top of the mounted post vise, throwing shadows, shining down on his hands. His hands were something else again. They were that big—and stubby? Looked about like they belonged to an old sawmiller, cottonpicker or something. Cracked and fissured all through, his fingers blunt as a square. He was missing the nail entirely on one finger, and the little tip was was gone off of one thumb. You wouldn't think, couldn't imagine, how he did what he did with them hands. They looked like bearpaws nearly, just big old awkward things, and he could do what he did with them. It was something. Well, his hands never paused an iota, and you know he was looking at me. He wasn't looking down at what he was doing, and here these hands went, just smoothing, smoothing that wood.

Well, maybe that was it partly. I don't know how come me to ask him what he was doing, but I did. It was strange then. He blinked, looked down at that piece of wood, and it was nearly like he just then found it sitting there. Like he never even knowed he was working it. Well, I blinked too then, looked down, got a good look at it. I seen it then. Clear as a bell. Cut-out piece of red oak, and the long end of it stuck way under the bench. Gun stock. That's what he was making. Most precisely, a rifle stock, and it was the old-fashioned kind, a muzzle loader—what you used to call your Kentucky rifle or your longrifle—and it went from here to yonder, but I didn't know it then. I couldn't see it, ever bit of it, from where I was standing, but I could see enough to recognize it. I didn't think nothing but them two words—gun stock—and I didn't know what else to think.

"What are you making, Mr. Lodi?" I asked him again, like a fool, but I couldn't think of nothing.

Still sitting there, looking down at his hands, looks up at me, surprised, like he don't even know. Just looks at me quiet a minute, don't say nothing. Then, like he's waking up from something, he shakes his head. Like a horse, you know, trying to shake loose the bit. Looks down again, starts turning that piece of red oak over and over across his lap between his hands. Says, looks up at me, says, "Why, son, I'm making you a gun."

Well, I liked to swallowed my breath. Oh, you know I'd been after my daddy and been after him, ever night nearly. I was good and growed up ten. I believed I was due a rifle for Christmas and I believed I was going to get me a rifle for Christmas—I'd just sucked down my pistol wishing, sucked down the fact I'd be done turned eleven by then—but now, people, I had my mind set on a pretty little Winchester. I'd seen one up at Lolly's was just what I meant to have. I didn't know nothing about gunsmithing, can't say I could tell you to this day much about it and I watched him start to finish, but I knew one thing in that minute: I didn't want no damn homemade gun.

I wasn't even sure but what he meant to give me a toy wooden gun, even if I could see that that stock was as long as I was tall. Looked about like a toy, somehow, the way it was cut out flat and square, like a outline or an idea of a gun. I was just heartsick. I guess I had a face on pretty bad. I don't guess I knew how to hide it if ever I'd cared to, and I just stared at the man. He leaned over right quick then, picked his hat off the bench and put it on his head. Well, Lord, that changed him, liked to scared me to death. Whatever face I'd pulled, I reckon I put back on another'n. Lodi looked at me fierce.

He says, "Come over here a minute, son."

What are you going to do? I's ten, and here he was, about my master as far as I knew, a big old growed-up man. Every inch of my skin was aching backwards to that door yonder where I'd come in at, but I did like he told me. Edged up to where he's sitting on that old nail keg, he gets aholt of my arm. I had this old bunchy brown coat on, I'll never forget that. It was my brother DewMan's before me and I reckon Clyde's before him. I hadn't growed into it yet, had to shove the sleeves up to get my hands out—well, that old cotton batting didn't want to shove up, it was bunched all around my elbow and arm. Lodi picks my arm up. I might've been trembling a little bit. He says, "Hold still a minute," kindly growls at me, "He-e-ere, now," stretches that arm out, bends it, sticks the butt of that stock up there in the crook. Well, my hand couldn't reach to the comb even, much less the place the trigger went, and Lodi eyeballs it, jerks it away, and now he just went jessie on it with the big rasp. Knocked, I don't know what, three inches and more off the butt, just laid it out the same woman shape, but shorter, near about like a half stock, and it didn't take no time. Half an hour maybe, I don't know. I was watching him close. He jerks my elbow up again, tucks the butt in there, wraps my hand around the rifle wrist. Lays my thumb on the comb. Well, you can believe it or not, people, but it was just a fit. He'd measured that stock out about like your mama'd measure you a new suit of clothes, and when he laid it back in there, it fit me like a skin.

Now, I'll tell you something, that little act turned a screw in me, and I can't explain it any better than this: I went from where I wouldn't've had a homemade gun laid out on a silver platter to where I felt it and seen it my own, same as if it was finished and cradled in my arms. Felt the heel snugged up there like I was born with it, plumb through that old heavy brown coat. I tried to lift it, sight along it, I couldn't do it—and it wasn't nothing but a stock blank, just the wood shape and nothing else to it, but I couldn't hold the sonuvagun up. Lodi had to help me. Now then, I'd had a half-dozen guns under my arm before that time—my dad's shotgun and Uncle Jack's and what-all—and I've probably had a flat hundred since, and I never in my life felt anything like it. I just changed toward it. I can't tell you how.

Well, you know what he done then, he went and fired up that forge. He did so, nearly five o'clock of an evening, he laid a load of coke in, shoveled it, went to work with the bellows. Now, you didn't do like that neither. Forges was just like anything: you didn't fire it up for a little while, you did it for the whole day's work and then you let it quit. Fuel was expensive, and it took a long time to get it hot enough where you'd want it, but you couldn't let it get too hot, you had to know just where you was at. But Lodi set that stock down, stood up and turned to shoveling a load of coal. Next thing I know he's over yonder at the iron pile, scraping and shoving things around. His back was to me then. I just had to do it, I reached out there on the bench and touched that piece of wood. That oak was as warm as a woman's belly, you'll pardon the expression, but, now, it was. It was just the very living wood. I reckon if I wasn't in love already, I sure was from that minute, and I just stroked it. Couldn't keep my hands off it. Here come Lodi, I jerked back, but he didn't even act like he seen me. He'd found him a long old piece of wrought iron, and he got them tongs cracking and put that bar in, laid on them bellows a minute. Like he's got a clock in his head or some kind of gauge, he knows just when to take it out. Goes to work with the big sledge on that heated barrel stock, he didn't have no mandrel or nothing, just laid it out on the anvil and pounded it around a broken piece of a brake rod. Just went to town.

I don't know how long we stayed in there. Wind howling. For a while you could hear sleet pecking that old wood-shingle roof. When we come out, there was a little dusting of snow on the ground. Wind had died some. The stars was out. Lodi didn't say a word to me, just picked up the lantern and hunked up his shoulders, walked off north through town. I know I got a licking from my mama when I come in the house—supper's cold on the table, fire's down, the whole rest of the family in bed. She got up when I come in, asked me where I'd been, I told her, Helping John Lodi. She said, Helping him what? I said, Finish up a new set of brake rods for Tarleton Maye's wagon; she said, My foot. She popped me a half-dozen times through that coat wadding, told me to get my hind end in the bed, but she never did tell my dad. My mama was partial to me, I know that. They all said it, and I'll allow it for a fact.

I might not would've stayed at the livery till supper much less way past midnight if my dad hadn't been gone to Brown's Prairie. I never was one to cross my dad. But look here, I'll tell you something. I don't believe none of it would've happened if my daddy hadn't been out of town. I've thought about it. I don't for the life of me believe Lodi meant to make me a rifle. He didn't have no sort of plan. It's just how life is, how you couldn't have one thing happen without what went before. Some of it's accident and some of it's intention, but one thing gets laid on another and it all keeps a-rolling from one thing to the next. But it's all tied up together, see—you don't just have this, and this, and this; you have this *because* this *because* this, even if you don't know what the because is. That's according to my reckoning, and I been watching it a long time. Like this, see: Lodi was working that wood on account of it wasn't six yet and he didn't have no regular work to get done. But see, he didn't have no regular work *because* my dad was out of town. If daddy'd been there, I bet you a hunnerd dollars there would've been somebody sitting around waiting on John Lodi to finish them a hound plate or something, storm coming or not. And if there hadn't been anybody waiting for work from him, why, my dad would've come in and told Lodi to knock off and go home. My dad wasn't a hard man. But he wasn't there to tell him, and Lodi wasn't going to take it on himself to go home half a day early, and so he had free hands and time to do something and he just did what he did.

After that night, it just laid like a secret between us. We didn't neither one need to tell it, but we was making that gun on the sly. Or anyhow, that's how I thought about it, but my dad had to know. I never come in the house before nine or ten o'clock of an evening; he'd just tell me to stoke the fire before I come to bed. Now, I'm going to estimate it took us about three weeks to make that gun. I say "us," and you know I didn't have a fat lot to do with it, only just held the barrel tight in the rings when he was rifling it out or whatever little job he showed me how to do. I don't think it would've took that long, even allowing we had to work on it after six or way up early in the morning, except he had to whittle him a rifling guide, and that was some job, I'll tell you what. But he made every piece of it, tang bolt to cheek plate, and he knew what he was about. Of course, later I could see that the main reason he was working that slab of red oak when I come in, the truth of it, was because he knew how. That was the prettiest gun I nearly ever witnessed in my life, I don't care if it was a muzzle loader. On top of that, it was the truest. I ain't saying that just because it was mine. I learned to shoot with that gun, kept it for years and years, and I never had to freshen it out but once. Sold it to Bob Martin for forty dollars in Nineteen Thirty-six, and that was a lot of money in that time. I'd give more than that to have it back now, I can tell you. John Lodi was a powerful artist at gunmaking, same as he was at anything else. I reckon he had been nearly all his life. You don't learn that business in a minute.

Okay, now this is something I didn't know for a long time—well, half a century nearly. Mama said it when she was right near to passing over. She was sitting on the porch one morning—by that time she didn't do much of anything but set around; Daddy'd been gone sixteen years—but Mama was sitting there rocking one morning, I was coming up the front steps. I don't know where I'd been, to the post office or something, and Mama just pops up out of nowhere, she says, "Grady, you remember that gun John Lodi made you?"

Well, I did a little turn then, because I never knowed any of them knew he'd made it for me special. I thought at the time they all reckoned he'd give it to me because it wasn't a manufactured Remington or Winchester, just an old homemade gun.

She says, "You remember that?"

I says, "Well, yes, Mama, sure I do."

She says, "You know what your dad give for that?"

I said no. My heart grabbed up a little tighter. None of them had ever mentioned anything about it. We made it. We had a secret. Me and Lodi. I never knew Dad gave him a dime.

She says, "Your dad give two dollars for that gun. John wouldn't take no more than that. What you reckon that gun'd be worth today?"

I said I couldn't imagine. I didn't want to think about it. Nearly killed me to sell it when I did, I just hated it, but me and Dorcas didn't have two red cents to rub together. You did what you had to back then. Told myself like this, said, Well, sir, you don't have a son to pass it along to anyhow, you'd just might as well. I sold it to Bob Martin for his grandson, or that's what he said.

"I bet it was worth twenty dollars," Mama says, "if it was worth a nickel. Your dad tried to make him take ten for it, but two dollars is all he would take. Just pert near give it away, didn't he?"

I said, "Well, yes, Mama, I guess he did."

Lovena Wixon

Granny Phelps come to the front porch, hollered clean through to the back.

"Loveeny, you better come out here! John Lodi's just this minute shot somebody in front of Dayberry's!"

I was doing the washing. I could hear her good as anything. She was hollering all the way through the house.

"They ain't even covered him up yet!"

Little voice squeaking, seemed to me like I could nearly see her, tipping up on her tiptoes. I was plumb out by the smokehouse.

"There's kids down yonder all ever one looking at him," she said. "Come on now. Quick!"

Well, quick as I could rinse the soap off, I went. Run down there with Edna on my hip and I'd left Jelly in the bed, I never even thought about her. I'd forgot she was home. Whole front of my apron was sopping wet with washwater, but you can't stop to think and change at a time like that. You never saw anything like it. Blood from here to yonder, half the men in town standing around waiting for somebody to do something. Ignorant things. Wasn't anything to do. The man was dead. Well, he was a white man, you could see that. They were going to have to wait for the federal marshal to come from McAlester, Choctaw law couldn't tell them what to do, though, yes, Tecumseh Moore was there. They were all there, half of Cedar, and what ones wasn't there was coming. That's how fast the news spread.

Well, we didn't know him, of course that's the first thing I thought of, but when I saw we didn't know him, I just went to trying to keep the children back. You want to be helpful. I could see those men weren't being helpful, they were just standing around. Sheriff Moore and Jim Dayberry were yonder in the stable doorway with their heads together. I didn't see John Lodi then. Sure did see the man he killed, though. He was laying on his back in the street right in front of the mercantile, and I guess John'd shot him with the shotgun, because the top of his head was blowed off. But Lord at the blood, you never saw the like, pooling in the dirt and it was still a-bubbling, worse than a stuck pig. You didn't believe.he lived two seconds. Half his neck was gone.

I'll swan to my time, those men stood around, stood around, I didn't believe anybody was ever going to think to cover the man up. I was about ready to go back to the house and get Hank's tarpaulin or something, but you couldn't keep the children out of there. They'd just slip under your arm, the boys would, and edge right up where they didn't have any business, and nobody was doing one thing to stop them, and I thought, Well, I better just stay here. If I'd ever thought about Jelly, I don't guess I would've seen any of it, because I would not of let her witness such an awful scene as that. I don't know where those other children's mothers were. Oh, directly here come one or two of them, Hattie Chessley and Nan Tannehill and some of them, but they didn't shoo their children off. People act so ignorant sometimes. Well, you can see I had my hands full, what with Edna bawling and me trying to keep those kids back, and I sure didn't aim to be like the rest of them and stand around gawking at that poor man, so I did not precisely examine the body, I just heard some of them talking about John Lodi'd shot him in the back. Well, I don't know about that, but I can tell you one thing: he sure enough shot him in the front one time, because his forehead was just a pulp. I got there quick as it happened, it must not of been over five minutes. Hadn't even a fly landed on him yet.

Well, it wasn't twenty minutes after that before they brought that girl around the side of the barn. Of course, I didn't have any idea then she was a girl. You can believe it or not, but that child had on britches. She isn't even a child really, I'd put her at sixteen or better—old enough to be settled down married and not messing with such fool-ishness as wearing britches and whatever-all else she's been at—but at first I thought it was a boy of twelve or fourteen maybe they'd caught back there doing something, into something he hadn't ought to of been. To my mind they were bringing this little fella around from the back —it was Angus Alford and Field Tatum had ahold of her on either side by the arm. Brought her over to where Sheriff Moore was standing talking to Dayberry, took that child's hat off—she had on an old slouch hat swallowed her face to the bottom of her ears nearly—and sure enough it was a girl. I liked to dropped my teeth. Her hair was twisted up in a stingy little bun, had her eyes scrinched up like a Chinese. But there wasn't any mistaking it was a female. The men kept on talking, hardly seemed to look at her. I believe they were embarrassed. She was just as still as she could be. Well, I had to scrooch over a bit—Hattie Chessley had got right in my way—and that's when I seen Lodi sitting on an old hay bale inside the barn. He was about as still as that child yonder, had a fat big-barreled pistol, I don't know what it was, some kind of pepperbox or something, appeared to me like, laying in his lap. He was looking at that girl, she was looking at him, both of them still as a dead possum, and I didn't know what to think. Afterwhile Grace Lovett sidled up to me and whispered that was his daughter. I wasn't any too surprised to hear it. John Lodi's always been about as strange as they come, didn't surprise me any to see he had him a peculiar daughter. I just said to myself then, I said, Well, come to the hearing, they're going to learn a whole lot more about it. Going to find out those two aren't the only strange ones in that family. Provided they get as far as a hearing. Provided somebody don't kill him before the law gets him to Fort Smith. Un-huh. You mark my words. That's just what I said.

So in another little bit, here come the other one. Walking down the street. Come from up north, around Lolly's or somewhere. I seen everybody looking, so I turned and looked, and here she come, sashaying down the street toward Dayberry's. Sashaying isn't quite the word, because she was coming slow, but there was something in it gave the *appearance* of sashaying. Had on a little old calico skirt looked like it had about nine petticoats under it. Had her hair all swooped up, no bonnet on nor nothing. Now, this one's about as pretty as the other one is homely, but you can see in a minute they're kin. She come slow; everybody just hushed up and turned and looked at her. She didn't blink an eyelash, never acknowledged a one of us nor the dead man on the street, just kept her eyes on her sister and come on. I wanted to slap her. I hate to say it, a time like that, but that child had a look on her face made me just want to slap her. That was her uncle laying yonder, she never even looked at him. Of course, I didn't know that yet, but I knew it was a dead man her daddy'd blowed to Kingdom Come, you'd think she could've had the decency to at least look a little scared or shamed or something. She walked right in amongst us and past us, went over by the little scrawny one and stood beside her, kept her eyes straight ahead. Like she was sleepwalking nearly, except she never wiped that look off her face. I'm telling you the truth, there was more than a few of us would've been glad to wipe it off for her.

It couldn't have been fifteen or twenty minutes then, here come the rest of them, just a-going lickety in a brand-new flatbed wagon. Had a highstepping team of horses, and I'm telling you what, here they come. The one boy was whipping those horses, they barreled up there and the boy in the cowboy hat and boots jumped down. I don't know how many of them there were altogether, the three boys and about a half-dozen grown girls on down to one little'un couldn't have been over seven or eight years old. The minute the horses jerked up, those girls went to wailing. It was the pitifulest thing you nearly ever saw. That was their daddy laying with his neck blowed out yonder, I didn't need anybody to sidle up and whisper me that. The one boy hollered at them to all stay put, and he jumped down, those poor girls just a-weeping and holding on to one another, and then the boy that was driving jumped down.

That first boy that come out of the wagon, the one in the hat and the fancy boots, he took one look at his daddy and immediately went to swooping and prancing all over that street. Couldn't be still a minute but he didn't know what to do with himself, and he just walked quick with his arms out, up and down and around, cussing. He didn't look at his father any more after that, just swooped like an old fighting rooster or something, up and down, cussing, like he was nearly blind. Well, I thank my lucky stars Jelly wasn't there to hear that kind of language, but every other child on the street surely was, on down to six and seven years old, and couldn't nobody put a stop to it. Looks to me like a few of those mothers could've took their children on off away from there and home where they belonged.

The one blond boy stayed in the wagon, held the horses, just sat there looking down, and then next thing I knew in all the commotion, he'd slipped down and come over to stand by the two girls. That was the first I knew he wasn't a part of that other bunch but one of John Lodi's. He's a big old kid, I bet you going on six feet nearly, and blond as he can be. Wearing suspenders. Good-looking boy, kind of gawky. I don't know what in the world he was doing riding up with the rest of them, but he come in with them, and then they separated after that. He stood with his sisters, and he did about like they did, which was nothing. Just stared straight ahead. In a minute Tecumseh Moore headed up to try and calm the cussing boy down some, and quick as his back was turned, the blond one went in the stable and squatted down by his father on the dirt floor. I didn't see him say anything, he just crouched down there by him in the dirt, and here in a little bit Moore seen him and went in and told him he'd better come on outside.

And of course along about then is when I remembered Jelly home sick in the bed, and I turned around with Edna on my hip and went on back to the house. I didn't see when that colored deputy showed up nor anything more about it, but I witnessed plenty enough to allow I didn't sleep too good that night.

But, now, there's one thing has got me completely baffled, and I want you to see if you can figure it out. You just calculate a little bit. All right. Now, I got there five minutes after the killing, maybe less even. Twenty minutes more, they found the little scrawny one. Five or ten minutes after that, here come the pretty one, and it wasn't fifteen minutes more till the whole rest of the bunch come in the wagon from Waddy Crossing. Maybe you can explain it to me. In less than an hour they was every one there but the dead fella's poor wife. You know and I know couldn't nobody send word eight or nine miles to Big Waddy Crossing and them children get back to Cedar in that amount of time. And that one girl was walking—you know it takes two hours and better to walk it. Those children had to know a killing was going to happen, don't you reckon? Long before it come down.

Grady Dayberry

Dad told it this way. Said it started back wherever they come from and there was another man in it besides them two, said there was guns mixed up in it some way, and old bad blood, and it was this third man somehow brought it all to a head. John Lodi never was one to tell his business, so I believe my daddy had to piece it together from one thing and another, whatever-all Lodi had told him and what folks around here said, and then, too, what Dad himself witnessed, which was pretty near start to finish of the killing—he was the main testifier at the hearing, I saw that myself—but if there's anybody knew anything about it to speak of, I believe it was my dad. So Dad said there was a running feud between these two brothers went way back to the land of their birth, and now, how it worked out them to be simultaneously fussing and living just practically one on top of the other—that's how my dad told it, said their houses wasn't fifty feet across the lot from each other, front to back—well, that part I don't know. This third man that was in on it, I don't believe he was any kin, but he'd known them back in the place they'd come from and been with them somehow on this deal.

So Dad said this fellow—his name was Tanner—said he showed up from Texas one evening. Rode into Cedar one evening on a big old bay gelding, leading a fine-looking train of fifty choice U.S. Army mules. Stolen, of course, but now I'll tell you something: that man didn't have to ride clear from the bottom to the top of the Choctaw

296 / R i l l a   A s k e w

Nation to sell those mules. He could have unloaded them just anywhere along the line, from Broken Bow to Talihina. Been a lot smarter to sell 'em down around Idabel or somewheres, the quicker shut of them the better, instead of parading them two hundred rough-going miles through the Kiamichi Mountains. There was deputy U.S. marshals crawling all around in these hills. I guess the man liked to live reckless, or else he was plumb ignorant, I don't know, but anyhow, here he come, paraded them critters right through town here and on up to Big Waddy Crossing. Word got around about this bunch of mules Fate Lodi had for sale, and folks come around and bickered and bartered and bought maybe a half dozen, and then this fellow Tanner went up to Muskogee or somewheres and unloaded the rest. I believe he got a little nervous to get out of town. Dad said the law at Fort Smith had also got wind of this fine bunch of mules Fate Lodi had for sale, but said by the time the marshal come nosing around, Tanner was already on the scout up to Sallisaw or someplace in Cherokee country, and the six or seven mules they'd sold hereabouts all had new traces, new harnesses, new masters—and new marking, I expect, burned into their rear ends.

Well, sir, that was the first of this fella Tanner coming, but it sure wasn't the last. Him and Fate Lodi, I don't know what-all they got into up yonder, gunrunning, horsethieving, bootlegging, no telling what. You'd hear about it, Dad said, like it was just a den of thieves at Big Waddy Crossing. That little community had quite a reputation at one time. Kept it up, Dad said, till that colored deputy carried Fayette to Fort Smith one time on a charge of introducing spirits into the Territory, but seem to me like Dad said they had to turn around and let him go again—couldn't find no evidence and wouldn't nobody testify against him. Old Tanner had already gone on the scout to Creek Nation, and that was all she wrote for them two's little partnership. But, now, what-all Tanner had to do with it I don't know, but I know it was something hatched up between them two, Fate and Tanner, that set a match to the feud between the two brothers. My dad told this to me in so many words, he said, "When Tanner showed up with them mules from Texas, John Lodi changed in his being from that day forward." That's just what my dad said.

I can't say that I noticed anything different. I can't recollect that I knew anything about it at the time—or anyhow I didn't hear about any mules Fate Lodi had for sale up at Big Waddy Crossing, because I was just a boy then and I had other things on my mind. And John

Lodi walked in from Waddy every morning and came on to work and walked home at night same as always, and he didn't quit that or miss a day of it, I reckon, from the minute he went to work for my daddy right up until the afternoon of the killing. I've thought about it since then, thought about what my dad said. "He changed in his being." I've tried to fathom what Dad meant.

After Lodi made me that muzzle loader I got to hanging around the stable pretty good, what time I wasn't out in the woods hunting or just whenever I thought I could get by at it without my dad locating me some little chore. I wasn't too work-brittle at that age. But I figured me and Lodi were pardners, and I'd go hang around when I could. He didn't perturb me like he used to, whether he had his hat on or off, and he'd showed me ever bit of the gunmaking from start to finish, explained to me just what he was doing as we went. Lodi never was much of a talker, and he didn't talk no more nor no less after he'd got that gun finished than I'd ever known him, so I didn't lay that off to him being changed in his being. All I figured was he'd just turned back normal, which for him was silent, and I didn't think a thing in the world about it then. Nor do I yet. That wasn't the kind of thing Dad was talking about.

Pondering on it, even now, all these years later, there's only one little incident I can think of. It was inconsequential to my mind at the time—or I shouldn't say inconsequential, because I remember I studied on it a lot—but what I mean, it wasn't something I looked at and said, Well, here's a man changed in his being. But later I thought back on it, and I believe this is part of what Dad meant.

I'd come in the livery one morning. Now, it must've been a Saturday because I know it was morning—I had a little something on my mind, that's how come me to remember—and I wasn't in school. We had us a little subscription school right here in town then, first white school around in these parts, I believe, and Mrs. Edith Hawkins was the teacher, what we called the schoolmarm, and my dad paid a dollar a month to send me and DewMan both, but DewMan quit. But I did go whenever Dad didn't need me, which was most of the time because he had Clyde and DewMan both still home till I was nearly grown, and my mama wanted me to and so I did. So I'm going to say it was a Saturday, and I come into the stable on this particular Saturday morning and Dad was there, naturally, bent over with a hoof grasped up between his legs, trimming a pitiful old white plowhorse belonged to Manford Slocum, and Mr. Slocum and two or three others was over in the new part, around the stove, waiting and talking, how I already told you folks were apt to do. Lodi was at the forge, working the bellows up good and hot, just huffing away. Well, the minute I seen my dad I kindly started backing up toward the doorway. I thought I might just go on to the creek bottom without any lead. I was entirely out of bullets, see, otherwise I'd a been long gone rabbit hunting—that's what I had my mind set on. There was a nice little new snow on the ground.

Right off, Dad looked up and saw me. I figured he'd say, "Step over here a minute, Grady, I need you to do this-that-'n'-the-other." But he didn't say a word, just went back to cutting on that old yella hoof. Well, none of the men over there seemed to notice me or pay me any attention, so I thought I might just as well stay, and I eased over to where Lodi was pulling a big old red froe blade out of the fire, and he laid it on the anvil yonder and went to town, bang bang bang bang. He didn't pay me any mind either, and of course that's what you want when you're a boy, ordinarily. You don't want grown men's eyes too close on you; it kindly embarrasses you, and besides, you figure if they're looking at you too hard they're going to pretty quick find something wrong. Except, see, I had this little business on my mind, and I was looking to get Lodi's attention without drawing any from my dad.

So up to that point wasn't a thing in the world unusual. Nothing was any different to any other time I went in that stable, except maybe how my dad didn't give me a job nor even blink at me hardly, but that's not what I mean to tell you about.

Now, I'll just be honest about it. It wasn't purely that nice little snow, which we didn't have every day in winter even back then, and it wasn't only that brand-new custom-made rifle that I hadn't had over six weeks or a month, but I also had me a brand-new beagle pup, and I was just about to have a fit to hunt her. She was coming up on half grown then and she wasn't this big, she could cut a trail through any kind of bramble, but oh, she was shy of humans. She'd duck and tuck tail and run off from any human being, me included; you flat couldn't touch her. That's how come Clyde to give her to me. He was going to shoot her but I talked him into letting me have her. I thought I could get her to come to me, but she never would do it. But I want to tell you something, people—now, that little beagle dog could hunt. Oh, she had a tender voice, and when she took the trail there wasn't no shaking her off it, and that pup never would run trash. Just a pure-dee rabbit dog from the word go; only thing wrong with her, she was just so timid to a human. I finally did have to shoot her, never could get her to come to me, but I'd just got her off my brother along about a day or two before this particular Saturday morning I'm speaking of, and I didn't have a whole lot else on my mind except needing to take her out. Wasn't going to do no good to take her out, the way I saw it, if I didn't have anything to shoot at a rabbit with when she run one around. So I had me a problem.

Here in a little bit, I got to thinking about these bullets, about what in the world was I going to do about being out of bullets, because I was just itching to take that pup out. Now, what I mean bullet, I'm not talking about these manufactured cartridges like you think of; I mean lead balls you make yourself. That's what you shoot in a muzzle loader, and all you need for it is a good bullet mold and a hot fire and some lead. But, now, I didn't have none of them things, and of course you know who did. He'd give me about four dozen when he finished rubbing in the linseed oil on that red-oak gunstock, made me a present of them in a piece of leather wrapped up like a tobacco pouch, only the sinew wasn't strung through any holes. You just unfolded it like a handkerchief, and there they laid, just as perfect and round. He taught me how to lay one in my palm and pour blackpowder over it till it covered it, and that'd be your proper load for one shot. Well, he just taught me how to shoot that gun altogether, how to shoot period, and of course I shot every last one of those lead bullets he gave me in no time, just pecking at songbirds and stumps and what-have-you, and now here I had me a new hunting dog and no ammunition and I was in a terrible fix. I only knew one way to get some more of 'em, and I couldn't no more go about it than I could've jumped over the moon.

Well, I got to hemming and hawing around there, and I don't know if I ever actually said a word but I know I stood there at his elbow the longest time with the words sawing at the edge of my mouth. I thought near about every human way possible to bring up the subject, and likely I got out a grunt or two even in between all them clangs, but I couldn't just come out and ask him, there was no human way. After a while Lodi went to douse that froe blade. He liked to tripped over me—I was standing just nearly on top of him, right in front of the trough. I jumped back, and something about that hot iron swinging or me jumping or something, I don't know what it was, but something unstuck my mouth and I blurted out, "Mr. Lodi, reckon I could borry your bullet mold and some lead a minute? I got to mold me some bullets for that rifle you made me. I got a new hunting dog I got to take—"

Oh, he give me a look durn sure shut my mouth. Didn't say a word, but he looked at me like he'd about wring my neck, and he turned with the tongs and plunged the blade in. Here that iron went to sizzling—oh, you could smell it—bitter, hotfire and burning, like hellfire itself. If I thought I was uncomfortable before, now then I was sure in a distress. I believe I was shaking. I didn't know what to think or how to act. You never saw such a look in all your life, or I hadn't, just a look as black as sin. Well, he never paused a second but went on about his work. I glanced over at Dad, and he didn't act like he'd seen anything. I looked over at the men yonder, and they had their heads together chawing and jawing; they didn't pay either one of us any mind.

I looked back at John Lodi. He didn't appear to act like he even knew I was there, just went on about his business, and I had the strangest sensation. I felt like I was crazy. Like I hadn't seen what I'd seen. I hoped I hadn't seen it, because it was murder I'd seen in that man's eyes. I knew it. I didn't know a name for it, but I felt it in every inch of my being: that man'd as soon choke me as look at me. But yet this was John Lodi here, standing at his anvil. I'd give up being afraid of him weeks back. I guess you'd say I was a little taken with him— you know how a boy'll make a hero out of somebody. Seemed like he could do so much more than my dad. I thought we were pardners, you know, and I didn't know what to do. My heart was bleating in my throat. In a bit he glanced back over at me—I was still standing there; I was too paralyzed to move, to blink hardly—and he said, "Come back this evening, son." He kindly rolled a look toward the other side yonder and back at me, like they was some kind of a new secret between us, picked up his hammer again.

I didn't go back that evening. I don't know how long it was before I went back. Not too long, I imagine, because that livery stable was about the center of my life, for one thing. Not to mention that empty muzzle loader carried considerable more weight than a look on a man's face I thought I'd seen but wasn't sure I'd seen and finally made up my mind I hadn't seen because nobody else acted like they knew anything about it, including Lodi himself. I guess I needed to make my mind up that way. The very idea of it disappeared until a long time later, when I got to trying to fathom what my dad meant. You know how a little fella's memory will do. I convinced myself I hadn't witnessed John Lodi's eyes blacken down cold under them eyebrows. For a little while around there, though, I was nearly sick. I remember that part. I just felt a hundred percent alone, because my mind wouldn't let me forget it. I'd go back over it and over it: had I seen him look thataway or did I just think it? There wasn't anybody I would talk to about it, not even Clyde or my mother. I don't know how to explain it to you, but I just felt like I was wrong. I wasn't supposed to know it and I didn't want to know it, and somehow knowing it made me a party to it. I was sick to my stomach that John Lodi wasn't what I'd cracked him up to be. And then I just made up my mind to forget all about it, and I did.

Man from Wister

I heard it like this. Heard the one brother came horseback from up around Latham or Sans Bois or somewhere, wherever they homesteaded. The two of them lived together, is how I heard it, just one right on top of the other and their children as well, and now, why, I don't know. Way too much land in this country for people to be living on top of each other, but I heard these two brothers did, and the one had a job of work at a livery over at Cedar and the other was a gunsmith deluxe or something up around where they lived, and made a pile of money off it too, from what I heard. So money was no doubt at the core of it unless it was a woman, but I never heard anything about that. There was bad blood between them anyhow, and I expect it went way back. Usually does, from all I've ever seen. So these two brothers were feuding and their youngsters as well, or this is how I heard it—it's an old story around here, folks have told it for years—and the one brother rode horseback down to Cedar one morning.

They tell me he was unarmed. Now, a man just didn't go around without a weapon hardly back then. Never mind outlaws and thievery and whatever else you might run into, there were still plenty panthers in these mountains then, and they weren't shy to tell. This is mean country, has been ever since the white man came in here, and still yet to this day these hills are crawling with snakes and ticks and chiggers, stinging scorpions, tarantulas, poison centipedes as long as your arm.

They didn't have so many ticks back then, but you can't shoot a tick anyhow, but what they did have was plenty of game, plenty of God's poison scourges, plenty of outlaws and Indians. A man had to be armed. There were wolves and bears and rattlers, not to mention you had to cross these old slow muddy waters horseback without benefit of a bridge, and these creeks have always been roiling with cottonmouths. You might happen across dinner under a six-point rack standing right in your path, and if you didn't meet dinner, you might meet your Maker in the form of a horsethief or any sort of old run-of-the-mill scoundrel. So a man just did not go around without a gun then, not to travel he didn't, excepting only one reason, and that'd be to lay down on his back like a dog and give up.

So I heard this one rode up in public, right out in broad daylight on Main Street, is how they tell it, and they say he called his brother out. This fellow wasn't armed, but he called his brother out the same as if he meant to fight him. Clearly he didn't expect his own brother to kill him, but now he sure did. Whatever bad blood it was between them must've been something awful, because, how I heard it, the one brother came out of the livery carrying an old pepperbox or some such contraption, and the other put his hands up in the air, put them up just like this. Said, I don't aim to do anything but just talk, Brother, I only come here to talk.

Well, the one put his gun down loose like he didn't intend to do anything but just hold it, and they stood awhile and talked. Then the one that had ridden down from Latham or Bokoshe or wherever it was, turned around and started to mount, had his foot in the stirrup and his back to his brother, and now I heard the brother raised that old eight-barreled pistol without a hi or a word of warning and shot the man in the back. Shot him down like a dog, he didn't have one chance in the world, that just how folks tell it. And now would you believe it? That man never spent a night in jail. They tell me Cedar's one town in Oklahoma you can shoot a man down in broad daylight on Main Street and never see the inside of a cell.

I know there's some folks need killing—some men are so sorry you can't do a thing with them but just put them out of their misery—but I don't care how sorry a fellow is, you don't shoot an unarmed man in the back. I don't care what. This wasn't any little pallid shootout; I guess that's why folks are still so apt to tell it. They tell me the one brother that did the killing was so eaten up with hatred he walked up to where that fellow was squirming dying on the ground and rolled him over with his boot toe, put them eight barrels right up against his brother's forehead and blew the top of his head off. Gunned him down unarmed like a dog and sauntered up to finish his work, and I guess the folks at Cedar just swarmed around and slapped him on the back.

Agnes Day Skeen

It was Brother Harland Peevyhouse who brought the word back to Big Waddy. I don't know what he was doing in Cedar in the buckboard that morning, waiting on the train from Wister maybe, but he must have been johnny-on-the-spot, because Otis said Mr. Lodi was not even good and stiff yet when he and the pastor raced back down there. He'd come directly to our house, Brother Peevyhouse had—didn't even pause in town, though there were men lolling at the hitching post in front of Lodi's store and I'm sure Jessie was there in the back—but he raced right on out here to our house, and you know, at the time I never questioned why. People just depended on Otis that way.

I stood on the side porch and watched the pastor's buckboard clatter around the curve and on through town in a cloud of dust like a storm coming, and I thought to myself, Well, my stars. Brother Peevyhouse was always what you might call on the excitable side, but I had never seen him in such a state. He lashed that poor old dray up the incline and into my cleanswept yard, which I hadn't ten minutes before finished sweeping, jerked him up tight with the reins just shy of the porch ledge there, and then sat leaning over the dashboard with his hand to his chest, trying to catch his breath as if it'd been him running and not that poor soapy creature he was driving. Otis was in the field, naturally—it was, I don't remember, maybe two or three o'clock in the afternoon; pretty well after dinner anyway—and I knew something big had happened, though I wouldn't have dreamed it was a tragedy. I thought maybe they'd finally pushed through statehood or something. I couldn't tell. But then the pastor caught his breath at last, and he practically shouted at me, "Where's Brother Skeen!"

I believe I was so taken aback I didn't even answer but just nodded my head toward the south field where Otis was plowing, and the pastor said, "Run out chonder and tell him to come quick. You come on too, Mizrus Lodi's going to be in need of female company."

I said, "Mrs. Lodi?" because it took me a minute to think who he was talking about. I'd never heard her called anything but Jessie, though we all called her husband Mr. Lodi, or anyhow I did.

He said, "Oh, Lord yes, Lord have mercy, John Lodi has just kilt her husband, shotgunned him to death on the streets of Cedar, Lord have mercy on this godless territory and the poor souls wretched enough to live in it."

I said, "John Lodi shot Mr. Lodi? Fate Lodi?"

And the pastor took off his little rimless glasses and wiped tears from his little eyes and raised them to heaven, or his hat brim anyway, and said prayerfully, "Kilt him dead as a lick log."

Those were very few words, coming from that preacher, and then he was quiet a minute, which was even odder, because he was one minister I certainly never saw at a loss for words. He sat in the buckboard looking skyward, weeping and shaking his head. Brother Peevyhouse hadn't been among us much more than a year at that time, and I suppose a killing on Main Street was something of a wonder to him, same as the Indians were marvels to him still. He'd come from Little Rock to save Indians, and I think he just never could get over there being so many Indian Baptists already, couldn't get over them having their own church with their own preacher preaching the gospel in Choctaw, and he would just shake his head over it while he skulked around the churchhouse at Yonubby when the Indians piled in for their all-day camp meeting and dinner on the ground. I believe he mistrusted the gospel in Choctaw. I think he had the idea that Brother Coley was preaching some hidden heathen doctrine from that Choctaw Bible. Brother Peevyhouse had had to settle for our little white congregation here at Big Waddy when he'd come to Indian Territory to save savages, and I think that might have troubled his mind some. I always laid much of Brother Peevyhouse's emotional nature off onto his disappointment over that.

So I can't say I was surprised to see him weeping in the buckboard over a murder, but I do remember being surprised that it was John Lodi who'd shot Lafayette, because if anybody had ever told me it was going to come to a killing between those two, I'd have surely said it would be the other way around. All at once the urgency came on Brother Peevyhouse again, and he put his glasses back on and twined them behind his ears, shouting, "Run fetch your husband, Miz Skeen, y'all come on quick!"

I thought to myself, Now, Pastor, where's your hurry? There's plenty time to lay the man out; nobody's going to try to raise Fate Lodi from the dead. If anybody needed killing in these parts, it was that one. And then I got ahold of myself. Sometimes my mind is just so wicked. I said a quick prayer for forgiveness and to please, Lord, bind my wicked tongue, which He's seen fit for the most part to allow me to hold silent in public in the years since I married Otis, but these bad thoughts He has never removed from my thinking to this day. So I didn't say anything, thank goodness, but just reached in the house for my bonnet and strapped it on, told Brother Peevyhouse to help himself to the water bucket if he cared to. I'd just drawn it fresh and set it on the porch, ready to take a drink to Otis. I scooped a dipperful and came down off the porch and walked out toward the field.

It was so strange how that killing worked on me, stepping with the filled dipper up and down over the furrows toward my husband. It was a drouthy spring that year, and the earth was hard as drypan and rocky as seven evils—this was just never easy farming country, never will be if a man carried a thousand rocks an acre out of these fields—and Otis had already busted two plowpoints trying to break it open. He was plowing along the creekline, making that swoop of *S* yonder —well, you can't see it now, the brush has grown up, but that's where he was, way off there. And I went, hollering. Well, just a little at first, calling him, hallooing him, but then the farther I went, the more that news worked on me, and the more it worked, the faster I stumbled, sloshing that little bit of well-water on the cracked rows—it would just turn black and sink in a second; by the time I reached Otis there wasn't a thimbleful of water in the bottom of that dipper—and I just went faster and faster until I was nearly running, holding my dress in one hand and the tin stem of the dipper high out in front of me, hollering, "O-oh-t-i-is! O-oh-t-i-is!"

Well, he never heard me, not for the longest. I could see him behind that old coal-colored mule we had then, which as a matter of fact we'd bought off Mr. Lodi, and that worked on me too. I could see the back of my husband's shoulders bowed to the harness and the sweat in big stains turning black, and somehow I felt my heart was just going to crack. There was a terrible feeling in me that if it could happen to Fate Lodi, it could happen to Otis. Could happen to every one of us, and I don't mean simply death but violence—a killing death. Murder. Not sickness or accident or the hand of the Lord working His mysterious ways on us, but the intentional striking away of a man's life by the hand of another, and these words came to me: *unto one of these the least my brethren,* and of course that Scripture is not about the least worthy brethren getting shotgunned on Main Street but Christ saying, *Inasmuch as ye have done it unto one of these the least my brethren, ye have done it unto me,* meaning charity, not murder. It made no more sense than a nursery rhyme for me to be thinking it, stumbling over that dunbrown field, but it sang in my head with no more control than I had over my wicked thoughts, and by the time I reached my husband, I was nearly hysterical.

Otis saw me at last, had reached the end of the row and turned the plow, and he'd stopped plowing and was still trying to loosen the checkline from around his waist and get free to come to me when I hollered—well, screamed nearly; I could hear it screeching up through the peachleaf willows on the creekbank—"Quit that plowing this minute and come quick! John Lodi's shot Mr. Lodi and killed him! Brother Peevyhouse's sitting in the front yard in the buckboard, wants you to come go with him!" Otis was still struggling to untangle the line, frowning—I don't know if he couldn't hear me yet or couldn't believe what he was hearing—but I didn't think he took my meaning or I didn't think he was moving fast enough, or I don't know what I thought, but I shouted, "Don't stand there gawking like a calf at a new gate! Lodi's killed Lodi! Preacher wants you to come go with him! Hurry up!"

I was nearly sick with fear and anger and that terrible rant in the core of my chest, going, *unto one of these the least my brethren, unto one of these the least,* and why, oh, why would I take it out on my poor husband? I don't know, but I did, God forgive me, more times than I want to remember, because while the Lord allowed me to keep my tongue from being quick in public, He sure never bound it from letting loose on the one I loved most. I'd nearly want to bite it off sometimes, and that was one of those times, because what I ached to do was throw my arms around him and hold him safe forever, and what I did was yell at him to come quick, hurry up. My husband was a slow man—I don't mean slow in his wits, for he had a keen, deep intelligence—but slow in his movement. He could plow all day and coonhunt all night and walk these mountains from Bald Knob to Big Ridge without tiring, but he went slow. He wasn't a man who knew how to hurry, it just wasn't in him, and in those days I went like a house afire all the time, hollering at him to keep up. He paid me not the least mind—he never fought with me—but went on how he went, slow and methodical, lifting one foot and setting it down in front of the other, and there aren't a half-dozen times I ever remember him getting in a hurry. But that day of the Lodi killing was surely one. He was trying to hurry even then, struggling to get the checkline off as soon as he saw me, and of course I could see that, but it didn't keep me from yelling. But when he came out from behind the plow, he started running toward me, his big boots clopping on that dry dirt, and I swear I thought my heart would burst right through my bodice, I was so torn up.

So I yelled again, "John Lodi's shot Mr. Lodi and killed him! Hurry up! Pastor's waiting!"

And he got close enough that I could see it rise up over his face—his understanding of what I was saying. He got within about three feet of me and just stopped. I could see it, the first thing: relief that it was not us, not me or one of his brothers I'd come running and shouting to tell him about. The second wave was the pure comprehension of what it was. I held the dipper out to him and he took it, his brows still furled in a question as if they hadn't yet caught up to what he knew, and whatever five drops of well-water had managed to cling to the bottom of that dipper he drained off and then slung the empty bowl sideways the way you would fling out dregs, and there wasn't a drop in it. I don't remember that he said anything then, I don't believe he did, but just stood directly in front of me and looked at me very still for a minute, and then he handed me that empty dipper, turned around, and went back to unhitch the mule from the plow. I didn't say anything. I was finished hollering. My husband wasn't going to leave his mule standing hitched to the plow in the field all day while he went off to tend to a murder; he got him unhitched pretty quickly, left the plow buried to the shaft in the dry earth and came on with the mule, slapping the reins on his black rump and the two of them highstepping crossways over the furrows, raising dust, moving faster than I believe I ever witnessed either one of them before or after, and I turned and started back to the house.

When I got there I saw the pastor standing in the yard with the drink bucket in both hands and that poor old dray's nasty muzzle buried right in it, but I didn't say anything, I just went on up on the porch and laid the dipper on the shelf. I could see men gathering in front of Lodi's store in town, and I thought, Well, word sure spread fast for the pastor to not even have stopped or said hidey. Pretty soon Otis came around the side of the house, because he'd moved that fast to unharness and turn the mule out in the lot, and he went and stood by the pastor and said, "Did anybody go in yet to set with Miz Lodi?"

Brother Peevyhouse raised his eyes heavenward once more, and I thought he was going to start weeping again. "She don't even *know* it, Brother Skeen. Don't none of 'em know it. I just not more than forty minutes ago witnessed the very killing—" He broke off and turned his eyes from heaven in the direction of my husband, and though he did have I believe the tiniest eyes I ever witnessed on a preacher or on any living creature except maybe a shoat pig, in that moment, looking straight on at my husband, Brother Peevyhouse's eyes swelled up large behind his glasses and got red. He said, "His own brother shot him dead right out in the street in front of the livery stable at Cedar. I mean, shot him down like a dog, may God have mercy on both of 'em. I never seen the beat of it. Shot him down like a dog." And the pastor was wiping his eyes behind his glasses, shaking his head. "I come right back to tell it, or let me say to break the news to the poor widow, as is my duty and responsibility as shepherd to this community, but I thought I better run up here and get y'all to come go with me." He was still so excitable he could hardly catch his breath. He looked over at me and said, "Miz Skeen, I'd be sure appreciative if you'd come go with us, a woman do need a woman at a time of grief and sorrow, it's a comfort to 'em somehow, I seen it ever time."

I just thought to myself, Rain on you, Brother. I didn't have one intention in this world of being part of that sad little delegation. By no means. In the first place, there was no love lost in me for Lafayette Lodi—well, I don't want to go into that, but just suffice it to say I didn't want to have to pretend some kind of sorrow I didn't feel—and in the second place, my job, as far as I knew, was to go right in the house and start cooking, because a woman's responsibility when there's a death in the community—doesn't make any difference if it's tragic or common—is to see to it that the food gets carried in. I kind of shook my head no at the pastor and backed up to the porch post, but he wasn't looking at me. He had his eyes turned down the road toward town and both arms wrapped around my oak bucket, holding it up for his horse. I looked at Otis to help me. He wasn't looking at me either but standing in the dirt next to the buckboard with his hat off, his lean shaggy head bowed to his chest nearly. At first I thought he was praying—I don't believe he'd even heard Brother Peevyhouse ask me to come go with them—and then I could see that it was working on him, what it meant: to go into Lodi's dark, cramped store behind the pastor and tell Jess Lodi and all those youngsters that their husband and father was dead—not from a tree falling on him, as Otis had gone with Cebe Gardner to tell Mrs. Jenkins, nor dead from the runaway team dumping the wagon and crushing the chest of Claude Wadkins, as he'd gone by himself to give the news to Claude's mother—but murdered in cold blood by the hand of his own brother.

"Reckon we better get a move on," Brother Peevyhouse said. "Folks is starting to gather."

A look came over Otis's face then that said, *Dear Lord, let this cup pass from me,* but all he said out loud was, "You want to wait till I saddle my mare or you want me to ride with you?"

The pastor hemmed and hawed a bit and said at last, not looking at either one of us but turning to set the water bucket on the lip of the porch, "I thought Miz Skeen might druther ride in the buckboard."

I knew then—I think Otis and I both knew—that he didn't intend to break the news himself but to place not just a deacon but a deacon and a deacon's wife both between himself and the telling. I would've argued or simply refused to go if it hadn't been for that look on my husband. I looked at him and then I turned and looked at the pastor. I said, "Wait till I get my apron off."

Otis had Sally saddled and the pastor's buckboard turned around by the time I came back out with my shawl and dress bonnet and a pan of cold cobbler from the last of the blackberry juice I'd put up last summer—it had a piece cut out of it from Otis's dinner, I'm embarrassed to tell, but it was all in the world I had fixed in the house to carry down there and I just couldn't make up my mind to go emptyhanded. It's hardly better than three-quarters of a mile, you know, from here across the creek to where Lodi's store was. See that old log house there where the mountain begins to rise? That's where John and his children lived, and Lodi's store was just down and a minute west from that, but I guess we couldn't walk it on a day as solemn as that one. I guess we had to lend the dignity of Otis's old saddlehorse and the pastor's buckboard both to the occasion, and we drove down the slope and across that old rock low-water bridge that lay over Bull Creek then. Otis hitched his mare and the pastor's dray in front of Lodi's store, where the townsmen—there must have been fifteen or twenty by that time—parted like the Red Sea for us to climb the wooden steps and cross the board porch and go in.

There was something that was strange from the minute we stepped inside the door. I could feel it, but I couldn't lay my mind on it. For there to be no customers was odd, certainly. I don't believe I'd ever entered that store, which was seldom enough anyhow—I didn't care to trade with Mr. Lodi and would only do so under the worst kind of emergency—but I don't believe I ever went in there once that there weren't at least a half-dozen men sitting around the potbellied stove, summer or winter, smoking and hiding their cob-stoppered jugs under their chairs. Oh, don't tell me they weren't, I'm not naive, and anyway this entire community knew. But it was not only that. I couldn't place it at first, because the store was as dark and crowded-seeming as ever, which the whitewashed walls and ceiling helped not a bit, and it was as close as ever with that smell of old smoke and unwashed men, but there was something else peculiar I couldn't seem to grasp.

Well, to tell the truth about it, just quite frankly, I was frightened. I don't know why. I don't know how to explain it. We walked in, Otis and then myself holding that ridiculous pan of cold blackberry cobbler, with the pastor bright and brave right behind us, and Otis called out, "Hello?" My chest knotted up sick with fear till the pan in my hands shook—at what, I can't say. I wasn't afraid that something was going to be done to me. It was just knowing I was going to have to look at Jessie and those youngsters, I guess—that in a minute I would watch them receive, hear my husband speak, the very words of tragedy. It didn't matter what I thought of that family—oh, I really don't want to get started on that, I really don't. I could write a book. And I tell you the truth, it didn't matter in that moment.

Well. All right. If you must know. Lafayette Lodi was a coward and a cheat and a pure out-and-out scoundrel, that's all. He sold bootleg whiskey to the Indians as well as half the white men in this country, which was a federal offense, you know, not to mention a lowdown dirty trick—you might just as well take an Indian and cram locoweed down his throat and wash it down with poison, it makes them that crazy and kills them that awful—and then he'd sell any kind of old gun or homemade ammunition to anybody he could get to turn loose of a dollar, and cheat them in the bargain. He did my husband and just about every man in this country dirty in some fashion—white, Indian, or colored, didn't matter—and if a fellow called him on it, he'd lie and say he hadn't done it and then turn right around and do it again. If a man called him on it a second time, Fate would begin to threaten—he was going to burn your haybarn, going to horsewhip the hide off your oldest-born. He threatened half the men in this territory at one time or another, though I don't know how much he ever carried out those threats, because he was an awful coward. He was.

Oh, I don't know what-all he did, I can't begin to tell you—a thousand things. Otis got into it with him over his hogs coming over on us and eating our corn. Otis tried to get him to put a fence up, but, now, Fate Lodi wasn't going to do it. "Free-range! This is free-range country, free-range!" he hollered, prancing up and down in my yard —and of course, he was right, this was all free-range back then, but nobody else's hogs came over on us the way his did; it was almost like they had the Lodi mind, to eat where it didn't cost anything and go home to digest. Jessie calculated mistakes to their favor on our ticket more than a few times so that I had to make Otis go back and settle with her over it. Their children were every one brazen and buck-toothed as gophers, they had the idea that they about ran this town, and the other one, the brother John, was a cipher and a mystery as far as anyone around here knew anything about him, whose own children were snatched up by the hair of the head and never taught—

Oh, see, now look how I'm talking.

I tell you it didn't matter. I didn't think such things in that moment, never for a minute considered the character of that family nor what the rest of the community said then or after—because we were walking into Lodi's store in the actual face and unfolding of death. We were its harbingers, we had come to tell it, and that made me just sick.

You know, it's very peculiar. I had that sense of something odd or strange, something simply not right, as I followed Otis's big back into the store, and I couldn't begin to place what it was, though I could see every detail in that building as clearly as if it were outlined in white thread. I probably saw Lodi's store in those few minutes more clearly than I'd ever seen anything in my life up to that point—of course, I know now that you can see nearly with the eyes of the angels in a moment of extremity and still be blind as a pup. Crisis, tragedy, anything like that can bring an acuteness of vision beyond anything you'd ever care to wish for—and still you'll miss the dead body in the corner. But then I didn't understand it, and I looked around those whitewashed walls cluttered with every kind of old such-and-so, trying to place what was strange. Lodi carried every imaginable salve and cracker and tool and meat and powder and drygood, hauled them up from the station on a flatbed and jammed them in his store sideways and upside down and just anyhow—absolutely no means of logical order—and each good he carried came in the door and sat there in its most raw and primitive state. That store looked about like an old sutler's supply at an army fort, and there was something in the smell and placement that made the room seem ancient, though I'm sure it hadn't been built over nine or ten years, and all of that, let me say, contributed to my distaste for trading at Lodi's. This was Eighteen Ninety-six, mind you, almost the turn of the century. You could ride the train to Fort Smith and purchase any kind of finery, lace curtains and silk hats with ostrich plumes and mercury-filled thermometers. In Saint Louis, where I came from, people had electricity already—and here was Lodi's store, primitive as an old corncrib and just about as rough.

I could see Jessie at the far end behind that old roughhewn oak counter they had, standing there with her arms crossed over her belly—it was swelled a little even then, now that I look back and remember, but of course that was not what I noticed. Any woman who's borne ten or eleven children is welcome to a big belly, I guess, though her arms and legs were no bigger around than my little finger, and the skin on her neck was drawn tight and ropy as a terrapin's. She didn't have a tooth left in her mouth, and I'll bet she wasn't a lot past forty years old. They say before she died her belly swelled up as big as a watermelon. They said it looked like she was going to drop a litter, she was swelled up so big—I know that sounds terrible; that's just how the people around here talked about it. We didn't have experience of such things. I wasn't there to witness it—I never could get myself to go in that place after Fate's funeral, I just never could, though I sent food in every day, right up to the end—but they say she died a horrible death, screaming and crying for her dead worthless husband and her mother.

Oh, well. I don't want to speak of all that.

So Jessie stood at the counter with her arms folded. Watching us. It was nearly as if she'd been waiting for us, and I believe perhaps she was. She didn't say a word. Her littlest girl was hanging on her skirttail; I could see the top of the child's head behind the counter. It came to me then that none of their other girls were around. There were usually three or four grown girls behind the counter to flop a bolt of cloth up on it and measure your drygoods or to scoop your coffee from the grinder into a sack, and they had a middling girl, seven or eight years old; even she was nowhere around. I thought then that that was what was strange in the room. I tried to think it—I wanted to let that be it so I could think it and get it over with—and yes, that was part of it, as the absence of men on turned-backward slatback chairs and nail kegs around the stove was also part of it. But neither was all.

We stopped a little way back from the counter, the pastor bumped up behind me, and Otis hitched in his voice a little, all of us waiting. I thought it was taking forever. My husband said finally, "Afternoon, Miz Lodi," and then hesitated again, standing there awkwardly with his hat in his hand. I wanted to just kick him. He'd never called her Missus, any more than anybody in Big Waddy ever did—he called her Jessie if he had reason to call her anything—and it seemed to me just wrong for him to do it then. Can you imagine? As if there were protocol to the delivery of a death notice which I knew better than my husband who'd been called on in the community to perform that service a dozen times.

Really, I can't tell you how a person gets to be called Missus or any other particular designation in this community. It's a mystery to me. You've got Mrs. Yanush called Granny Merl by the whole community and old Mrs. Withers called Franny by even the little Indian children, yet they called me Miz Skeen from the day Otis carried me in here from Saint Louis perched high on my Aunt Elgis's featherbed in the spring wagon—I was twenty-three, which is old to marry, perhaps, but not *old,* and as childless on that day as I'll go to my grave —so it's not solely a matter of age, though getting old helps if you care to become a Mister or a Missus. It's not entirely tied to respect either, because, as I told you, most folks called Fate Lodi Mister, and I don't think you would say he had this community's respect. He had this community's something-or-another—fear a little, certainly, but not just that. He had our . . . minds . . . our imaginations, is the best way I know how to put it. People talked about Fate Lodi more than any other living individual in this country. Thought about him, complained and griped about him, and maybe, for some of the men, bragged about him as well. Some people—men, I should say; I never heard any woman but Jessie say one word in Fate Lodi's favor—but some of the men around here admired him, and I guess that's a kind of respect. He did always seem to get hold of just about whatever it was that he wanted. Seemed able to get anybody to do what he wanted, either through bullying or pigheadedness or charm—at least that was true up till the last couple of years, when he turned so cowardly and full of threats—and some men are prone to admire that kind of lording it over everybody, if they haven't got the gumption to do otherwise.

But in any case, such was the condition in our community that Fate Lodi was Mister, and Jessie was Jessie, and I wanted Otis to tell it right, do it right. I could hear the pastor breathing hard and mumbling behind me, and the cobbler pan was shaking in my fists, and I took the edge of it and poked Otis in the back, Lord in heaven forgive me. He was the best mortal man, I promise you, that the Creator ever allowed to draw breath, and I couldn't leave him alone for a minute. I had to try to make him do as I wanted, act and move and speak as I wanted, hold his head over the bucket when he took a drink of water. I stayed on him all the time, and he just took it and went on. Never one time argued against me. I was high-strung, he called it, and he laid it off onto us never having children, but the truth is, I had the devil in me and I didn't know how to quit.

He was a big, handsome man, you know, my husband—over six feet tall and broad in the chest, with slender legs about as big around as turkey sticks and the prettiest head of black hair. When he took his hat off, his hair sprang up wild and ragged; he couldn't keep it tamed with a quart of hair oil. He had the deepest-set eyes I ever saw on a man outside of pictures of Abe Lincoln, and Otis's were nearly that brown and sad. Picture him standing before that poor widow woman who was so newly widowed her husband's blood was yet pooling on the dirt street in Cedar, who did not yet know she was widowed but only that trouble had come calling with his hat in his hand and sweat-stains blackening his shirt back. See him standing awkward in the middle of that cramped whitewashed store, saying, "Miz Lodi," while he holds in his mind and his misery this terrible information, trying to think how to deliver a message of horror and sorrow which he no more wanted to be responsible for than he'd care to jump off a barn roof—trying to come up with the right words how to tell it, his pastor no help at all but grunting and heaving behind him, and his good little wife right at his side, using a tin cobbler pan to poke him in the back.

They say He's a merciful God, some say it, and I surely hope it. Every day I draw breath I pray God's mercy, pray Otis knows what was in my heart, because I surely never got the chance to tell him.

Oh, that's not true.

There was a chance every minute for seventeen years, until the day he died walking out of the cornfield. I was standing right here on the porch. I saw him, he was walking this way toward the house. The crops were laid by, I don't know what he was doing—checking to see if they'd tassled yet maybe—but he was just right there coming out from between the green rows, and I heard him say, "Oh, no," and then he fell. After that, no word out of my mouth or frown or hissed whisper was ever going to be taken back.

But you didn't come to hear all that.

Jessie stood real still with her arms folded, and when Otis said Miz Lodi the next time, she turned an arm loose and reached down and placed her hand on top of the child's head. I could hear the pastor huffing, trying to say something behind me, going, "Luft, luft, luft," and I could feel Otis's misery, his tongue like a knot in the back of his mouth, and oh, I wanted to help him and I wanted to run out of there, and I wanted him for pity's sake to hurry up and quit calling her Miz Lodi and say it right.

In a little bit, Jessie said, "Well?"

I believe she knew. I really believe she did. Or she knew something anyway, because that little girl started whimpering, and when I looked I could see the child wiggling and clutching with both hands at her mother's palm pressing down on her, squirming and crying, trying to get out from under the weight of her mother's hand.

Otis said, "I'm afraid I've got some pretty bad news."

Jessie didn't say anything. Her mouth was collapsed together like an old woman's; it gave her the strangest look, because she didn't have a gray hair on her head.

The preacher went, "Luft, luft, luft, luft."

It was then I felt the men's eyes behind us in the store doorway. I didn't have to turn around to see them. I could feel they were there.

"There's been a shooting in Cedar," Otis said finally.

She stood quiet the longest time, no sound but the little girl crying, the pastor huffing, the men holding their breaths in the doorway. Then she said, very soft and slow and steady, the way you'd talk low so as not to wake a sleeping child, "Which one is it?"

"Well, Miz Lodi," Otis said, "it's your husband."

Jessie didn't bat an eyelash. She didn't ask if he was dead or living, who'd done it, nothing about it, which is another reason makes me believe she already knew. The little girl kept crying—not at the news, I'm sure; she probably was not yet even talking, and there hadn't been enough words passed for her to understand if she was—but because the bulk of her mama's hardtack weight was pressing down on her head. The men began to murmur behind us. The pastor, too, finally got his tongue loose, and I heard him say, "Lift 'em up to the Lord in prayer," which is I suppose what he'd been trying to get out for ten minutes.

"Did anybody yet send for my boys?" Still soft as a whisper.

Well, the pastor's voice was unstoppered pretty well I guess at that point, because he proceeded to declare that the two oldest were down yonder already—never did he explain where "down yonder" was or how they'd got there, but perhaps she knew more about it than I did, because she didn't appear the least surprised, whereas I kind of blinked when he said that. The girls were yonder too, the pastor said, or most of them, near as he could count. He'd stayed a minute to pray with them, knelt right down in the street to pray with them to give God the victory, and then he'd come right on back to lift her up to the Lord in prayer, she needn't worry, if the family needed anything, anything at all, just call on him as shepherd and friend, our church community would be there to provide for her and the children in this time of grief and sorrow—

Oh, I don't know, he went on for the better part of twenty minutes, but I was just glad. I didn't want Otis to have to utter another word. The men had started nudging inside the store by then. I stepped forward and set the cobbler on the counter, and then went back as quickly as I could and stood beside Otis. I just don't have the tongue for it. I don't know what to say, even at a regular time of bereavement. Death embarrasses me. Still yet it does to this day. I didn't know what to say to anybody when they came out to the house after Otis died. My husband was lying dead on the cooling board in the parlor, what was I going to say to some woman who says the Lord moves in mysterious ways or she's praying for me or she knows just how I feel?

Anyway, I was glad Brother Peevyhouse took over. He wasn't weeping, or saying anything about anybody getting shot down like a dog, but just answering a few questions from the men who'd come on in by then and were milling around. I never heard Jessie ask him anything, but the others did, and I have to say the pastor handled it very well. Otis made his way over and stood by a big pickle barrel against the wall, and I followed him. He was just waiting, I think, for what the pastor wanted him to do next.

In a little bit he said, "Agnes, if Brother Peevyhouse needs me to go back down yonder with him to fetch Mr. Lodi in the buckboard, you reckon you could ride Sally home on that old saddle?"

I'd never taken much to riding since I came into this country, though I could drive a team from here to Houston if I had to, but I just never did care much to sit a horse. But any time I did ride, it was in the pretty little sidesaddle he'd sent to Fort Smith and bought me, it most certainly was not in an old cow-pony man's saddle like Otis used for his old mare. But I said, "Yes, Otis, I believe I could." I thought to myself, Well, I can walk that mare up that hill.

Then he said, "I don't know, what do *you* think he did with them?"

He turned his eyes expectantly on me, as if we'd talked about this already, as if this was the middle of a conversation we'd been having silently all afternoon and just now got around to speaking out loud. I didn't have an idea in the world what he was talking about.

"What did he do with who?" I said, because I knew the "he" was Fate Lodi—not because he was the man who'd just got murdered but because he had that kind of effect on people: lots of times you'd hear people talk about *he*-this and *he*-that and never once pass his name, but you knew who they meant. But I didn't know who the "them" was that Otis was talking about, and I looked at him and asked that, and now it was his turn to look at me as if he didn't have an idea in the world what *I* meant.

"Why," he said at last, and swept his big deep-set eyes around the cluttered whitewashed boardslats, pausing at last on the lone empty west wall, barren and pale as a burn scar, which was of course the source of that strangeness I'd witnessed and not witnessed because I had not been willing to see it. "Why," he said, "what'd Fate do with all them dozens of guns used to hang on the wall over there?"

Grady Dayberry

Now, you need to understand something here. Killings was not all that unusual in this part of the country at that time. I don't mean you'd see one every day, but you'd hear about one onced a week nearly, but usually it'd be connected to a bank robbery or a shootout between a posse and some little gang of outlaws or somebody got shot down delivering the mail. It's hard to imagine how much outlawry and killing it took to settle this country, but, now, it sure did. The majority of the time there'd be some famous person at the heart of it, or if he wasn't famous to start with, he'd get famous on account of it. Those were the kind of killings that traveled. What I mean, if Cherokee Bill shoots some stranger at a bank holdup and it was a fellow just happened to be standing around, curious, watching the robbery, how any fellow might do, why that's the kind of killing you'd hear about. That happened up at Lenapah in the fall of Ninety-four, I think it was, and we all heard about it in a week or two. Heard they made a law afterwards that Cherokee Bill was to pass unmolested in Lenapah from then on. That's one outlaw was allowed by law to come and go in a town any how he pleased, on account of the people were so scared of the man. Now, that wasn't the killing made Cherokee Bill famous, but it was one that sure traveled, and you know a bunch of them did. I could tell you a hunnerd stories, but they'd near ever one show off Henry Starr or Belle Starr or the Cook Gang or the Daltons or somebody. If you heard about a killing way off up at Chandler, it had to have a outlaw in it, and if you heard about it for years and years after, it generally had a outlaw and a posse and like as not some kind of famous marshal.

So I don't know why folks around here tell the Lodi killing so often, or they used to, maybe they don't so much anymore. But it didn't have any outlawry in it, no robbery or posse, no marshal even to speak of but that colored deputy out of Woolerton and old Tecumseh Moore. May be we're partial to it on account of it's our own, you know how I mean. Like family. Like how you might have an ornery son who's mean as the dickens but you're a little bit partial to him as well. You know they tell the Sabe Cutler killing, and the Starkey boys, both them killings, plumb up to this day. But still not to the degree of the Lodi killing, and what I think, I think it's on account of they were brothers, and on account of them girls. A killing in a family, between the members of a family, now, that's a terrible thing. They tell me it's the most usual type of a killing, I don't know about that, but I do know it's a type that can tear the heart out of some people, just rip a family wide open, and from there on out to the town. How else are you going to act?

Well, what my dad told me, the first he knew anything about it, Fate Lodi was standing out in the street one morning, hollering for his brother. Going like this: *soooeee soooeee*—hog-calling him, you know— then he'd throw his head back and gobble like a turkey. Now, that's an old Indian trick. I've always heard Indians would do that if they aimed to kill you or die trying, and I reckon that's what Fate meant by it and I reckon John knew it too. Dad did, and he didn't know just quite what to do. It was kind of a cool day in March, but it was bright out. Bright and still, no wind to speak of, and Dad had the stable doors open. This'd been along about ten o'clock. Here the one brother is, hammering away with his crosspeen, minding his own business, going about his work; here's the other'n outside in the street gobbling like a turkey, or in other words calling him out.

Now, as it happened, there wasn't any customers in the livery yet that morning, and I don't know if folks just hadn't got there yet from wherever-all they had to drive a team from or if word had got around there was going to be trouble—though that's generally more liable to draw folks than to make them shy away, near as I've ever seen it—or I don't know just what happened, but anyhow they wasn't no customers, only Dad and John Lodi inside the barn. According to what my dad told me, Lodi never so much as lifted his head from the anvil, not even at the first sooey, just kept on working—he was beating out a new plow blade, if I remember right—and on the surface of it acted like he didn't even hear all that carrying on his brother was doing outside on Main Street in public daylight. But ever time Fate would cut loose with one of these animal sounds, John'd bring that hammer down harder. Just blam and blam! and *blam.* Ruint that piece of metal and kept on hitting it anyhow. Slower, and harder. The sound ringing out in that empty barn, Dad said, clanging slow like a dead church bell, echoing high in the rafters. In a little while John put down the crosspeen and picked up the sledge. Blam. *Blam. Blam!* BLAM!

Well, my dad, you know, his temper'ment was always to be a peace-maker. That's just the kind of man he was. Folks around here know it. Some people—now, I don't want to say who—but some people are forever hankering for a fight, and I don't mean to be a fighter their-selves but I mean to watch other folks fight it out. There's some people, if it looks like something is stirring, they'll just stand over to the side and holler sic 'em, but my dad was never that type of man. Not to mention John Lodi was his employee and had worked good and faithful for him for close to nine years. So Dad felt like he had to do something to prevent what looked like was going to be trouble, and he studied on it a little while to see what he might do. He knew he was up against something, though of course he didn't yet know the half of it, and he knew he'd have to figure some way to handle it. The day was bright out, like I mentioned, and Dad would be at a disadvantage the minute he stepped out that open doorway until his eyes settled, so he wasn't interested in just walking out yonder to see what was going on. If a man hoots and sooeys and does all that animal rigmarole to a fellow, well, you know a thing or two about it, and one thing you know is, he is full of contempt to his eyeballs, and the reason he's full of con-tempt is on account of he's scared. And a scared man is a dangerous man, everybody knows it, and my dad didn't aim to put himself un-armed and blinded in the middle of that.

So Dad went on about his business, kindly kept an eye on John Lodi while he was at it, and did pretty much like him. Acted like he couldn't hear a thing. But he told it like this, said, You could slice the air with a sawblade—and by that he meant the tension, I imagine, and the anger, and them clangs getting louder, and he believed John Lodi was fixing to blow. So he says to himself, Well, now, I'm going to have to do something. He stepped over to the stalls—I forget now what he'd been working at that morning, if he ever told me—but he quit whatever it was and went over and commenced to harnessing our old mare, name of Vergie, and I don't even know how come her to be in the stable instead of out in the lot. She was a pitiful old thing, and I believe Dad had to shoot her not long after, but he went and caught her up like he was going to hitch her to the wagon. Now, we had the prettiest matched team at that time, a pair of highstepping trotters, and of course Dad's saddlehorse and DewMan's and Clyde's, but they were either all ever one out in the lot or else Dad figured Fate Lodi was liable to shoot whatever stuck its head out the door first and he figured it'd ought to be Vergie as anything else, but anyhow Vergie it was, and Dad told John Lodi he was going to meet the train, which was a story didn't hold an ounce of water because the train didn't come till twelve-oh-one and you sure didn't need no horse and wagon to get to the depot unless you meant to carry a load back because the depot was just up the road a little ways, and you sure wasn't going to carry no big load with that Vergie—she was all broke down in her hips, I don't know if she could've hardly pulled a buggy at that point, much less that old wagon, much less tote any kind of a load inside the wagon—but anyhow John didn't look crossways nor pause a minute beating that poor pitiful plow blade, and Dad eased old Vergie to the door. Or "eased" is not just the right word, because Dad told me he liked to jangled that harness to pieces trying to make a little noise.

Paused a minute at the doorway with Vergie's nose stuck out there, just a-jingling and a-jangling to beat the band, hollered at John again over the banging and sooeys and gobbling, "I'm headed up yonder to the de-pot. Anybody comes looking for me, you tell 'em I'll be back in a little bit." Thinks about it a second, hollers as loud as he can holler, "YOU TELL THAT DADGUM MARSHAL WHEN HE GETS HERE I WAITED HALF THE MORNING, COULDN'T WAIT NO LONGER, BUT YOU TELL HIM TO STAY PUT, I'M GOING TO BE RIGHT BACK."

He thought that might do some good. He figured if Fate Lodi was ever going to hear or believe it was J. G. Dayberry coming out the door and not John Lodi, he'd of done it by now, and Dad noised his way on out. Kept Vergie in between him and them turkey gobbles, which hadn't let up a iota, and stopped in the daylight to get his eyes back. Peered up the street over Vergie's back. Fate wasn't a hundred yards away, there in the street in front of Tatum's store, and Dad said he could see right off Lafayette Lodi was armed to the teeth and soused to the gills. That's just how Dad put it. Said he had a Winchester in the saddle holster and another'n laying acrossed the horn. Had a pistol belt strapped on and a Colt stuck in each holster, one in the front of his britches, and one in his fist, waving it around. His other fist had aholt of a whiskey bottle, waving it around too, which goes to show how drunk he was, because you know that was a criminal offense. This was Indian Territory, people, liquor was strictly against the law anywhere inside these borders. These deputy U.S. marshals were liable to be on your tail in a minute with a warrant for introducing and selling liquor in the Territory, and we're not talking about no piddling little offense neither, you were going to go see Judge Parker on that one, that was sure. Which is not to say folks didn't drink plenty whiskey, run plenty of it and sell it—bootlegging and horsestealing was the two main ways some folks got their start in this country—but a fellow didn't go prancing around on Main Street waving it around.

Dad said Fate didn't appear to be worried about a deputy U.S. marshal showing up, nor shook up any about an old white nag creeping out the stable door in full harness and no wagon in sight either. Said he hardly appeared to notice excepting to crow louder, but said Fate's horse was sure jumpy, but Dad kept on anyhow, a little bit and a little bit. That horse was a little old blue roan, nervous as a flinder, and every time Fate would throw back his head to gobble, it'd flinch and dance. He had it lashed to the rail in front of Tatum's and he'd rare back to yodel and fall back against the saddle and that horse'd shy and buck and Lodi'd cuss awhile and take him a swig. He was making a pretty little scene for hisself and too drunk to care, I reckon, though folks was cleared off the street entirely. Dad said you couldn't have roused a mouse. People ain't blind to a powder keg when they see it, and Dad said that street was dead as Sunday morning. Wasn't nobody visible about. Said he allowed there was plenty watching from somewheres but nobody aiming to mix in it, and Dad could see he was just on his own. Well, he kept on north, easing along a little, kept that old mare between him and Lodi, and my dad didn't have a sign of a gun on him. Would you call that a brave man? Brave or plain stupid, that's how my mama told it, but Dad said he did what he had to do. Said a man sees what he's got to do, now, he's just got to get up yonder and do it, can't go wavering and misguessing about. So Dad eased along the street to where he was about even with Fate Lodi wallowing and carrying on. He stopped then. He had to do a little more studying on it, see, contemplate something or another to talk about.

In a little bit he says, "Morning, Fate." Just as calm and friendly.

Like they was just passing on the street in front of the bank. Now, my dad had a nodding acquaintance with Fate Lodi, or you might even call it speaking, and I guess about everybody in these parts did. Fate ran that mercantile store up at Waddy Crossing and folks around there traded with him for feed and drygoods and all, but the main thing he sold out of it was guns, and folks from all over this country would trade with him on that. They'd come about as far to buy a gun off Fate Lodi as they'd come to have his brother fix their singletree, and I don't rightly know why unless it was just the amount he kept on hand and the kind and the price. He claimed to be a gunsmith but I don't believe he ever made any guns that I knew anything about, but I do know he repaired them, freshened out barrels and re-set sights and what have you, but mostly he just sold 'em. A gun trader, that's all there was to him. He wasn't no gunsmith, the way John was. Nobody told me that. Didn't anybody have to tell me that, I just knew it, and I was just a boy. But people all around would go to Big Waddy Crossing to buy guns off Fate Lodi, and I'll allow my dad might have even, once in a while. So Dad had some acquaintance with the man, but they wasn't what you'd call friendly, and then too, it was Dad's own employee and friend Fate was trying to call out. But Dad proceeded to the best of his ability.

"Turned off kindly cool this morning, ain't it?" he says.

Well, I guess Fate didn't quite know what to make of it. Dad said he blinked a couple of times, held real still, stared out in the street at Vergie.

"Reckon it'll get hot enough soon enough, don't you reckon?" Dad says, friendly like, just passing the time of day, you know.

Fate stood as still as an old souse can stand still, is how Dad put it, and stared at Vergie's face.

"I'm about to head up to the station yonder. Y'all come go with me," Dad says, just lilting his voice up so nice and light. Thought he might persuade him with honey, I suppose, but you know there's no persuading a drunk. The way Dad told it, he said Fate kindly grunted or something, like an old boar. Said Fate raised that pistol, or tried to, the muzzle dancing around yonder, said he couldn't keep it steady for nothing, you know how wavery a old drunk is, but Dad said he didn't believe Lodi could hit him by aiming for him but he might hit him by accident and Dad just ducked down a little tighter behind Vergie's neck.

Said Fate hollered across to him, "You go to hell, horse!"

That was the first Dad knew Fate thought it was Vergie talking to him. Then my daddy understood he was in a pretty bad fix. Said he knew if he stepped out from behind Vergie, not only was that going to leave him without a ounce of protection but it was liable to startle Lodi so bad as to set him off sure enough. Said on the other hand, if Fate believed it was a horse trying to sweet-talk him, said he—meaning Dad—said he didn't like to be standing anywhere near around it. Said he'd seen a old drunk wood-hauler one time nearly beat his wife to death with a piece of hickory trying to mash the crawling snakes off her, said he reckoned if Fate thought it was a talking horse, he was sure enough going to commence firing one or more of them many firearms, and then no telling what. So if Dad was unsettled before on how to proceed, now he was sure enough stumped. But you know, sometimes when you're in it there's not a thing in the world for it but to just go ahead on.

"Yessir," Dad says, "reckon it'll be hot as the dickens here before we kno—"

Blam. Blam. Blam.

Lodi fires off that gun.

Dad said them bullets went ever which way. They was one lodge in the wooden sign over the front door of the stable—I seen it myself, that very afternoon when I come in after the shooting was all over with—and that sign was eighty yards or more off to the right of where Lodi was standing and close back. Slug stayed in it till the building burnt down in Twenty-nine, I reckon; I don't know that anybody ever climbed up there and dug it out. One of 'em went off some other direction, one zinged right over Dad's head. It was about then that Dad said he thanked his lucky stars and fool tender heart he'd kept that old pitiful mare for me to ride around on even when she went rheumy in one eye and got hard of hearing, because that horse never batted a eyelash. But said that blue roan liked to pitched a fit, whinnied and snorted and jerked around yonder, said it sounded like a big old buck snorting fear, and if that's not a sound that'll chill you, but Dad said he just gulped him in a deep breath of air and went on.

"Good day for setting around the stove—"

Blam. That's four, Dad thinks.

"—partaking of a little corn whiskey—"

Blam. Five.

"—provided a fella might know whereabouts to find him a little nip."

Blam.

That's six and the last one, and Dad nor Vergie neither one hadn't
been shot yet. Says to himself, says, Well, I can either get around
before he pulls out another weapon, or else I can lay down and quit.
You know my dad was nothing like a quitter, not ever, and he jumps
around Vergie there, got his mind set to rassle Fate down, he thinks
he can take him before he gets another gun loose, he's so wavery
drunk.

But, now, Dad's got another think coming. The minute he jumps
under and around that nag's neck, Lodi's got the pistol in his belt
buckle pulled up nearly, and Dad just stops straight up. Goes,
"Eeeeeasy now, easy," smooth and softlike, how you'll talk to a snaky
horse. Puts his hands up where Lodi can see them, comes on, walking
so slow maybe Fate can't even see him coming, but I guess he did, or
else just got too fed up trying to pull that pistol loose from his belt
buckle, drunk as he was—it's a wonder he didn't blow his buckeyes
off, you'll pardon the expression—but all at once Lodi just quits messing with that pistol, turns around to reach for the butt of the rifle he's
got strapped to the saddle, or that's what Dad thought. Dad paused
then, sure enough. He's out bare in the middle of the street, mind
you, no horseflesh between him and Eternity nor nothing, he says,
"Well, now, Mister Lodi, I don't mean a thing in the world—"

Fate stands around to face him then, peers across the road, trying
to focus his eyes, says almost like he regrets it, "Reckon I'm just going
to have to shoot you."

He's got him a weapon in his hands now, sure enough, and it ain't
no Winchester rifle and it ain't no Colt forty-four. Dad said he didn't
do a lot of speculating at the time on where the devil it come from,
but later he reckoned it must've been stuck down in the saddleholster
the other side toward the store, but however or wherever it come from,
Fate Lodi was drawed down on my dad with the evilest-mouthed-
looking weapon Dad said he'd ever eyeballed in his life. Said it was
one of these old-time contraptions called a pepperbox, used to be
popular back before Sam Colt learnt the world how to make a cylinder
turn—a bulky old pistol with a whole bouquet of barrels on the end.
They ain't worth a damn for accuracy but some of them can fire all
six or seven barrels at once. You don't need aim with such blasting
power as that. Can't even a blind man miss a target at twenty yards
with one of those things, and Dad is maybe twenty feet away from
Fate Lodi and it don't matter a bit in the world that the man is knee-

walking drunk. Fate goes to draw down on him, Dad just goes to praying in his heart, says, Lord Almighty Sweet Jesus, help me, and if You ain't going to help me, take care of my wife and children and make her see to it them boys gets trained up in the way they should go, Jesus' name, Amen.

Dad gets him an idea then. He says—real calm, real easy and nice, hands up, just a-smiling—says, "Don't mean to bother you, Mister Lodi, I sure don't. I just thought you might want to come help me drink that quart of bonded Tennessee whiskey I got coming in on the noon train from Fort Smith."

Well, you know my dad was not a drinking man, but he'd been around it enough to know that about the only thing interests a drunk better than a good fight is a good sup. Thought he might wet Fate's whistle enough with the thought of that imported whiskey to get his mind off shooting him—now and again folks did get themselves some good bonded whiskey smuggled in over the border, but most the time they had to settle for this old popskull liquor these moonshiners around here used to make—and for a minute it did nearly look like it was going to work. Fate squints his eyes at him for a while, lets them gunbarrels droop down a little bit, and then he says, low and mean, "Go to hell." He proceeds to lift the many-mouthed muzzle of that gun.

Dad said he didn't know where in the world John Lodi come from, nor when, which by that he meant he didn't know how John got out the livery door and between himself and Fate so quick. He pretty near just materialized in the dust of the street, that's what Dad said. Said he must've been coming the whole time, from the second Dad stepped out from behind Vergie—this all happened in less than a half a minute, mind you, just takes long in the telling. Long in the living, for that matter—you know how facing death is—and that's just what Dad said it looked like, said the barrels of that pepperbox looked like seven kinds of death coming. That's how many barrels was in it, Dad said, he counted them, you can bet he did. But Dad said just the very single second Fate raised that gun, John was standing there between them, his back to Dad and his front to his brother. Said John said, "All right, Brother, give it here."

And then it was quiet. Dad said you could hear Clara Belle Whitford's chickens up the street scratching in the yard, said you could hear that roan breathing, and the morning bright and still. Dad said next thing he knew, John was walking away from him. Said he just took two steps forward and got aholt of that murderous gun. Another step, he turned and walked back down the street and in at the stable door. Dad said he thought then, Why, you so-and-so, if that's all there is to it, why'd you let me make a fool of myself hiding behind that old broke-down horse? He was put out with John right in that moment, but of course that all changed later too. Said Fate was left standing there leaning back against that pony's flank, turning the bottle up to take him a snort. Dad said the poor old fellow—those were just the words Dad used when he told it, and now, that's the same poor old fellow was ready to loose seven barrels of gunshot upon him a minute ago, which goes to show two things: one, how tender a nature my dad had, and two, how pitiful old Fate Lodi finally looked when his brother took that gun away from him, don't matter if he did have about eleven others strapped and tucked and wedged all around—but Dad says the poor old fellow turned bleary eyes upon him, all the meanness gone out of him now and nothing left but pure bafflement, like he didn't know what in the world just happened. Dad said Fate turned around and took about six tries to get his foot in the stirrup, mounted that little blue roan and rode off back up Main Street toward the north.

Now, all this happened around ten o'clock of a Tuesday morning, and Dad said it wasn't five hours before Fate Lodi come back. All right. Here's where the real mystery comes in. Nobody seen him come.

Field Tatum

N̲o, sir.
No, sir.
No, sir.

I can't testify to that, sir, I didn't see a bit of it. All I can tell is what I saw when I come out of my store.

Well, it was Mr. Lodi faceup in the street and a gun laying beside him. Just sort of cradled beside him, sir, kind of snugged up against his pantsleg, the barrel—or barrels, I mean—all pointed down at his boots.

Well, sir, it was unique-looking, I never saw another one like it. Might've been fifty caliber, say, four barrels to it. I didn't take that good a look. I couldn't tell you if it had been fired, sir, Mr. Moore might be able to tell you that.

Three. I heard two right close together, shotgun shots, or that's what I thought then. Just immediately I thought it was a double-barreled shotgun fired one barrel and then the other right close together, but not both at once, just *pow, pow.* And then I heard the pistol.

Well, I'm pretty sure he was, Your Honor. I didn't check him, but I don't see how anybody could be alive in such a condition as that.

No, sir. I didn't see John Lodi at all, not at that time.

Just right quick, I mean, quick as I could get there. I don't believe he could have run back to the livery and got inside it in that amount of time. I really don't see how.

I'd say not more than thirty seconds. I mean, it just went like this: blam, blam, and then pop, and the boy ran out the door, and here I came right behind him in time to catch him sprawling sliding headfirst in the road.

No, not Mr. Lodi, the boy Jack.

In my own words? Who else's words am I going to tell it in?

What's that? Said, yessir, my own words, sir, I'll do the best I can.

Well, I was cutting up a side of beef at the time, Your Honor, in the back of my store. Tatum's Mercantile. I been running that store going on eight years there on Main Street, Town of Cedar, Choctaw Nation, Indian Territory—got my permit papers up to date, signed by Chief Gardner himself, December the eleventh, Eighteen-ninety-fi—

All right, yes, sir. I will.

Well, so, I do some butcher work for a few folks in addition to what I cut up regular to sell in my store, so that's what I was doing, I was working on a beef for my brother-in-law Willis Willowby, which means I was back behind the butcher counter pretty well in the back. I couldn't see out the window at all, sir, from back there. I didn't have an idea there was anything going on in the street. Now, I had Jack Slocum's boy Jack—he works for me afternoons, sweeps up and stocks shelves and makes deliveries and that, and I let him run the register some when I'm too bloodied up butchering to wait on the ladies—but we were slow Tuesday afternoon so I had the boy Jack stacking tomato tins up near the register when the gunshots went off. Well, as soon as we heard it, the boy flinched and tried to jump and run out there, and I shouted, "Hold it, son!" because you don't know if it's a bank robbery or what. You don't want to run into the big middle of something, and you don't want your employees doing it either—Jack Slocum would have my hide. So I said, "Hold it, son!" and came out quick, but that boy had got to the door before me and he'd already run out. I got there just in time to watch him leap off the front steps and trip and roll right over Mr. Lodi's body. He didn't know he was there, couldn't see him on account of how high the porch is and Mr. Lodi was of course flat on the ground. His horse—Mr. Lodi's horse—was tethered to the post in front of my building, sort of jerking and prancing, I think more on account of that boy running out the door so quick than anything else. Well, that's all I saw. The boy tripping over the body and sprawling facedown in the street with a mouthful of dust. When he twisted his neck around and got a good look at what he'd tripped over, now, I'm telling you what, he scrambled up pretty quick and lit out. I never saw that boy move so quick.

Yes, sir, now, he might have. That might have disturbed the body some, I just couldn't tell you that. All I can testify to is what I saw. Mr. Lodi was laying on his back in the street, and the gun was right close beside him. That'd be about it. Folks started gathering just right away, I guess we all heard the shots. Sheriff Moore there, he could probably tell you as much as I could. Time I got down on the street good, he'd already come from somewhere, and there were plenty others saw about what I saw, some of them maybe even more.

Oh. Well. That. That was a while later.

Yes, sir, Your Honor. Well, it was Angus Alford fetched me.

Sir? Maybe a half hour, maybe a little less. It hadn't been too long, I know that, just long enough that the buzz had died down some but not petered out altogether. Folks were still coming. We were—some of us—we were waiting to see if there was anything we could do, notify the family or carry him home or anything. I mean, clearly there wasn't anything anybody could do for Mr. Lodi. Somebody said somebody had already sent word on to McAlester here, I don't know about that, but Sheriff Moore was in the stable talking to Mr. Dayberry and John Lodi, and the rest of us were just sort of milling around. There didn't seem to be anything a fellow could do. I'd already took my butcher apron off and tried to put it over him, but Mr. Moore said no, I don't know how come, so I wadded it back up. Somebody did finally go up and spread a handkerchief over the face at some point, quite a little while later. I didn't see who it was. But I was standing in front of the store, my little mercantile there, with my apron rolled up in my hands, couldn't think to put it in inside, and Angus—Mr. Alford here—he hurried up from somewhere and motioned me to come go with him. He was making it out kind of secretive.

I don't know, sir. You'd have to ask him that.

Well, sir, a situation like that, all kinds of people around, somebody comes up and motions like it's urgent and secret you ought to come go with him, you just quit and go. I followed him into the little alleyway there that runs between my store and the livery stable, and on around back. That's when we seen—saw—the young lady yonder and—

Yes, sir. That's her. She was—I'd have to say she was dressed different to what she is today, but yes, sir, that's the one. I didn't know she was Mr. Lodi's daughter. I—Your Honor, I'm just going to have to tell you the truth about it, I didn't know it was a girl, or a female, I mean. She was—she had on what you'd just have to call man's clothes, you couldn't tell what it was.

Why, broadcloth britches, Your Honor, a man's shirt, man's hat. Had a gun holster buckled around her, and the woman she was rassling—

Well, I'm trying to. That's what I'm trying. It was that girl, or that young lady yonder, and a Indian woman rassling out back of Dayberry's barn.

I didn't know her, Your Honor. Just a little short fat Indian woman.

Just regular, just how any of them dresses. I don't remember. Just some kind of a dress, didn't have on no blanket or shawl or nothing, had her hair braided on top of her head. Just a normal-looking little squaw woman. I couldn't say who she was.

Well, they was rassling fit to feed a circus. I mean, that kid, that young lady yonder, was whipping herself around like a snake with a hoe on its head, just *whip wh-h-i-i-ip!* That little old Choctaw had aholt of her by both wrists, clamped down and hanging on like a snapper, she wasn't going to let go, talking Choctaw at her just as hard and fast as she could talk it, and the kid turning and whipping and snapping like crack-the-whip, the two of them whirling around inside that extry feed-lot Dayberry's got set up out back of his barn.

Well, of course I figured it had to do with the killing. You just—you just automatically think it. You don't see such a strange sight every day, and if you see it not a half hour after a murder, you naturally think the two events are connected. But I didn't know what to do about it. We—the two of us, me and Angus—I guess we just stopped and gaped awhile. I didn't want to go jump in the middle of it, I thought we'd just wait it out a bit, see what come of it. At first, you know, we thought it was a kid—a boy—maybe an Indian boy or a little half-breed—that woman was rassling with. She was talking to him, or her, in Choctaw, that much I knew. Well, and he was armed, or I mean she was, the kid was, so that was one reason not to jump in there, and then plus too, the Indian woman had a good hold so it was just about a draw as far as I could tell, I wanted to see how it turned out. But Angus—Mr. Alford—he begun to sidle in that direction, kind of easing over, getting close to the rails. Along about then the kid, the young lady yonder, whipped her head in such a way as to send that man's hat a-flying, which then we seen it was a young lady, Your Honor, so we got to moving quick. What I mean, it was clear the child was white then, you could see her whole face, it was clear it was a female. Angus run and jumped up on the rail fence, I run around to the gate. He got there before I did, grabbed that squaw around the throat. Time I got there, that kid—the young lady, I mean—she was . . . well, Your Honor, she was cussing a blue streak. There's no nice way to put it. Angus had aholt of the Indian, the Indian had aholt of the kid, never turned loose a minute, and I know Angus had him a good grip—

Well, you thought you were protecting her. We meant to be. You don't know what you're doing, you can't think something through, you just react by gut instinct. What we seen, a Indian had aholt of a white girl, you don't spend a lot of time asking yourself who's doing what or why. I guess Angus nearly choked— Your Honor, if I could, I'd just rather Mr. Alford testify for himself.

No, sir.
No, sir.

That's—I don't know what happened exactly. The Indian woman turned loose of the young lady, and I had the young lady by the back of the belt, she turned away from the squaw and proceeded to fight me, Your Honor, just whaling away with both fists. I didn't see much after that—I was just trying to protect my face. Next thing I knew, Angus was holding her, the young lady there, around the waist, had her about half lifted off the ground. I saw the squaw get up off the floor of the feedlot and walk off west out of town pretty fast—moving fast for an Indian, what I mean.

No, sir. I didn't see where; just west. I had my hands full, you might say. Angus held her, the young lady, while I took the pistol out of the holster. I tried to get hold of her fists but I couldn't, I finally just gave it up and sort of waded in underneath. Finally got hold of it, the gun. I put it under my waistcoat—well, I'd dropped that butcher apron a long time ago, finally found it the next day trampled to pieces underneath Jim Tarplin's mules, but—

Yes, sir. All right. Well, that's about all I can tell you. I got hold of the pistol and hid it under my vest, some of the fight seemed to blow out of her then. We just, the two of us—I mean, there didn't seem to be anything to do but just take her around to where the sheriff was. We didn't know what else to do with her.

Yes, sir. I knew Mr. Lodi. Both Lodis. Of course, everybody knew John, he'd worked for Dayberry since long before I ever even went to Cedar. Yes, sir, I knew the victim as well. Recognized who it was as soon as I got a look at him after Jack's boy Jack tripped and fell over him. I think most folks around in that country knew both men.

Well, I wouldn't want to say about that. I did trade with Mr. Lodi some. I mean, I'd gone up to Waddy to buy a Winchester off him one time, and I'd buy shells and powder along—he had a good price to his guns, a lot of variety, a lot of people would shop guns off him. But I can't say I knew the man. I sure wouldn't want to say if he had any enemies, I wouldn't know anything about that.

What I knew about John, I knew him to be a good worker. That's about it. Quiet man, for the most part, just, you know, he'd say hello and how are you, but I just wouldn't know a thing about his business, nor his brother's. Oh, you hear things, but what I understand, you can't enter hearsay in a court of law, and well, that's about all I'd know would be hearsay.

Yes, sir, Your Honor. I'll sure do that. Un-huh.

Thank *you.*

Grady Dayberry

Nobody seen nothing. I believe your court records will tell you that. Even Dad didn't see but the tail of it, and he was the primary witness. Folks tell it six ways from Sunday, and don't any of them know the truth. That's what's so strange. Fate come riding back into Cedar—this'd been around two, three o'clock in the afternoon, see, bright clear day out, it all happened right out here on Main Street on a Tuesday—and nobody seen a thing. Dad said it was pretty near like them two had a invisible cloak on till it was over. He didn't know how to account for it, and I don't. Not really. They's some things I guess there's no accounting for, ever, but I got my ideas. Now, I'm going to tell you just what Dad told the judge at the hearing, and this is how he told it all his life:

Said he heard a little pop. This was well after dinner, see, long after the Twelve-oh-one and a little after the Two-oh-seven come through. Dad said he knew it because he heard both whistles, he didn't have any doubt. He was up in the loft pitching hay down, and he heard a gun pop. Now, you know that wasn't no shotgun, nor even a rifle, had to be a pistol, and small caliber at that, but Dad said he heard it— *pop*—and then it all happened this quick: he looked and seen Lodi gone from the forge and knew in half a heartbeat who it was and what it was. Said he jabbed the fork in a pile and jumped down, didn't even wait long enough to use the ladder, just leapt down off the loft onto the stack he was pitching and run for the door. Said the second he landed hands-down in the haystack he heard rifle fire and right on top of it an explosion, like dynamite nearly, just BOOM, heard another'n as he was running, and just as he reached the door, he heard a third. Said time he got out the door in the daylight the smoke was thick and John was crouched in the dirt on the street in front of Tatum's, lowering the muzzle of that pepperbox he'd taken off his brother not five hours before. Said Lodi stood up after a little bit and walked over and stood still, looking down at his brother.

Now, folks'll tell you—I've heard this story till I'm nearly sick—some folks say John went yonder and stood over his brother and put the seven barrels of that gun right on Fate's forehead and pulled the trigger and blew his head off. That is just not how it happened. I don't know why folks are so ugly as to tell a tale like that. My dad seen it, or seen the end of it, seen John in the street protecting his life like any normal man would, a dozen yards away. It was as fair a killing as any, fairer than a lot of them, and Dad told the judge that. The top of Fate's head was off, sure, but that's just the pitiful accuracy of them old contraptions. What Dad thought, he thought John was aiming high, trying to shoot over Fate's head to warn him, make him come to his senses, and accidentally took the top of his head off with that old muzzle-heavy gun. Said John never tried to run nor nothing, said he just got up and went and stood over his brother, looking down, like he was watching a bobber on a still pond. Folks started piling out of buildings and houses. Fate didn't twitch or nothing, probably died right off, or anyhow he was sure enough plenty dead by the time Dad got there, much less the rest of the town. Eyes open. Bleeding head to foot, top of his head off and his throat ragged. We all seen that. I seen it when I come in from school.

But see, there's all these little peculiar things about it, and I think that's partly how come that killing won't lay down and die. Some of it's things Dad never mentioned at the hearing, and I only heard him tell onced or twiced. One thing, Dad said Fate had unloaded himself from about half the weaponry he had strapped on in the morning. Oh, he still had guns, no question he was armed and dangerous, but—don't make a lot of sense, but Dad said Fate had took his gunbelt off, didn't have a pistol anywhere about him. Said he had a rifle in the saddleboot, and it was still there. There was a gun laying beside him —not in his hands; those blasts knocked it out surely—but laying next to him in the street was a weapon, looked about like a four-barreled sawed-off shotgun with a hand grip or something, if you can imagine such a thing. Well, it was some kind of high-caliber gun, Dad said, but it wasn't a pistol exactly—made like a shotgun nearly, I reckon, or anyhow you had to load it from the breech. Four barrels, had to be a mighty nose-heavy gun. Dad never did know what become of it. They said somebody had it a day or two at the hearing and then it just disappeared.

Another strange thing: old Heck Woolery said Fate passed his house up at Bull Creek about a hour or so before the killing, said he wasn't drunk in any way, shape, or form. Said he spoke to him and Lodi didn't answer back but to nod afternoon to him, said he looked mean as Satan maybe, but he was sober as a nail. Well, and not only that, but Heck said he didn't see a one of them children pass his place, and you know the wagon road ran right by his field. Said he was out with the turning plow all afternoon, didn't leave the field from dinnertime till way up close to dark, yet them youngsters, nearly every one of Fate's and all of John's that were still living, they all got from Waddy to Cedar somehow or another. The other peculiarity—nobody ever did account for this, though I have my ideas on it, same as everything—but when they went to move Fate that evening to put him in the wagon to carry him back up to Big Waddy Crossing, Dad said he seen it himself, what folks talked about later and how come some of those stories to get started. Fate had a little ragged hole, looked like a twenty-two hole, in the back of his skull.

But to me, the most mysterious part of it is how come there to be nobody to see it. To see what actually happened. Did Fate draw down on him with that big gun or cuss him or what? Did John try to talk to him or did he go to shooting the minute he come out the door of the stable, and how'd he know Fate was out there? Fate didn't make none of them turkey sounds like in the morning, otherwise the whole town would've heard. I guess somehow or another we all want to see it. If we ever just heard somebody tell it, somebody who'd seen it, we could settle it in our minds and let it go. But it was that peculiar turn, where everybody had disappeared from the windows and streets of Cedar for those two or three minutes. And folks tell it and tell it, and don't none of them know what they're talking about, except my dad. I've been studying on it for three-quarters of a century, and I come to this little bit of a conclusion: what I think—I think it was a event wasn't meant for the public to witness. I believe it was between them two and God, wasn't none of the rest of us's business, though folks sure made it their business after the killing, or tried to, you never heard so much talk. But I believe the Lord arranged it for Fate Lodi to slip into town in a little envellup of time when everybody's back was turned because them two brothers had business between them that had to be reckoned.

I don't believe anybody is ever going to know what really happened, because them that could tell it are dead. But you look how it went: Dad was in the loft pitching hay when the shooting started—he wouldn't ordinarily do that till feeding time along about five o'clock— and he jumped down and run as fast as he could run, but he still got there after it was finished. Field Tatum was in the back of his store cutting up a hog. Ordinarily he'd a been right up there at the cash box where he could see anything went on in the street. Mister Upton at the bank said he was putting the day's receipts in the safe when he heard gunfire. The streets were as empty as they'd been at ten o'clock in the morning when Dad was trying to settle Fate down, and now this was an active town then, just as lively as a junction. There wasn't hardly ever a moment between daybreak and sundown when there wasn't folks about their business all up and down, and here it happened twice in one day. Lovett's Hotel was right across the street yonder, wasn't nobody loafing in front of it. Nobody come forward to say, "I seen what happened," not even old Sour Waters, and you know he claimed to witness ever bank robbery and shootout from here to Kansas. It goes beyond peculiar.

All right, now, I'll just tell you a little thought I been having for a mighty number of years. You're going to tell me I'm crazy, but I'm eighty-seven years old now, and I don't much care. I been called plenty things in my life, crazy won't hurt none on top of the rest of it, but, now, here's what I think: I believe if my dad hadn't mixed up in it in the morning, the killing would've happened then. Right there ten o'clock in the morning, John Lodi without a gun to his name and Fate Lodi armed to the armpits and drunk as a lord. Furthermore, I don't believe it would've been John that did the killing and Fate that got killed but just exactly the other way around.

Now, hold on, hold on. I'll tell you why. You look how the streets were empty then and later, how they wasn't no customers around. God cleared the platter for them in the morning, and then my dad mixed up in it and changed everything. I believe that. And then the good Lord had to go to work and bring Fate on back later and arrange it all private, the streets empty, all over again. So then it happened and they wasn't no witnesses. I believe in my heart the Lord intended it like that.

But, now, here is what I don't know and won't never know, I don't reckon, till come time to meet my Maker, but this is what I been wondering for seventy-five years: Did the Lord use Dad as His instrument to make sure the right one got killed? Or did Dad mix in it and mess up the Lord's plan?

BOOK FOUR

Revelation

Then shall he kill the goat of the sin-offering,

that is for the people, and bring his blood within the

vail, and do with that blood as he did with the blood

of the bullock, and sprinkle it upon the mercy seat . . .

LEVITICUS 16:15

I was standing at their well turning the windlass when I first heard him. The sun was high overhead, still too far south yet to crack the treebuds, but coming. Small black strips of shadow ribbed the dead grass at the foot of the well. I stood in the cold sunlight, turning the shaft by rote motion, my mind stale and inward, my eyes seeing nothing though they were turned toward the bare back of Waddy Mountain before me. The day was bright and still. I heard the hoofbeats, a ragged canter around the base of the mountain where the road curved, and I turned then, still cranking, and saw him coming along the road from Cedar on the back of the blue roan. He was still far off yet. I didn't think anything then except to crank faster, because I didn't like any of them to see me draw from the well. There was only the one well and we shared it, though I hated it, because it was another way he tied us to him, another way Papa allowed it because he did not dig us a new one when the first one ran dry, and I didn't dig one because I believed, always, we were not going to be there that long. I made the children use rainwater for washing, and in the months Bull Creek ran high I toted our drinking water, too, when I could, because I hated drawing up that bucket in sight of their front door. But I'd watched the cousins drive off together in the wagon in the early morning and I knew Jessie would stay in the back of the store the whole day, so when I came outside for Jonaphrene's washwater and found the rain barrel tipped over, I had allowed myself, out of sloth and haste, to come to the well.

My uncle was drunk, leaning heavily in the saddle, which I could see even from such distance, but I didn't think anything about it. Not yet, in the still, bright sunlight, did I think this day different from any other. I watched him as I turned the crank so hard that it sang, and still I turned harder, until the full bucket rose on the slimy rope to the lip. I pulled it to the side, watching, my thought only to finish quickly and get back to the log house. He leaned forward like he was asleep nearly, but he was not too drunk to think to turn the roan's head away from the boggy place and walk him on the high ground toward town. The horse had his head down, but Fayette pushed him, coming over the rough ground at a fast walk. I poured the bucket into the wash pail quickly, the water splashing my shirtfront, and they came on, past the closed mill and the livery, and I could see something odd but I was in a hurry and I didn't try to make out what it was. The horse was coming faster, so that Fayette bounced and swayed in the saddle, past the post office, the horse trotting on his own now because he smelled the barn.

I saw then what was different. I stopped, let the well bucket drop, the rope singing, the hickory handle spinning around. I balanced the wash pail against my belly on the rock lip, held it in my arms, and looked at him. My uncle was laden with guns, weighted with them, his shoulder and chest and belt clotted with gun butts; he had rifle stocks shoved into saddleboots at his kneecaps, others wedged cross-ways before him like sticks. He came on, past the store, and I ducked down that he might not see me, spilled Jonaphrene's water on the ground. He didn't allow the roan to turn up the path toward the rock barn, though the horse tried, and Fayette jerked the reins viciously, held him to the roadbed, the roan's head trying to twist to the left, so that he was nearly trotting sideways. They passed below where I hid myself behind the well, and went on beyond the log house toward the old path on the east side that climbed to the foot of Toms Mountain. Fayette bobbed in the saddle, and the guns were strapped and draped about him as their wagon had been strapped and draped with their belongings on the morning we all left Kentucky, which I did not forget, ever: Fayette's ghost wagon, laden, seeming to follow but in truth driving us out and away from our home. And so when I saw him on the blue roan on the last morning of his life looking the same, decked and strapped hat to boot with a glut of guns in his drunkenness, I left the water bucket and went across the earth behind the log house and along the rise where he had disappeared, and I followed him along the path up the rise and into the ragged shed of the old barn.

He faced me in the barn darkness over the back of the blue roan. The horse was outlined against the square of daylight which was the opening at the back of the barn, and he was lathered and trembling, you could smell the fear on him. My uncle stood on the back side of him and wallowed drunk across the saddle, hung over it with both arms, one hand holding tight to a whiskey bottle. He heard me, raised his eyes and looked at me, his eyes filmed, and then he lifted his whole face and the bottle, raised both, and both empty as dry retching, and he looked at me, did not see me, but I saw him. You could be dumb as a fist and still see it. You could be blind even and smell it: his fear. I recognized it but I didn't know what it meant and so did not respect it, for the reason that I had seen him wallow and slur for too long. He raised his bleared eyes to me, not seeing, and then he threw the empty bottle down, lurched away from the horse, and stumbled to the remains of the front stall. I heard him slamming the wood, cursing, because he'd forgot what he'd done with it. And then he remembered, and I waited, quiet, while he came out of the front stall and stumbled toward the back. I could hear him back there flinging the old moldy hay about, and then I saw him against the square of daylight showing the foot of Toms Mountain, lurching toward us, me and the roan. He came clutching in his fist a brown patent-medicine bottle with the label still on, and he sat on the three-legged milkstool and pulled out the cork stopper so that it popped weakly. The stool was the old one I'd sat on beside the hearth throughout the dark swirl in the beginning, which from that time forward never served beneath the warm flank of a cow. Fayette had brought it up here for drinking when he buried his still. The still was long gone. He'd had Moss dig it up and haul it off someplace when he heard the law was coming, and they filled the floor in. I don't know what they did with it; the thump barrel and copper cooker are still boiling and reeking somewhere up on Toms Mountain, I guess. My uncle tipped the milkstool back on two legs and leaned his shoulders against the stall slats to raise the bottle, his horse still saddled and sweaty and laden with guns, and then my uncle fell off and sat on the barn floor in the moldy dust, drinking. Within only a few swigs he'd drunk himself blind. He sat with the bottle dangling from his hand and his eyes open, seeing nothing. The bottle dropped and lay on its side, spilling liquor, and Fayette did not rouse even to save his corn whiskey, so I knew he was blind and would not wake up.

I went to the roan and began to unburden it of guns. The horse stepped and snorted, jerked his head up, but I just held to the bridle ring with one hand and slowly lifted a cartridge belt from the saddle-horn with the other and eased it over my shoulder. The horse calmed some, still trembling, and I slid the rifles from their boots and leaned them against the west wall, unstrapped the shotgun and the great un-wieldly volleygun and stacked them, loosed the remaining cartridge belts and holsters from the saddlehorn and dropped them in the straw. I went over to where Fayette sat staring blind. He roused himself, or tried to, rolled his eyes up toward the place I was standing. *You old goat,* I thought. I wasn't afraid of him. I reached to pull the pistols from his belt, and the stink of whiskey and vomit knocked me back. I held my breath long enough to pull the two Colts butt-first out of the holsters, but the gun Papa made was locked under his belly, his white shirt bulging over it, round and swelled up tight as a dog tick, hanging bloated dirty white over it and down over his belt so that I would have had to lift and pull, and that was enough. I quit. The gunbelt, too, I left on him. I tossed the pistols I could reach easily on the soft, black barn floor, loamy with decomposed straw and old horse dung, so that they made only two mute little thuds, but I didn't take the gun Papa made, I wasn't thorough and I should have known better, and this is a mistake I made because of contempt. I just went on about what I was doing, turned to the stack of rifles and hoisted the volleygun, sighted along that ancient contraption, that enormous old thing, which I also held in contempt because it was Fayette's prize he cherished above all others—or above all but the gun Papa made—because it was the first one and no other owned one like it, because no normal man would hold and treasure such a useless gun: too heavy to carry, too heavy to aim, its mouth partitioned and multiplied to spit twelve balls at once like the teeth of a manyheaded serpent spewing brimstone. *Pah!* I laid it back down and reached for the others.

Once or twice I glanced over my shoulder as I gathered the guns. He sat slumped with his eyes open, white spots of sunlight from the unchinked log walls mottled over him, and I believed him unconscious, powerless, sotted with drink. I gathered up all I could carry—but not the volleygun or the gun Papa made, which was still wedged beneath the bulge of his belly—and I went out of the barn with them, believing that in this, as in all things, I carried my family's lives in the hold of my hands. You see what it is? I could laugh nearly. We have each of us our sin and our folly marked on us as clear as the print of bone beneath our faces, and pride is mine, and God will beat me down for it. He has done. He will.

I waited a moment in the dust of the old barnyard, looking south toward Waddy Mountain, plucked bare and gray and pimply as the skin of a chicken. The barn stood on the rise north and east of the log house where my family stayed—no, it was not our house. Not ever. I did not ever in my life call it ours. I stood in the barn's mouth with my eyes gazing south but my memory on the wagon where Papa had left it around the east side of the log barn. I could see the sumac growing up through the wheelspokes. I didn't need to walk around there to see. An old awful sickness came on me, and I removed it in the way I had found to do, meaning I turned my mind stale. I looked south awhile, and then west, staring at the scattered paintless buildings of Big Waddy Crossing. I could see smoke from some of the houses standing still in the bright, unmoving air. The sawmill was quiet. They'd logged out the valley, logged Bull Mountain a long time ago and Waddy Mountain last summer, and now they were started on the line of Sans Bois behind us, but the mill only ran about half of the time. Soon it would be cheaper to carry the mill to the timber than to haul the logs in with oxen. Soon enough Blaylock would pack up his sawmill-set and go someplace where there were still trees.

I laughed, standing there in that noontide, shaking away the gray taste, the staleness, turning my eyes south to the humped back of stump-ridden Waddy Mountain. I laughed for the sun coming back to us and the cold bright air and Fayette crumbling in his drunkenness so that I could strip him of guns and walk out and stand laughing in the yellow dust. I tried to think where to put the guns I'd taken off him. Nowhere in Big Waddy Crossing, surely, nor Fayette's fancy frame house or rock barn. Not his store. Nor the corncrib or smoke-house or chicken coop nor anywhere around the old barn. If he wasn't hunting weapons he'd be hunting his bottles, and no hiding place anywhere around close was safe. The log house was not a place I would even think to consider because I wouldn't sleep with the taint of those guns even for so long as it would take him to come off his drunk. I looked west toward the dug well between the log house and their house, a few dozen yards from the back of the store. I could see the lip of it and the wash bucket on its side in the shade of the stone wall. I imagined standing beside that wall and dropping the guns one by one, to hear them splunk deep in the darkness, to dream of them rusting in that dark pit, shells softening and releasing their powder, cartridges greening with slime, reddening, blackening, spoiling their drinking water. The urge was strong in me to do that—not to hide his guns till he dried out, but to get rid of them completely, to sneak in the store in the night and take them from their nails on the walls, from the case behind the counter, from the locked room in the back; to gather his stores of blackpowder and smokeless powder, his carbines and rimfire cartridges and shells, to take all of it and destroy it so that there might be nothing for him to wave about when he cursed and threatened Papa.

At once I knew what I would do, but not in the dug well, because I didn't know what seven guns would do to well water but I didn't intend to find out because I could never keep Jonaphrene from using that well—she was too lazy to tote water up the rise from the creekbank—and anyhow, come August, we would all have to drink from it. Come dog days, Bull Creek would lie stagnant with fever and none of us dare drink from it, and I had lived long enough to know that dog days would come. I laughed again, out loud, my arms full of weapons, because I knew where I would go.

I made my way through the stubbly yellow grass down the slope. The cartridge belts and holsters were draped around my neck, and I carried both Winchesters in the crook of my right arm, the barrels weighing on my forearm, the two guns together heavy and unbalanced. The shotgun was beneath my left arm. I walked with the muzzles pointed to earth as a hunter walks, as Papa had taught me, the Colts tucked in my pantwaist and my hands free to steady the barrels of the long guns. It was just over a quarter mile to the place on the creek. I walked carefully, stumbling sometimes from the weight of the guns and the size of my boots, which were not my boots but an old pair Jim Dee left behind when he went. Down along the creekbed, easy, easy, to the great crumbling sandstone slab where once I'd taught the children.

The place was unchanged, but for the soft bank and loose stones tumbling, eaten by water, but the sandstone slab was just the same, and the trees around it, echoing Mama's memory. I stood on the rock above the water, the muscles in my back and neck burning, and let the rifles down slowly, touching the muzzles to the stone and allowing the barrels to slide along my arm to the face of the rock. I knelt as I lowered them, until at last they lay blueblack and shining on the sparkling brown slab. On my knees then, I raised up, kneeling, held the shotgun over my head, hoisted it prone in both hands like an offering to heaven, and heaved it into Bull Creek running then in the weeks of springtime swift and moiling clear. Triumph was in me in that moment, and I laughed in it, out loud, to the clear sky and bare branches budding. The shotgun tumbled once, stock over barrel, and lay in the creek bottom, wavering against the stones.

So, I thought. *There, and so much for your **power**, Uncle, which is not your power. Which exists in the strength of itself from the hands of another and only for a time, and it is not **yours**. See it lying snuffed and fouled in clear water, powerless in water, without purpose but for the stock to grow soft and green with slime to feed the nudging mouths of perch. Fool. Another man made it, Uncle. Another man pissed on the earth for his saltpeter and dug in the earth for his iron ore, another smoked wood for the charcoal to make the blackpowder which imparts it its strength, which gives the mouth its fire and its mystery, and it is not **yours**. Another man forged those barrels, as my papa could have forged it, as my papa would fire it and beat it into life with the strength of his hands if he chose to, and he does not choose to, and you cannot force him, Uncle, and you have no power but what explodes from the mouth of that which another created, which you can hold only for a time in your hands. It is not **yours**! You bought it to pretend to own it, but it is not your strength, it is not your might, and it can never be. See it cold and useless, stiff on the bottom, gelded. Let it release its power there. And this also.* I pulled one of the pistols free of my belt and dropped it in the water. It rolled a little with the current and sank to the bottom. I plunked the others singly, pulled them from the holsters, my pantwaist, held each above the roiling water by the triggerguard and released it, and one fell straight away and one tumbled and wedged against a branch and one rolled downstream a yard or more and settled in a shaded spot.

I stood up then, and I felt the power in me as if it were righteousness. I lifted one of the Winchesters, raised it high, and heaved it as far out as I could. It hit butt-first against a log on the far bank and went off. The report sounded in the creekbed and repeated itself once against the mountain, but I didn't care. By the time I looked, the rifle had already disappeared beneath the rushing water. I lifted the last gun, and in that gesture, in the cold sunlight with the creek singing to the fingering branches above it, the emptiness swept over me. That quickly, with that little warning. The air and joy and power were sucked from me in a twinkling, because it was ever that way, the emptiness; from the first day of its coming it could suck me hollow in a breath, like bones sucked clean of marrow: dried out, scooped out, brittle and useless as a brown locust shell. I flung the last rifle without looking. I heard the splash above the creek's sounding, but I had turned away already and started back up toward town along the near bank.

North from the treeline along the creekbank I walked, one foot before the other, by rote motion, the way you chop cotton, do the milking, churn butter, any tedious activity you go through without thought because it's got to get done. I didn't care anymore. I came up onto the road and turned toward the path up to the old shed barn, with the intention of carrying the volleygun and the gun Papa made back down to drown them in Bull Creek with the others. I thought of the gun Papa made, the big four-barreled pistol, with its flat casing jammed beneath the round mound of Fayette's belly, and I tried to think how to retrieve it without touching him. It was my next job, I thought, to rid the world of them forever, those two that were old among us, Fayette's treasures he prized above all others. When he was not drunk he kept them mounted on the rock face of the chimney inside his house, mounted together as if they were equals, and they were not and could not be, excepting only in how he went for them first to fire them when he got drunk. That volleygun was not true, it exploded and sprayed without purpose, would hang fire and misfire; it was nothing but an old blackpowder muzzle loader with a dozen firing channels to foul and clog, a worthless gun, the first of Fayette's guns-with-many-barrels, and he kept it on iron hooks above his fireplace, where it hulked like something deformed, some distorted notion of weapon, above the gun that Papa made. The gun that Papa made. A perfect gun. A nearly perfect gun. Which caused us to leave Kentucky forever.

I looked for some kind of pleasure within me, to heave those two guns into Bull Creek, but the emptiness was on me bad, and I couldn't find any. I climbed tired toward the barn, empty, separate from caring, because the old hollowness had swept me and sucked me dry. That is how I account for it. That's why, when I looked up and saw Jonaphrene in her shirtwaist on the log porch with her hair down to wash it, saw my sister shoeless in the shade of the overhang with her dark hair spread across her shoulders, I only looked at her and through her and did not tell her to get on in the house. I didn't stand a moment outside the barn door and watch and wait and listen. I took no care when I entered the darkness from the sunlight. The hollowness had come unbidden and settled upon me on the creekbank, as it had come from the first dawn when the cedars bled, to foist its emptiness upon my life and spirit, to leave me unprotected from living, from work I had to do, and that is why I was not in any way prepared or protected when I went into the barn.

He stood against the west wall, at the head of the blue roan. He had walked the horse around to where I'd stacked the rifles, and for a minute I wasn't sure I saw what I thought I saw, because I was deadened still, and hollow, my eyes were not adjusted to the darkness, and anyhow I didn't believe it because it wasn't possible. I stopped inside the mouth of the doorway, and I looked at him. He looked back at me. He was not blind now. He didn't even appear to be drunk. The gun Papa made was in his hand, retrieved from his belt, from beneath his belly where I'd been too prissy to touch. The volleygun was strapped again to the saddle. He didn't sway on his feet, nor did the gun waver. At first my mind couldn't grasp it, I could not receive it, because I knew he couldn't have dried out in the short time I'd been gone.

"Oh," he said, and his breath blew soursweet with old whiskey, his organs steeped in it like brine. "It's you." I knew then how close I'd come to dying in the instant I stepped from the daylight into the darkness of the barn. The emptiness poured out of me entirely, and I was alert.

He'd expected a man when he heard my boots rustling in the dry grass, stobbing the dung dust of the barnyard. He thought it was a man who had robbed him, a man coming back now to catch him naked without his weapons, and I didn't know which man he feared, or if it was all men, but, "It's you," he said, and breathed again. He was glad to see me. I wanted to laugh when I knew it, because if I had contempt for him, he had an equal portion for me, as female, as John's daughter, and he was glad enough to see me to smile a little, breathing whiskey through the crack of his beard. He'd swum up out of his black stupor and found his whiskey spilled, found that which was God to him, his guns and his whiskey, gone from him, and the fear had clamped around him and brought him to his feet—not the gaping black fear he'd come in with, but a honed fear, particular, focused on one certain man or men, I did not know who, and it was that fear which roused him to a steady appearance. But he was drunk still, don't mistake it—insane drunk, mad drunk—and the stink was bad in the barn.

"You better watch sneaking up on a fellow like that," he said. He swayed a little, standing in one place, the top of his body dipping a half circle.

"Jessie sent me," I said. It was all I could think of. "She wants you to come down to the store."

"What for?" His eyes showed blue and red even in the barn darkness, eyeballs soaked red and the blue parts dull within the red swimming. His nose was swelled to a ruddy blob between his cheeks. "Wha's she want?"

"I don't know. She just said for me to come tell you."

He squinted, lifted the hand with Papa's gun in it, and pressed the heel of it against his forehead, the four heavy barrels aiming skyward. I could see them wavering. He lowered his hand, coughed once, and cleared the phlegm from his throat. "Tell 'er—" Smacking his cracked lips. Trying to act normal, trying to say it normal, when his mouth was warped with slurs and sickness. "Tell her I'll be down directly." And of course he was lying, because he had no intention of going down there, because his store and wife and business were beyond him, even whiskey making was beyond him, even selling his guns, because my uncle was half the time too drunk to work.

"All right," I said, nodding, beginning to back toward the front of the barn, thinking, *I'll get my rifle and wait for him.* Thinking, *He'll wander out in a little bit to hunt a bottle, I'll wait for him out there.* I turned to walk out in the daylight, and it was then, in the turning, that I saw the union of barrels rising.

"Wait—" he said.

My blood dropped. The dark barn went darker. Every thread of blood in my body sank to my feet, so that it felt my insides would fall through the barn floor. A sound hummed in my ears, a high skirring like gourd shells shaking, unceasing. I stood very, very still, my back half to him. I couldn't turn, and yet I saw the angled black shape outlined in the barn darkness, lifted toward me. From the side of my mind I saw it, not with my eyes. I didn't breathe, though even with my nostrils stayed and my chest unmoving, the rank smell seeped in me, bringing in me barnscent, horse lather, the odor of old haydust and manure; bringing in me, so I could not hold my breath against it, the sour taint of his smell. Slow, and slow, I turned my face to look at him, easing my eyes around. He blinked at me, the gun Papa made steady now, not trembling, drawed down on me. He was maybe fifteen feet away.

"What're you doing with them belts?" he said.

It was only then I realized I still wore them, the empty holsters stiff against my ribs, because the hollowness had come on me unbidden so that I didn't finish my work. I cursed myself—even in that moment, yes; even with the blood draining and the sound buzzing and the fire twisting in my chest—for being so stupid as to walk into the barn darkness unprotected. To stand now, unarmed and dumb, outlined against the bright day in the doorway with the cartridge belts and empty holsters draped around my neck. I had nothing to answer.

"You been scheming on this for years. Ain't you?" His blue eyes narrowed in the poor light. "Answer me!"

"Found them," I said.

"You been planning it."

The muzzles were not quite leveled at me but aimed just a fraction above my head. I gazed at the four barrels as my uncle lowered his hand and lined them up with the place where the fire was burning in the center of my chest.

"Where is he?" Fayette said.

"Who?" My voice came from a great distance.

"Your pardner," he said, slurring the word out a little.

"Partner?"

I thought for an instant he meant Papa, or Jim Dee maybe, though Jim Dee had been gone for two years. But his eyes squinted down tighter. "Where's Tanner?" he said.

That, too, came from a great distance. "Tanner?" I felt like my brother Thomas, to echo his words so, but I couldn't find any core within myself to think. It had been years since I'd heard the word Tanner. I saw the outline of the skink stranger on the porch in the blue moonlight, but the memory was from so long ago, floating.

"Y'all been hatching this up a long time, ain'cha?"

I was silent, staring. The memory was flickering in me, but I couldn't grasp it.

"Ain'cha!"

I shook my head.

"Y'all think you can catch this old boy napping"—and now his torso swayed a little, but the gun did not waver—"you got another think coming. Blow your damn head off." Suddenly his eyes narrowed again, filmed over, shining. He wagged his head and the gun side to side, shook his head and the four barrels in unison. His voice was slurred and gleeful when he said, "Tell you what. Blow your head off with your own damn gun. How you like that?"

My voice was stopped. I couldn't answer him. I was looking at the red webs of veins across his cheeks, at his eyes filmed like uncooked eggs. I was looking at the way the yellow scarfskin drawn across his bones quivered, how his pores leaked sweat and whiskey. We were caught in a tunnel, which was the dark length of barn open at both ends, dotted here and there with those still, white spots of daylight. I could see even in that darkness. And yet the fear never left me. It is hard to explain, because I saw all this, and felt it, and I could feel the smooth handle of the gun in his hand, sleek, balanced, I could feel the power in that hand. At the same time I understood for the first time what it was that made him crave guns with many barrels—and it was because of what I felt not in him but inside myself, because the death in the four barrels was plainly visible in the four muzzles yawning black and plumbless toward me, perfect circles for killing, made powerful, made perfect and complete, by the hand of my father.

"Kill you with your own damn gun," he said. "Call it suicide." He laughed once, a terrible sound, and then he threw back his head, stretched his neck, gobbled deep and wet in his throat.

Still I didn't understand that in his twisted, besotted brain he thought I was Papa. There were other things I didn't understand because I could not think, because just then, standing with my uncle facing me in the shabby shed barn, mad-dog drunk and drawed down on me, I felt and knew only one thing: that he would kill me. If you have stood unarmed with the open muzzle of a gun aimed hard on you, then you know what it is, and if you have not, no amount of telling is going to proclaim it, but I will say it anyway, tell you how black terror swells on you beyond the blood drop of the first moment because you comprehend helplessness, because you know in the fullness of yourself the truth of your complete and abject powerlessness, which if you had a gun you could at least be calculating to shoot first, you could just shoot. You could shoot. So it is powerlessness swelling on you, and terror, and disbelief, because you cannot fathom you are going to die, and yet it is complete belief that you will die, in the next second, in the next instantaneous union with all men who have died thus, all men and women who have died thus, in terror, disbelieving, believing, facing the mouth of a gun. I did not think about God. I didn't think about Mama, Thomas, my sister, anything of my life, but only the dead mule—not Delia, the other one—because I saw my father turning in washed amber air, the gun lifted, the flat side of it strange because it was like the flat tang of a Winchester because there was no cylinder to bulge out, the four barrels welded as one when Papa raised them, turning them in the sunset air, and the big mule's forehead exploding red.

I waited, my body numb, and when the gun fired I waited still, to learn where he had shot me, because I could feel nothing. I waited to feel the warmth of blood oozing, so that I might know where the wound was. I waited to fall down. The gun fired again, the sound thundering, and the shriek of wood splintering, exploding behind me and a little above my head, coming more sudden than the thunder ceased. I could smell the salt smell of gunpowder so I knew I wasn't dreaming, but I was not joined with my body then but floating a little above it, and so I thought I might be dead. Still, my body remained upright, and the gun fired again, and the loamy barn floor exploded to the side of where Jim Dee's boots stood.

"You goin' to show me just right precisely where you put 'em." His tongue was thick, but the words came clear enough. "You goin' to walk out in front of me, in case your pardner gets any fancy ideas, and we'll just go fetch my own legal property before you make me go ahead and shoot you. I didn't mean for it to have to happen but you been at it for years and years. I told Daddy I might have to kill you. I told him ever since you started setting yourself up so high and mighty, but you and him won't neither one listen." His eyes narrowed. "Y'all think you can rob me blind, you think I'm too dumb to see it. Been robbing me for years, haven't you? Taking what's rightfully mine. Make a jackass outa me right out in the damn street. Hush! Hush now. It's a damn rat snake, that's all, shut up. Quit your sniveling before I whup you. Shut up now, Daddy'll hear. You want me to lick you?" And then he stopped abruptly, blinking slowly in the barn darkness. His tongue snaked, liver-colored, out between his cracked lips, from beneath the coarse hairs curling, swiped sideways across the lips' creviced surface, and he narrowed his eyes. "Stand right where you are." He was quiet a moment. "Th'ow me that belt." He waved the gun at the cartridge belts around my neck.

Still I didn't understand what was in him. I was stupid with fear—and yet fear is better than emptiness. I tell you it is. I knew only that he was crazy drunk and I wasn't dead, and if I was not dead yet, maybe I would not have to be. I was at once rejoined with my body, and when my uncle motioned again, said, "Th'ow it here!" I lifted the top cartridge belt over my head and tossed it toward him. It thunked on the soft barn floor.

"Not that one!" He waved the gun again.

I lifted the next belt, and the fat cartridges lined up in their strip pouches of leather clinked a little metallically when they hit the belt on the floor.

"All right now, turn around," he said.

There was something worse about the gun in his drunken hand trained on my back instead of my belly, and I began scheming again, trying to think. I said, looking straight at him, "They're just right out yonder," and I nodded my head, easy, toward the daylight behind me, thinking now that it could be in my power again, the power of my mind and my words, that I could bend him to my will if only I was smart enough, quick enough, because it was my pride again coming on me, and my contempt. And then for some reason I turned my head to look out the door. My sister, barefoot on the cold stubble of grass, was climbing the path toward the barn. Before I knew I would do it or had done it, I shouted, "Jonaphrene! Get back to the house!"

She looked up at me, her eyes that slow slate gaze, stubborn, and yet uncomprehending.

I screamed, "Right now! I'll be there in a minute!"

My sister paused for just an instant, hardly even perceptible, and then she came on, picking her way barefoot up the rise along the path. In the relentlessness of that gesture I saw the whole of our lives, the threads pulling as they had been pulling from far back, as long as I could remember, and even before, back through my mother's and father's memory, and their mothers' and fathers' before them, infinitesimal threads raveling, drawing together, relentless as my sister picking her way up the path. I saw cedar trees bleeding their smoked seed into the cold dawn air as the blond specter coughed, bending over, holding a pencil in unfleshed fingers, and my cousin Fowler's eyes slitted deep in envy, deeper, disappearing, and then I saw the black woman's pink bitten flesh, which I had caused, the triangular wedge gouged from her flesh by the force of my own driven will, and behind me my uncle reeling into the abyss.

"Jonaphrene!" I screamed, helpless. "Get back to the house!"

"What—?" Fayette said.

I turned to see him, and knew that he'd been whipped suddenly to the log barn, jerked back from black time and distance by my voice or Jonaphrene's name or the cunning tricks of the whiskey, I don't know. He held the gun Papa made loose and reckless in his hand, no more controlled by him than the cold eye of the sun outside crossing heaven.

"What—" he said again.

Blinking, and the word not even a question really, not to ask anything of reason in the still, rank air of the barn, but an empty echoing word of void and despair. The word came again—"What?"—and its echo, rasped away, dying as the last voice of locust dies in the distance, fading, thinning, to become air and silence, and I wanted to move, turn and run to my sister or walk backwards away from him out of the barn, but I did not and could not move backwards, because I reeled forward, dark, *into darkness, swept in. I was sick, roiling, trembling, in my soul and my body, the taste in my mouth foul, reeking poison from my tongue inside my mouth, the backs of my nostrils, my rotted teeth and belly, blinded, my head split across the front like an axe in it, and I wanted to vomit, I wanted to lie down but I could not because of the terror because something would happen in the next breath, the next instant, irrevocable and hellish, the end of the earth forever because the gates of hell would groan and the earth beneath the rise on which the barn stood would split open to swallow my hated self in my skin hating my bones reeking with the scent of me wanting to die and not dying but only the earth opening to explode me out of my guts and the sordid sinew of my body into hell when there was only one thing to save me, and it was not God—*

Fayette turned.

I fell back, stumbling, and he stumbled, but only a little, and then he went carefully, as if he were not sick, as if he were not drunk even, to the side of the blue roan and lifted the leather flap of the saddlebag with the butt of his hand, the gun loose in it pointing wildly sideways and then up toward the shed roof. I turned quickly and went out the open door to stand in the acrid dust of the old barnyard and breathe deeply the still, bright air.

I should have run right then. As quickly as I was freed and outside of the sight of him, I should have run down the slope and swept my sister back to the log house. I should have got Papa's muzzle loader and come back to the barn lot before he'd found his flask to drink those last few drops to stave the sickness. I should have, I should have, but instead I stood listening to the whisk of the uncapped flask, the long sucking pull. I listened to the whisper of the metal cartridges slipped from their leather pouches, heard the breech snap open to receive them, the slide of cold cartridges into warm steel chambers, one and two and three, and then the click shut. There was a sudden clink of spurs, and the creak of saddle leather when his weight pressed into the stirrup. The horse stepped back once and sideways before the reins lashed its flank and the spurs stung and it leapt forward. Still I stood, unmoving, leaning back against the shaved logs in the sunlight, the last cartridge belt knuckled beneath my shoulder. I stood there still when he whipped the blue roan out the barn door. Stood calm in the harsh sunlight, watching my sister scramble off to the side of the path in her bare feet, my heart lifted in a strange unfathomable rejoicing.

He saw her. I know that he saw her, but he lashed the rein ends on the blue speckled haunches, drove the roan, hard, down the path directly at her so that Jonaphrene scrambled and leapt to the side with no more grace than a frog, and she wasn't trampled only because she rolled sideways, her skirt twisted around her legs like clothes wrung from a wringer, but I saw as she fell what it did to her face. My uncle pulled up at path's end and turned around in the roadbed, the horse dancing a circle like a trick horse at a fairgrounds because Fayette had the reins cinched up so tight, the horse's head lifted, ears back, eyes rolling, and my uncle turned and looked up at me, his eyes like nails, and I knew where he would go then, what he would do.

I watched his hatless head turning as the horse turned in a circle, his eyes burning on me for a long time, what seemed a long time, and he'd jerk his head around fast when the horse had wheeled too far for him to keep his eyes on me. I heard Jonaphrene's soft moaning sounds, *oh,* and then *oooh,* and I saw the cartridge belts I'd dropped on the barn floor hooked over Fayette's shoulder, the crosshatched grip of the gun Papa made protruding from its place beneath the gray swell of his belly. He didn't let go my eyes until he spurred the roan once and jerked him west on the road. They disappeared from my sight on the far side of the log house. Only then was I able to move.

I went to my sister. She lay in the bitterweed along the side of the path with her head pointed downhill, her dark hair loose and tangled, her legs wrapped around, caught cocoonlike in the web of her skirt. "Stand up," I said.

She released the little moaning sound again, and it was not really a moan but just the word "oh" let out on a long breath.

"Get up, Jonaphrene," I told her. Her eyes were on me and I could see the mark coming already on her cheekbone, but it hadn't broken the skin. "Hurry," I said.

She didn't let out the sound again, but it took a while for her to begin moving. I could hear Fayette talking loud to someone on the road in front of his store, but I couldn't see him because the log house was in the way. I reached a hand down to my sister and she took it, and then she began to try to stand up, but gravity and the twisted wrap of her skirt kept her because she was slanted the wrong way downhill, and I had to bend over and try to hoist her beneath the shoulders, because I knew she was hurt.

All the things that happened next took place in probably no more than a few minutes, but it seemed such a long time because I was swimming through it because it was like one of those dreams where you try and try and try and cannot get where you are going, and it was like the whole long years in Eye Tee of waiting and trying and expecting to go home to Kentucky, which I'd been striving for years to take my family and my mama home and still we were no further east than on the morning I found the empty wagon, no closer home than on the day the man shot Delia, and so I helped up my sister, and when she stood finally, hunkering over a little to lean on me, I looked and saw Thomas where he stood on the back porch of the log house. He had his Sunday hat on and Papa's suspenders. He was standing with his arm on the corner post, looking at us. And then I heard the horse again and turned my head to see Fayette trotting along the wagon track that ran on the far side of the store past their house to the barn. The horse danced and pranced sideways because he wanted to go on up to the rock barn, but Fayette held him, and he was bellowing, Fayette was, dancing the horse into their yard, and then Lottie came out on the porch, and I heard him shout at her, "Right in yonder under the spoolbed in that front bedroom! My carbine! Fetch it out here! Right now!"

It was then I saw Jessie come out the back of the store and walk swiftly up the footpath they kept soft between the back door of the store and their front porch. She had Myrtis on her hip but it didn't seem like she even knew it, because she walked right up close to where

Fayette's horse was jerking and prancing, and she was talking to him but I couldn't hear what she said. Lottie stood big on the porch. When Fayette hollered at her, she'd turn and start to go in the house, and then Jessie would say something and she'd come back away from the door to stand on the porch ledge. Then Fayette would holler again and she'd go back again, and she went back and forth like that two or three times, but she never did go on in the house and bring him the gun.

I shouted at Thomas where he stood gawking at us dressed up for Sunday meeting—I could see his hair slicked back behind his ears beneath his good white felt hat—I shouted, "Get the gun, bring it here!" because Jonaphrene couldn't go down the path any faster, and I wanted to laugh again, because I could still hear Fayette shouting at Lottie to fetch his carbine rifle, and so there we were: my uncle calling for a gun in his yard from his daughter, and me doing the same from my brother as we neared the yard of the log house, and I thought, even then, that it was just a question of whether I could get Papa's muzzle loader out of the house fast enough.

"Hurry!" I hollered at Thomas, and he just stood there.

Jonaphrene, over my shoulder, leaning down on me, said, "What is it? Martha, what is it? What's he done?"

"He ain't done it yet," I said, and now we were in the yard, and I could see the tipped-over bucket so plain behind their well. "He's fixing to."

"What?" she said.

"What," Thomas said.

"Kill Papa. Thomas, hurry up and bring me the gun."

On the rise—it was not so far, a hundred rods maybe—clear as day, I saw Fayette slash the reins at Jessie trying to grab for the bridle, and he cursed her once, one soft word, and then he spurred that poor horse back down the wagon track to the roadbed, and I couldn't see him then, for the log house and the store both were in the way. But I knew he was started for Cedar already, and I was still swimming, I just could not move any faster. I felt Jonaphrene's weight ease off me and, turning, I saw her standing up straight, the old look rising on her, sweeping her face beyond sorrow, whatever it was.

"Thomas!" I said. "Move!" because he just stood there, his mouth open, gaping at me, and oh, the hatred swelled on me, I cannot tell you, to look at my brother staring, comprehending nothing, and my sister with that look on her, and Fayette on his way to Cedar to kill

Papa—I believed that, I still believe it. I knew what was inside him. Thomas turned to go in the house then, but I saw already it was no use. Time was fleeing too fast, Fayette was gone already, and I tried to be quick, tried to think, and I could think nothing because we had no horse or mule, only the weathering shell of wagon. I didn't know how I would catch him fast enough—and then I knew I must run, swift, run, directly over the land, and head him off at the narrow place where the two mountains ebb toward one another on either side of the road. I had to outrun the blue roan, and so I couldn't carry the longrifle. Already I was backing away from them down the slope toward the creekbank, and I said, "Sister, go down to Mewborn's and tell him it's an emergency, see if you can borrow his rig and come on in the buggy. If he won't let you, see about Skeens or somebody, but hurry!"—because I was thinking that if I didn't catch him at the Narrows, we could catch him with a rig if we had to chase him. "Hurry up now!" I said, backing, already beginning to run. "And bring the rifle! Don't let Mewborn see it!"

She seemed to be waking then, coming awake from a long sleep. I was backing, fast, and she looked at me, put her hand to the bruise blooming blue and red across her cheekbone, already swelling, and then she touched her loose hair let down for washing, ran her fingers through it, said, "I can't go to Cedar looking like this."

"Hurry!" I said.

I looked no more at either of them but turned and ran over the road in Jim Dee's boots. Even in the March-hard roadbed the sharp bootheels broke the pan and released the ocher dust, and I could see the dust from the blue roan also, trailing on through town nearly to the boggy place. I looked no more in that direction either but ran down into the trees along the creekbank, ran through the underbrush. Sap-softened willow twigs bent with me, cold jackoak fingers cracked and snapped when I passed, snagging at the cartridge belt across my shoulder. I came to the sandstone slab without stopping, slipped off the bank beside it and waded into the water. I could only see one of the pistols—not either one of the Colts, but an old single-shot Remington, but it was good enough. I didn't stop but waded directly toward where it was wedged against a tree branch. I reached my hand in the cold rushing water, and the pistol rolled a little as if it would sweep away from me, but I grabbed for it, scooped it up, dripping, and held it against my shirt, rubbing the side of the barrel against my chest as I continued to try to run, splashing against the current, and now I was truly swimming, though my feet scrabbled along the bottom, because Jim Dee's boots were weighted with water, sucking me down with water, willing me to surrender and allow them and the force of the water to sweep me downstream. But I would not. I would not! I clambered up the bank, and never for a minute had I stopped running, nor did I slow or stop or ease for a second but ran straight across Faulks' fresh-plowed field, the cartridge belt thumping against my chest, my brother's boots squishing and dragging, rubbing, my heels burning fire, and I ran on, spinning the cylinder once or twice to rid it of water, and I didn't know if it would fire but I believed that it would. I thought I could beat him to the foot of Waddy Mountain and shoot him from the side of the road, but when I reached the clotted underbrush that marked the turn of roadbed, I saw the roan's dust sifting away south behind the curve. I stopped long enough to take my brother's boots off, flung them to the side of the road and undraped the belt from over my shoulder. I strapped it around me—it was twice too big, and so I wrapped it around twice—and buckled it. I jammed the gun into the holster and ran on, the weight of the gun beating against my thigh. I ran with the tan ruts and small rocks retreating beneath me, ran in the bright air so still I could hear crows laughing on the far side of the mountain. The dust of the roan stood above the earth long after they'd passed, and I ran through it, my lungs burning hot. The sharp pain thrust its knife in my side, but only for a short while, and then I grew light in my body so that I skimmed over the earth almost like dreamflying, and the rejoicing came back on me. I couldn't feel the stones. I ran as a deer runs, swift, on my small feet.

So I gained on him, came up behind them. I could see the roan's dark tail flicking flies in the distance, because he had slowed to a walk. Fayette held himself straight in the saddle, and I slowed, walking fast still, but not running, and I was silent. I meant to get within pistol range and kill him, that was all—only I thought suddenly it would be better to get around him and shoot him from the front, because I was thinking how they tell Belle Starr's killing over and over because she was ambushed, shot in the back, and to this day they don't know who did it, and that mystery has kept her alive because they talk about it, say it was her son, her lover, a neighbor who shot her, and worse, it has sanctified her in people's minds because they say the killer was a coward and she didn't get to face him, even she didn't know who shot her—or maybe she did. But I was unwilling that my uncle be sanctified and kept alive by people talking. I was unwilling to be called coward even if none knew my name. And so when we came to the place where the road curves back to the east around the base of the mountain, I cut south straight across the land.

I had to run again, to get around him and head him off before he got to a place where there would be others to see us. That part of the valley hadn't been logged yet, and the trees were tall—pine mostly, and red oak, a few giant hickories, their bottom branches so far above the earth a man could ride a horse beneath them and never have to hold his hat—and so it was easy to run. The earth was soft with pine needles and crumbling dead oak leaves, but there were acorns and pinecones to jab my bare soles or roll beneath them, and the trees were many and I had to weave in and out. It was dark in the pine shade, and cool, because I was sweating. I tried to angle continuously south and east, but it was hard because the trees grew in their untamed pattern and wouldn't let me keep to a straight line. Still, I felt that strange joy, even in the pine darkness, running, half thwarted, with murder in my heart.

In time, I saw the lightened space ahead between the tall trunks, and I headed directly toward it. I came out from the pine woods abruptly, like running out a barn door, onto the beaten road, and there, a half mile or so to the south, the rock and wood buildings of Cedar rose up on either side of the tan strip to nestle and hold it, and there on the road itself, maybe fifty yards past me, was my uncle's back, jostling on toward the town. He didn't turn; I guess he didn't hear me, though my breath was shuddering so loud. I drew the pistol and stood in the roadbed, held the gun in both hands and aimed at the matted brown hair on the back of his head. I lowered the muzzle and aimed at the broader target of the dirty white shirt stretched across his back. I was in good range, easy range. I pulled back the hammer with both thumbs, held it, watched my uncle's back jimmy away from me along the road.

I don't know why.

I don't know why.

I had every intention.

I wasn't afraid. I was in some kind of high glory that drove me beyond even the comprehension of fear. I ask myself to this day, as I question all the if-onlys, because it was my last chance and I knew it, even if it meant I had to shoot him in the back. I just didn't, that's all. I don't have an explanation. I wasn't afraid, I tell you; I wanted to kill him. In hatred I wanted to kill him, for all of it, from the gray dawn of the morning it would not turn morning, for the sake of my mama and Grandma Billie and Jim Dee and Thomas, for that look on my sister and what was in his black sodden heart about Papa, which I tell you I knew.

No. That's not it.

All right. I will tell it.

I could not squeeze the trigger, because I had been made to go inside him. The hellish stink and loathing of him lifted my soul in the barn darkness and soothed me, gave me that power to run barefoot without tiring, rejoicing, but the same instant that gave me power and gladness was the same that stayed my hand an hour later from killing him, and it wasn't anything like what we know of the word compassion, don't think it. It wasn't because I loved him or grieved him or felt sorry for him to ride drunk on a blue roan and be shot in the back— it was because my soul was made part of his, and his mine, so that I could not un-know him, because he was me, because that was made to happen to me, though I had refused it, I'd turned my back on it the dawn the cedars bled.

I don't want to remember that. I don't want to.

Walking. I was walking and it wasn't dawn yet, it was not even the lifting just before first light, and I was in the valley east of Waddy walking alone, not even Ringo was with me, though he was still alive then. I was fourteen, it was spring. It was after the camp meeting where they say I did such things but I don't remember. I was fourteen. Thula tried to warn me, she told me time and time again. *The Creator give you that job to do, you going to die you ain't done it.* In English she told me, and again in her language, and I was willful. It wasn't my brothers and sister I set my face against. It was God's face. Because He gave it to me, Thula told me, and I turned my own face away.

I walked before daylight in the place of tall grasses where the thousand rocks are hidden just under the dirt's khaki crust, and the grasses are tall and sweeping there, I don't know why; it isn't a place of blackberry brambles and sumac as other open spaces are, but just those tall grasses in the little prairie east of Waddy and the cedars dotted here and there, so much distance apart, as if God planted them for the shape of His eye's pleasure, and the cedars are shaped like cones, peaked at the top and rounded full on the bottom, not as a pine tree is formed, but in the shape of a child's top. They were burnished copper still with winter, the drouth of that winter, and it was the time of the earth's turning with springtime, the loop dropping down. I walked toward the sun which had not come yet, but light was quickening east, and I saw it happen to the cedar tree to the right and just a little in front of me. The cedar tree smoked. I saw it and stopped, and I held myself in the still air, so still the grasses did not even hint to whisper, so still I could hear the fluting thrushes starting in the deep woods far off on Toms Mountain. Smoke seeped from the silhouette of the cedar. It was like the burning bush in the desert, the smoke shimmering around it the same shape as the tree itself, as if the heart of the tree was on fire, and yet there was no flame, and it was not consumed. Off to the north, I saw another. And in time, farther east, another: the cedar trees bleeding their lifeforce in smoke shimmering to the still, predawn air. I stood motionless in the still valley, held my breath to not stir the motionless air. Way off, I could see another, and later, another, as if singly, one at a time, touched by God's finger, they must burst into flame, but it was not the flame of fire but something else, I don't know what it was: their blood. And then I heard the song.

It was not humming now, not a high keening at the edge of hearing, but a real song. I could hear the voice of it, I could hear words, and they were not words of English or Choctaw but I knew them as we know dreamwords, and the song rose and fell, it was in the air, the smoke, the light coming from the east: piercing, beautiful, like water trickling, like light shining, the sound of spirit walking in the world. The song pulled from my very breast, the hard core heart of me, to my nipples and fingers and the soles of my feet. As I listened the song became smell; it didn't die or transform but became smell also, embraced smell, and it was smoke then, it was light then, and taste, and the smell of some place on the earth I had been and forgotten, which I cannot describe to you any more than I can name you the sound, but it was a little like watercress plucked from a stream and crushed at once in the teeth and fingers, the green smell of plant but not of earth, of water but not the mud and dank that goes with it; a smell of longing, like craving, to prick at the nose like crushed cedar and become in the back of the mouth and throat a taste like green apples and honey, and the song was mine, the smell was my before and after, what was given to me, what I was supposed to do: it was my life, singing in the air and earth and sky around me. The pain came then, sudden, an eruption in my limbs like they would be torn asunder, and I heard a voice saying, *See this, you must follow. Be still.* There was

Light then, and Presence, and around me in the valley the cedars bled.

I turned my face away. Kneeling—I was kneeling then, I don't know when it happened—kneeling, I lowered my face in my hands to block it. I put my thumbs in my ears to not hear it, but the song was inside me and outside me and still it sang. I stood up with the sun rising over the rim of the world, rising white light, red with spring coming, the bleeding cedars before me turning red with the light of the sun rising, and I shook my fist at heaven, because it was God in the red light of heaven, which I knew then, and I roared and shook my fist over my head because He had killed her, or at least He had not saved her, and everything, every last bit of it, followed from that. I turned away from the east and walked back to the log house.

From that day on, the mystery did not come on me.

From that day on, I went in shame and defiance and anger, the hollowness a cold permanence to ebb and swell as it would, and I just went on, taught the children and schemed and prepared. I didn't tell Thula. I wouldn't tell her, though she knew, or she knew something, because it was right after that she left. She knew always, from the beginning, because she tried so many times to smoke me. She tried to make me sweat. She talked to me, in English and Choctaw. She said I would die. But I did not—you can see that I did not—but something was not right, because every preparation I made to go back home was stripped from me, but I wouldn't see what it meant. I believed that I knew what I was doing. I'd seen her black eyes on me many times— watching me in judgment, I told myself then. I grew to hate her so bad. I blamed her for it, as I blamed Fayette for what befell us in the living world, what befell me. I wouldn't see that it was just those old threads pulling from all directions for eternity, just our lives spun by God's mind telling Himself a story with the pitiful substance of our pitiful selves. I wouldn't see my part in it, and I hated her because she told me. She tried to make me understand. She would come to me in dreams, bending over me as she had bent over us in the red darkness, her flat brown face with eyes like black seeds in it, coming down, telling me in dreams of torment that I couldn't keep from remembering, so that it got to where I stayed out and gone from the house at night, wouldn't sleep on the pallet with Jonaphrene because of Thula breathing the same air in the shell of the log house. I said to myself she was a devil, and I know she wasn't. Even then I knew it, because He gave her to me for a guide—not a spirit guide, because I wouldn't hear the Spirit, but a flesh-and-blood woman talking bad English, saying, "The Creator handed you that job to do, you going to die you ain't done it."

I followed them on the white horse miles and miles going slow on the wagon road to Latham because her eyes told me, because her mouth said, Come go with us, but her eyes said, You are going to die if you do not. And I did die to something, because I fell unconscious for seven days, they said a death mask came on me, Jessie said I was dead, she wanted to bury me, but Thula told them I was not dead but in the other world receiving my instructions, and I remembered what it was then, for a little time I remembered. I cannot tell you now because it was stripped from me that red dawn when I shook my fist at God. From that moment I did not enter another, willing or unwilling, until the afternoon my uncle faced me over the back of the blue roan in the darkness of the barn shed.

Why?

Why would He make me enter that man who was my enemy? Why, when He should make the mystery come on me again, would it be only to know the rank self-loathing and fear and hatred in my uncle, who only hated and loved my father as Esau hated and loved his brother for stealing his father's blessing, as Cain hated and loved Abel in the weary old sin of envy for his blood offering more pleasing in God's sight, as all men have hated their brethren and loved them for eons in the spinning out of God's tale? Envy is not my secret sin set forth in the light of God's face. Pride is. And contempt, which is only a guise of the same thing. And anger. I have owned them. I confess them. Why make me bear witness to Fayette's sins?

I stood in the roadbed aiming an old single-shot twenty-two at the back of my uncle, whom I loathed as fiercely in that moment as in the twinkling instant on the creekbank with my arms lifted, hoisting his guns into the water, as on the nights I listened to him outside the log house, standing in the yard or down on the road, hollering at Papa, cussing Papa, and sometimes walking around and around the house firing his pistols and the gun Papa made, which we knew what it was because it made such a loud sound. And Papa on the far side of the room in his blanket, just lying there, listening, never answering him back or doing anything but to lie awake looking up at the dark dome of log ceiling and listen to his brother curse him and make threats and fire his guns in the night air.

I wanted to kill him, and have believed all these years I should have killed him because if I'd killed him when I could have, any moment when I could have, alone, before he reached Cedar, before he came face-to-face with Papa, then they would not have all had to pay. I watched my uncle ride away from me. After a long time, the mottled hide on the roan's rump growing ash-colored in the distance, I let the hammer back down.

The town toward which the man rode was no different from hundreds of other white towns springing up in that time, spontaneous life spawned from invisible spores scattered along the newly laid rails crosshatching the whole of Indian Territory—except in this manner: the spawning ground which was to become Cedar, I.T., had been, from the time of the Choctaw people's coming, a gathering place for consensus and punishment, for the meting out of Choctaw justice at the site of the old courthouse and whipping tree, in the rule of law brought with the Choctaw people from their homeland. The place had held from the beginning a certain life, marked by the echoes of Choctaw words spoken, the force of which lay on its soul and in its dust and could not be erased.

It stood at a crossroads, where the new east-west road beside the train tracks crossed a north-to-south section of the old stage route, and for this reason Cedar, I.T., held within its encasement the shape of the Cross as well as the reaching out of arms to the Four Directions. The streets were laid out square, as white men plat their towns: a radiating grid of smaller squares emanating from the central chiasma, the grid fading into smaller crossroads of smaller, poorer houses outward, until the edges of the town blurred back into the little plain whence it had arisen. The gleaming blueblack rails of the train tracks appeared to slice into and bisect the town, separating itself from itself, but in fact the whole of the town had emerged from the ocher earth on either side of that steel intrusion, as matching fungi will spring up on either side of the gash in lightning-struck wood. The log and brick and native stone buildings had sprung up in a line perpendicular to that gash, sprung oxblood-red and umber and burnt sienna from that yellowbrown dirt, a transformation of rolling flaxen earth into triangulated redbrick bank and square train depot, created from uniform rectangles of baked red clay dug from the red earth in the very coreheart of the land of the red people and drawn east by mule train to be laid and stacked in patterned squares along the main street, as dark redbrick buildings were being raised, distinctive, throughout the Indian Nations. No different. Hardly different, except in the minds of those who lived there, because it was home.

South of the rail tracks were the wagon yard and the hotel, the post office and mercantile and a new white steepled churchhouse, which had raised up on either side of the old livery stable and stage stop; north of the tracks, a half mile above the old commissary, the remains of the Choctaw courthouse still stood. Yet even that portion of Cedar was changing, for O. L. Upton had caused to be built on the northwest corner of the intersection a triangular-shaped two-story redbrick bank. It was toward this building Thula Henry walked, crossing the east-west road slowly, her skirts lifted in one hand above the swirl of khaki dust. She stepped deeply to mount the high plank sidewalk that ran in front of the bank, and then she stopped a moment at the corner, looking north.

In the distance, beyond the last house that marked the limits of the town, she saw the man riding stiffly, elongated in the saddle, the fine horse stepping slowly, stirring dust. Through some trick of alignment and that very moiling dust, Thula didn't at first see the girl coming behind him, and so for a moment she merely looked at the white man with unaffected eyes, tracking his approach as she might watch a silent crow flapping across a cleared space in the sky: a curiosity because of its solitariness and silence, but not so strange as to be a sign, necessarily. Fayette hardly swayed with the saddle motion, and there was something nearly formal in the erect dignity of his posture, the arc of his wrist as he held the reins above the horn. The woman stood a moment, watching him with recognition but without particular interest, and then she continued on toward her destination, which journey carried her in the man's direction, for she was only coming from the mercantile south of the train tracks to join her son George at the general feed supply store known as Lolly's.

She moved unhurriedly in her soft shoes along the plank sidewalk which united the three buildings on that side of the street: the brick bank building on the corner, the old native stone commissary to the north of it, and finally the roughsawed front of Lolly's Guns, Farm & Feed. Beneath her arm, Thula carried a brown paper-wrapped bundle containing a few yards of calico encasing a spool of thread, a length of ribbon, a tin of sardines, and a second, smaller, brown-wrapped square, the paper folded in fourths around a neat stack of white-flour crackers. These few small purchases had, up until that moment, satisfied her belief in a reason for her presence in Cedar, I.T., on this particular bright early-spring afternoon. In the next instant, however, her own leisurely motion and that of the roan shifted the brief alignment of horse, man, and girl, and through the obscuring dust Thula saw Matt coming along the road behind Fayette in her man's hat and breeches, shoeless, wrapped twice around her narrow hips with a thick leather gunbelt. Immediately Thula understood why she'd said yes when her son George drove into her yard that morning to see if she wanted to come go with him to Cedar to pick up the new turning plow he had ordered, because she understood that the deep trouble she'd been feeling in her mind for many days and nights now was connected to the girl.

The woman hurried forward and stepped into the narrow crevice between the old commissary and the feed supply, her soft leather shoes whispering across the splintered surface and down onto the damp earth between the rock and wood walls. She peeked around the corner of Lolly's, and now Fayette was within the compass of the town, passing in front of the remains of the old courthouse. As he rode nearer, Thula saw that what had at first seemed an erect dignity was, in fact, something more like a stupor, or a trance. His blue eyes held directly in front of himself, focused somewhere in the middle distance; the reins were doubled between middle and forefinger in his left hand, and his right hand rode loosely, palm-down on his denimed thigh. Thula could see the crosshatched grip of a pistol protruding from his pantwaist, the cartridge belts draped over the saddlehorn, the big volleygun strapped down. Several horses tethered along the street stirred restively as the man and horse passed, though her son's mule, standing with head bowed before the shabby wagon parallel to the front of Lolly's, did not stir. It was then that Thula realized the emptiness of the street, except for the stirring, snuffling horses, the head-bowed and forbearant mule. Nowhere was there a wife waiting impatiently in a wagon, sitting on the spring seat with her snarled knitting while her husband completed his business at the gun and feed supply. Nowhere was there a child playing, a loafer loafing, a drummer selling. No Indians were sitting on the plank sidewalk across the way watching the town's comings and goings, and there were no comings and goings here on the north side of the crossroad and train track, nor, turning her head, did she see people moving about the street to the south. Within Thula the familiar dread she'd fought against in the nighttime began to rise, here in the damp alley, in cold daylight. For seven nights Thula had awakened at the deepest hour, soaked and sweated in that dark dread. Each of those nights she had lain in her bed as the low white pricks of stars on the black horizon faded from her window and the air in the room blued, the shapes in the room darkening, and then graying, becoming distinct. When the eastern sky blanched in preparation to receive its color, Thula would still be lying on her shuck mattress, watching, unable to name or know what it was that made her feel afraid. She had risen on each of those troubled dawns and got the stove started, gone through the day irritable and restless, quick and harsh with her grandchildren, which had never been her way, and filled with a vague, directionless sense that something very bad was going to happen, a cataclysm, a terrible event. In bed again at night, she would pray, the cornhusks whispering beneath her restless and shifting body, pray staring into the black room as it turned blue into gray into light. *Chitokaka ma! sai yimmishke; nan-isht ik a sai yimmo ya is svm apelvchaske.* But she remained dry and full of dread. Thula thought that it would be her own family that would suffer the cataclysm—her grandson Moss maybe, who seemed doomed for it, or one of her sons—and so she was for that reason glad to see the armed man and the girl walking behind him, and in another way, she was even more afraid.

From the day Thula had silently gathered her herbs and tobacco within her leather satchel and returned to her own house to live, she had thrown herself more deeply into the Baptist church at Yonubby; she had prayed at revivals and for revival and carried her Choctaw-language Bible with her at all times. She'd quit making medicine, for she feared it was not pleasing to the Lord. She feared that it might be true what Christian preachers preached: that the old ways were the ways of Satan; that the people had to turn their face against the old ways because it was only through belief in the name of *Chisvs* that their souls might be saved. For five years Thula Henry had lived doing as she believed she ought to do, but without peace. Always she carried the discomfited sense that she had forgotten something or neglected something. She would see the girl sometimes, with her family at a camp meeting or walking along the road with the old beagle, and often the girl would appear, but for her small size, nearly normal, and other times strange, but Thula would turn her eyes away. Now, standing in the well of alley between the rock building and the rough-timbered wall of the feed supply, watching Fayette Lodi pass before her and continue south on the dirt street, Thula did not turn her eyes away. She did not have the desire to, nor could she, perceiving, as she did, without turning her gaze, the force of the girl coming along the street trailing the man, tethered to him nearly, as the younger children had trailed the wagon home from camp meeting on Thula's son's white plowhorse in the cold new-moon darkness five years before.

The girl still bore that look of hollowness, like a cornhusk doll without features, but for the yellowbrown eyes staring ahead at her uncle. She was lean, hard-muscled, bony, and her chest was as flat as the day Thula had first seen her when she was ten. Thula realized with a start and then a slow deepening of the dread within her that the girl had never received her womanhood. Watching from her creviced place, the woman teetered between believing it was a sign of the girl's emptiness that she'd never got her womanways and, in the next instant, thinking it signified how powerful was the girl's medicine: a mark from the Creator that the girl had been charged to do powerful things. It was as if Matt exemplified and bore in her body the duality that had grown up in Thula, so that the woman could only watch in secret trembling as the girl—armed, barefoot, hardly taller than a fourteen-year-old, her face blank beneath the soft brim of the tan hat —passed in the street and continued on south midst the pawing, whickering horses.

When Matt neared the crossroad beyond the bank that ran east and west beside the train tracks, Thula Henry stepped up onto the plank sidewalk, crossed it swiftly and, holding the parcel to her chest and bending her knees deeply, and grunting once, for the distance was nearly two feet, she stepped down into the dirt street, where none but her son's long-suffering mule witnessed her movement.

There were none but that mule's eye, warm, brown, slanted, comprehending, and God's eye, perhaps, to see the short Indian woman moving along the street in a long dress of faded cotton, her hair crowblack still, and braided, looped in a black circlet crowning her head, a pale knitted shawl about her shoulders, the paper-wrapped parcel pressed to her chest, and on her small feet the soft leather shoes that were not moccasins but something more like house slippers hand-stitched of cowhide, raising a thin skein of dust behind the thin boyish figure walking steadily, neither swiftly nor slowly, behind the armed man mounted on the nervous, evenly gaited blue roan. None but God's and the mule's and the Indian woman's eyes to see when the figure lifted its trousered knees and stepped barefoot over the railroad tracks that appeared to slice through the heart of the town. But it could have been God's eye alone that saw the chert-eyed sister, her hair a dark mane flying, the bruise dimmed beneath a flour coating upon her cheekbone, as she snapped the reins above the rump of the little bay mare belonging to the Waddy postmaster Clay Mewborn, harnessed to the neat, shining buggy belonging to that same Mewborn, the yellow-painted spokes on the four wheels seeming to swirl backwards as the vehicle rolled swiftly toward Cedar on the old Butterfield road.

The *what* of what happened is so simple. The *what* takes place in the warp of time that is God's time, or perhaps it is not God's time but only the peculiar distortion of the human mind's belief in Time, forged and lived in each consciousness as it goes on forever retelling, shaping, trying to grasp and change the unchangeable. A man is killed. A man was killed. A man is being killed forever. And there is none but the eye of heaven, or the sun, or the all-seeing eye of the Creator to bear witness to the affluxion of lives and moment, drawn together in the mystery of unrelenting orchestration, for now, in the center of the khaki street forming the spine of the cross, its color paler than the transverse, bleached and aged with the numbers of coachwheels and iron shoes that have ground and parted its dust, the Indian woman hurries forward, seeing, on the far side of the tracks, the armed man halt the blue roan before the false front of the mercantile; seeing the wraithlike figure of the girl step to the side and conceal itself behind the red walls of the deserted brick depot. Now, thirteen miles away, in the swept yard of a small cabin a half mile south of Woolerton, a deputy U.S. marshal turns his smooth high-domed forehead to the eye of the sun, his burnished terra cotta skin seeming lit from within as he flips the stirrup over the fine leather seat of the saddle, the whorls and nubs at the back of his closecropped head now revealed to heaven as he bends to tighten the cinch around his stallion's inflated copper belly. On the far side of Waddy Mountain, the white woman stands on the porch of her husband's store, gazing south, her youngest child whimpering on her hip, the flattened ridge of her mouth deflated, and a dark tumescent swelling, unknown to her except in the deepest unwilling reaches of her consciousness, already rising in her belly, as the boy Thomas, in his pale dress hat and his father's suspenders, runs south along the road toward the place where he has seen his sister disappear in the postmaster's buggy, while within the dark sepulchre of the livery stable, John Lodi pauses, his arm raised, the great shaggy mallethead hammer poised, his ear cocked to the open door of the stable, where the bright still air stands yellow.

Jonaphrene drove fast around the curve through the pine woods, but she slowed, pulling up hard on the reins as soon as she saw the buildings of Cedar ahead. An overpowering shyness swept her, a self-consciousness born of vanity and confusion, and the terrible isolation in the confines of the log house on the edge of the little fading community of Big Waddy Crossing. As she passed before the remains of the old courthouse at the north edge of town, its rock chimneys standing empty at either end of the pile of rubble, the charred columns on the slab porch holding up only sky, she thought she could go no further. The long yellowbrown street before her was empty except for the few tethered horses and, far in the distance, the moving figure of the Indian woman, whom the girl did not recognize. Her experience was so barren that she did not even think it strange the town was empty, silent; she only feared someone would come out of one of the buildings on Main Street and see her with her tangled hair and marred face, and so at the cross street just past the cotton gin, Jonaphrene turned the bay's head to the left, and then, at the next corner, right again, taking the turns slowly, the mare walking, following a nameless side road parallel to Main Street through each of its small crossroads, south.

On the floorboard beneath her highbutton shoes, in the well of the buggy, lay a carbine rifle—the very one Fayette had called out to his daughter Lottie to bring him from beneath the spoolbed in the front bedroom. The one Jessie had brought out of the frame house after her husband's departure and carried, the crying toddler stumbling after her along the step-softened path, the rifle dragging muzzle-down and weighted through the bright motionless air, into the whitewashed and crowded interior of her husband's store, where she'd laid it upon the oak counter for no reason present within her own mind. A simple carbine rifle in no way tied to Lafayette Lodi's mired obsession with weapons of many chambers and barrels and complex firing mechanisms; it was merely another weapon he owned, as yet unblighted with the palm sweat and hunger of the man who owned it: a gun possessed of no more significance than the fact that it had been there, on the oak counter, when Jonaphrene went into the store because she could not find her father's muzzle-loading Kentucky rifle inside the log house.

Her sister had told her to borrow Mewborn's buggy, bring the muzzle loader, not let Mewborn see it, and Jonaphrene had followed meticulously each instruction, but for the bringing of the muzzle loader, which was not in its place on the two iron nails above the front door, and which she did not spy in a quick sweep through the downstairs, and so she'd gone to the store, where she knew—or expected—there were rifles aplenty. Jonaphrene, struggling to comprehend a world no one would explain to her, had developed into a very literal-minded young woman—more literal-minded, in fact, than even her brother Thomas, who took all the world at its word. Matt hadn't told her to bring Thomas, and so Jonaphrene had left him, running fast away from him across the field. Her sister had told her to hurry, and she had hurried, and yet when she couldn't find the muzzle loader, it had seemed to her no betrayal or peculiarity to go to her uncle's store. It had been, after all, Mewborn she'd been instructed to not let see the gun. Jonaphrene couldn't hold within herself the division and loyalty Matt carried, because she did not understand it. She'd been taught words long ago about a dead mother she could not remember, had been told she must haul water from the creek when there was a perfectly good fount of well water a hundred yards across the pasture. To her mind it wasn't betrayal to drink from her uncle's well, to wear her cousins' cast-off dresses, to go to Jessie and tell her she could not find the muzzle loader she was supposed to carry in Mewborn's buggy to Cedar. It was Jessie who had lifted the shiny carbine rifle off the counter and handed it, wordlessly, to her niece.

When Jonaphrene came to the junction of east-west crossroad hugging the train track, she halted the leather-trimmed buggy, climbed down with difficulty over the yellow wheelspokes in her ballooning volume of six overlayered skirts, and stood a moment looking west. She waited for the unfamiliar soreness to settle before she reached into the buggy and lifted out the carbine rifle and, holding it awkwardly before her in both hands, began to walk toward the depot along the bare rails. She walked slowly, stiff in the litheness of her limbs because of the violence of her fall: a girl of fifteen, beautiful, with no inkling of her own beauty but only an overweening self-consciousness that made her, even as she stepped along the crossties in a forced, uneven gait, believe there were eyes watching her from the houses on the far side of the road. She had no notion of the clownishness of her six layered skirts donned in lieu of petticoats, her face powdered with white flour, dusted on hurriedly in one quick, peering glance into the triangular piece of broken mirror wedged into a chink of log wall above her pallet in the dim upper room. She had no knowledge of the startling, nearly painful symmetry of form and bone and color beneath that flour-caked surface, the impossibly long fringe of lashes, straight, serge brown, above which the straight slash of brow seemed to give a scowl to the perfect features—a frown belied by the wide taking-in of the graygreen eyes, changing, transforming, shifting color as she walked, turning her head slowly, glancing self-consciously side to side at the invisible watchers she believed must be audience to her journey. For all the inward-turning of her awareness, she could have no idea of the strange juxtaposition on the creosote-blackened rails of girl and gun and awkward beauty, which alone would have captured all eyes to witness her part in the unfolding—had there been any human eye turned upon it.

For not even Matt turned her head to witness; not even Thula Henry, who could have seen Jonaphrene from the moment the buggy turned the corner, had she not been so locked onto the thin figure kneeling on the wooden platform behind the depot. The Indian woman had been flung drowning into the place of her soul's division, so that, watching in the harsh still glare of midafternoon sunlight, she saw not the bony nineteen-year-old in a man's hat and breeches hunched behind the brick wall of the depot, but the fourteen-year-old walking from the east in the wanner light of midmorning, up the slope and into the clotted yard beside the log house, where she sat down on the dun grass and put her arm across the rolling back of the fat beagle: the fourteen-year-old Matt, thin, pale, parched-corn yellow, her hair pulled back tightly from her face in a leather thong at the base of her skull, and her eyes entirely empty. Thula's fear was not dry now but a swamp like the black aimless sloughs of the Fourche Maline river bottoms, rising, changing, transforming solid earth to quagmire and bog.

"*Impashilup*," she said, out loud.

John Lodi, emerging from the stable then, walked alone in the street toward his brother. He was not afraid, walked without anger even in that moment, but merely in weariness at the relentlessness of the trouble between them, which was not hatred, to John's mind, but only the old tie of brotherness, raveled and worn raw by the chafing of Fayette's sickness. He carried the seven-barreled pistol he'd taken off Fayette five hours earlier; he didn't believe his brother meant to kill him—had not thought it five hours before, didn't consider it now—but he carried the pepperbox anyway, as both pacifier and threat. He might hoist it and brandish it when the other began waving his guns around, or he'd offer to give it back to him as a sweetener to get his drunk brother to settle down. Even when Fayette, standing perfectly steady, apparently perfectly sober in the dirt street beside the blue roan, pulled the big four-barreled howdah from his waistband, John did not change expression or pause but came on at his steady, unchanging rhythm.

It was in the soul of Fayette Lodi himself that the turning of the moment began. The man stood in the harsh sunlight manifest in the soiled flesh of his body, but his mind was locked away from that world in a darkened place, a cavern of pictures, words, imagined slights, and the profound, spitting, unsatisfiable outrage at what others had done to him. The words wrung themselves out in his shriveled being, inescapable: a ceaseless, monotonous rant against his sons who'd betrayed him with their worthlessness, against his wife who'd betrayed him with her lack of faith, against the community of Big Waddy Crossing which had betrayed him by not becoming the big town he'd wanted, against his partner Tanner who'd betrayed him by quitting him altogether. Above all, first and last, most ancient and new and forever, the litany belonged to the brother walking toward him on the dirt street, whose very skin and eyes and hair, whose very tilt of head and living bones were an effrontery to Fayette's soul. He aimed to kill him. To kill him now in the final blasted outrage of his soul's festering, or to die trying, or to do both. Fayette was perfectly calm, perfectly placid, as he raised the heavy muzzle of the howdah in the still sunlight.

And the girl was with him. The two were joined as one—not yoked in a bonding as it existed between the two brothers, but as if their souls' impermeable borders, having touched in the dark remains of the shed barn, must now merge with one another, overlapping, united in the void of consumed self never to be filled. And yet there was a difference: in the man the soulsickness was enlarged by the alchemy of whiskey past the certain sin of envy, beyond his first belief that his brother would forever have something he did not, into the pure unsatisfiable lust of hatred that made him aim the four-barreled howdah at his brother's face and pull the trigger. But it was a separate cause whereby the girl Matt slowly squeezed the trigger of the twenty-two pistol a full heartbeat before the howdah's first explosion—a full half second before her father fired the seven-barreled weapon at his brother's forehead, just as Jonaphrene, the literal-minded and self-conscious Jonaphrene, raised the light carbine to her shoulder and, another heartbeat later, while her uncle turned in the still, cold light, falling, fired the shot that blew out his neck.

She was coming behind me. I turned my head a little maybe, or I didn't turn it but only glanced over my shoulder with my eyes, or I don't know what I did but I knew she was coming along the street, trailing me. I could see her skirt stirring little dustdevils, I could see the tiny, tiny cobwebs of hairs escaped out of her braid. I didn't care. I crossed the road and went on, and I went up the little slope of bank to the tracks, the little embankment, a mild raised place of black cinders and dirt to hold the bed of rails, and the rails were shining dull in the sunlight but the crossties themselves were slag black, and I could smell the creosote and the iron leavings of trains that had passed and would pass over them, sparking steel, a splinter coming in my sole because I did not lift my foot high enough, and I didn't care. I could see him pulling up on the reins, his shoulder raised, though the roan would have stopped if he'd only just let him, because that horse was spent. He stopped in front of the mercantile store this side of Dayberry's, and I could hear the leather creak when he put the weight on his left side, put his drunken weight into the stirrup so that I hurried as fast as I might, I did not care about that splinter, though later when I took it out with Papa's hunting knife it was three inches long. I hurried to the next building, the depot, to hide, and why, I don't know, I don't know that either, because I tell you I was not afraid.

So he stood down, and I felt Thula crossing the empty road behind me, stirring dust, and I did not know her part in it, I didn't believe she had a part in it, I couldn't think that, she was not blood, not even half-blood, not any kin to me or my kin, and so she was like a spider in the road or an old terrapin, not even there for a witness because she would not see it any more than a terrapin would see it, and then I saw Papa. He was coming out the door of the stable, just walking out blinking a little in the light. I thought, *He don't know. He don't even know Fayette means to kill him.* I thought that so fast. Lightning. Faster than it could ever take now to say the words out loud. I just saw it in him, Papa, coming out of the dark square into the empty street with his hat on, and he had one of Fayette's many-mouthed guns like it was just an old ancient thing that would go on forever in us, my uncle and his guns, that I could never find them all and drop them in creekwater, I could never uncover all the pieces of death he had stole and bought and bartered and garnered unto himself, nor ever bury them deep in the earth. There could be no pit of earth deep enough to take and keep all his guns. One would poke out or stick out somewhere, like bones buried too shallow that the dogs keep digging up, so I felt defeated, though I should have been glad my Papa was armed coming out into the street with his brother ready to kill him.

The pistol was in my hand again. For a while, walking, it wasn't, but there behind the depot it was again, the grip smooth and the keen weight of it balanced, and the back of my uncle's head was only a couple of hundred yards away. And so I aimed again, pulled back the hammer, Papa walking in the still, bright daylight, and it was not to save Papa in that instant, though I have said for years that it was, because the black violence and rage in me was *at Papa, there was no separation, Fayette's hatred was mine in the gaping maw the vast open black emptiness so that I hated him with a lust of violence to KILL him to KILL him in outrage for the effrontery of his self to conflict with Myself and my self crying out to hurt, to kill that which would hurt would take from me rob me to leave me soulless barren and without, and it was not this joined portion of self I would kill but that other in the street coming as he had always come to rob me cross me deny me so that I fired* as Fayette fired or before Fayette fired, the pistol making a fine sound an instant before the explosion from the mouth of the gun in Fayette's hand, one barrel, and immediately the second barrel, Fayette's aim going wild because he was already falling, because it was only accident or the hand of unseen forces that made the small neat twenty-two cartridge lodge in the back of my uncle's skull on its way to Papa's face.

I didn't know what the clamp was around me, the weight of something squeezing my arms and chest, tight, so tight to take my breath so that it was like the dream where I am locked in a corpse of body, the unwilling shell of body, paralyzed, that will not move, and I struggled to cry out because I could not breathe or move, though I saw Papa walking toward Fayette's body in the dirt street with the gun in Papa's hand hanging loose at his side, Fayette's throat bleeding, the left side of his neck vanished where the red pulsed and spurted, and above his eyes the bone still showing white, a white visible sliver an instant before the red welled and drowned it, the red spurts from his throat becoming halfhearted, slower and weaker, and all of it clear before my eyes, going on forever, because I could not move, until the sound came when I knew it was not the dream but her holding me, Thula's arms vised around my arms, pinning them, and the sound of her voice chanting, which I didn't know what she was saying but I understood she was not talking to me because it was almost like her song when she smoked me, gave me the clay cup, but it was not that either. My strength returned then because I was not caught living in the dead unmovable shell of my body but only grasped around the chest by a little Indian woman of no strength, so I burst the clamp, raised both of my arms with all my power, twisting on the wooden platform to face her, twisting, breaking free, and she never hushed up chanting or praying, whatever she was saying, and the clamp was not on me, but in the next instant she had me by the wrists of both hands, pulling me along the platform on the track-side of the depot, pulling me, hard, fast, west along the platform, away from the center of town.

But the coiled hoop of time is not stopped for the dead or the act of death; it spirals relentlessly forward, and the living, willing or unwilling, must turn, move, perceive, open their mouths or shut them, locked each in the cavern of self, so that John Lodi, unaware of his daughters, walked in the still and gleaming light toward the body, aware only that his brother was dead by his hand; stood over the corpse knowing only that in the rushing eternity in which his brother fired at him, he, John, had gone cold with the familiar black and icy rage that allowed him, or forced him, in the same rushing instant, to pull up and fire the seven-barreled gun at his brother's forehead. Jonaphrene started forward, stopped abruptly, seeing a young boy dash out of the mercantile and trip over her uncle's body, seeing in the next instant the store owner come out onto the gallery wiping his hands on his bloody apron, and she whirled in the horror of her self-consciousness to run with the awkward carbine back along the ties to the place where Mewborn's mare grazed, untethered, nipping the yellow grass in the ditch beside the track.

The people of Cedar began to pour forth from the square buildings, drawn each to the place where death had been committed, the livery owner J. G. Dayberry in a sharp-faced rush of intent to protect his employee, and the others, in the excitement of news and event and the fading echoes of the sounds of violence, to gawk. Five miles to the north, the boy Thomas stood in the dirt road waving his arms and crying as his cousin Caleb, approaching with his brother Fowler and six of his sisters in the wagon, slowed the highstepping young team, while, two and three-quarters miles farther north along the old Butterfield road, Jessie, inside the store now, suddenly bent double at the waist, her gut stabbed with a searing pain. A mile east of Woolerton, Burden Mitchelltree turned his big stallion's head onto the Fort Smith road. And on the train platform, a hundred yards from the bleeding shell left by a soul's departure, two figures, facing each other, skimmed westward joined at the wrists.

The woman moved smoothly, swiftly backwards along the platform, pulling the girl who was not girl, nor woman, nor any sexed creature but an incarnation of human will in a small, nut-hard body, unfathomably strong. And yet Thula Henry was stronger. The two glided along the platform, joined at stiffened arms' length as two partners face one another over the momentarily stilled handle of a switchman's cart while it glides along the rails. The gun was between them, still clutched in Matt's hand, the muzzle pointing to the side wildly, and Thula's hands were clamped around the girl's wrists, snapped tight. When they reached the end of the platform, Thula rushed forward and grabbed the girl around the waist before she had the chance or perception to resist, and immediately half dragged, half carried her off the platform and around the side of the depot to the dirt track of alley that ran behind the buildings on the west side of the street. She didn't hesitate before the gun, or fear it, or care about it, because she was compelled to drag Matt away from the town and the intrusion of white eyes by the same force that had made her drop her bundle and clamp her arms around the girl's chest in the instant she'd known the girl would fire the gun: upon the crouched, thin figure in front of her Thula had seen a vision, an overlay of strange bone and flesh, and she had thrust forward in the very instant of expulsion of sound from the pistol, followed immediately by explosions from three directions, and Thula had found herself moving backwards along the platform without thought of what she was doing or would do, knowing nothing except to whisk the girl away from white eyes. Her fear was entirely broken, discarded, not dark and swelling but cut from her by the rush of blood and breath needed to move the girl. Awkwardly, bearlike, she trundled her as far as the back of Tatum's Mercantile along the two pale tracks of alleyway behind the store, and there the girl suddenly twisted around, jerking out of her grasp.

The two stood in the dirt alley, breathing hard, looking at each another. Muted sounds came from the other side of the building behind which the two stood: men's voices, someone shouting, footfalls thudding in the dirt street on the front side of the store. The girl and the woman panted, their chests rising and falling in union. Thula said, "You come go with me." There was a minute's silence, or silence between the two of them, for the sounds on the street were swelling, rising in staccato excitement. But the girl answered Thula nothing.

"We not finish," the woman said.

Slowly their breaths calmed, slackened, their pounding hearts each began to settle. The girl's eyes were not hollow now but alert, alive, glowing in their strange yellowbrown color of earth. Slowly she returned the twenty-two to its casing in the leather holster. Still she did not answer.

"He aims us to do it," Thula said.

The girl's narrowed gaze began to dart then, to the left, where there was an old corral behind the stable, to the right, in the direction she and the woman had just come, over Thula's shoulder, where there were several frame houses set flat to the earth and wide apart, and beyond that the open sweep of the little prairie where the town stood.

"The Lord knows," Thula said. "It's only the Lord knows what it is we didn't get finish. We got to depend upon the Lord," and she went on talking, nearly chanting, a mixture of English and native tongue. "He set it out for us to do it. You can't mess with that, same as you can't mess with medicine. You can't mess with holy, *holito-pashke,* it's going to do you real bad." Her voice was low, almost monotonous, but there was urgency in it, until she ceased all at once, staring hard at the girl's face. A mask of bones lay across Matt's features, and then, as Thula watched, the bone mask was supplanted with the softened flesh of a human infant. This was the same image she'd seen on the girl's face in the instant before the gunfire, and it was her own vision, Thula understood that, given her by *Shilombish Holitopa,* the Holy Spirit. But she did not know what it meant. As quickly as it had appeared, the vision fled.

For a time there was the ringing voice of silence, a bell of silence descended around the two figures, the Choctaw woman and the white girl in a dirt alley back of the mercantile in the new town arisen for its little time between blue humps of mountains on the face of the ancient and spirit-filled prairie. In the silence Thula Henry's ear pulsed with her blood beating. She stood on the earthen track, listening, breathing.

From a great, undeterminable distance, she heard a sound: *tock-tock tock-tock tock-tock tock-tock,* the clocking sound of striking-sticks, in rhythm, in rhythm, the old beat of blood. The sound changed then, and deepened. Thula heard a lone voice calling, the sound answered, repeated by many voices, and the rhythm and the song were the sound of her own blood. This was not a song of her father's people, not a song from the Green Corn ceremony carried on, undiminished, at Nuyaka and Okfuskee, renewed in the *saka-saka* of the shell shakers, the singing and drums; but a sound more distant, beyond her own memory, to the remembering of her mother's people, the *Chahta* people—to the sacred ceremony in the old homeland in the place the whites called Mississippi, the homeland Thula Henry had never seen.

Slowly, Thula's mind filled with a new vision, an ancient vision: an image of fire, and then daylight, and the people dancing. She heard the call of the singer's voice rising in a song already forgotten, being forgotten, because the preachers said the people must—not the white preachers only, but Choctaw preachers, speaking in native tongue the Holy Word of the Lord, saying, We got to purge out the old leaven, that we could be a new lump. Saying, This cup is the new testament in *Chisvs'* blood. Saying, We got one ceremony here now, *Chisvs* give us this ritual, it's *Chisvs'* blood, *Chisvs'* body, His blood been shed for us, His blood been spilled on the mercy seat, that's the Blood sacrifice from here on out, that's all we got to know. Saying, If it had to be white people coming to take everything to bring us the Word of the Lord, so it is. The Lord works in mysterious ways. Saying, We got to forget all that old stuff, just not think about it, we got to depend upon the Lord.

But within Thula's bloodmemory the vision rolled forward.

Though she stood in the cold bright sunlight, her sight closed down in darkness, a flickering darkness, and she saw men and women stepping, turning in the great hoop of the circle; she heard the striking-sticks, the gourd rattles, and the voice of the singer calling, the men's voices answering, and the women's voices, while the people went on stepping, stepping in the unending circle as if they would go on forever, as if the singer must sing forever this song of purification, of acknowledgment and honor and worship, singing in the voice of the people, the song given to the people, the dance shaped by the hand of the Creator to honor all that has gone before and will come after, as the *Chahta* people had done from the beginning—

Abruptly the song stopped. The dance stopped. In the same manner that the mask on the girl's face had fled, so disappeared the dancers: snuffed as a lantern wick clamped off by damp fingers.

A welling of grief came on Thula Henry, unfathomable, a stuffed and swollen sense of loss beyond sorrow at the soul's edge of remembrance, and she didn't know what it was. She stood a moment blinking, longing, praying for return, and she didn't know what it was she would return to or have returned to her, but only felt it: the gaping, expectant sense in her of something gone. When Thula looked, there was only the girl standing before her. Just the thin, strange-eyed white girl standing barefoot with her back against the wooden building in her britches and man's hat, the gunbelt dragging down on the narrow hips, the hard, flat chest rising and falling. Within Thula the dread began to rise again, dark and fingering, licking, even as the old unwilling sense of responsibility returned to her, called forth by the rumblings of men's voices rising louder from the street. Without a word she reached a hand toward the girl.

Matt stared at her, expressionless, her eyes not empty as before but with the meaning in them unrevealed, and Thula, helpless and urgent, aware then of a gray-mustached white man in overalls standing in the crevice between the mercantile and stable, where excited voices filtered from the street, knew nothing but to say the words again.

"You come go with me."

The girl was silent.

"It's not too late," Thula said. "We go up yonder to Yonubby, you come stay with me."

"No," the answer came finally.

"We ain't done it!" Thula said. "We not fully understand. *Chihowa* not give us that understanding!" She could not say these things in the backwards language of English, the paltry language of English that did not have the meaning in any of its tongued and spitting words. "We are not finish!" she tried to tell the girl. "You going to die from it. Me too maybe. Or something worse."

The girl, staring at her as if she did not see her, as if she looked through the woman's solid cotton-clad body to the sleeping weeds in the valley behind her, said, "You seen me." The girl's voice dropped to a whisper, again the hoarse sound of whisper, saying, "You seen me in the red darkness." The focus of her gaze changed, though the ocher eyes never moved direction, but seemed only to pull back, to retreat behind themselves.

Thula watched the girl in silence, in the slow opening of recognition, but what she saw was not revealed in the face of the yellow-eyed girl, not revealed in vision or memory but only in the glimmering of a soul's reckoning, to be received for an instant and later forgotten in the word-mind but remembered in the soul's hope. Thula understood in that glimmer the meaning of the bone mask and its afterpart; she remembered what her people had known from the early time: how the Creator had bid them honor the bones of the dead in the sacred baskets had bid the people paint their living faces in honor of rising up from the dust for a little time—not separate from the bones of the ancestors or the unborn soft and new in their flesh to come, but the manifest union between each, in their unbroken place on the unbroken hoop in the eternal unfolding. For an instant her soul understood what the people, without their songs, were in danger of forgetting, and then the recognition was ripped from her as the girl suddenly turned and began to walk away.

Matt moved quickly toward the crevice between the stable and the mercantile, and then as abruptly changed course, turned on her bare heel and headed toward the corral fence at the end of the wagon tracks. She shinnied over the top rail and jumped to the trampled dirt, headed across the open space toward the other side, and Thula, compelled by the force she could not comprehend, followed after. When she reached the corral fence she did not climb over but crawled painfully between the bottom and mid rail, hurried on, skimming swiftly through the skein of powdered dust after the girl walking away from her across the empty open square. Acting, not thinking, not understanding, Thula rushed forward and caught the girl by the arm and swung her around. She clamped on, snapped tight at the wrists once again, and Matt fought her, hard, pulling back with all the wizened strength in her calf muscles, her knotted forearms, but Thula Henry would not be shaken loose. The two jerked and swirled and turned about the dirt track, Matt Lodi twisting and whirling, and Thula Henry, unshakable, hanging on.

Thula did not know when the two white men first appeared, was unaware of them entirely until her throat was locked fiercely from behind by a flannel-covered arm, choking her wind off, so that the white man accomplished what even the ferocious whirling and jerking of the girl's strength could not do. Thula let go. There was no more than a heartbeat when she saw the bald short man bleating, as he circled the girl with a blood-spattered apron held up in front of him, "Behave now! Behave yourself, here!" and then Thula's breath was gone completely, the world darkening, and she went down.

When the light came again, she was lying on the feedlot floor. She was aware, as through a fog, a clouded mist, of the two white men. One of them—the mustached one in overalls she'd seen in the little alley—was holding the girl by the back of her trousers; the other still circled the girl helplessly, ineffectually, with his hands in the air. Coughing, gasping, the choking not from her lungs but from her throat where the man's elbow had pressed tight, Thula pulled herself up to sit in the trampled dust a few feet from the strange, excited circling of the two men around the girl who was like a she-fox caught live in the teeth of an iron trap, leaping and snapping in pain and terror and fury. Thula knew that these white men did not see her. Her presence was nonmaterial to them, dismissed, a disappearance. For a moment she felt the old welling of rage at the men's ignorance, at their mindless ruthlessness to nearly choke the life out of her and then dismiss her from their sight as if she were a whipped dog panting in the feedlot dust.

But in the next instant, watching the girl snarl and spit and spin in her pitiful shrunken fury, Thula Henry was washed entirely of her hatred. She felt it ebb from her as cleanly as a lanced wound. What it was, she did not understand in that moment; she was aware only of a terrible sorrow for the thin form whirling about and cursing and lashing. From that sorrow, deep within her, emanated a kind of letting-go, a forgiveness, *aheka*, so that Thula could not hold in herself the bruise of hatred. The washing away came not from inside her but through her, as the working of medicine came through her, and she understood her part had not been for the sake of the white girl only, but that she, Thula Henry, might remember in the fullness of knowledge what had long been given to the people—not separate from the Fourth Part, not in fear as the fear had been taught her—but in union, in oneness, as it had been given from the beginning of the world. In that moment, the woman's peace was restored. Thula's mind did not comprehend it, her tongue did not know how to tell it, yet her *shilup*, her immortal spirit, was one with it, so that she knew that whatever the joining-together had been, it was finished now.

From a great, peaceful distance she watched them, heard the men's curses rise above the girl's curses from the little whirlwind of dust stirred by their turning feet. While the white men rattled their awkward tooth-filled tongue in loud voices and danced fearfully around the girl, trying to hold on to her without coming inside the range of her flailing arms, Thula Henry drew her weary legs beneath her. She lifted her sore and weighted body from the dust and limped slowly to the corral gate, left standing open. She walked out of the feedlot, across the faint dun-colored wagon tracks behind the town buildings. The profane voices faded behind her as she started out north and west across the prairie to begin the long walk home.

She'd seen me in the red darkness, her brown face coming down, round and flat, soft as doeskin, while I lay fevered on the hard pallet. She witnessed me, saw me pray one into death, one into life. She knew it was Mama's baby suckled by a black woman I turned back. To keep Thomas. It was only to keep Thomas, my brother, whom I loved. I have tried to say it, tried to make justice of it, but God turned back the bitter joke on me, made him an idiot, to stay a knee-baby forever, and not that only, not only that. Because I was charged with the gifts of the spirit, and it was not in the manner of the tongues of men and of angels nor the gift of prophecy, but to enter the soul of another, for the sake of union. For the sake of mercy. And I turned my face away. I chose first my family, and then my own will. And so it was stripped from me, scooped out of my soul when I shook my fist at heaven the dawn the cedars bled. Given against my will, taken from me against my will, returned to me in the barn darkness with my uncle, and you have seen what I did with it. Even as Thula had seen.

I couldn't bear to breathe a moment longer the air of her presence. She had witnessed me in the black shade behind the depot, even as she'd seen me in the red darkness, the same: her eyes open, her arms clamped round me the very instant my finger began pressing lightly, squeezing gently, so easy, the smooth plate of the trigger easing back —and then it was her two hands pulling me away from the place of killing, the dirt street of Cedar, where the voice of my uncle's blood cried out from the ground. Her two hands holding me in the dirt tracks behind the town, her mouth in the other tongue saying, Come go with me. I would not go with her. I would never go with her. I would have to kill her if I did.

I turned to run. I thought if I could get to the creek bottom on the far side of the fence rails, she couldn't keep up with me. I knew the creek bottoms of Eye Tee, the tangled depths and mudwater sloughs; I could weave among the grapevines and swamp willows as clean as a river snake. If I could make it to the water, she couldn't grab me again.

It was them, whoever they were. In the dirt square Thula held me, her strong hands clasped round me, but I would have broken free. I could have. I would. But the men came, and it was not what they did to me but to her when the one locked his arm on her throat, took her life's breath and Thula fell back into darkness, so that for a dying instant I fell with her. Unwilling. As I had ever been.

I stood on the rib of earth in the crimson darkness. There was someone with me, a presence with me, to the left of me, and I did not know what it was. It was not to hurt me or help me, but only to be with me. I faced north and west. Below was the red roiling place, lit crimson with the light of earth and heaven, and the earth was glutted with its live things, its teeming curl and scent, living, blood dark. From a small rounded place there rose up long-legged birds lit red in their own light, shooting toward heaven, streaking as stars streak toward heaven, until I knew they were not birds but spirits flying heavenward without wings as the soul moves in arrow flight, lit red from within in the red darkness, and behind each, others rising, in an endless eternal stream.

For this there is no translation.

I fought then, cursing, railing, crying out against it. It was not men I struck against. My uncle's blood cried out from the ground. I fought the unspeakable mercy.

Burden Mitchelltree sensed a killing before he'd even ridden close enough to the town to see the crowd. A half mile ahead, at the crossroads, he saw a lone figure dash across the road from the north side to the south side; behind that figure, a few moments later, another one darted. Above the drumming of his horse's hooves he heard a rising thrum of voices, off to the south a little, out of sight behind the buildings on that side of town. Killing or bank robbery, he thought. Or both. Those were the two events that could put that rise in the air, that particular high-pitched murmur of turmoil and excitement. He pressed his heels tighter against the stallion's belly, though he was already pushing the sorrel at a steady lope, much harder than he ordinarily would just heading out for Fort Smith. But he'd got a late start—a peculiarly late start to be setting out on that sixty-mile journey—and he meant to stay over at a boardinghouse on the far side of Wister operated by a certain light-skinned, sweet-faced daughter of a Choctaw freedwoman. Already he was going to be hard-pressed to get much past Fanshawe before dark; this little sidetrack would set him back further, and cursing silently, glancing a hundred yards ahead at the blank bank building where no crowd stood about, and so satisfying himself that it was indeed a killing he was looking at, not a bank robbery—which was something at least, he thought—he chucked softly at the sorrel as he dug in his spurless heels.

Thus it happened that the nearest deputy U.S. marshal, unsent for, galloped into Cedar from the west in a swirl of dun dust within an hour and a half of the Lodi killing. The deputy wheeled his tremendous copper-flanked stallion around the turn by the brick depot, rode into and scattered the clutch of gawkers gathered around the corpse sprawled faceup on the street. Mitchelltree ignored the scowls and glares of resentment from the scattered onlookers as he gazed at the dead man from his great height astride the quivering, sidestepping stallion. He could see that the man had been dead for a while. A blood-soaked handkerchief had been spread over the face, and it was black and fidgety with flies even this early in the year. The pooled blood in the dirt road had already sunk into the dust, jelled mulberry. The handkerchief didn't cover the ragged neck, flagged with scraps of torn flesh, or conceal the blood-matted brown hair spreading flowerlike from the blasted scalp. Mitchelltree dismounted, handed the reins to a boy standing by the hitching rail, and made his way through the knot of onlookers who had regathered around the dead man as turkey buzzards, scattered but unmolested, will return quickly to the scavenged kill. The deputy's resonant voice rumbled over the rising buzz from the townsmen.

"All right, folks, all right. Let's have a look at him."

Bound to be a white man, he thought, although he'd spotted the old Choctaw sheriff in the livery doorway nearly as soon as he'd rounded the corner. He'd love to find out it was an Indian shot by an Indian, so he could nod knowingly at Sheriff Moore, say, Well, if you need anything, and go on about his business. But Mitchelltree knew it had to be a white man. Two reasons, he thought: one, to make good and sure to mess up this little stopover at Miss Marilla's; two, because the last bill passed by Congress in its ever-loving pursuit of control over the Indian Territory was so all-fired complicated already, demanding Mitchelltree to be in two places at once, plus keep track of which cases still belonged with Parker, which to the new district court at McAlester, that he sincerely needed a clear-cut white-on-white murder in a little white town with no law and no jail that had to be investigated right here late in the afternoon when he had to be in court the next day at Fort Smith to testify in a year-old murder case before Judge Isaac Parker as part of finishing off the loaded dockets under the old federal court's authority—so just naturally it had to be a white man there dead on the street. Mitchelltree nodded at a bystander, who squatted down and peeled back the congealed kerchief. The deputy took a step forward, bent his knee and knelt beside the corpse. Shotgun blast to the skull. Another to the neck, it appeared like. Dead before he hit the ground. A white man.

Mitchelltree stood up, brushed his neatly laundered corduroy trousers free of dust, turned and walked toward the livery stable, where he'd seen the old Choctaw sheriff Tecumseh Moore. He hadn't recognized the man he'd hired on to for a day and a half nine years before, though he'd seen Fayette Lodi more than a dozen times since. That ill-favored trip with the sandstone-filled wagon had been one of his last wage jobs before he'd received his appointment as deputy U.S. marshal under old Jacob Yoes, and Mitchelltree had every reason to remember the man, even if he hadn't seen him in the years in between. But the top of Fayette's skull was gone, the brilliant blue eyes were closed—someone had thoughtfully weighted the lids with pennies before the kerchief had been placed—and the former mass of brown curly hair and the rufous beard had grayed considerably since the last time Mitchelltree had seen him, and grayed strangely: not in swatches at the temples or interspersed throughout with wiry strands of white or silver, as a brunette ordinarily grays, but the entire head and beard faded, washed out, the way a redhead grays, as if the pigment had been bled away. Then, too, the face, what was left of it, was nearly covered with blood.

It was not until he spotted John Lodi inside the stable, sitting on a hay bale with his hands dangling between his knees and a blank, numb expression on his face, that Mitchelltree began to get a glimmer of what had unfolded here. This Lodi he recognized immediately as the man in the slouch hat who had climbed the ridge, shot the big charcoal mule, and handed the four-barreled pistol back to Mitchelltree without a word before he'd gathered the two strange little girls by the shoulders and guided them before himself down the path to the bottom of the ridge. Even before Sheriff Moore and the little hawk-faced livery owner emerged from the dark interior of the stable and came over to speak to him, Mitchelltree began to perceive in a slow dawning that the dead man on the street was the other Lodi, the one they called Fate—the reckless impatient white man who'd had his barns built before he got his stones hauled, the old bootlegger and horsetrader that Mitchelltree had twice served warrants on for introducing ardent spirits into the Territory. And he knew just as well, in that same slow dawning, that it was the brother inside the barn there who'd killed him, knew it as perfectly as if he'd been told it would happen just this way that evening on the ridge behind Big Waddy nine years before. Immediately the deputy U.S. marshal began to relax, and he sauntered toward the sheriff and the livery owner with a pleasant, casual expression. This wouldn't take much time, then. You had the dead man and the killer and the weapon, it appeared like, for the sheriff was coming toward him holding an old-fashioned pepperbox pistol, and the only question was self-defense or murder; it was just going to be a matter of having the brother bound over to go before the grand jury at McAlester—yes, this new killing would go to the Central District Court at South McAlester. Just a clean ordinary simple killing.

Then he saw the two girls and the big hulking blond boy in shabby suspenders and a snap-brimmed dress hat emerge from the shadows within the depths of the stable as the sheriff and the livery owner walked out. The three young people glided in union over to where John Lodi sat with his hands dangling between his knees. At once Mitchelltree knew the two females were the same two rat-headed little girls in gaping gingham dresses who'd stood accusing him in singsong on the ridge that evening, and the absolute strangeness of them then complied with the strangeness of them now as they gathered behind their father, the short one in britches, the other in many-layered petticoats, and the boy hulking between in unraveling suspenders and the new-looking hat as if his body were too big for himself.

"Had us some little excitement here this evening," Tecumseh Moore said.

"That was self-defense, now. I'm a witness," the liveryman piped in. "You just ast anybody. See if you don't find out how crazy that Fate's been acting, he was looking to kill somebody. He was bound to kill somebody before this day was over if somebody didn't kill him first." And the livery owner turned to the crowd standing now in front of the dead man so that the body was obscured. "Am I right?" Silence from the onlookers, who'd begun to weary of the livery owner's self-proclaimed proprietorship over this murder, but the small man waved his arms, thrust his face forward at his neighbors. "Y'all going to back me up on this, or am I going to have to do all the testifying myself?"

There was a low rumble from the crowd then that could have been mumbled agreement, could have been grumbling, but Mitchelltree paid it no mind in any case, and he reached for the gun the sheriff held.

"This it?" he said.

"Might be," Moore said.

Burd Mitchelltree examined the pepperbox. Certainly this contraption could have done that kind of damage at close range, but when he checked the barrels there was something troublesome about it. The pepperbox was an old seven-barrel percussion-cap muzzle loader, and only one barrel had been fired. Inconceivable that the man would have paused to reload the one barrel before he fired a second shot. Yet clearly Fayette Lodi had been killed with two powerful gunshot wounds. An inaudible groan rose from Mitchelltree's belly as he realized this was not going to be as simple a little killing as he'd thought, and he swerved the sound into the soft tremolo of his bass voice, saying, "Mm-huh. Must be some kind of gun to make two holes like that with one shot, say?"

"Must be," Tecumseh Moore said.

"Well, look here," the livery owner nearly shouted. "You ain't seen the other'n, the one Fate pulled. That'll explain you a thing or two."

And he marched on banty legs toward and through the crowd of townspeople, the big Negro deputy marshal and the shorter, broad-backed Choctaw sheriff following until they stood rimming the body again, and the livery owner Dayberry began to shout, "Where'd that gun go? What went with the gun, it was laying right here a little bit ago!" He looked up at Mitchelltree, his bright blue eyes comprehending and furious. "I seen it not ten minutes ago. Laying right here!" and he tapped the rounded toe of his boot up and down in the dust a half-dozen times. "You can't trust nobody in this town." His eyes swept the clutch of onlookers. "I tell you what," he said, addressing the two lawmen but never taking his eyes from the circle of neighbors. "Before all these farmers and squatters come in here, you didn't hear of such stuff. You didn't hear of some little weaselly thief going into a dead man's house while the family was all gone to the funeral and stealing that dead man's carpentry tools and his prize fiddle like somebody"—his eyes swept the circle again—"*somebody* done to Jemson Lovett last Wednesday was a week ago, and this whole town knows it." Then he seemed to catch himself. His face relaxed a little; he tilted his head up, peering through half-closed eyes at the crowd. "Before we had all these white people come traipsing in here," he said in a low, confidential tone to the sheriff and deputy, as if the crowd around him were not listening; as if he himself were not white as a biscuit, with sparkling blue eyes and sandy hair and a faded dusting of freckles that swore his kin had come from Scotland by way of Ireland not many generations before, "you only had one kind of thievery in this country: plain old out-and-out bank robbery and murder. A man'd shoot you to take your boots off you, but he wouldn't come sneaking around filching tools off your widow's front porch like a old weasel while you laid up at the churchhouse, dead in your coffin." He looked at the crowd again, spoke clearly. "Jem Lovett was my friend, and not a man in this town but knows it. I ever find out who took that toolbox and fiddle, somebody's going to be mighty sorry." He narrowed his eyes again, stood with his hands on his hips and his intelligent face thrust forward. "Not to mention I hear tell of who picked up that dadgum gun!" Then he turned, disgusted, looked at the deputy marshal with a shared sense of their lone, mutual integrity, said, "Reckon you'll have to inquisite 'em yourself, mister. I'm liable to bust somebody's nut." And he marched off to stand by himself a short distance from the gathered townsmen, noble, dignified, fed up.

Mitchelltree looked at the sheriff, who seemed to be studying a cloud formation off in the distance over the back of Bull Mountain. "You know what he's talking about?"

The sheriff, never taking his eyes away from the northwestern sky, nodded once. His face, unconcerned beneath the broad brim of his felt hat, told that he was a man in high prime, the eyes bright, the dark complexion entirely unseamed, and yet the thick hair that bushed out from beneath that hat was a fine silvery gray; he could have been anywhere from forty to sixty. He did not volunteer any further information, and Mitchelltree, figuring the old fellow would offer what he cared to when it suited him, gazed around at the circle of onlookers. There were forty or more, men and boys mostly, with a few white women in sunbonnets standing back near the mercantile's porch ledge. Their eyes did not meet the deputy marshal's eyes but seemed intent on the dead man or the dirt road or, like the sheriff himself, some peculiar cloud formation overhead.

"Somebody want to explain to me what gun he's talking about?" Mitchelltree gazed calmly at the crowd and waited.

There were a few things he'd learned in his years riding for Parker. One was, no white crowd was going to jump up and join forces with a black marshal unless its interests lay with him successfully executing his duty. It didn't matter what the law was, what crime had been committed, how many federal warrants signed by Judge Parker he had in his hand; that bunch was going to be cooperative if it was outraged over the crime, and entirely silent if it wasn't. Another thing, when you asked a question from a bunch of folks gathered together, no matter what kind or race of folks that bunch was made up of, there was such a thing as wait-time that had to follow. Even if somebody was itching to volunteer an answer, you had to wait for him to get up the gumption to do it, had to wait for him to make up the words in his own mind, had to let the silence string out long and uncomfortable until that somebody would open his mouth and say something. If you didn't wait, you were liable to step on what was coming, shut it down before it ever got started. A lot of times they didn't intend to tell you what you asked, but whichever one finally piped up and said, "We don't know what you're talking about, mister," that was the one you cut out from the herd when nobody was looking and headed off by himself so he could tell you what he was secretly busting a gut to tell you.

So Mitchelltree waited, and the silence lengthened, punctuated by the scolding of a raucous bunch of bluejays off south among the trees along the creekbank. The Choctaw sheriff gazed placidly at heaven, chewing on a pine splinter; the townspeople shuffled their feet, cleared their throats, now and then coughed a little. Mitchelltree held the pepperbox with the bouquet of barrels lying flat against his palm. At last a grizzled, barrel-chested, heavily mustached man in overalls stepped forward.

"I guess I can answer that if everybody else's memory's too poor to remember," he said. He looked around at his fellows with an expression that was half accusation, half a petition for support. The crowd met this one's eye, as it hadn't the deputy's, though not with the support he seemed to ask for, but rather with a kind of detached curiosity, as if they were mildly interested in what he had to say about this business. Finally a voice called from the back, "Well, go on, Angus. The old lady's got supper waiting."

Angus Alford glared at the voice's source an instant, then turned to the deputy once more. "There was a pistol here," he said. "Or I guess you'd call it a pistol, I don't know. Wasn't much like any pistol I ever saw. Flat-sided. Four-barrel. Appeared to be a high-caliber type of a thing, but it had a hand grip like a pistol, and I guess it was one Fate brought with him same as he brought that monster there," and he nodded through the crowd at the weary blue roan still tethered to the hitching post in front of Tatum's Mercantile. It took an instant for Mitchelltree to comprehend that the horse was Fayette Lodi's, and then to realize that the monster the man referred to wasn't the horse but the grotesquely fat volleygun strapped to the worn saddle on the roan's back.

"I'll just tell you the truth," the man said. "It's a wonder more than one of them didn't get killed. I don't know how John Lodi kept from getting blasted into the next century from the sound and the size of it. Unless what Dayberry claims happened is what happened." His bushy mustache twitched side to side as if his nose itched him, and he began to scratch with stubbly fingers in the coarse grizzled hairs. He paused a moment longer, and the deputy marshal in his calm patience awaited him, until at last the man said, "J.G. claims Fate shot his own self in the neck." Angus Alford shrugged his shoulders. "I wouldn't know. I was around back, loading my wagon. Time I got out here, there wasn't a lot to see but a dead man and them fat barrels getting clogged with dust." He looked down at the scuffed dirt beneath the dead man's open palm. "Well, it was right there, mister." He nodded at the empty hand, glanced up briefly in the direction of the open stable doorway. His expression turned smoothly blank. "It's all I can tell you." He stepped back into his place among the onlookers.

Another voice came from the back of the crowd, not the first one but a second, higher-pitched one, goading as one goads a fight in a tone of high glee. "Tell him the rest of it, Angus! That kid you and Tatum drug around from the back yonder! Tell him 'bout that squaw y'all was fighting with!"

For the first time Sheriff Moore stirred as if the goings-on in the street held some interest for him. He moved into the center of the circle, spat the pine toothpick off to the side as he spoke. "Maybe you want to talk to John Lodi," he told the deputy. "He been sitting in yonder pretty calm a long time. He could probably tell you what you want to know."

The sheriff's bright obsidian eyes moved coolly around the circle of white faces, and then he looked up at the deputy U.S. marshal, whose composed face revealed no impression of the last few moments' revelations; disclosed nothing of the way in which, within Mitchelltree's mind, several unconnected thoughts wheeled and collided, raucous as the jaybirds on the creekbank, saying, Yes, that would surely be the gun he'd sold Fayette that evening on the ridge at sunset, with the two dead mules and the spilled wagon sprawled hopelessly down the hillside in the dying light, sold for thirty-five dollars, an outrageous price, which Mitchelltree then had attributed to the man's drunkenness but was not about to pass up, and he had waited until past dusk while Fayette went to get the thirty-five U.S. paper dollars, and he had tested them by feel and taste in the growing darkness before he finally handed the unloaded pistol to Lodi and said, Now, I buried the shells yonder by that black mule's hind end, you can come dig 'em up tomorrow if you want 'em, and walked off down the back side of the ridge north in the darkness, thirty-five dollars richer but weaponless and afoot, and, Yes, he was certainly going to have to miss this night's stopover at Miss Marilla's, which thought swept him with alternating waves of relief and regret, for he had in his secret heart thought he'd ask her to marry him this visit, which accounted for his late start, as he'd packed and repacked his saddlebag a half-dozen times, and watered the stallion and brushed him and oiled the saddle and fooled around, making up his mind a different way each time he considered the idea through to its conclusion, and now the decision was out of his hands, he thought, with that commingling of relief and regret. His attention returned to the men before him, in particular to the Choctaw sheriff with whom he shared an unnamed affinity in the face of these white onlookers, and he nodded at Moore to go on.

The sheriff said again, his eyes steady on the brown man's eyes, "Maybe you want to go yonder and have a talk with John."

They entered the stable doors, trailing a little ragtag crowd of men and boys who'd broken off from the main crowd and followed them down the street. J. G. Dayberry alone stood in the archway and shooed the men back, saying, "Y'all go on about your business, now. You got no call to come in here." The deputy marshal was already striding the few steps into the dim interior to where John Lodi sat, unmoving, expressionless, with his offspring lined up behind him, and the Choctaw sheriff, who routinely detached his interior life from the goings-on of white people, did not even glance back. Dayberry stood with his arms crossed, leaning against the scarred piece of timber that held up the crossbeam, his hatchet face turned now to the bunch of men and boys outside in the fading sunlight, now cocked the other way to watch and listen to the three men inside his barn.

Mitchelltree spoke first. His resonant voice rolled in the grayness, echoing nearly to the rafters, though all he said, standing a little to the side of where John Lodi sat, was "Evening."

No answer from Lodi.

"Sorry to hear about your brother," the deputy said, as if Fayette had dropped dead of natural causes and had already been planted out north at the Waddy cemetery, instead of lying fifty rods away in the street with his head and neck blown to tatters. The deputy reached up and took off his big white Stetson hat, held it loosely at his side in one hand, the pepperbox pistol pointed floorward in the other. In a few moments he went on. "Got a few questions I wanted to ask." His face was turned up as if he were searching the rafters for the source of that rolling echo which was only his own vibrating voice. The deep color of his skin blended with the dimness of the barn's interior, so that even the burnished light that seemed to illuminate it on cloudy days was extinguished, and Dayberry couldn't see any expression on the lawman's face, only the lift and turn of features, the coal-colored mustache a black slash above the white teeth. Tecumseh Moore stood a few feet to the other side of Lodi, and his face bore as little expression as Mitchelltree's, so that it seemed to the livery owner that the darkness in the barn had wiped their features blank. They stood so casually, so relaxed and nonchalant in the grayness, that one could easily believe they'd sauntered into the barn on other business and had just paused a minute before the man seated on the haybale to pass the time of day.

Dayberry's attention was taken by a couple of boys outside as they scuffled in the dirt, each elbowing the other out of the way in order to claim a spot in the row of men edging nearer the barn door, and the livery owner called out, "Here, now. Y'all quit!" And then he recognized his own youngest son at the back of the row, the boy's woolen cap poking out underneath Tarleton Maye's elbow, and Dayberry cried in a sort of subdued shout (for he did not want to disturb the serious proceedings taking place inside his stable), "You! Grady! You get on in the house! I'll tan your hide in a minute. Right now, hear?" He saw the red cap duck back and disappear behind the row of onlookers, and not really satisfied but too torn by his divided attention to pursue the matter further, he turned back to peer inside the barn.

Mitchelltree spoke in a low, almost secretive tone to John Lodi, but the deputy's voice was too rich and resonant, and Dayberry recovered every word.

"Folks tell me he had a weapon. Some unusual type of four-barrel breech loader." Mitchelltree paused an inordinately long time between each word, as if each carried particular significance. "A unique type of a weapon." He paused between the sentences as well. "Now, it do sound to me like we got a self-defense situation here. Trouble is . . . somehow or another . . . that gun disappeared."

John Lodi did not raise his head, lift his face, acknowledge the man's presence in any manner, and his youngsters stood perfectly motionless behind him as well, although all three pairs of those eyes were focused keenly on the deputy U.S. marshal, and Jim Dayberry, his head cocked as he looked birdlike through one eye at the interior of his stable before he turned his sharp gaze back to the street again, noticed that the skinny scrinch-eyed female in boy's trousers glared at Mitchelltree with animosity and what appeared to be a kind of familiarity, or at least acquaintanceship. Recognition. That was wonder enough to the livery owner, but then Mitchelltree did something that took him fully by surprise, and Dayberry forgot all about the little gaggle of onlookers outside his stable, forgot about his son Grady, who'd ought to have gone straight in the house after school and not come hanging around this unfortunate business; forgot, in fact, about John Lodi's youngsters as well.

Burd Mitchelltree squatted down in the straw and dried manure, laid the pistol on its side carefully in the dusty leavings, and brought his face to a level just even with John Lodi's—just almost exactly as if John Lodi was a little child, Dayberry thought. And when the deputy spoke, his bass voice had that gentleness and coaxing in it you might use with a child who's too scared or too shy to answer. Dayberry sucked his breath in through his teeth because he thought sure as anything John Lodi was going to haul off and knock that deputy marshal head over heels.

"What I need to know," Mitchelltree said in his patient, deep-timbred voice, "is how it happen your brother end up with two holes in him. I'm going to go on and do my investigating here, but I'll know what I'm doing a little better if you explain how that come about."

Still no response from Lodi. The youngsters might have been a row of oddly dressed store mannequins behind him. Over in the stable portion of the barn, a horse snuffled softly. The silence spun out long. Tecumseh Moore reached up and scratched the side of his head beneath his hat, and even that soft scritching proclaimed itself loud in the darkness.

"You wouldn't know what become of that gun, would you?" Mitchelltree said. He balanced his big Stetson on one knee. Dusted the ghostly brim. After a while he said, "I don't guess you would've sent somebody out to get it, would you? That wouldn't probably make much sense."

For the first time, John Lodi raised his eyes from the barn floor, looked over at the deputy marshal, the two men's faces on a parallel plane, and Dayberry saw that his employee had no notion of what Mitchelltree was talking about, and he saw that Mitchelltree also saw it, because the deputy nodded his head once.

"Well," he went on after a bit, "you don't have to tell me anything. Save it for the grand jury. I just thought you might help me out. Now, you know what I'm going to tell the judge in terms of what I see here going to sound pretty shaky, not the self-defense type of situation could keep a man from getting hanged. I do believe it to be that, I think so. But all I see, I see an unarmed man dead in the street from two big-caliber bullet holes, and we got a weapon here"—he glanced down at the pepperbox pistol lying dull and bulky on the barn floor, but he didn't make a move to touch it—"hadn't been fired but once, one barrel, and if we don't find that other gun we got us a mystery that won't lay down very quick."

J. G. Dayberry was aching to remind the lawman that there were forty witnesses in the street this minute who could testify that Fate Lodi had been armed; he wanted to point out that those same witnesses were any one of them a potential thief, any one of them could have had the opportunity to filch that gun out from beneath the dead man's fingers; above all, he was itching to pipe in with his opinion that Fate Lodi had shot his own self in the neck. But Dayberry was as stilled by the rolling music of Burden Mitchelltree's voice as John Lodi seemed to be, as all the people present appeared to be, for even the Choctaw sheriff turned his black eyes to the smooth plane of the deputy's forehead, listening. And Dayberry, lulled as he was, thought of how a snake charms a bird with its side-to-side swaying, and he thought the rise and fall of that voice was exactly the same, the hypnotic rhythm of words and the timbre, the soothing sound of it, almost singing, almost chanting, but pitched low and vibrating; it might have been thunder, the low roll of thunder from the far side of a mountain where the cloud that contains it cannot be seen, and Dayberry forgot to think about the ragtag bunch of men and boys behind him, but he remembered what he'd heard of the black deputy's reputation, remembered he'd heard that Bird Mitchelltree (and Dayberry, like nearly all white men, thought his first name was Bird; the Woolerton paper and the McAlester *Journal* even printed it that way) could smooth-talk an outlaw into surrendering if he could get close enough to talk to him. There was another colored deputy, old Bass Reeves up at Muskogee, who was famous for his sly disguises that let him get the drop on any outlaw he set out to serve a warrant on, and Deputy U.S. Marshal Bud Ledbetter—who, of course, was white anyway—was known all over the Territory and half the nation for his pure-dee bootleather toughness, but Burden Mitchelltree's reputation was of an airier nature, and it was marred by hints of impropriety—rumors that he was too quick to arrest a man who crossed him, too slow to act on a warrant if it was a Negro or an Indian he counted as friend—old stories Dayberry himself had never paid much mind too, laying them off onto the fact that the man was colored, and white folks in this part of the Nation were bound to talk that way about a colored marshal. But on the other hand he'd never believed the tale of how the lawman had talked all nine of Rafe Buckhorn's gang into surrendering after their murderous three-day rape and robbery rampage from Oklahoma Territory to Creek Nation all the way down to Gaine's Creek south of Woolerton, talked them into it without a soul, lawman or outlaw, firing a single shot at each other, which was a story that had gone around for six or seven years. Listening in the barn doorway, unable to open his mouth to pipe in with his well-founded opinions about Fate's killing, and thinking ironically that maybe it was true what folks said, that this was one bird that could charm a snake, the livery owner listened to Mitchelltree speaking low to John Lodi, and he was not the least surprised when his chronically silent employee, who hadn't spoken a word since the very moment of the killing, now opened his mouth and said, "I reckon Fay's gun went off when he fell. I guess it was that howdah did that to his neck."

It was only then, as if the spell had been suddenly broken, that Dayberry could blink his eyes clear enough to realize that the taller of John Lodi's two daughters, the pretty one with the pale face and the piled-up mass of dark hair and the many petticoats, was twisting around silently in the dim light of the stable, grimacing as she tried to peel her sister's bony hand off where it was clamped over her shoulder.

"Well," Mitchelltree said, and dipped his high-domed forehead once, running his great blunt fingers around the pale brim of his hat. He had not yet looked up at the two daughters; his eyes were on the barn floor. At last the deputy nodded again, seemed to be thinking. "That sounds reasonable," he said. (And J. G. Dayberry, thinking, See, now, that's what I been saying, what I been saying, grunted softly and nodded his head, and behind him the row of men and boys, who had crept close enough while the livery owner was distracted to hear this last part, also grunted and nodded, and the boy Thomas in imitation of the onlookers also grunted and nodded, and none of the witnesses present, with the possible exception of the Choctaw sheriff, disbelieved for the moment this implausible, nearly impossible explanation.)

"Mm-huh," the deputy said, and unfolded himself from where he'd been squatting; he rose to his full six-foot height with a sort of languid uncoiling motion, shook his corduroy pantslegs back down over his boot tops, replaced the Stetson on his head. "Well, you know I have to carry you to the federal jail at McAlester. I guess in a month or two they'll hold the preliminary, see if the judge believe there's enough evidence a crime been committed to bind you over for the grand jury." The pepperbox still lay on the stable floor in front of his feet. Mitchelltree glanced at it. "Probably they going to find they got enough evidence," he said. He raised his eyes, glanced at the two daughters, let his gaze slide past them as smoothly as if he did not see the elder's hand clamped upon the younger in gritted silence, past the big blond boy in the felt hat, and on around to Tecumseh Moore, who stood looking at the row of men and boys blackening the stable door.

Mitchelltree followed the sheriff's gaze. He spoke again, his eyes on the bunch of onlookers, though he did not appear to be speaking to them. It was hard to tell, really, just who he was speaking to when he said, "I got two little problems here. One, I got to be in court at Fort Smith tomorrow, one o'clock. Two, I don't intend to leave here till I find out what become of that gun." He paused just an instant. "If there was another gun." He gazed casually at the onlookers, who shuffled and gazed back, and there followed then the long wait-time that was such a part of the deputy's habit, which pause gave opportunity for the elder daughter to slip her hand from the younger girl's shoulder, and the two stood then in the lengthening silence with the older one's arm around the waist of the other, her mouth moving imperceptibly against her sister's ear. The boy stood beside them, waiting as the others waited. Still the deputy did not look at the youngsters but kept his eyes nonchalantly and carefully trained on the men outside the door. He went on after a while, saying, "You got any farewelling to do, you best go on and do it. Need to eat or use the privy or anything, you go on now. We likely to be traveling a long while after dark."

His eyes were so focused on the men in the doorway that it took even Tecumseh Moore an instant to realize the deputy marshal was speaking to Lodi. Mitchelltree said, "Get your horse saddled, do what you got to do, meet me out front soon as you get ready. We might get as far as Poteau this evening if we start pretty quick," and he reached down to scoop the pepperbox into his fist. It wasn't until then that everyone, John Lodi and his daughters and the little livery owner included, understood what the deputy meant. He aimed to take John Lodi with him to Fort Smith.

Dayberry said, "He ain't got a horse."

Mitchelltree said, "Reckon you'll have to give him one, won't you?" and walked directly into and parted the little crowd in the doorway, striding out into the reddening light.

The divided, grumbling men turned and fumbled like newly hatched ducklings into a line behind him as the deputy strode rapidly along the street, back toward where the larger crowd still milled about the corpse, and he scattered that bunch as well as he knelt once again beside the body. He was, to all appearances, oblivious to the covert glares and low, murderous mumbles that followed him. For twenty-five years there'd been only one place on the continent where a black man could arrest a white man—could, in fact, kill a white man if necessary—without causing a riot or a lynching, and that place was Indian Territory. But such conditions were rapidly changing. From his first days on the bench, Judge Parker had recommended Negroes, particularly Indian freedmen, for appointments as deputy U.S. marshals because of their known reliability and bravery, because they often spoke native language, because of the fact that Creeks and Seminoles trusted a black man about a thousand times sooner than a white man and would therefore be less likely to resist, defy, or shoot him outright the minute they saw him trying to arrest one of their people. Even now, as Parker's court was being stripped of all authority, there were still more than a dozen Negro deputy U.S. marshals under appointment in I.T., but Burden Mitchelltree had never achieved the harmony and grudging respect that Grant Foreman, Bass Reeves, Poorboy Fortune, some of the other black deputy marshals held within the swelling white population. And it was precisely because of this abruptness in his actions following those long, calm silences, which the white settlers thought of as highhandedness (or, more commonly among those who'd migrated from the Deep South, as many of the whites in the Choctaw Nation had, uppitiness), combined with that barely detectable tremor of irony or contempt in his voice, that the rumors and glares and little grumbles of resentment followed him almost anywhere he went. Now, as he knelt on the street in the riotous dying light, several of the white townsmen slid sidelong glances at one another, or mumbled beneath their breaths and spat. But Burd Mitchelltree paid them not the least attention as he rolled the stiffening body onto its side to examine it from the back.

He had to lay the pepperbox down in the street in order to use both hands, and as he lifted, the pennies slid off Fayette's eyelids and plunked softly in the dust. Unseen by the deputy, the blue eyes slid partially open, and the townsmen standing nearest stirred uneasily, looked away from that empty gaze. Fayette's head flopped sideways as if it could be wrenched from the trunk by no more than a light twist of the wrist, and Mitchelltree had to hold the skull up by the matted hair to keep the neck wound from gaping further. He grasped the left shoulder from beneath by one hand, hoisted the skull in the other as he scanned the wound; the deputy quickly saw what he looked for, was confirmed in what he'd suspected the minute he'd made that first swift appraisal of the body: the bullet that had made the neck wound was high caliber, high powered, and had come from behind.

Or he thought so.

It seemed so.

But then, the ragged wound was tremendous, blood-covered, the flesh shredded and pulped mulberry where the blood had gushed from the pulverized artery. The shot could nearly as well have come from the front, or even, almost inconceivably, but not impossibly, from below. There was of course the option of hauling the body to Woolerton to be examined by Doc Boot for an opinion on the source's direction, but that would have to wait until day after tomorrow, and by then the decomposition and smell would have set in. And then, too, there was the obvious choice to scout the area for the exploded cartridge, because clearly no .45 or .54 caliber cartridge was lodged in that gaping ragged mass of shredded flesh. But then Mitchelltree's same dilemma of having to be two or three places at once: here, Woolerton, McAlester, Fort Smith—which was the consequence of the damn Congress and its incessant meddling in the jurisdiction and affairs of the Indian Nations—added its reckoning to his calculations. His casual, unruffled demeanor unchanged, Mitchelltree examined the neck wound without touching or probing, for even the hoisting of the body had made new pools of half-congealed blood ooze to the surface. But the old calculating thought process was firmly in place, and the deputy marshal weighed the evidence as he saw it in those few moments, giving credibility to one possibility, then another, trying to make up his mind what he thought.

On the surface, Burden Mitchelltree kept always the calm, deliberate appearance that so infuriated some white men, drew respect from others, but in his mind he'd never changed from the essentially cautious, shrewdly calculating gambler he'd always been. It was only when he'd weighed his possibilities a dozen times and reached an ambivalent but final conclusion that he would burst forth with those abrupt, decisive gestures that some found galling. Just now, though, he was immersed in the weighing process, and he held himself still as a sunning lizard, eyes slitted, pondering, while the townspeople edged closer, trying to see what the deputy marshal was seeing in the exploded throat. The town's secret mind knew that if the deputy was examining from the back, it was because he thought Fate Lodi had been shot from behind. With the same ease with which it had been persuaded by John Lodi's implausible explanation, the town was now convinced that the dead man in the street had been shot in the back—and this without a word from the deputy, not even so much as a musing grunt. Craning, elbowing one another for position, they watched over Mitchelltree's shoulder. None saw the small, neat hole in the back of Fayette's skull, hidden as it was in the waste of blood and matted hair cradled in the deputy's big hand; none, including the deputy, even entertained the possibility that there was a third wound, regardless of how many conflicting stories were already circulating about how many gunshots had been heard. The two apparent ones had been so clearly sufficient for the work.

Lost in his unhurried deliberation, his narrowed eyes drawn by a flicker of movement, Mitchelltree glanced up to see the three young people emerge from the stable, the taller girl and hulking boy now on either side of the wiry figure in boy's britches, their arms wrapped around each other as if to form a shield. They did not approach further but stood just outside the doorway. Watching them, watching in particular the small wiry one in the middle, whose yellow eyes glared at him now as they had in the sun's dying flare on the ridge nine years before, Mitchelltree understood in a moment's revelation why the younger girl had twisted around beneath the bone clamps of the elder's fingers: if not for the dominance of her sister, the younger one would tell what she knew. The deputy recognized immediately the one he would have to cut out from the herd. But not here, not in the presence of the father, or the sister.

Abruptly Mitchelltree made his decision, though he'd have to keep the man in custody until he could find an opportunity to speak to the girl. The deputy would have risen immediately and followed through with his habitual, unapologetic haste, if he'd not been holding the dead man's head in his hands. With great gentleness, he eased the corpse back down, rubbed his bloodied palms against the dust of the street, clapped away the dirt. In one smooth decisive sweep then, Mitchelltree stood, scooped up the pepperbox, strode the few steps to his sorrel, untied the leather thong from the saddlebag, and placed the gun inside. He turned toward the stable just as the livery owner came out leading a pitiful-looking broken-down old white mare, saddled and bridled, with John Lodi following behind. Behind them came the Choctaw sheriff, smiling a wry smile that hardly touched his lips but made his obsidian eyes glint brightly in the ruddy light. They came on along the street, Dayberry scowling as he led the old mare, Lodi with his hat and a cotton jacket on, his face expressionless, and the half-grinning sheriff, followed at a slow distance by the three young people still linked arm in arm. Before they'd covered the fifty rods or so, the grin broke through on the sheriff's face, and then as quickly disappeared.

"What time you say you got to be at Fort Smith tomorrow?" Moore asked when they'd drawn near enough that he did not have to shout. His tone was gravely serious, but the wryness still crinkled about the eyes. "Looks like you going to be riding about all night."

"What is this?" Mitchelltree said, and for one of the few times in his life, his smooth, decisive action petered away into an indecisive, flailing halt. He eyed the white mare.

"This," the livery owner answered, "is Vergie."

"And what, you don't mind if I ask, you got a saddle on that piece of pitifulness for?"

"You told me to give him a horse. All right, I give him one."

"That ain't a horse, that's a piece of dog meat or something. Give the man something he can ride or—" Mitchelltree suddenly turned to the crowd. "Anybody got a horse they care to rent and can get saddled quick? I ain't got time to mess with this fool."

"He can ride that horse," Dayberry said. "She's done saved his life once this day, I reckon she can take him to meet his Maker."

Mitchelltree, unwilling to waste time and breath explaining he was taking John Lodi to Fort Smith not to stand trial but simply to keep him in custody till he could get him to McAlester, ignored the livery owner. He glanced at the blue roan in front of the mercantile, saw instantly that the animal was too ill-used to set out on a fifty-mile journey, and turned back to Moore, ready to make a deal with him. But the bright crinkling about the Choctaw man's eyes, coupled with that too-serious expression, made him unwilling to ask the sheriff anything, and the frustrated deputy turned to face the crowd again. But the livery owner went on in his reedy voice, unstoppable:

"You ast anybody in this town what happened ten o'clock this morning! Ast anybody. That durn Fate Lodi come in here on that blue pony armed to the teeth and soused to the gills. He stood right in the street yonder and gobbled like a turkey. What do you think he had his mind on, a nice little play party? He come down here to shoot his brother, and everybody in this town knows it—I don't know why they got their durn tongues gummed to the roof of their mouth." His eyes raked the little crowd of townsmen, turned, glaring, to the deputy again. "I had to come out here and use this poor old mare for a shield to see if I couldn't talk some sense into him, which you can bet I could not. She served that purpose good enough, I reckon she can take a man to his hanging, if you so all-fired sure you got to take him—because I never seen a man yet go to Hanging Judge Parker's court and come home to talk about it—so if you ain't going to listen to me when I tell you and tell you Fate Lodi was aiming to kill him, been looking to kill him the whole durn day, which I might's well be talking to a pinestump, then you just go on and take him to Fort Smith then, but you needn't get in such a damn hurry to get him there. Vergie'll get him there plenty quick enough to suit me." And the livery owner reached up and stroked the scraggly yellowed mane while he glared at the deputy, his chin lifted, blue eyes blazing, their brief moment of shared integrity, for Jim Dayberry's part, now entirely a thing of the past.

"Oh, for the love of—" Mitchelltree started, and then broke off. He turned his eyes to the north side of town, the far side of the railroad tracks, where the eyes of the townspeople were turned, focused on the new-looking flatbed wagon with two erect figures in it approaching in the distance.

"Jiminy Christmas. Here he comes again," a voice said behind him. "Going to be fireworks this time, you hide and watch."

"That ain't him, that's the other'n," a second voice answered. "And one of them grown girls."

There was silence in the street a moment as the people watched north along the road.

"No, sir. That's that wild one, sure as I'm standing. Marshal, you better get your prisoner back in the stable if you want him strung together in one piece when he goes before Parker. That boy's liable to tear him to pigfeed."

"That ain't him, I tell you, it's the other one."

"Which other one?"

"One got him calmed down."

"Hunh. You want to call that calm. You hide and watch."

"Y'all hush. Who's that coming behind 'em?"

And the eyes of the townspeople and the liveryman and the sheriff and the U.S. deputy marshal all squinted through the coming dusk and rising dust at the buckboard clattering along behind the wagon.

"That's that Waddy preacher driving. Man alive, he made good time."

"What I tell you?" a voice whispered. "That's the oldest boy in that wagon. Look there, he's dressed common."

"Tell you one thing, I never seen the like of that other'n, swooping around here like a old tom turkey in hat and spurs. I thought they never were going to get him calmed down enough to get him back in that wagon. I thought we were just bound to have another killing before evening."

"Hnnnh. Ain't evening yet."

"What I want to know, did that gun of Fate's disappear before that wild boy left or after?"

Silence a moment as the wagon neared the crossroad in front of the bank.

"Oooh, Lord," someone breathed.

"That's not no grown girl, now. Is it?"

The three offspring of John Lodi did not look at the approaching vehicles but at their father, who stood with his head bowed, almost as if in prayer, so that he might not have to look at his dead brother; they did not see when the flatbed wagon, springs squeaking, box swaying, crossed the train tracks and came on, rolling to an easing stop a hundred feet above where the many denimed legs had shuffled and drawn closed in front of the body when the crowd saw, as one witness, that it was not one of the daughters in the wagon but the dead man's wife seated on the spring seat beside her red-eyed son.

"Somebody going to answer me that?" a voice hissed, insistent. "Anybody seen that four-barrel pistol since that wild one left?"

"Hush. Hush, now. That's his wife."

The Reverend Harland Peevyhouse drew up his sagging dray behind the wagon, holding one hand toward the crowd, palm out, straight in front of him, in a sign either of halt or of benediction, and a tall shaggy-headed big-shouldered man with deepset brown eyes and a face lined with a great sadness and compassion climbed down from the buckboard and walked front to where the widow had one foot already on the hub, and reached a steadying hand up to help her climb down.

Caleb sat in the wagon, staring straight ahead, his mouth working. The preacher struggled to ease his considerable weight over the side of the buckboard as Jessie came wordlessly forward. She carried a shiny black patent-leather handbag snapped together in her two hands in front of her. She wore a new navy calico bonnet and a freshly starched white linen apron over her gray skirt. Her mouth was collapsed flat. The man with the sorrowful eyes followed a few steps behind her, his hat in his hands, his eyes averted from the place where the curtain of men's legs had drawn together. With the continuing approach of the widow, the curtain parted again, and Fayette's body was revealed in its grotesque distortion, for, despite the gentleness with which Mitchelltree had laid it back down, the examination had left the broken body more damaged. The head lay at a loose, impossible angle from the torso, the jelled blood welling from the neck and the sharded gash on the forehead; the right arm was twisted beneath, the left cocked peculiarly across the chest, and the half-opened eyes stared blindly at heaven, the mouth dumb and open, spilling blackness, like a ripped-open scarecrow, unstuffed and unstrung. The woman walked toward it as if it were no more than that: a lifeless replica of humanness, come undone.

When she drew within a few yards of her husband, the women on the mercantile porch began to ease slowly forward, their faces shadowed in buckram, as the townsmen drifted south along the street. The men settled at a comfortable distance near the hitching rail between the mercantile and the livery barn, close enough not to miss any words spoken, far enough to get out of the way if bullets began to fly. But the woman neither spoke nor pulled a derringer pistol from that patent-leather pocketbook to turn it on John Lodi, as more than a few of the men watching thought and muttered among themselves that she would. Rather she looked calm and still at her husband for only a moment, turned her eyes then, not to the brother-in-law, who stood with his hat on, head down, eyes not meeting eyes, but to the tall pretty sister with the bruise darkening her cheek, leaking its livid color from beneath the flour coating: the one, as Burden Mitchelltree instantly noted, who would have released her voice from beneath the clamps of her sister's fingers. He saw then, watching the strange yellow eyes of the elder as she stared at the woman, that both of John Lodi's daughters knew the source of, were privy and party to, the shot that had blown out their uncle's throat.

He'd known. Of course he'd known; the fact had simply not pushed through the cacophony of thoughts crowding the deputy's mind. The younger girl did not return her aunt's stare—not, Mitchelltree saw, because she refused it, as the father with his head bowed refused all eyes, but because her slate gaze was too occupied, the graygreen lights beneath the serge fringe now flicking sideways toward the townsmen on her left, now darting up to the townswomen on the porch, back around self-consciously to the men again, to see if they were watching her. Still the deputy waited—that age-old biding of time that was both his gift and his torment, for it was in near paralysis sometimes that he waited, caught by that unrelenting need to weigh and balance and figure, as if, could he only know more facts, perceive a situation from more angles, he might in some way comprehend the incomprehensible, control what was entirely out of his hands. Just so Burd Mitchelltree tarried, watching from beneath his quiescent surface, waiting for the players to act.

A wiry auburn-headed boy in a red knit cap, with the same fierce expression and clear blue eyes as his father, sidled up and stood at John Lodi's elbow, but J. G. Dayberry did not growl at his son Grady to go home. The livery owner stood with a gnarled clutch of knuckles twined in the mare's halter, the other hand on her yellowed muzzle, his scowling gaze focused protectively on his employee, standing slump-shouldered, head bowed, off to the left and a little in front of him. The Reverend Peevyhouse, alighted from the buckboard now, came waddling toward Jessie, dabbing behind his round spectacles with a white handkerchief, but the man with the sorrowful eyes took a step backwards, reached a lanky arm out to the minister to keep him from going any farther, so that they stood then a few feet behind the widow, each on either side of her, connected by Otis Skeen's staying arm. Angus Alford, his thumbs hooked in the galluses of his overalls, detached himself from the clutch of townsmen beside the hitching rail and moved up to where he could see better, and in a bit Field Tatum stepped down off the mercantile porch, edged slowly forward, the bonneted women following, whispering, behind him, as the town, entirely unconscious of itself, moved slowly to re-form its loose circle, its great misshapen hoop, with the Lodi children, their father and dead uncle and their aunt, with her calm eyes, in the middle.

The town grew silent, listening: no longer did it murmur its soft chorus of gossip and judgment. Particulate selves melded into the whole, as individuals may lose self in a gathering of souls come together to commit violence, or to worship. The town of Cedar was joined to bear witness to that which no individual could have preserved: the whole forged as one to give testament to what none outside the closed shell of the family, facing itself within that gathered circle, understood.

In the purpling twilight, in the center of the circle, the woman looked at the brother who had killed his brother, and beyond him to the three offspring who stood linked together behind him, blood of his blood; blood of her husband's blood, and her children's. She held herself in that calm stillness as if this were no more than she expected, accepted; as if she'd known her whole life that each breath and heartbeat within the cage of her chest would lead to this moment, no more escapable than the truth that one day those very breaths and heartbeats would quit. The distant argument of jays on the creekbank was silenced by dusk's coming; the nightbirds had not yet begun to call. In the quiet of the town's watching, Jessie stood, her face shadowed by the navy bonnet so that only those nearest and in front of her saw the change coming. As those few watched, the calm stillness began to depart from her, and what settled over her expression was even then beyond the unified mind of the town to comprehend. Never did she take her eyes from the children, and now Jonaphrene's fidgety gaze held steady, looking back at her, as Matt looked at her, and the boy Thomas, watching her, and yet the woman knew they did not perceive what she remembered, unwilling, in that moment: that she had wordlessly, four hours earlier, handed the carbine rifle to her niece, knowing, even then, what would come next.

Slowly, John Lodi raised his head. His eyes—the shape and cast of his eldest daughter's, the ungraspable color of the younger's, and none like, none like the guiltless pallor of his son's—met the woman's. They stood a long time, forever, eternity; stood no longer than the pulse of one heartbeat, one breath, recognizing each other: each knowing the other and the whole, all that had happened, not in the details of bullets and barrels and who had fired in the moment of killing, but that truth beyond particulars as it was made manifest in themselves and their children: that law which says we shall tear down in the same portion with which we forge and hone and make; and the second law, its equal: the old baffling determinant whose truth is that we have been given power to destroy life yet not to create it—but only to act as the vessel for it, a little while, sometimes. Jessie's eyes went to the children again. They stood tightly bound, the strange boy on one side, the awkwardly beautiful younger girl on the other, her lips silent now, subsumed to the will of her sister, and in the middle, her thin arms tight around each of them, the eldest: small, wizened, unmercifully strong—and yet her eyes as empty as they'd been when she lay curled, hollow, on the pallet years before. As she looked at the children, and remembered, Jessie's chapped knuckles began to whiten against the clasped pocketbook.

In the street, as the town watched, the woman began to tremble, her slatted bones heaving beneath the shirtwaist as if she could not get her breath—in wrath, the town thought; in an outraged paroxysm of grief. Only Otis Skeen, whose gift and curse had been compassion, saw, in the trembling slope of the woman's shoulders, in the knotted bones beneath the gray cotton on her back, that it was not rage, not personal loss or sorrow that made her tremble so, but a terrible, hopeless grief at humankind's ruthless paltriness on this earth—and her part in it. Her terrible part in it. Jessie turned away from the children and began to walk toward her husband's body. With each step she seemed to sink lower, as if she were melting, as if the thin legs beneath the gray skirt were dissolving into the earth. Within four steps she was on her knees; with the next gesture of propelling herself forward, she sprawled flat on the ground, the shiny patent-leather purse caught beneath the white apron as her arms stretched, her hands opened, closed again, clutching her husband's legs.

"Ma!" Caleb leapt from the wagon, covered the distance in a few bootclops to bend over his mother, saying, "Ma! Mama! Ma!" And he put his arms across his mother's arms, his hands on her hands, his head lifted, saying, "Ma! Ma! Ma!" like a distressed crow cawing, and after a breath, "Mama!" and then, again, "Ma! Ma!"

The town, its eyes on the prone woman and son sprawled over the body, was silent a moment longer—only a moment, but long enough for Burden Mitchelltree, seeing the man's shoulders heaving, to hear the working out of the sound. It came hard and deep at first, from a place unused, frozen inside him, barking into the air in short hard chops, as of an axe breaking ice. John Lodi was not bound, and yet he stood with his hands clasped at the wrists, his feet together, as though both were shackled. The great shoulders heaved with each chopping sound. And then the barks began to run together, rose from the frozen chest and spilled from the throat in harsh, dry shudders, the sobs of a drunkard on his knees in the garden, but still John Lodi stood upright in the street, hands and feet together, as if he were powerless to move. The blond boy began to sob. Beside his sisters, joined without expression in the violet dusk, in his new felt hat and ragged suspenders, the boy sobbed in the manner of the father, tear-less, shoulders shaking, hands and feet together. The town began to move again, and softly murmur, the circle drawing tighter, while the son Caleb went on cawing in the twilight, "Ma! . . . Ma! . . . Ma! . . . Ma!"

Coda

The descent is quick from the bony blue ridges of the Sans Bois to the open prairies in the heart of Oklahoma—quick, and yet gentle, for the Sans Bois are the most northern of the great Ouachita Mountains, and they long earthward toward the sweep of plains from which they arose. A rider on horseback can travel north from the hidden caves and rock ledges of the Sans Bois, winding down in a slow, sloping decline, and within no more than a few hours find the surrounding land gently rolling, the horizon arcing away above a sea of goldentop grasses. It is hardly thirty miles from the deep mysteries of the Fourche Maline creek bottoms to the broad, meandering sand banks of the Canadian River crawling west to east across the prairie, where lone sandstone bluffs rise above the grasses and the few trees are of the short, clawed variety: blackjack and shinnery; where the ocher earth begins to darken, taking on the rusty hues that will deepen to blood red farther north and west along the ruddy waters of the Cimarron and the Deep Fork.

Here, to this prairie landscape, the remains of John Lodi's family came and settled in late summer, 1896, taking up residence in a Creek freedman's abandoned cabin a half mile north of the salmon-and-buff-colored sands of the Canadian. They never returned to the log house at Big Waddy Crossing, for there was nothing to retrieve there. Together they traveled in a buckboard borrowed from J. G. Dayberry, directly from the hearing at the Central District Court at South

McAlester to the town of Eufaula in Creek Nation, where John Lodi entered first the feed supply and then the local livery stable to purchase with his last earned dollars a used turning plow and a mule.

The court had ruled, based on the findings of the grand jury, which had been lullingly swayed by the testimony of Deputy U.S. Marshal Burden Mitchelltree, that the killing of Lafayette Lodi in the town of Cedar, I.T., in early March of that same year, had been a case of justifiable homicide. According to the deputy's interpretation of the evidence, the deceased had been in the process of reaching toward his saddle for a tremendous twelve-barrel volleygun he had strapped there, for the clear purpose of murdering the defendant, and although in the court's opinion there was an unsatisfactory amount of contradictory testimony, and though there was a great deal of suspicious whispering in the crowded gallery and a strange resistance on the part of the widow to testify against her brother-in-law, nevertheless the jury found that there was insufficient evidence to hang the man, and the court, unwillingly, ruled the killing self-defense. The accused himself never took the stand.

John Lodi, in fact, took no part in the proceedings whatsoever, but sat with his hands folded on the polished oak table before him, silent, throughout the hearing, and when it was finished, he gave no indication of gladness or relief. He merely stood, looked to his eldest daughter, seated with her siblings on the hardback bench in the front row, and walked out of the hearing room with his offspring trailing an odd, formal tail behind. They climbed at once into the waiting buckboard without a nod, without so much as a satisfying glance at the little ragtag crowd of citizens who had traveled by wagon and horseback fifty or sixty miles from the communities of Cedar and Big Waddy Crossing to attend and bear witness to the end of the story. The Lodis left the mountains, disappeared from the lives of those communities—but never from their minds or memory—and traveled to the prairie country east of Eufaula, where the earth speaks with different voices, planted themselves in a cabin near the Canadian's changing sands.

John Lodi turned his skilled hands to the tasks of farming, and the loamy soil in the bottomlands of the Canadian River were rich for that purpose, but whatever wisdom or grace had once been in the tough palms and blunt fingers, those gifts had entirely disappeared now, and the plow would not plow straight, the chopping axe glanced off the gnarled jackoak, and the ears of corn, when the hands reached to pluck them, shriveled brown-kerneled and hard within the green shucks.

Whatever task the man turned his hands to, fruitlessness spilled from it, and yet he did not quit. All human will had departed from him with the flight of his brother's soul from the broken body in the street at Cedar, and yet John Lodi had no power but to keep on in the motions of living until his own soul should do as the will had already done. It took seven years. The body is an incorrigible creature, driven to survive, sometimes, even in the loss of all hope.

As for the girl who had never become woman, his daughter, Matt Lodi, she survived, as the father survived, and her will and power increased in direct proportion to the loss of his own. She carried the other two with her, fed them on corn pone and goat's milk, directed their every breath. As the man shrank, growing smaller and older—incredibly frail and aged for his forty-odd years—even so, the daughter grew stronger, though no less wizened, but with a gristly, gnawed strength that allowed her to gather the others to herself and make them survive. It took so little to save them: shelter in the shape of a former slave's cabin, two porched rooms with a dogtrot between; chopped wood for warmth in winter; wild turkey, quail, and rabbit, and the fruits of the earth for their bellies, preserved for the length of the short winters from her memory of her mother's ways of canning and drying. The boy Thomas grew taller, put on weight, until he grew past his father's former size and began to soften to a shapeless bulk. Jonaphrene, too, began to soften, though not in the doughy manner of her brother, but with the rounding of the angular adolescent limbs into the softer forms of womanhood.

The hair rope hoop coiled, and coiled again, the seasons spiraling into years, into the unfolding of a new century, and little changed. Their lives were only lives now, hardly lived. In some way, for each of them, everything had ended on the dirt streets of Cedar. As John Lodi's gifts had disappeared from his able hands, so had Matt's gifts departed; no longer did she search in the darkened spaces behind her eyes but kept every particle of her being focused in the arid, sun-spun world, to the gathering of food, the filling of bellies, the making of crude wooden furniture: to the keeping of her family together in a hard-gritted penance, as if once, long ago, she had made a grievous mistake.

Twice a year she hitched the plow mule to a neighbor's borrowed wagon and drove the seventeen miles to Eufaula to trade for supplies. There were few goods that the family needed which could not be taken from the earth, but for those items—plow points, kerosene, turpentine, coffee—Matt grew a small patch of cotton; she carried two bales to the gin in autumn, saved back two bales to buy supplies in the spring. After the first season, Matt traveled alone to Eufaula, or accompanied only by her father, for she had seen how the bustling streets worked on her sister, how Jonaphrene would be stirred by the sight of white women in plumed hats and fine dresses, by the many rich odors, the sounds of jangling harnesses and the rumbling of the board sidewalks beneath the boots of men in broad-brimmed hats. Remembering the lost Jim Dee, Matt forbade her sister to go with them; she made Thomas, too, stay behind. The younger girl protested, but only faintly, and only for a short time. There was only one will in that household, Matt's will, and it determined all of the comings and goings, the days of planting and harvest and which day should be wash day and which hog-killing or canning, which morning the cotton-filled wagon should set out for Eufaula. This is why there were only the two of them, the father and the daughter, in the borrowed wagon traveling west on the old Briartown road toward Eufaula on the cold spring afternoon in 1902 when someone shot John Lodi in the back.

I knew the sound first, it could have been the explosion of voice in my own throat, a crack of sound from my own gut. I'd been hearing it a long time. I just didn't remember what it was until it exploded a little ways back over my shoulder, and Papa fell. I did what you must do when there is gunfire, tumbled backwards and sprawled flat into the bed of the wagon, but not before I saw him. Not before I recognized the source of the sound. He had to be close, only a little ways off the road behind a little clutch of scrub oak. I saw his horse even, a chestnut tied to the clawed branches outlined against the clear sky because the horse was big and the trees small and scrawny, because he had to be close to the road in order to kill him. That was always the condition with the gun Papa made, whose sound I recognized as if it were my own shout, I'd heard it so many times. It did not have distance, did not have accuracy, its perfection was a lie because it was no good in a country of such distance, a lie of perfection, as so much had been a lie—but the sound did not lie, the explosion of powder, or its killing strength when Papa fell.

I lay flat between the bales of cotton, waiting. I wasn't afraid. I think I was glad nearly. The mule kept walking, her slow balking pace. I don't think she was deaf but just stubborn, to not buck and run at that sound.

I couldn't see Papa. I thought maybe he had fallen off, knocked to the earth by the force of the explosion. I lay looking up at the pierced blue sky above me, swaying with the motion of the wagon. Waiting. I thought he would come on and kill me. I heard the metal jangle, the horse snort once as he mounted, and I thought, It will be finished now. Papa's old muzzle loader was still beside the spring seat, loaded, yes, but I knew there was not time to reach it. I wouldn't try. The mark was on us, each Lodi, unto the last one, and I was in no way surprised. I was only surprised when I heard the chestnut's muted hooves against the road dust, loping away from the wagon toward the east. The sound faded to a soft drumming and then disappeared altogether. Still I didn't sit up. I didn't reach for the reins to stop the mule walking. I lay between the bales, looking at the sky arcing above me. I'd seen his face, for that one turning instant. Bearded. He had grown fleshy, as Fayette had done in his last years, the son's face transformed in seven years into a mirror image of the father's, even to the eyes, which I did not remember Fowler's eyes blue like Fayette's eyes, but they were, there on the road to Eufaula where he stood with his hand stretched out before him, the four-barreled gun dark in the cold sunlight, his eyes as light and clear as the plains sky.

No one tells the story.

The daughter drove home with her father's body resting beside the bales of unginned cotton in the bed of the wagon, throughout the cold day and on into the evening. The sun sank winter-red and purple behind her, behind the bare reaching fingers of blackjacks low on the horizon, but Matt did not see it as she drove east, back over the wagonroad to the two-room cabin near the sandbed river, where her brother and sister waited. It was cold dark when she and her father arrived there. No official was notified, no death certificate issued. John Lodi's death was never listed as a murder in the annals of Indian Territory, never recorded in any way at all.

Acknowledgments

My first thanks go to my family for their abiding faith and support, in particular my parents, Paul and Carmelita Askew, who willingly answered at all hours all manner of questions about guns, cookstoves, ways of living and doing and talking; my husband, Paul Austin, who from the beginning has given me faith, freedom, keen-eyed criticism, and love; and, especially, my sister, Ruth Brelsford, who received these pages in daily missiles sent south and west from the mountains of New York to her home near Tulsa. She read with commitment, openheartedness, and tremendous forbearance, for she'd agreed to make no comment but only receive the story as it spun forward, and to her great credit, she asked no questions, made no judgments during the years of messy and tortuous creation. Her silent partnership is all through this work.

I'm deeply grateful to my agent, Jane Gelfman, whose enthusiasm and tenacious commitment are unparalleled, and whose gratifying first phone call will forever be the high point for me in this book's journey, and to my editor, Courtney Hodell, who read with probing intelligence and a deep comprehension of the work's intention; her contributions have without doubt helped to make a better book. Thanks, as well, to Jessica Treat for her skillful feedback and enduring friendship, to W. Roger Webb at Northeastern in Tahlequah for giving me the opportunity to come home and stay a while, and a special thank you to Ida Stallaby of Red Oak, Oklahoma, for sharing with me her language and her good company as she struggled, with great humor, across the gulf of two worlds and two tongues to help me understand The Word in Choctaw. Above all, my thanks to the Creator, for giving me this job.

—Rilla Askew

A PENGUIN READERS GUIDE TO

The Mercy Seat

Rilla Askew

A Merciless Land

Against the background of the American Civil War, slavery, Indian removal, manifest destiny, outlaw legends, and the ordinary, everyday rigors of frontier life unfolds a story of two brothers. John Lodi is quiet and honest, dedicated to and gifted at his blacksmith's craft, while his brother Lafayette is loquacious and shrewd, harboring a penchant for bootlegged liquor, underhanded deals, and illegal guns. As different as they are, these two men and their families are knotted together by blood, a knot inevitably to be dissolved by blood. The Lodi clan rattles out of Kentucky one foggy midnight to escape retribution for breaking a gun patent, heading for the lawless Indian Territory destined to become Oklahoma. The abandonment of home and kin, and the journey itself, seem to take more of a toll on John's family, the worst loss being the death of John's wife. Numbly grieving, tattered, and sick with scarlet fever, John Lodi and his children do not catch up to Lafayette in Indian Territory until six months later. In this new land, forcibly relocated Native Americans, freed slaves, and hard, circumspect white men form an uneasy community poised between suspicion and tolerance, which erupts at times into violence. The gulf between cultures is emphasized by the discordant relationship of the Lodi brothers, who are irrevocably bound to one another, and yet between whom there is hardly a moment's understanding or harmony.

John's eldest child, a girl called Mattie, has inherited her father's relentless will, and from her mother an urgent—if mysterious—mission that she believes will save her family and deliver them safely back home to Kentucky. Her child's perception deepens and broadens, and we see that a mystical gift of vision sets Mattie apart from her brothers and sisters. Awash with painful memories that belong to a liberated slave-woman, Mattie struggles against her own compassion to maintain the racial enmity she feels is necessary to safeguard her family from the woman's alien influence. Another time, sitting amidst the ash and dust of her family's destroyed possessions, Mattie relives the deaths and thwarted desires of her ancestors. Yet with her pragmatic pioneer's mind and will, Mattie rejects her spiritual gift of sensitivity with all her might. Just as in the Bible the Mercy Seat is both the place of atonement and the place within the Ark of the Covenant from which God speaks, in the novel atonement and communion are required in order to find mercy. Caught between the violence of human will and the capriciousness of Fate, with both longing and antipathy in their hearts, the characters in *The Mercy Seat* refuse to become what nature, or their Creator, intended them to be, and their legacy transforms their country utterly.

Rilla Askew
A Brief Biography

Both of Rilla Askew's novels to date, *Strange Business* (1992) and *The Mercy Seat* (1997), are situated in her home state of Oklahoma. She was born in the foothills of the Sans Bois Mountains in 1951, a fifth-generation descendant of southerners who settled in Indian Territory in the late 1800s. The western landscape and history that is a part of Askew's heritage live on in her imagination and her work. *The Mercy Seat* is based on Askew's own family's relocation from Kentucky, and many incidents materialize into fiction from a distant past that was kept alive through family stories. Askew's deep connection to her surroundings is evident everywhere in her work. In *The Mercy Seat*, she says, "This country. Oklahoma. The very sound of it is home."

Askew originally moved to New York to become an actress, but turned instead to writing plays and fiction. Critical and popular response to her work was immediate and overwhelmingly positive, her first book winning the Oklahoma Book Award. *The Mercy Seat* was nominated for a PEN/Faulkner award for fiction and the Mountains and Plains Award for fiction, and won the Oklahoma Book Award and Western Heritage Award for best novel of 1997. Askew now moves back and forth between the southern Catskills and the Sans Bois Mountains of Oklahoma.

Questions for Discussion
The Mercy Seat

1. The book begins, "There are voices in the earth here, telling truth in old stories. Go down to the hidden places by the waters, listen: you will

hear them, buried in the sand and clay. . . ." In what ways does the geography of the U.S. tell the story of the Lodis or help to forward the plot? How is landscape a character in this story, as well as the setting, active in unraveling its plot?

2. This is both an essentially American and a recognizably ancient story, with allusions to the Biblical account of the brothers Cain and Abel. How does this book's theme of exile work in the Biblical and in the American sense? What is it the Lodis long for and wish to return to?

3. According to the Native American healer Thula Henry, there is an essential "Fourth Part" missing from the white man's spirituality, a part that sets nature in balance and maintains Thula's own soul in harmony, at least until she joins her destiny to Matt Lodi's. Could you argue that the author is hinting that Native American people are privy to an Edenic existence, an existence desperately sought and simultaneously rejected and destroyed by the encroaching whites? How does Mattie's rejection of her gift effect that argument?

4. Mattie fears and is feared by the life-sustaining women she encounters: the black woman who nurses Lyda; Thula, who saves Matt's life on arguably three occasions; and even Jessie, who is bound by a sense of duty greater than her own unwillingness to help John Lodi's children. How does this explain or complicate Matt's failure to "become" a woman? Why does Matt systematically suspect and reject the nurturing gestures of others and her own compassionate urges?

5. Demaris Lodi is an elusive character, dying early and leaving a restless mission to her eldest daughter. Was this a consciously bestowed legacy? Do you agree with Matt that her mother "died of a broken heart"? How does the tin box and its contents illuminate Demaris to her daughter? How do these ancient clan loyalties and betrayals cast a light on Mattie's own angry devotion to her family?

6. John Lodi is a miraculously skilled gunsmith and Matt Lodi has "gifts of the spirit." Why do each of them reject their gifts? Does John's more clearly spelled out reasoning shed any light on how Mattie feels about her gift?

7. How does the incident of the mules witnessed by Burden Mitchelltree pose as both foreshadowing of and a metaphor for the showdown that will occur between John and Lafayette nine years later? How does it inform Mitchelltree's understanding of the brothers' relationship and influence him in his crucial role in John's trial?

8. We see John Lodi's four surviving children as both contrary and complementary to one another. The two girls serve as nearly polar opposites to one another, as do the boys, yet amongst their differences there is a strange harmony. How are they necessary to one another's survival? How does Jim Dee's abandonment of the family effect its balance?

9. Fayette Lodi's name is shortened to "Fate" by the terse Oklahoma dialect, making one wonder if he is truly an instrument of fate. What are Fayette's motivations? How do John's differ? Matt's? Jessie's? What is the relationship between fate and human will in this story? Which seems to have the upper hand in the unfolding of its plot?

10. To what do you attribute John Lodi's relentless silence, which he will break neither to instruct his children nor to retaliate against the threats, challenges, and accusations of his drunken, gun-loving brother? What keeps John from deserting Fayette? To whom, and how, does John show affection?

11. In the Bible's Book of Leviticus, when Aaron's sons offer "strange fire before the Lord" (that is, offer the wrong sacrifice, the wrong penance) the fire devours them. The exacting god of the Old Testament then demands the blood sacrifice for atonement: the "sin offering" which will be sprinkled on the Mercy Seat. In what ways does this symbolism resonate with the novel? Which characters offer "strange fire"? What would be a suitable offering?

12. In the last scene, Jessie becomes aware of ". . . a terrible, hopeless grief at humankind's ruthless paltriness on this earth—and her part in it. Her terrible part in it" (419). How would you define Jessie's part in it? In what ways does she contribute to the rift between the two brothers? Why did she give the carbine to Jonaphrene?

13. At one point, Jessie becomes aware that "the sins of the fathers are visited upon the children." If this is true, what are the sins of Fayette and

John Lodi and how are they visited upon the younger generation? In a larger sense, what are the sins of the American forbears and how are they manifest in the major characters? Are the African-Americans and Native Americans in this story somehow exempt from, if victim of, these original American sins?

14. Distrust and judgment between races abound in this book. Analyze the interactions between Mattie and the black woman, Mitchelltree and the Lodi Brothers, Thula and Jessie. How does the communication and understanding between races, or lack thereof, add tension, intrigue, and conflict to the story? Could these dynamics correspond to race relations today?